CHEATING
AT SOLITAIRE

THE GREGOR DEMARKIAN BOOKS
BY JANE HADDAM

CHEATING
AT SOLITAIRE

———

A Gregor Demarkian Novel

JANE HADDAM

ST. MARTIN'S MINOTAUR
NEW YORK

This is a work of fiction. All of the characters, organizations, and events portrayed in this novel are either products of the author's imagination or are used fictitiously.

www.minotaurbooks.com

Library of Congress Cataloging-in-Publication Data

Haddam, Jane, 1951–
    Cheating at solitaire : a Gregor Demarkian novel / Jane Haddam.—1st ed.
        p. cm.
    ISBN-13: 978-0-312-34308-8
    ISBN-10: 0-312-34308-6
    1. Demarkian, Gregor (Fictitious character)—Fiction. 2. Private investigators—Massachusetts—Fiction. 3. Armenian Americans—Fiction. 4. Celebrities—Fiction. 5. Massachusetts—Fiction. I. Title.

PS3566.A613 C44 2008
813'.54—dc22   2007049770

First Edition: April 2008

10 9 8 7 6 5 4 3 2 1

CHEATING
AT SOLITAIRE

PROLOGUE

1

There were things that Annabeth Falmer understood, and things she did not understand, and among the things she understood the least was what she was doing on Margaret's Harbor in the middle of the biggest nor'easter to hit New England since 1853.

Actually, she didn't understand what she was doing on Margaret's Harbor at all, but thinking about that made her head ache, and the last thing she needed in the face of snow coming down at two inches an hour was a headache. She was only about a mile from the center of Oscartown, but she didn't think she'd be able to make it in for a spare bottle of aspirin.

It was two o'clock on the afternoon of Tuesday, December 31st, but it might as well have been the middle of the night. The world outside Annabeth's window was not black, but it was impossible to see anything in. The snow was so heavy, she was in a kind of white-out. The only visibility was to the east of her, where the ocean was, and even that was like something out of a surrealist aesthetic. She could see waves, white-tipped and agitated. She could see snow piling into drifts against the tall metal parking meters that had been set out along the beach for people who came in from the landlocked towns. Most of all, she could see the tall oceanward tower of the Point. There was a light on up there, the way there always was now that Kendra Rhode had taken up residence for the duration.

"Who in the name of God names a baby Kendra?" Annabeth said, to the cat, who was the only one besides herself at home. She was talking to the cat a lot lately. It was probably inevitable, but it still made her feel oddly sick at the pit of her stomach. Things had not worked out as badly as she had thought they would, back in the days when she lay awake night after night not knowing how she was going to get through another week, but they hadn't exactly worked out as a triumph, either.

The cat's name was Creamsicle because that's what he looked like: oddly orange and white the way the ice-cream bar had looked in Annabeth's childhood. She tried not to wonder if there were Creamsicles for sale any longer—everything seemed to disappear, except the things that didn't, and those tended to be around forever—and got the cat off the ledge of the landing window. He was a small cat, less than a year old. Annabeth wasn't sure he had ever seen snow before.

"Trust me," she told him, dropping him down onto the kitchen floor as soon as she walked through the door. "You only think you want to go out. It's cold out there, and wet, and there isn't a single cat treat for miles."

Then she got the cat treats out and gave him three different colored ones on the mat next to his food bowl. She was a compact, middle-aged woman, thinner than she should have been, with hair that had gone gray so long ago she couldn't remember what color it had been before. Even so, she didn't think she was really becoming one of those people, the ones who spent all their time by themselves and talked to their cats and knitted things they never used, the ones who were found dead after a month and a half because the neighbors smelled something odd coming out of the apartment.

For one thing, Annabeth thought, she didn't knit. For another, this was not an apartment, but a house, and an expensive one, and her sons called four times a day trying to make sure she wasn't completely suicidal. It was one of the few things she didn't mind about this nor'easter. It had reduced cell phone reception to absolutely nil.

She filled the kettle full of water and put it on to boil. She got her violently orange teapot down from the shelf over the sink and dumped two large scoops of loose Double Bergamot Earl Grey into the bottom of it. The tea was a bad sign, but the teapot wasn't. It hadn't occurred to her, when she'd told John and Robbie that what she really wanted was to spend a year on Margaret's Harbor with nothing to do but read, that she would actually spend her time worrying that she was turning into a cliché out of something by Agatha Christie.

Or, worse, something out of Tennessee Williams, or William Faulkner. The neighbors would come in, drawn by the smell, and find not only her dead body on the floor of the kitchen, but the dead bodies of all her old lovers buried in the root cellar right under the basket of fiddlehead ferns.

"I'm going slowly but surely out of my mind," she said, to the cat again. The kettle went off, and she poured the water from it into the teapot. Then she got a tray, a mug, a tiny mug-sized strainer, and her copy of Gertrude Himmelfarb's *The Moral Imagination* and headed on out for the living room. The storm could scream and moan as much as it liked. She had two industrial-sized generators. She could keep her electricity going in the middle of a nuclear attack.

She put everything down on the coffee table, poured herself some tea through the strainer, and curled up in her big overstuffed chair. This was the way she had imagined herself, last year, when she had been talking about this to her sons. She had seen herself, comfortable and surrounded by books and cats, reading without having to think about anything else in the world. It hadn't occurred to her that the utter sameness of it would get boring faster than watching *The Sopranos* had.

3

The cat jumped into her lap just as she heard the first of the heavy thuds against her kitchen door. She put her hand up to stroke him and said, "I'm an ungrateful idiot, do you know that? They gave me absolutely everything I ever wanted, and some things I didn't even think of, and I'm about ready to plug my fingers into a wall socket, it's so out-of-my-mind dull."

There was another thud, and this time she paid attention. She put the mug away from her and looked around.

"Do you think it's an animal?" she said. "I can't imagine it would be a person out in all that. Even Melissandra Rhode isn't as crazy as that."

The third thud was heavier and more dangerous than the other two had been. Annabeth could hear the wood straining under whatever was hitting it. She put the book down and got up. You could see the ocean from the kitchen windows. Whoever had built this house had wanted to watch the waves at the breakfast table. Still, it couldn't be the sea coming in. Not this fast. And it couldn't be a tree branch blown loose by the wind. It sounded like something soft.

"I should watch television," she told the cat. "At least I wouldn't be rewriting Freddy Krueger movies in my head."

She went back to the kitchen and looked around. She looked out the big windows at the sea, but it was comfortably far away, although choppy. She looked at the walk that wrapped around the house at that side, but saw nothing but untouched snow. She looked around the kitchen, and wondered what she had been thinking when she bought two complete sets of Le Creuset pots to hang from the hooks over the center island.

"One of those is going to fall on my head one day and give me a concussion," she said, not even to the cat this time. The cat was still in the living room, curled up on a cushion. Then there was another thud, and this time it was distinctly accompanied by giggling.

"What the hell," Annabeth said.

She made her way out into the pantry, its four tall walls covered floor to ceiling with shelves. She went into the little mud area with its benches and pegs for holding outerwear so that it didn't muck up the rest of the house in bad weather. She stood very still and listened. The giggling really was giggling, not just the wind, she was sure of it. Sometimes it sounded not so much like giggling as it did like crying. The kitchen door had no window. There was no way to tell without opening up.

"What the hell," Annabeth said, thinking that if there really was some half-crazed homicidal maniac out there, ready to rip her into body parts before he disappeared into the storm, she almost owed it to him to cooperate. Anybody who wanted anything badly enough to go through that storm to get it, ought to have it.

"Not really," Annabeth said. She missed the cat. It gave her a cover so that she didn't have to recognize the fact that she had started to talk to herself.

She grabbed the knob of the door, turned it to the right, yanked the door forward, and stepped back.

She was just in time. The young woman who came falling through at her couldn't have been more than five feet tall, but she fell hard nonetheless, and she fell far, too.

It took a minute or two, but Annabeth worked it out. This was definitely somebody she recognized, even if she couldn't remember what the woman's name was, but that was the least of it. The most was a toss-up between the clothing—a pale blue-silver, sleeveless minidress, hiked up to beyond beyond—and the hair. Annabeth thought she'd go with the hair. It would have been long and blond under other circumstances, but at the moment it was black and sticky and covered with blood.

2

Marcey Mandret was pretty sure that Stewart Gordon was mad at her—furious, in fact—but the information made no sense, and she was too tired to think about it. Besides, what did he have to be mad at her for? He wasn't her father, for God's sake, or her uncle, or even her agent, and this wasn't a working day anyway. The snow had started coming down like crazy hours ago, and everybody had just packed up and gone to what amounted to home. Marcey hated Margaret's Harbor with a passion. It didn't matter to her that presidents had vacationed here, or that Kendra Rhode's family had had a summer place here since before the Civil War. Nobody cared what people like that did anymore. People cared about Kendra only because she had started hanging out with people like Marcey, although Marcey was fairly sure—there it went again, that weird zinging in her head, as if there were a live electrical wire up there somewhere—that that wasn't the way it was playing in the papers. It made her furious, it really did, that the papers and the television stations all made it sound like Kendra was the Most Important Person in the History of the World, even though Kendra didn't do anything except wear clothes and look really tall.

Stewart Gordon was over there against the wall, staring at her. His head was as bald as if he'd shaved it, but people said he'd lost his hair when he wasn't even twenty years old. He was a lot older than that now. He was ancient. And he was a snob. He was always carrying around the kind of book Marcey was sure nobody actually read; they just liked to be seen carrying it because it made them look smarter than everybody else. She didn't care how smart Stewart Gordon was. He was a loser in the only way that counted. He was getting only five million dollars for this picture, and Marcey was getting seven.

Money. Liquor. The dress was coming off, again. The straps kept sliding down her shoulders. She was the only person in here with straps. Everybody else was dressed as if they were about to pose for an L.L. Bean catalog. Who bought things out of the L.L. Bean catalog? It was all such clunky stuff, and that other place, Harbor Halls, was even worse. All those pastels and twin sets and espadrilles, except in the winter, like now, when it was parkas and snow boots. Marcey had never worn a pair of snow boots in her life, and she didn't intend to start now.

She got the strap adjusted on her shoulder and made her way

6

slowly in the direction of the bar. She wasn't walking very well. Her head hurt, and she was very dizzy. She tried to remember the number of champagne cocktails she'd drunk since they'd shut down filming at eleven, but she couldn't do it. They'd shut down filming. She'd come over here with Arrow Normand and Kendra and some other people. She'd started drinking and then she'd started watching the snow. Kendra was gone now. Arrow seemed to be gone too. Arrow's boyfriend—Marcey looked around, and blinked. The only other person from the film who seemed to still be here was Stewart Gordon, and she would swear on her life that he was still be nursing the same big mug of beer he'd bought when he first walked in the door.

There was a bar stool in front of her. This was good news. She sat down on it and tried adjusting her strap again. She was fairly sure she could not be really drunk, because Kendra had told her that it wasn't possible to get drunk on champagne. She felt drunk, though, and her right breast seemed to be completely exposed. She pulled at the strap again. The bartender had started pouring another champagne cocktail without being asked. He wasn't much older than she was and he was looking straight at her nipple.

Somebody squeezed in against the bar between her stool and the one on her right. She looked up and saw Stewart Gordon handing her cocktail back to the bartender.

"Do something about your dress," he said.

"Why is it that everybody on this island wears bow ties?" Marcey asked him. "Have you noticed that? They all look like Porky Pig."

"Have you been running a tab?"

"It's okay," the bartender said. "That guy from the film comes over once a week and settles the tabs. You know, the guy—"

"Shit," Stewart Gordon said.

"I bet you don't run tabs," Marcey said. "I bet you pay for that beer right when you get it and then you drink only one. You can't take my drink away. You're not my father."

"Your problem is that nobody is your father, not even your father."

7

"I make more money than he does. I make more money than you do. You can't tell me what to do."

The bartender was standing right there, holding the champagne cocktail in his hands. Marcey leaned across the bar and got it. Then she tilted her head back and swallowed almost all of it in a single long gulp. This was not the best thing she could have done. She hadn't realized until she did it just what kind of a mess her stomach was in. She was probably going to throw up. This was all right, since she always threw up, but she preferred to do it without an audience. It was practically the only thing she preferred to do without an audience.

"Arrow does everything in public," she said, looking at the third button on Stewart Gordon's dark blue chambray shirt. God, the man was tall. He was enormous. "She even vomits in public. Don't you think that's pathetic?"

The bartender coughed. Stewart Gordon took what was left of the drink out of her hand. It didn't matter. Marcey had won this round. She'd drunk most of it. Now if she could just stand up and get another one. She could go home, or up to Kendra's, but she didn't want to. The party wasn't due to start for hours. There would be nothing to do up there.

"It's New Year's Eve," she said.

"I know," Stewart Gordon said. "And you're going to keel over before the ball drops. Do you have a coat?"

Marcey waved into the middle of the room. "I've got my jacket. You know. My blue jacket."

"Your blue jacket is made of glitter and silk thread. Do you mean to say you came all the way out to New England in the middle of the winter without a decent winter jacket?"

"I hate coats," Marcey said. "They make me look fat."

Somebody came up with the jacket. Marcey didn't see who it was. She really wasn't seeing much of anything. Stewart Gordon handed it to her.

"Put it on," he said. "At least it will cover your breasts, one of

8

which, at the moment, is waving in the breeze, to the enormous satisfaction of half the people in this room. And only most of them are men."

"It's not just the breast," Marcey said. "Don't you know? Kendra and Arrow and I made a pact. We're all going commando for the whole year. This year. Until midnight. We're all going commando to show that we're, that we're—"

"Ass," Stewart Gordon said. "Kendra Rhode got a one-hundred-million-dollar trust fund the day she was born. She doesn't need a career. You do. And you're not going to have one by the time she's through with you."

"Kendra Rhode is my friend," Marcey said. "She's my best friend. We'd do anything for each other."

"Kendra Rhode is a psychopath who likes to play with people's heads. Button that jacket and I'll take you home."

"I don't want to go home. There's nothing to do at home. And besides, I'm supposed to be out at the Point for a party. You weren't invited to the party, were you? Kendra invites only the best people to her parties."

"Come into my parlor, said the spider to the fly."

"What?"

"Never mind. Let's go."

Marcey looked around the bar. There were a lot of people there, and most of them were looking at her. That was reassuring. That really was. Sometimes, when she got drunk enough, she began to feel as if she were trying to walk on water. It was all right as long as she didn't notice that that was what she was doing, but when she did she suddenly realized that she couldn't, and she was way out over the ocean and about to drown. She hated that feeling, that about-to-drown feeling. It made all her nerves go crazy and it made her want to cry. She wanted to cry right now. Crying seemed to be the best thing she could possibly do. Crying had substance, and she had no substance. Everybody said so. There was something coming up her throat. It might be vomit, but it might be something else. If she didn't get Stewart Gordon away from her, he would start giving her a lecture about how she should have gone to school.

"School isn't important," she said, leaning very close to him. Leaning was not good. Leaning was like falling. "What does school get for people? Jobs in offices. That's it. Jobs in offices. Or mechanics. Or things. School—"

There always came a point when the air looked slick and solid, when it could ripple. It was rippling now. It made her think of mayonnaise, and of the first time she had ever been in a movie, when she was seven years old. Her mother was always sitting in one of those folding chairs at the edge of the set, leaning forward with her elbows on her knees, tense. Everything was always tense. That was the year she had been interviewed by Katie Couric. She had been given a big solid chair to sit on, and her legs had dangled from the seat without reaching the floor.

"I can't walk on water," she said, as loud as she could, past Stewart Gordon to the room at large.

Everybody was watching her. They really were. Everybody was always watching her. They would always watch her. This was what life was like and it would never end. Never never never.

Somewhere at the back of her mind, though, there was that ocean of water she was walking on, and the thought that it was ending for Arrow. It was ending right now.

Stewart Gordon was holding her up with one hand. She was standing up. She had no idea how she had got that way. She gripped the bar with both hands and wrenched herself away from him. Kendra got paid to go to parties. That was not fair. Arrow was starting to look like a fat slob. That was not fair either. Nothing was fair, and she deserved better than this, although she was not sure for what. The most unfair thing was Stewart Gordon, who was like the voice of doom, or something, all the time. Somebody ought to do something about Stewart Gordon. Somebody ought to put a stop to him.

Even so, when she finally decided to throw up, Marcey was careful to do it directly onto the bartender's pink-and-green, tiny-fishhook-patterned bow tie, and not on Stewart Gordon's chambray shirt.

3

Once, when he was younger, Carl Frank had liked to tell people that he didn't believe in God but did believe in the devil. He didn't tell people that anymore, because somewhere along the way it had become true. God was, as he understood it, a benevolent being, a cosmic Superperson whose first and most important characteristic was to wish his people well. Carl had been around for a long time, and he didn't see any sign of anybody wishing anybody well. Even on a purely mundane level, the here and now, the day to day, all that was in evidence was bad luck and bad faith. Even the good luck was bad, more often than not. When he thought about the people he worked for, and the people they had him looking after, he sometimes wondered if there wasn't a malevolent Superperson out there somewhere, making sure that everything turned out as badly as possible.

About the devil, though, Carl had no need to get metaphorical. The devil was a person just like you and me, except not, and she lived in a cloud of celebrity she had done nothing to earn. In fact, she had never earned anything in her life, unless you counted the money people paid her to go to their parties, which was considerable. It made Carl stop and wonder every time he thought of it. A million dollars just to show up at a party, when you didn't sing or dance or act or even sling hash in a cafeteria? A million dollars just to sit there and be. That was not luck, it was sorcery, and the devil's name was Kendra Rhode.

The pain-in-the-ass's name was Michael Bardman, and he was getting hard to hear on this cell phone. Cells never worked all that well on Margaret's Harbor, but in weather like this they were about as reliable as a schizophrenic on LSD. Of course, it was impossible to explain that to Michael Bardman, because he had never been on Margaret's Harbor in the winter, and wouldn't come. Michael liked L.A. Michael liked New York. Michael liked some place in the Greek islands where he could spend all day on his boat making phone calls to people he could have been screaming at in person if he weren't so intent on taking a vacation. Carl wondered what it would be like if somebody decided to give Michael Bardman a taste of reality, and then he didn't. The Michael Bardmans of this world, like the Kendra Rhodes, lived in an alternative universe.

The snow looked like a solid sheet of white outside the big front windows of the Oscartown Inn. Carl took a long sucking pull at his Scotch and water and waited for the tirade to be over. It was the same tirade he had heard yesterday, and the day before, and the day before that, and the only reason he wasn't scared to death that he was about to lose his job was that he knew that Michael Bardman knew that there was nobody out there who could do it any better.

"Let me try to explain this to you again," he said, when Michael's screeching had subsided momentarily. Michael Bardman had made something of a career of screeching. It was what he did instead of actually producing movies.

"You keep explaining things to me," he said, "and I keep telling you I don't want your explanations."

"You also don't want me to walk out of here in the middle of everything, so you're going to have to listen to them. We're in the middle of some kind of huge snowstorm. They call it a nor'easter—"

"I don't understand why everything has to stop because of a little snow."

"It's not a little snow, it's a lot of snow. Half the island has already lost electricity and the rest will probably go before morning. We can't film at all, outside or in. And it's not your problem anyway. We're not a month and a half late because of a snowstorm."

"It's costing a fortune. And on a movie that isn't going to make all that much. I mean, it will do all right, but—"

"But it's not going to be *Lord of the Rings*. Yes, I know, Michael, I know. But nothing is going to get any better, or any cheaper, as long as that woman is here screwing things up. And she's not just screwing things up, Michael, she's doing it deliberately."

"I don't see why my actors have to drink like fish just because Kendra Rhode drinks like a fish. If Kendra Rhode jumped off a cliff, would they all just jump in after her?"

Carl looked down into his Scotch. His glass was half empty. He would never have been so fatuous as to describe it as half full. He couldn't believe he had just heard what he had heard. He was having a very hard time not bursting out laughing.

"Listen," he said. "Kendra Rhode does not drink like a fish. She gets other people to drink like fishes. She's never late to appointments. She gets other people to be late to appointments. And, like I said, she does it deliberately. She likes to see people crack up."

"Don't be ridiculous. You make her sound like, I don't know—"

"It doesn't matter what I make her sound like, Michael. It's true. And as long as she's here, Marcey and Arrow are going to be shit out of control more days than not. And the longer that goes on, the more money you're going to lose. You ought to be grateful as hell that Stewart Gordon is a thorough professional, because if he'd been less of one he'd have walked off this picture weeks ago."

"He can't walk off the picture. He's not important enough."

"He's something better than important," Carl said, thinking that it was completely useless trying to explain to Michael that some people did not judge the success of their lives by how well they were doing in the movies. "He's independent, Michael. He's stashed most of the money he's ever made—"

"It can't amount to much."

"It's more than he needs to live on," Carl said, "which means he doesn't have to work if he doesn't want to. And the pair of them are driving him nuts. And I don't blame him. You've got to do something to get those two away from Kendra Rhode, at least for the next few months, or you're not going to have a picture at all. And that's assuming that Arrow doesn't run away and get married to the latest toy boy."

"Oh, God," Michael said. "I thought we got rid of the toy boy."

"We got rid of the first one, more or less. The divorce is in the works, at any rate. But there's a new one, one of the camera people, not a serious one—one of the grips, I think—"

"Can we just fire him and get him off the island?"

"I'm already on it. But I stopped in at that little pub place on my way here this afternoon, and Marcey was all by herself at a table drinking champagne cocktails and letting her dress fall off her, and Arrow was missing in action completely. So I don't think the news is good. You've got to let me do something about Kendra Rhode."

There was a very long silence on the other end of the line. Carl wished he could be surer of the cell phone reception in the inn. He needed to get himself a refill. Michael Bardman's voice came back on the line.

"You can't do something about Kendra Rhode," he said. "She's a Rhode. They're, what, like the third-richest family in America?"

"Hardly. It's a whole new world these days. Old money barely makes the cut. I'm not talking about having her whacked, Michael. I'm talking about hiring her."

"Hiring her for what?"

"For a picture. You've got to have a picture somewhere that she could be some use in. Or at least, seem to be some use in."

"I can't hire her for a picture. And besides, even if I tried, what makes you thing she'd say yes?"

"Make it a big picture. Brad Pitt. Sean Connery. Make it a picture she can't refuse."

"You must be out of your mind. Whatever in God's name makes you think that somebody like Brad Pitt would agree to work with her?"

"You don't actually have to hire her, Michael. You just have to pretend to hire her. Ask her out to the coast for exploratory conversations. That kind of thing."

"Sometimes I think you're seriously in need of medication. The woman can't act. She can barely speak, from what I can see. And that family has lawyers. You can't just go jerking her around and then thumb your nose at her. She'd sue."

"By which time you'd have your picture in the can and it wouldn't have cost more than a single arm and leg. A few more weeks of what's been going on out here and your totals are going to look like the Social Security budget. You won't even need to inflate the expenses to make it look like it's been losing money, because it will be losing money."

"I don't see what Social Security has to do with it," Michael said. "It's a young picture, except for Stewart Gordon. Young actors. Appeal to the high school set. Rated R so that they'll all feel good about themselves for sneaking in under the rating."

The Oscartown Inn looked out onto a picturesque village square, picturesque because it had been calculated to look that way, square because it had been hacked out of a tangle of existing streets when the Powers That Be decided that they wanted the town to look like the "real" New England. That would have been in the 1930s, when people like Kendra Rhode tried as hard as they could to stay out of the public's sight, and places like Margaret's Harbor were important because they were places where rich people could go to live richly and not be observed by anyone doing it.

"It didn't matter in Hollywood anyway," Carl said. "Even then."

"What?" Michael said.

"I was thinking about the Great Depression," Carl said. "People were scared to death that there was going to be a violent revolution. Rich people were. So they hired public relations experts to keep their names out of the newspapers. But it wasn't like that in Hollywood even then. Stars ran around looking rich in public. They always do."

"Social Security. The Great Depression. I think you're cracking up."

"I'm going to crack up if you don't do what I tell you. Find some way to get Kendra Rhode out of here before she pushes those two right off the edge of the world and brings down your movie with them. She does it deliberately, Michael. I'm not making this up. She likes to see people crash and burn. I think it's the only thing on earth that doesn't bore her."

"Shit—," Michael said.

And that was all he said, because the service had cut out. Carl folded up his phone and put it in his pocket. He liked the Oscartown Inn. Marcey and Arrow complained about how stodgy it was, and Carl was sure the inn's management complained about them, but he just found the place comfortable, and that was all he needed to be satisfied. It did occur to him that there had been a time, not all that long ago, when he had needed a lot more to be satisfied, but it was like the man said. You can't always get what you want.

He took his empty drink glass across the lobby and through the tinted-glass, mahogany-lined doors of the inn's bar. He went up to the bar itself and sat down on a stool. The bar had the television on, which was a miracle. The cable company up here had to be the best on the planet. The set was turned to a news channel. A woman reporter was standing in the snow in a pastel green parka with fake fur around the hood, talking into a microphone and shivering.

"You want another one of those, Mr. Frank?" the bartender said.

The bar was dark, the way so many bars were. It was as if most people couldn't really drink in the full light of day. The people around him, sitting at the little tables, all looked like the kind who nursed a single drink for an hour and then went home. Some of the women had tote bags next to their chairs with books peeping out of them. Over on the far wall there was a huge fireplace that went through to the common room on the other side, the fire in it fully stoked and blazing. Carl had seen Stewart Gordon down here some nights, all by himself with a book of his own. There had to be something better he could be doing with his life than what he was actually doing with it. The problem was, he couldn't think of what.

16

He made a gesture at his glass and said, "Give me a double this time. I think I'm in for the night."

4

There were people on Margaret's Harbor who said that Linda Beecham was a living history of the island. If you needed to know who fell down sloppy drunk on Main Street on Christmas Eve in 1924, or who was and wasn't at the Montgomery's Gold and Silver Ball in 1933, all you had to do was to ask Linda. She wouldn't even have to look it up. She sat there on the second floor of the Harbor Home News Building, looking out her big plate glass window at the people of Oscartown, and it was as if the island had its own fairy godmother, the Spirit of Christmas Past in chinos and fisherman's sweaters and big clanky suede snow boots that she'd certainly never bought in any place you could get to without driving over water.

The thing was, though, that any picture of Linda Beecham as the Spirit of Christmas anything had to come from people who knew her very little, and then mostly as a decoration. It was true enough that she knew everything there was to know about the island. She had been born and raised there, which was incredibly rare, at least until recently. For most of the world, Margaret's Harbor was a place to take a vacation or to own a second house. People came up from Boston and New York in the summer and sat in the hole-in-the-wall coffee places with copies of *Forbes* and the *New York Review of Books,* and even their waiters were from off-island. There were times when it was possible to think that there was no such thing as a native of Margaret's Harbor. The whole place was just a repository for old New England money, new New York money, and the families of presidents too famous for their own good.

Linda's family had been fishermen, back when she'd had any family, and some of them had owned stores in the small towns in the island's center, away from the ocean, where property was expensive. If she bothered to remember it—and she almost never did—she could feel the air on her face biking out to Oscartown to see the rich people when she was still in grade school. The girls had all looked to her like space aliens because they were nothing like the girls she knew, and nothing like the girls she saw on television. Back in those days, Margaret's Harbor got exactly two television stations, both of them out of Boston. They showed the standard sitcoms and westerns and game shows and the Boston nightly news, which made even less sense to her than the rich people did. The only thing that did make sense to her was her plans for the future. None of those plans had included spending the rest of her life on Margaret's Harbor.

The reason that Linda Beecham couldn't be the Spirit of Christmas anything was this: she never smiled, if she could help it, and she never acknowledged Christmas when she was away from the office. The office was always decorated to the hilt, including strings of lights around the entryway that faced Main Street, but home was blank and bare of even so much as a holly wreath. If people sent her Christmas cards, she threw them away. If people showed up with plates of cookies or fruit baskets full of navel oranges, she waited until they'd gone away and then put everything but the oranges down the garbage disposal. She was not an evil-tempered and embittered woman. She didn't put a lot of venom in her systematic exclusion of all things sentimental. She just went about her life as methodically as possible without actually being transformed into a robot, and when people tried to get her to do more than that, she pretended she hadn't heard them. Linda Beecham had learned a lot of things in the fifty-five years of her life, but the most important one was this: it was very dangerous for some people to be happy.

At the moment, since it wasn't even New Year's Day yet, the decorations were still up on the premises of the *Harbor Home News,* including a small tree in a wooden pot with bows and candy canes all over it. The tree sat in the window that looked out onto the street, and Linda tried her best to pretend it wasn't there. In some ways it was too bad that she wasn't evil-tempered or embittered. If she had been, she could have told the silly little intern who had brought her the tree to shove it up her gilded rich girl's ass.

On the other side of the office, her best reporter—her only full-time reporter—was setting up a presentation on a tripod. The tripod had an easel on it and the easel was covered with photographs, most of them in color, even though the *Harbor Home News* never published anything in color. Linda had a big cup of coffee that she wanted to bury her face in. She sometimes thought that if she ever decided to become a legend in her own time, she'd start spiking the coffee with gin.

"You know," she said, "there's a major storm out there. You could go home."

"You could go home too," Jack Bullard said. "It doesn't matter for either of us. We walk. I want you to look at these photographs."

"They're very nice photographs. They're just photographs of silly people."

"Photographs of silly people fetch a lot of money these days. I've got one I haven't developed yet of Arrow Normand falling into her car dead drunk and probably worse not an hour and a half ago, and I'll bet you anything I could sell it to the tabloids for a few thousand dollars. And Arrow Normand isn't even a big deal anymore."

"Was Arrow Normand ever a big deal?"

Jack Bullard sighed. "These people may be trivial, Linda, but they're not unimportant. At least, they're not unimportant to the people who have money to spend on photographs of famous people. And we've got lots of photographs of famous people. If you don't want to run them in the *Home News*—"

"I don't."

"At least consider the possibility of selling them to somebody who does want to run them. These people are here. We get the pictures nobody else gets—"

"How do we do that, Jack? I've been meaning to ask you."

"I just don't look like a paparazzo. Because I'm not one. Although lots of people probably have the same pictures, they just get them on the cameras from their cell phones and they're not very good quality. Mine are excellent quality. She wasn't wearing any underwear."

"Who wasn't?"

"Arrow Normand. She had on a miniskirt cut up to, well, wherever, and she wasn't wearing any underwear. I've got at least one picture in my camera nobody could print anywhere. Except they do, you know, they show them on television with the wrong place just sort of fuzzed out. It's really incredible what they'll do on MTV these days."

"When I was growing up, the *Home News* used to run society pages. Parties, you know, and debutante things. Nobody seems to do any of that anymore."

"Nobody seems to care," Jack said. "Look, I know what you think and I see your point. These are not stellar examples of human beings. They're not distinguished except by their publicity and they haven't accomplished anything you'd say was important."

"Most of them haven't accomplished anything at all," Linda pointed out. "I mean, you can say what you want about the old robber barons, but they built industries. They provided jobs for millions of people. They were good for the economy. What you're asking me to do is to run stories on people who—"

"On people other people want to read about," Jack said. "It's no use, Linda. Not everybody has your high-minded idea about what should be news, and not everybody is more interested in George Steiner and Steven Pinker than in Arrow Normand and Marcey Mandret. Maybe they should be, but they're not."

"It's like high school. The people who are accomplishing something are invisible, and the people who are visible are all, well. . . . You see what I mean."

"I do see what you mean. But this is a good story, Linda, and we should use it. And if we don't use it, we should at least sell the pictures to a tabloid that's willing to pay money for it. But I say we use it, because it really is a good story."

"Arrow Normand falling into her car dead drunk is a good story."

"She didn't just fall into her car. She was with that guy she's been all over, one of the camera crew people she took up with. Mark Anderman. That's it. They were together."

"I thought they were always together."

"They are, but this time they were fighting. She kept kicking him and screaming at him that he was a bastard—"

Linda cleared her throat.

"Sorry. But that's what she called him. Then she took her nails to his face and ripped a couple of good-sized streaks in his skin. He was bleeding. It was incredible. I got pictures."

Linda took another long and deep drink of coffee. She liked Jack Bullard. He was young, and he was definitely from the rich people part of the island, but he was direct and without pretensions, and he didn't try to make her something she was not. That made his obsession with the movie people all the more stupefying.

"It's incredible that Arrow Normand scratched the face of Mark Anderman until it bled," she said. "You do realize you're not making much in the way of sense."

"I'm just trying to make money. Although, I'll admit, the whole scene was weird as hell."

"I think the very idea of these people on the island is weird as hell. The world isn't what it was when I was growing up. Lord, Jack, really. Thirty years ago, somebody like Kendra Rhode would no more have been seen in public with somebody like Arrow Normand than—I don't know than what. It's the sixties. I'm sure it is. That's what changed everything."

"The sixties have been over for forty years," Jack said, "and that's not what I meant. I meant there was something about the scene that was weird. It can't be that she was fighting with him or scratching him. She does things like that all the time. It was . . . I don't know. Something about the car. Truck. It was a truck. A big purple pickup truck."

"So the scene wasn't just incredibly vulgar, it was also incredibly tacky?"

"You talk like an etiquette book sometimes, Linda. An old etiquette book. Come and look at these pictures. We could run a story about the movie. We could talk about how it's affected life on the island, having the movie people here. It would sell a lot of extra copies—Alice could probably even sell some extra advertising around it."

"I'm not going to print a picture of Arrow Normand's private parts in the *Harbor Home News*. Not even on an inside page."

"I haven't developed those pictures yet," Jack said. "Come ahead and look at these. I wish I could get into the party tonight. That would be a coup. Kendra Rhode's New Year's party on the society pages of the *Harbor Home News*."

"There haven't been society pages in the *Harbor Home News* for twenty years."

"Come look," Jack said again.

She got up from behind her desk and started across the room to him, thinking that he got too enthusiastic over everything. He had yet to learn that enthusiasm, like happiness, could be dangerous.

She had just reached the point where she could see the photographs clearly—Marcey Mandret doing one of those over-the-shoulder hooded-eye poses that had been a staple of Marilyn Monroe's; Kendra Rhode carrying her little dog into an accessories store called Mama's Got a Brand-New Bag; Arrow Normand looking like she was about to throw up—when Jack straightened up and frowned.

"What is it?" she asked him. "Is one of the photographs that bad?"

"The photographs are fine," he said. "Maybe I'll stay behind today to develop those pictures. I wish I could put my finger on what's bothering me so much about that scene. It's like I almost saw something, but then I didn't. I didn't really see it."

"You should go home and go to bed," Linda said, and she meant it.

She really wasn't either evil-tempered or embittered. She liked Jack, and she wished him well, even more than she wished most people well. She just needed to keep herself in check, so that she didn't do something to destroy the first resting place she'd ever found.

She looked at the easel and the photographs pinned to it, the pictures of people who did not matter in any serious sense but who would always matter more than they should in every other sense.

Then she told herself she really ought to start spiking her coffee with gin.

5

Stewart Gordon thought of himself as a sensible man, and he was certainly sensible enough to know that different nationalities had different ways of dealing with common problems. That was the kind of thing they had taught him at St. Andrew's, and that was the kind of thing he stuck to when he experienced the inevitable collision between Scottish sanity and Hollywood lunacy that hit him every time he worked in the States. This time, though, things had gotten far beyond out of hand. If he had been the parent or guardian of any of the spoiled brats being paid hefty seven-figure salaries to work on this project, he would have locked them up on food and water for a year, long enough to beat some sense into their heads. As far as he could tell, though, none of these people had parents or guardians. They had fathers who were off somewhere—in at least one case, in prison—and mothers who hit the bars as hard as they did. And they all hit the bars. Stewart Gordon liked his ale, and he liked his Glenfiddich even better, but he'd never understood why anyone wanted to get drunk enough to suffer through the headache on the following morning.

Not that he hadn't suffered through a few in his time. He had. He was normal. But that was it. He was normal. These people were—

"Stupid," he said, out loud, and on his back, Marcey Mandret giggled.

It was still the middle of the afternoon. There were lights on here and there, but that was only because the cloud cover was so thick that everything was hazy. He could have gone right down Main Street and deposited the woman in the lobby of the Oscartown Inn, but he was uncomfortably aware that Marcey's behavior had attracted an audience. There would be photographers out any minute, if there weren't already, and that was all he would need. He did not get his picture in the tabloids. He didn't hide. He didn't surround himself with forty people whose only purpose was to run interference between him and the press. He just went around living his life, and people mostly left him alone. People did not leave Marcey Mandret alone, mostly because she spent so much time getting their attention.

He looked around. He was off the track, he was sure of it. He was too close to the water. The girls had rented a house, and he'd thought he knew where it was, but now he was slogging through snowdrifts and he could hear the sea. He was cold, too. He'd wrapped his jacket around Marcey's ass when he'd first hauled her onto his shoulder—why didn't these women wear knickers? why?—and even his wool commando's sweater wasn't much help in this weather.

The houses around him looked mostly closed up. He always had to remind himself that most of the people with houses on the island used them only as vacation homes, in good weather. There was the Point, but not only was it too far away, he didn't like the idea of asking Kendra Rhode for anything. The only other house with lights on was a relatively small one, and it had lights on everywhere. He made a calculation. In his experience, Americans were pretty good in an emergency. They took you in and dried you off and warmed you up and gave you a phone. He could only hope that the house with the lights on had an American inside, and not some visiting twit from Paris.

It was hard to figure out how to get where he needed to go. The snow was high enough to be obscuring the sidewalks. He tried a direct route, moving carefully, hoping that he would neither fall nor provoke Marcey Mandret into another bout of vomiting. My God, that girl could spew it out. He stumbled a little here and there, but the house continued to come closer, and he started to worry that he would look too threatening for even an American to let in. Of course, the American might recognize him, which was usually a good sign— but it happened less often on Margaret's Harbor than in other places he'd been, because Margaret's Harbor was Sophisticated.

He started to come up to what was obviously the walk to the house's front door, and the first thing he saw was a small ginger cat sitting in the window. Cats were good. He liked cats. He plowed along, judging his way by the indentations in the snow, and the cat stood up and stretched. It was like the start of some kind of silly movie: there's a knock on the door, and you open up to find this enormous muscled bald man carrying a half-naked girl to your doorstep.

There was no proper porch. They didn't do much with porches on Margaret's Harbor. He thought about knocking and found the bell instead, which at least wouldn't have connotations out of horror movies. He rang once, and waited. He rang a second time. Maybe there was an old lady in there, peering at him from somewhere upstairs, too scared to open up.

A moment later, a woman appeared next to the cat in the window. She was not a particularly old lady. She looked him up and down and then withdrew. A second later, the door swung open in front of him.

"Ride 'em, horsey!" Marcey Mandret suddenly shouted.

The woman in front of him blinked. Stewart thought he was probably blushing. "Excuse me," he said. "Excuse us. I'm—"

"Stewart Gordon," the woman said. "From that science fiction thing. One of my sons used to have a poster of you on his bedroom wall."

"Good. I don't mean to bother you, but—"

"No, come in, come in." The woman stepped back hurriedly. She was, he thought, somewhere in her early fifties, and very neatly put together, like Judi Dench in the best of her middle age.

Stewart brought Marcey into the front hall and looked around. It was a standard Margaret's Harbor colonial except for the built-in bookshelves, and they were everywhere. There were even two in the hall. They were filled with books, too. He wondered if this woman owned the house or rented it.

"Excuse me," he said again. "She's—"

"Oh, come into the living room and put her down on the chaise. I'd put her on the couch, but here's the thing. I've got one too."

"Got one what?"

"Girl. I've got a girl," the woman said. "She came to the back door about twenty minutes ago, in practically no clothes. And she looks sort of familiar, but I can't put my finger on it. And I think she's been raped. She's lost her underwear."

Stewart sighed. "She probably wasn't wearing any. None of them do."

"None of them?"

"The young women I'm making this movie with. Sort of. We spend an awful lot of time chasing after the young women and not much time making the movie."

"This one has blood in her hair," the middle-aged woman said. She was leading them into the living room, which was large and once again almost completely lined with bookshelves. It was not the room he had seen from the hall, which made him think that the dining room must be completely lined with bookshelves too. The woman pointed him toward the chaise and he put Marcey down on it. She was having a fit of giggles. Then he looked over at the couch and saw Arrow Normand, passed out as completely as it was possible to be without actually being dead.

"Arrow Normand," Stewart said, pointing to the girl on the couch. Then he pointed to the chaise. "Marcey Mandret."

"Annabeth Falmer," the woman said, holding out her hand.

Stewart processed the information. It took longer than it should have, because he wasn't used to that form of the name. "Anna Falmer?"

he said. "*Abigail Adams and the Birth of the American Nation*? You do own this house."

"What?"

"The bookshelves. I was wondering if you owned the house or rented it. If they were your books or if you'd rented the place from somebody—this is going around in circles."

"No, no. I understand. Yes, I do own the house. I mean, my sons bought it for me and put the bookshelves in. I said it was a silly thing to do, just to spend a year on the Harbor, but my younger one, the one who's the lawyer, said that buying was better than renting for some reason, I'm not sure what. Writing history doesn't make a lot of money, you see, so I've never had any, and I don't understand it. She's got blood in her hair. And she says there's a man somewhere, in the snow. I've got the kettle on if you don't mind tea. I could put brandy in it."

"Tea with brandy sounds wonderful. You sound like you could use it yourself. Are you all right?"

Annabeth Falmer sighed. Stewart decided that he had been right in his first impression. She was a neatly made woman, and he liked her general . . . way of being. He liked her books. He could see some of them, and they were not the books of a self-consciously "intellectual" person. There were intellectual books in great numbers, of course, but there also seemed to be a hefty selection of Terry Pratchett and virtually all the Miss Marples Agatha Christie ever wrote. He also liked the fact that she really had no idea who Marcey Mandret and Arrow Normand were, or why she was supposed to care.

She had been leading him out to the kitchen without his noticing it. He looked around and saw that there was even another bookshelf here, although it contained mostly cookbooks. The kettle was screaming. She got a clean cup and saucer out of the cupboard and a bottle of Metaxa Seven Star out of the bread box. He let that one go.

"Here's the thing," she said. "I was going to go out. I mean, I tried to call the police, but there's no use, not in this weather, everything is

27

such a mess and there aren't very many police. But I should go out. Somebody should."

"Why?"

"Because that girl, the one with the blood in her hair, she said there'd been an accident. She'd been with a man, in a truck, and it went down an embankment, over on the beach somewhere. I think. It was hard to get her to make sense. But she did say she was with somebody, and he's probably still down there, and I can't just leave him there, can I? If he's already dead it won't matter, but if he isn't he needs to get medical help somehow or he will die, and—you probably think I'm a lunatic."

"No," Stewart said, thinking that this was one of those people with a tremendous sense of personal responsibility for everything. He recognized it because he was one of those people himself.

He took a tea bag from the box of them she was holding out to him and picked up the brandy bottle.

"Let me get some of this into myself. Then let's go see if we can make Miss Normand make enough sense so we can find this person she thinks she left out in the snow."

6

Kendra Rhode did not speak to people she did not want to speak to, except for policemen in patrol cars, when they thought she was both driving and drunk. The truth was that Kendra was never drunk. She was never high, either, beyond the buzz you could get from sharing a single joint. In all the tens of thousands of pictures that had been printed of her since she had first decided to make herself a celebrity, not one showed her bleary-eyed and stumbling, or fallen asleep on a table in a bar somewhere while somebody poured beer in her hair. Blood will tell, Kendra's grandmother used to say, and Kendra thought that it was true—even if her grandmother had been trying to get something across about her mother, who was another story altogether.

28

Kendra's grandmother would have said that she should have taken all three of the telephone calls that had come in in the last twenty minutes, and the other one that had come in over an hour ago, but Kendra knew something her grandmother did not. It was never a good idea to make yourself too available to people who had launched themselves into free fall. Failure was a particular thing, but it was also a cliché, and Kendra could see it coming a mile off. There were different kinds of failure too, and some of them she didn't mind, or was at least willing to put up with. She didn't care if a movie tanked or a song sold almost nothing or a prize went to somebody else, somebody stuffy and snotty and older, whom she wouldn't want to know. She did care about disintegration, and she was sure that everybody on earth was capable of disintegration. She'd seen it happen. They fell over some edge somewhere, or were pushed, and then they couldn't remember where they'd been the night before and they stopped meeting the obligations that really mattered and they got maudlin and wanted to cry on you when the night went on too long.

She stopped looking at herself in the mirror and looked out her window instead. Her bedroom at the Point was the big one with the circular extension that looked out into the Atlantic Ocean, away from the quieter waters of Cape Cod. There was nothing quiet about what she could see out there. The snow was coming down in a steady curtain. The sky had almost no light in it at all. She bit her lip and poked at the diamond barrette she had used to clip back her hair for the afternoon.

"There's going to be trouble getting people out here from the mainland," she said.

Her mother, sitting on the other side of the room with her legs curled into an overstuffed chair, looked up from her copy of *Vanity Fair*. It was Kendra herself who was on the cover, holding Mr. Snuggles up to her chest and blowing a kiss onto the top of his head.

"They're not going to have trouble," her mother said. "They're not going to bother. Half your guest list is going to be stranded until the storm is over."

"If they let themselves be stranded until after the party, they won't be getting into the house." Kendra went back to the mirror. Weather was boring. Most things were boring. "Some of them will make it in time, though, just watch. They know I'm keeping a list."

"You'd really punish people for not making it to a party in the middle of a major snowstorm."

"I'd punish people for a lot of things. They all know how important this party is to me. I've been planning it for months."

"You could postpone it, due to weather. People do that kind of thing all the time."

"I don't. And there's no reason to postpone it. There are plenty of invited people already on the island. It's not like the storm is a surprise, Mother. They've been talking about it on the news for days. If it mattered to you to be here, you'd know that and make your plans accordingly. I can't help it if some people don't find my party very important, but I don't see why I should rearrange my life to make it easier for them."

"Sometimes I think it's entirely understandable that your grandmother approved of you. Even after you dropped out of high school."

"Education is for swots," Kendra said. "And even the most successful swots don't bother with it. Although I've noticed something about success. It comes and goes. I wonder if it always did that."

Kendra's mother's name was Maverick, which was only one of the things Kendra's grandmother had had against her. By now, she had put down her copy of *Vanity Fair* and was openly staring. Kendra was used to that. Everybody stared at her. Her family had been staring at her since she was in the seventh grade. Kendra stared at herself very hard, trying to look directly into her own eyes, as if by doing that she could see into something that was otherwise always hidden. It never worked. She knew herself well enough to know that everything she was was available on the surface. The mystery people thought they saw in her was actually disbelief. Nobody took her seriously.

"I don't understand your relationships with your friends," Maverick said, finally. "That girl who called, what's her name, she's a friend of yours."

"Which girl who called?"

"The second one."

"Marcey? She used to be a friend. I don't think she's going to be a friend very much longer. She's going to hell."

"Yes, I know. I can see that. You drop your friends when they go to hell?"

Kendra bit her lip. "They're not friends like that. They're more like business acquaintances. Do you know what people pay me to come to their parties?"

"To come to their parties? That's it? Not to, oh, I don't know, promote a product, publicize a clothing line—"

"Just to come to their parties," Kendra said. "Even private parties. They pay me a million dollars. This year, I made almost as much money on my own as I get from the trust fund, and next year I'll make more. That's because I'm the center. I define what it means to be one of the hot people. I can't afford to have Marcey Mandret throwing up on my shoes. Besides, it wasn't actually her who called."

"Claudine said—"

"She said it was about Marcey, not from her. It was from Stewart Gordon. God, I hate that man. I really hate him. He's so—"

"Intelligent?"

"Don't be ridiculous."

"It's true, though, you hate intelligent people."

"It's not true at all. I find smart people fascinating."

"There's a big difference between intelligent and smart."

"Mostly what he is is impossible," Kendra said. "They hate him too, you know, Marcey and Arrow. There he is every day, telling them how to live their lives, lecturing them when they're just a minute late for a rehearsal or they have trouble memorizing their lines or something. He's impossible. I didn't invite him to the party. I didn't want him around to bring everybody down."

31

"But you did invite him to the party," Maverick said. "I saw the invitation list. What did he do, turn you down?"

"Nobody turns me down."

"Maybe he's even more intelligent than I thought he was."

Kendra ignored this. She did not think Stewart Gordon was "intelligent," and she didn't really "hate" him in the way she usually used that word. He made her uneasy, that was all. She couldn't be around him without starting to squirm, and she didn't know why. She did know she didn't like it. For most of her life, with most people, that would have been enough—except that she'd never had this kind of feeling about anybody else that she could remember. Teachers in school, clergymen at the various churches Maverick had dragged them all through when she was having her spiritual phase, even the bankers and trust lawyers who handled her money, Kendra could take any and all of them in stride. They only thought they knew more than she did. Stewart Gordon just made her want to spit.

"Marcey got drunk in that place downtown and threw up on the bar," she said. "That's the message he left with Claudine. I don't know why he left it with me. I don't know what he thinks I'm supposed to do about it."

"You could take her in. Dry her off. Make sure she didn't freeze to death in the cold."

"She won't freeze to death. She'll show up here right on time, just watch. And she'll be sobered up enough to get drunk all over again. So will Arrow. I just wish we didn't have to put up with the dopey boyfriend."

"You could have not invited him."

"Not inviting people doesn't necessarily mean they won't show up." Kendra got up and walked over to the great curved wall of windows. This was a Victorian-era house. The ceilings were not just high, but majestic, and that meant that the stories were higher than they would have been on a modern place. She could see the rocky promontory far below her, the tip of it sinking and rising as waves of water washed over it. That was boring too. It was incredible how much of what went on in the world was just plain boring, and there was nothing she could do about it.

"I wish something exciting would happen," she said. "I wish we could have a ritual murder."

7

There was a moment at the end there, right before the two of them walked out the door, that Arrow Normand thought she was going to lose it. She couldn't figure out why she hadn't lost it. She'd heard a lot in her life about self-control and self-discipline, and there were times when people said she had both, but she'd never really understood either, and she didn't understand them now. What she did understand was that she was going to be in a lot of trouble, and waking up to tell them all about it wouldn't help her situation at all.

It wasn't as if they hadn't tried to get something out of her, or that she had been able to play completely dead. Stewart Gordon could play completely dead. She'd seen him do it. He could lie there, so lifeless you thought he was dead, and you could poke at him and yell in his ear and he wouldn't move. This was "acting," he'd told her when she'd asked him about it, and she'd known right away that he was being sarcastic at her expense. There were times when Arrow felt as if she were nothing more than a big, bad ball of resentment. She resented nearly everyone she could think of, all those people, like Stewart Gordon, who didn't understand what was important. They didn't understand that she was important, that was the thing. She was famous, and she was rich, too. Money was very, very important. It was stupid to pretend that it was less important than things like if she knew where Switzerland was, or if she'd ever graduated from high school.

She waited awhile in the silence before allowing herself to open her eyes. She had to be careful. The world seemed to be full of people who didn't understand what was really important. Besides, she didn't want to talk to Stewart Gordon twice in one day. It was hard enough to talk to him once. He always looked at her as if she were some kind of bug.

She felt the cat come up next to her on the couch and then rub his side against the top of her head. She really liked cats, although not as much as she liked dogs. Too many people were allergic to cats. She opened her eyes and watched as it walked down the back of the couch behind her. It was just a matter of thinking straight. That was all. She just had to think straight, and act like herself, and everything would be all right. It would help if her head wasn't so fuzzy and her stomach didn't hurt.

She made herself sit up, just a little, and look around the room. It was the kind of room she remembered from home in Ohio before she'd come out to Los Angeles to be famous, except for the book-shelves and the books. Nobody back home in Ohio read much in the way of books, and Arrow had the sneaking suspicion that nobody else really did either. People just pretended to read books, most of them, to make other people feel stupid, and to pretend that books were more important than money, too. The woman who lived in this house must be either very poor or very ugly. She wanted to make the whole world feel stupid.

Marcey was lying curled up into a fetal position on the chaise lounge, which was really a "chaise longue," which Stewart Gordon had lectured her about just that morning on the set. Only stupid people said "chaise lounge." The real word was "chaise longue," which meant "long chair" in French. It was Stewart Gordon who was stupid. Some people looked cool in bald heads, but he didn't. And nobody made any money doing one-man shows off-Broadway.

She forced herself all the way up and swung her legs off the couch. Everything hurt. She was probably running a fever. First the truck had gone off the road and onto the beach, and then it was later, and cold, and the snow was pouring in the open window next to her. She didn't see why anybody bothered to live in New England. Snow was horrible, no matter how neat it looked in the movies. Winter was horrible too. This island was the most horrible thing of all. That was because everybody watched you here, but not like they watched you in L.A. They were like schoolteachers who thought you were stupid, stupid, stupid, and they were always making mental notes about what you'd done so they could tell you all about it afterward.

She stood up, very carefully. She did not think she was going to throw up. She was past that. She was not sure she could stand for very long. She really did have a fever. Her whole face was hot. She'd probably come down with the flu and shut down the filming and make everybody mad at her again. She leaned against a small table. The woman who lived here had left a book and a mug on it. Arrow couldn't read the title of the book, because her vision was blurred. It didn't make sense, anyway. She wondered what time it was. It had been dark when they'd been driving around in the truck, but storm-dark, not night-dark, and as far as she knew it could still be the middle of the afternoon. That would be bad. She needed it to be night. The closer it was to night, the better off she would be.

She got to the chaise longue and sat down on the edge of it. She couldn't have stood up much longer. Marcey was covered with a blanket that was just like the blanket Arrow had had on her on the couch. The woman who lived here must buy matching blankets. Marcey seemed to be snoring. Arrow put out her hand and touched her on the shoulder.

"Marcey?" she said. "Marcey, you need to be awake."

Marcey groaned a little, and turned, and looked up. Arrow bit her lip. They all got pretty drunk, partying. Arrow had been pretty drunk herself just a little while ago. Every once in a while, though, it was important to sober up, and then you—

And then what?

Arrow pressed down on Marcey's shoulder and shook. "Marcey," she said again. "You've got to wake up. It's important."

"Fuck that," Marcey said.

She hadn't opened her eyes. The longer Arrow stayed upright, the more she was sure there was something terribly wrong with her. She was so hot she was burning up, and she was dizzy. It wasn't the kind of dizzy you got when you were drunk. It was the kind you got when you spun around and around and around without stopping, or went on one of those rides at the amusement park where it did that for you. She shook Marcey again, hard this time. There were all kinds of things she felt she had to say.

Marcey turned over, flat on her back, and opened her eyes. She turned her head from one side to the other, which couldn't have helped much, because the chaise had arms on both sides. She sat up a little and looked around. Arrow held her breath.

"Where are we?" Marcey said.

"I'm not sure," Arrow said. "It's a house some woman owns, in town, I think. Nobody we know. I just—Mark and I had an accident in the truck, and it was cold, and I was walking, and this place was here. I think. I was sort of wasted. This woman made me lie down on the couch and put a blanket on me and tried to get me to drink tea, but I wouldn't, and then Stewart Gordon brought you here."

"Stewart Gordon brought me here?"

"Carried you in on his shoulders. With his coat wrapped around your middle. I saw it. I was pretending to be asleep. I didn't want to talk to her, you know, the woman who lives here, and then Stewart Gordon was here and I didn't want to talk to him. I don't think it's right that people like that can call you stupid. Do you know what I mean? I don't think it's right."

Marcey was suddenly a lot more awake than Arrow was, and Arrow could see it. She was sitting bolt upright and her eyes were clear.

"I threw up," Marcey said. "At that place, the bar place on Main Street. Not the inn, the other place. I threw up on the bartender because he had a bow tie. Crap, crap, crap. Where the hell is Stewart Gordon now?"

Arrow looked away. "They went out. Stewart Gordon and the woman who lives here."

"Out? Isn't there some big storm or the other? Why did they go out?"

"I don't know."

"And what about Mark? Where's Mark?"

"I don't know."

"God, isn't it just like the jerkballs you go out with, there's an accident in the truck and then he just dumps you there to go walking around in the snow. Are they coming back?"

"I guess so," Arrow said. "They'd have to, wouldn't they? Or the woman would. It's her house."

"It's a really dinky house," Marcey said. "You ever noticed that about this place? Most of the houses are really dinky. Except Kendra's, you know. That one's good."

Arrow took a deep breath and almost immediately started coughing. Her chest hurt. Her head was on fire. "Listen," she said. "We have to find out what time it is. We have to get out of here."

"We can get out of here no matter what time it is."

"No, listen, Marcey, be serious. We have to get out of here and we have to go somewhere. Somewhere safe. We have to go to Kendra's house."

Marcey was suddenly very still. "You know how that works," she said. "Kendra's getting ready for the party. She's not going to let anyone in there while the setup is going on. You know what she's like."

"She's supposed to be our friend. We should be able to go there if we're in trouble."

"What trouble? I get drunk all the time, Arrow. It's not like I committed a felony."

Felony. That was one of those words. Arrow wished that the air would stop moving. Her chest really did hurt. Really, really, really. All her muscles hurt too. She didn't know what "felony" meant. People used it all the time, but she had always been too embarrassed to ask. If she asked Stewart Gordon, he would call her stupid stupid stupid. That was always, too. Out there in the snow with the window

37

open on her side of the truck, she had been able to see the sea. It was not the same sea as the one she saw in California, and it didn't feel the same. It was angry and dark. The beach was full of rocks.

"I have to get to Kendra's house," she said stubbornly. She was sure that was the right thing. She was sure of it. "I have to get there now."

"If you try bursting in on her when she doesn't want to see you, she'll cut you off. You know she will. She cuts people off all the time."

"I have to get there now," Arrow said.

She stood all the way up. Her legs felt like water. The skirt of her dress was hiked. She could feel a cold breeze between her legs. There was something about that, about having that part of herself exposed. There was something deeply shameful about it, no matter what Kendra said, but it was one of the conditions, it really was. The snow was coming in the window of the truck and the wind was very strong and very cold and then there was blood in her hair. There was blood everywhere, but there was especially blood in her hair.

"I have to get to Kendra's," she said.

And then she passed out cold.

8

Jack Bullard's life had been an exercise in delayed gratification. If being about to work and wait was what it took to be successful, he thought he was due to overtake Bill Gates before he was thirty-five. Underneath it all, he had never really believed it. It didn't seem to him that people who succeeded did it by working and waiting. A lot of them were, like Kendra Rhode, just born to it, and anybody who had grown up on Margaret's Harbor could name a dozen more like her. The trick, some of the people on the island joked, was to know how to pick your great-grandparents, and that was the only trick they wanted to know. The other trick, the one that ended up making multimillionaires out of people like Marcey Mandret and Arrow Normand, was not the kind of thing you were brought up to believe was worthwhile if you lived on the island.

Right now, Jack was having a hard time knowing just what was and what was not worthwhile, and he was covered with snow. Everything was cold. This was the largest nor'easter he'd seen in years. There were people on the island who said it was the largest in a century. Whatever it was, he kept going out in it, and that was not a good idea. He was behaving like a tourist. The tide was coming in too, he was pretty sure of it, and this house—his parents' house, the one he'd grown up in—was too close to the water. If this had been a summer storm, he'd have been pumping out the basement for weeks.

He put his gear on his kitchen table and went to the window to look out. The curve of the beach was visible in the darkness mostly because of the streetlamps that lined the road that ran along it. He could see, on the other side, what looked like a car and people moving among the rocks. He stared at them for a while and then dumped the contents of his backpack on the table. The house was not the way he had remembered it. Once his father died, it was as if the old place had given up. It had been in the family, after all, for over a century. It was odd to think that Kendra Rhode's grandparents and his own had come to the island at the same time, or at least built houses there at the same time. He wondered what Kendra Rhode's family had thought of it, in the beginning. It was one of the things he liked least about rich people. They liked to go where the primitive was. They liked to think they were roughing it.

He went right up to the kitchen window and looked out again. There were people moving along the beach. His throat felt very tight. He had a chill. There didn't look as if there were any police lights there. Oscartown did have its one police cruiser, complete with lights. It didn't look as if there were any ambulance lights, either. Maybe it was one of the movie people moving around, seeing something strange, poking at it to see what she found—but Jack did not believe that. The movie people were just too stupid. They were stupid to the point of stupefaction. Jack had never really believed the publicity that came out of the entertainment magazines, that actors and singers and entertainment people were all morons, that the entire celebrity world was just a grown-up version of high school, but there they were. He couldn't deny it anymore. He had file cabinet after file cabinet of pictures to prove it.

The file cabinets were right there, with him, in the kitchen. He did not use many of the rooms in the house anymore, because they were filled with junk. He just couldn't seem to keep it going. It embarrassed him a little because he had been brought up with more than a belief that Old Money was the only kind that mattered. It mattered to people on the island to keep their places up. Sometimes he thought he was going to suffocate here. Linda would miss him for a few days and send Jerry Young, and Jerry would knock on the doors and look in the windows and finally let himself inside, and there Jack would be, stretched out on the floor in front of the stove, blue from the lack of oxygen that was Margaret's Harbor.

He looked out the window yet again. There really were people over there. They were making their way down toward the beach. He bit his lip and rubbed the flat of his left hand against his cheek, the way his father used to. He was beginning to look like his father. He was beginning to look old. It wasn't supposed to be this way. He had worked hard in school. He had gotten good grades and good board scores and good financial aid. He had gone off to a reasonably good college. And then what? The college was supposed to fix everything. Instead, he had just turned around and come home, and home had been what it always was.

He went to his file cabinet and used his little key on it. Here was something the movie people had done to him. He'd never locked anything around his place before. The summer people locked their places. Those places were huge, and there were lots of valuable things in them. Somebody said the Rhodes actually had a Renoir. No burglar in his right mind would bother with a place like Jack's when he had the Point to invade, and Jack knew for a fact that security at the Point was a lot less good than Kendra liked to pretend it was.

Jack looked through the little stack of manila envelopes, all of them full to the breaking point, all of them lumpy, and picked the one marked "Las Vegas." He opened it up and dumped the contents on the kitchen table next to the contents of his backpack. His backpack was full of photographic equipment. Some of the photographers from the big media companies who hung around town these days, waiting for Marcey Mandret to fall out of her dress, had talked to him about it. There were professional carrying cases and things that professional photographers used. He looked like an idiot carrying his gear around in a backpack. Jack thought he looked like an idiot in any case, because he was older than some of the guys working crew for CNN and CBS, and yet they were there, and he was here, and never the twain would meet.

Except that they would, if Jack had his way. He was suddenly aware of being wet as well as cold. The collar of his parka had soaked through. He didn't know why he was still wearing it. He unzipped it and shrugged it off. It hit the floor behind him, and he didn't notice. The pictures from Las Vegas were good ones. He could get some decent money for some of them. There was the big picture of the whole lot of them when they'd first arrived, Kendra in the center, because she was always in the center, and then the two toy boys, Steve Becker and Mark Anderman. Steve had his hand on Kendra's ass. You couldn't really see it in the photograph, but Jack had taken the photograph, and he knew. Anderman was less intrusive, but his left hand was over Kendra's right shoulder, and the big thick ring on it had spoiled the lighting.

Jack pushed that picture away and tried another one. The one he came up with was the picture of Arrow and Mark in the living room of the Hugh Hefner Suite. The Hugh Hefner Suite had come as a revelation to him. A hotel room that cost ten thousand dollars a night? That was nine thousand square feet? Who could afford things like that? Who would want to? Kendra had stayed in an ordinary suite, without all the bells and whistles, and even that had seemed too garish for her. Las Vegas was not the kind of place debutantes, or ex-debutantes, ought to spend time. The lighting was all wrong.

He went through the pictures one more time. They were good pictures, the kind of pictures the tabloid press really loved. It bothered him that he would never be able to use them. Las Vegas was a tabloid dream. It was a place where nothing was really real. It was supposed to be that kind of place. It was on purpose. What he felt he himself was by accident, or bad luck, or karma: a facade without anything to back it up. That wasn't exactly accurate. Las Vegas was a facade, but he wasn't even that. He was—something.

He'd been too cold before. Now he was too hot. There was sweat trickling down the back of his neck. The Las Vegas photographs were fanned out in front of him, and they looked like a movie set. All the people in them were too pretty. He thought he should be happy about his anonymity, at least for the moment. Without it, he would never have been asked to go on that trip, and he would never have gotten those photographs, and he would never have been able to sell that one of the whole group of them together to the *Star* for $7,500. It was the most money he had ever made for one photograph, and it had ruined his life.

I have not ruined my life, he told himself. Then he got up and went back to the kitchen window. He had a very clear memory of his first day at Colgate, his father's old station wagon pulled up as close as it could get to the door to his dorm, his stuff coming out of the back in boxes. He was not hopeless. He knew enough, just from living on Margaret's Harbor, to have come in chinos and a polo shirt, and good ones, too. There was still no way to mistake the difference, and not only the difference in cars (that old Ford of his father's, next to the new Volvos everywhere) or in the way the other fathers looked. It was Jack himself who was insufficient, and he knew it. He lacked that thing these people had, the ability to be really real all the time, to anybody who saw them. It was the same thing people like Marcey Mandret and Arrow Normand had, although they did not have anything else: the ability to be visible. They would not have it for very long, but as long as they had it they would be worth taking pictures of. They were careful, though. Visible people never took up with other visible people if they could help it. It worked out badly.

Jack went back to the table and began to pick up the pictures, one after another, very carefully. In some of them, everyone was smiling. In others, it was obvious that Arrow and Marcey were drunk beyond belief, and so were Steve and Mark. Kendra Rhode always looked upright and cool. All the interiors were too shiny and garishly colored, as if he'd used cheap film, which he never did. He went back to the first picture and looked at it again. There they were, standing in a semicircle, Kendra in the middle, the men on other side of her, Arrow and Marcey on either side of them. Kendra had told him, that night, that none of the women were wearing underwear. Jack had no idea why she would think this was something he would want to know.

He put the pictures back in their envelope. He put the envelope back in the filing cabinet. He closed the cabinet drawer and listened to the click as the lock snapped into place. It wasn't much of a lock. Anybody who was determined could destroy it in a second. It was a good thing that nobody he knew would care enough about anything he had to try to steal it.

He went back to the window one more time. He pressed his forehead against the glass. There really were people out there, more than one, but they must have come on foot. There was no car parked on the road that he could see, and he would have been able to see the headlights. The lights were coming from the beach, and some of them were moving around, like flashlights. He felt so enormously sick he wanted to throw up right there, but he knew he wouldn't. It was part of his pact with the house never to get it certain kinds of dirty. It was part of his pact with life never to ask it for more than simple survival, but that was what was wrong. That was what was killing him.

He had spent every single second of his existence trying to escape from Margaret's Harbor, and he was absolutely certain that this was his last chance.

9

In the middle of it, plowing through drifting snow in her calf-high black suede L.L. Bean snow boots, Annabeth Falmer began to wonder if she'd been out of her mind. It was one thing to have a sense of responsibility, to feel that it wasn't right to leave somebody to die in the cold when you had the capacity to see if you could help him. It was another to go blundering around when you had no hope of providing assistance at all. It had been many years since Annabeth had been out in a storm like this. She didn't like to drive in snow, and wasn't good at it, so when it got like this at home she always just stayed put with Creamsicle and her tea. She wondered if it was worse here because of the sea. She seemed to remember something about the Gulf Stream, which she was sure didn't come all the way in to Cape Cod. She wished she'd pulled out a snow hat and made Stewart Gordon put it on his very bald head.

"I can see it," he shouted back at her.

He wasn't really very far away. He always stopped and checked to make sure she was coming on. She sped up a little now, still thinking about the hat.

"There it is," he said when she pulled up next to him. "They must have spun out. It's pointing the wrong way for this side of the road."

She followed the line of his outstretched hand and saw it: an enormous pickup truck with oversized wheels, painted a violent and uncompromising purple.

"My God," she said. "Has somebody been driving that thing around town? You'd think I'd have noticed it."

"He's been driving it around some, yes," Stewart Gordon said. "It's Mark Anderman's."

"Who's Mark Anderman?"

"I told you, up at the house. Arrow's latest boyfriend. Not the guy she married, and not the one after that, but a new one. Maybe a couple of weeks old. She met him on the set."

"And he's probably in there."

"No way to tell from here. Why don't you stay up here and let me go down and see?"

Annabeth Falmer was not a woman most men had found a need to protect, but she recognized the impulse when she saw it. She wondered what he was protecting her from: the climb down, or the fact that this Mark Anderman was very probably lying in the driver's seat stone-cold dead. Either way, she didn't want to be protected. When Stewart Gordon started down the long bank toward the pickup truck and the beach, she followed him.

It was a bad climb down. Margaret's Harbor was not Maui. It was not a gentle place. The slopes that led from the roads to the sea were covered with scattered rocks, and steep. Annabeth kept hitting her ankles against hard things, and sinking her legs far into the snow so that the wet came in over the tops of her boots. The sea would have been beautiful if she hadn't been so afraid of it. It reminded her of that poem by Matthew Arnold, of the death of religious faith, with the waves crashing against the shore under the great white chalk cliffs of Dover.

They were almost at the truck. Stewart Gordon had stopped to wait for her. "What were you thinking about? You looked like you were thinking about something."

"I was thinking about trying to write in my office at home when the boys were small, and it would be so cold I'd try to type with gloves on, and it wouldn't work," Annabeth said. "It would go down to three degrees Fahrenheit and nothing I did could make the house warm, and I'd be aware all the time, you know, because heat's expensive and I'd be running it at full blast, that the bill was going to come in and I wasn't going to be able to pay it. But it was so cold I pumped it up anyway, and then it took forever to get my work done, because it was so hard to type."

"And your husband? What did he do?"

"Oh, he was dead by then. He died when the boys were small. Three and seven, I think they were. He—my husband, I mean—he worked with computers and things."

"And your sons are now grown up and they're, what—a doctor and a lawyer?"

"A cardiologist and a litigator, yes."

"And they like you enough to buy you a house on Margaret's Harbor just because you wanted to spend a year to read?"

"I should have thought of going to Italy. I like Italy. I've been thinking of writing a book about Italy. About Lucrezia Borgia, maybe. At least there wouldn't be this kind of snow."

"That's very impressive."

"A book about Lucrezia Borgia?"

"No. The fact that your sons like you enough to set you up this way after you did whatever it was you had to do to get them where they are. I've seen women like that. Most of them survive by getting hard. You didn't."

"How do you know I wasn't set up with enough life insurance to choke a horse?"

"The fact that you were afraid of paying the heating bills."

"Fair enough," Annabeth said. "I was thinking of something else, though. While we were coming down. There's a poem by Matthew Arnold, called 'Dover Beach.'"

"'. . . for the world, which seems
To lie before us like a land of dreams,
So various, so beautiful, so new,
Hath really neither joy, nor love, nor light,
Nor certitude, nor peace, nor help for pain;
And we are here as on a darkling plain

Swept with confused alarms of struggle and flight,
Where ignorant armies clash by night.'"

Annabeth stopped still. "Exactly," she said. "That's amazing. Very few people know that poem. Even English majors of my generation—our generation, really, I'm fifty-five and I seem to remember—"

"Sixty-two."

"Yes, well, even English majors of our generation weren't asked to read that, and nobody else ever does except in graduate school. Maybe it was different in England—"

"Scotland," Stewart Gordon said. "I'm Scots. You've got to keep that straight, or men in kilts will storm your door and beat on it with large swords."

"Right," Annabeth said.

"But you didn't go to graduate school in English literature, did you? It must have been history."

"Oh, it was. But then I taught as an adjunct for a while in a small place and they had me teaching everything. They put it in textbooks for undergraduates now. 'Dover Beach,' I mean. And, you know, I know that the night of the poem isn't supposed to be a storm. The moon is out. But then there's all that at the end, and it just feels more like a night like tonight. I'm babbling."

"No. You're doing what I'm doing. You're slowing down as we approach the goal."

"He's going to be dead in there, isn't he?"

"Probably. There's no telling how long he's been in the cold. If we could have gotten some sense out of Arrow, we might have a rough idea when it was the accident happened, but as it is, as far as we know, it could have been hours. It could have been any time since about eleven this morning."

"Why eleven this morning?"

"That's when they threw Arrow off the set and she took off with

Mark. Both of them, by the way, already fairly out of it. Not to say she was as out of it as she pretended to be at your place."

"Did you think she was faking? I thought she was faking. I just couldn't figure out why I thought that."

"You thought it because she's a damned piss-poor actress," Stewart Gordon said. "I thought about pushing it, but I didn't see the point. There's one thing all those girls are good at, and Arrow in particular, and that's turning mulish and shutting up. It made more sense to come out and see. Here we are. We're not going to be able to get to the door on the passenger's side. The trade is almost rolled over onto it and it's jammed against even more rocks. This place is unbelievable with rocks. It's worse than the shingle at Brighton."

"We'll have to climb up to the driver's door," Annabeth said.

"I'll do it. Later on, I'm going to put a shot of Scotch into your tea and tell you why Arrow Normand is the inevitable product of late-stage corporate capitalism. That was a good book, the one about Abigail Adams, but your understanding of economics is up your ass."

"Right," Annabeth said.

Stewart Gordon had been pulling himself up to the truck's driver's-side door all the time he'd been lecturing her about Arrow, rocks, and capitalism. The windshield was frosted over, but they could see well enough through it to see that there was a man in there, and blood. Annabeth thought about the blood in Arrow Normand's hair, and then she thought of something else.

"You know," she said. "This truck is practically on its side."

"I can see that."

"I know you can. It's just—she must have climbed out. Arrow Normand, I mean. She can't have been thrown from the truck, which is what I thought she said. She must have climbed out. Except, I don't know. That doesn't make any sense."

"Huh," Stewart Gordon said. "Stand back a little. If the door is frozen shut, it's going to take a good yank to get it free."

Annabeth stood back. Stewart Gordon yanked. He yanked again. Annabeth came forward a little and touched his arm.

"Look," she said. "The little post thingee, the thing that locks the door. It's down."

Stewart Gordon stopped and looked.

"That doesn't make sense either, does it?" Annabeth asked him. "I mean, she couldn't have been thrown from the truck if the door was locked, and the door wouldn't lock itself. And I can't imagine that she thought to lock it while she was climbing out."

"Just a minute," Stewart Gordon said. He leaned over and went at the windshield with the side of his arm, brushing off the thin layer of frost in great leaping arcs. The wind was getting worse. Annabeth thought that it was coming straight through her coat and going out the other side.

Stewart Gordon grunted, and stepped back again, staying on top of the truck so that he looked like some kind of fearsome statue in honor of something—Annabeth was very aware that she was making no sense. Stewart Gordon had his hands in his pockets and was looking straight down. Annabeth moved slowly and got herself onto the truck, scared to death that she would slide off into the snow and then need rescuing herself. She got up next to him without his making any sign that he was aware she was coming. She looked down and saw the streaks of red and something else everywhere.

"He hit his head," she said. "But that doesn't mean anything, does it? Head wounds give a lot of blood, even minor ones. He could still be alive."

"He's not alive," Stewart Gordon said.

"How do you know? We ought to at least check."

"We're not going to check anything. We're not going to touch anything. We're going to go get the police no matter how busy they are in the storm. We're going to get them now."

"We should get an ambulance, just in case," Annabeth insisted—

and yet, even as she insisted, she knew that he was right and she was wrong. Here it was, she thought, here it was, those ignorant armies clashing by night. Except that it wasn't night. It was only late afternoon. If she looked hard enough she could still find the sun behind the dark clouds that choked the sky. That was why they could see the purple of the truck, where it was exposed.

She was about to ask him why so much of the purple of the truck had not been covered by falling snow when he stepped back again, turned to her, and said, "He didn't hit his head. Somebody put a gunshot through it."

PART I

ONE

1

Gregor Demarkian had been born and brought up on Cavanaugh Street, and married there when he was in his twenties. He knew everything there was to know about how this place reacted to the expectation of a marriage, right down to the superstitious things the Very Old Ladies would do in the privacy of their living rooms when Father Tibor Kasparian wasn't around to scold them. He had no idea why he had thought things would be different, now, for him. Maybe it was that Cavanaugh Street was so very changed from the way it had been when he had grown up here. There had been a lot of rising tides raising boats in the course of that something-more-than-half-century, and what had started as a cramped blank space of tenements and peeling paint had ended, now, as one of the most upscale gentrified neighborhoods in the city of Philadelphia. The building where Gregor had been born didn't even exist anymore. Howard Kashinian's development company had had it torn down, nearly a decade before Gregor moved back to the street, and replaced it with three four-story brick town houses, each offering a single long apartment on each of its four floors. The disintegrating brownstone where Lida Kazanjian Arkmanian had been brought up did exist, but the fifteen other families that had lived there were gone, and Lida had bought the place, had it gutted, and turned it into a showplace that had been featured on the cover of *Metropolitan Home.* It was a different world, with different expectations. These days the wives expected to spend their winter vacations in the Bahamas and the children expected to go to college when their time came—and a good college, too, not just whatever was on offer locally in the community college system. Sheila and Howard Kashinian's daughter Deanna had had a huge, expensive party for her sixteenth birthday that was featured on a televison show called *My Super Sweet Sixteen.* Elda and Michael Valadanian's son David had just been appointed, at thirty-two, the youngest federal court judge in the history of the Eleventh Circuit. Susan Kasmanian, Hannah Kasmanian's niece, had been accepted to study for a doctorate in mathematics at the Massachusetts Institute of Technology. This was not the kind of place that insisted on wrapping up the bride and groom in flower garlands so that widows could spit on them for luck.

Maybe Gregor had simply assumed that all that kind of thing would be ignored because the woman he was marrying was not herself Armenian. In fact, Bennis Hannaford was nearly the polar opposite of Armenian, in spite of the fact that she was eerily small and dark, as if in revolt against generations of tall, pale, blond English ancestors. She was a Hannaford of the Main Line Hannafords. That great pile of a house was still sitting out there, in Bryn Mawr, waiting for her brothers to decide what to do with it. She had come out at the Philadelphia Assemblies. She had graduated from Agnes Irwin and Vassar. She even sounded more like Katharine Hepburn than anybody else Gregor had ever heard. He couldn't imagine anybody thinking she could spit on Bennis for any reason at all, and he had a sneaking suspicion that before she allowed herself to be wrapped in flower garlands, Bennis would insist on being naked.

Still, here he was, on the second of January, months before there was going to be anything like an actual wedding, letting Donna Moradanyan Donahue wrap a tape measure around his head.

"Stop making such a fuss," she said. "I'm the one who should be screaming bloody murder. I've just had a baby."

"That's true," Gregor said. "You should be home with Martha Grace. You should be fighting with your mother-in-law about what church she's going to be baptized into."

"I'm letting Russ fight with his mother," Donna said. "It's counterproductive when I do it. I just need to get the proportions right here. I mean, you don't want your head to be up on Lida's roof looking like Charles Manson or something, do you?"

"I don't want my head up on Lida's roof at all. And you can't claim this is some kind of Armenian tradition, because I know better."

"It's my tradition," Donna said. "Just wait till you see what I do for the wedding. I'm going to cover the entire street. Well, except for the church. Father Tibor—"

"You cannot wrap the church in shiny paper," Tibor said. "It's not respectful."

"I wouldn't think it would even be possible," Gregor said.

"It won't matter," Donna said. "The church will have lots of flowers. We're going to have banks of them going down the stairs straight to the sidewalk. We've got to work on your entrance, though. Usually there are limousines, and that does for ceremony, but with both of you coming from the same street, we'll have to think of something else. Maybe we can work up one of those processions with children, you know, that they have in the villages. I always think those look beautiful."

"That is because you have never had to live in a village," Father Tibor said.

"Here's more coffee," Linda Melajian said, putting the pot down in the middle of the table. "Bennis called to say she's going to be held up at the lawyers this morning, and you're supposed to stop complaining."

Linda Melajian stomped off, and Gregor watched her go. It was nearly noon now, and outside the big plate glass windows of the Ararat Restaurant, Cavanaugh Street looked clean and cold and mostly empty. Donna had finished her measurements and wrapped the tape measure around her hand, and she pushed against him a little to give her room to sit down. The remains of the lunches Gregor and Father Tibor had tried to eat were still sitting on the table. Father Tibor never ate much, but Gregor used to, until all this thing with the wedding. Now he'd left a great big stack of grape leaves stuffed with lamb sitting on the plate, and Donna Moradanyan started picking at them.

Sometimes—and, for some reason, much oftener now—Gregor Demarkian thought that Cavanaugh Street was someplace he had imagined for himself on the worst and darkest days of his life. It wasn't someplace real. He would wake up in an hour or two and find himself still in that awful apartment near the Beltway, the place he had gone to wait for Elizabeth to die. Then he would turn over in bed and look at the numbers on the clock he had always set for five, so that he could be at the hospital before she woke up, if she woke up. Day after day, week after week, for almost a year, with nothing else to think about, and nothing else in his life. It was when he had first realized that he was not good at making friends or keeping them. He was too closed in on himself, and for all the time between the day he had married Elizabeth and the day she had died, he had lived as if they were the only two people in the world. Work didn't count. Work was something he was good at, but when he walked away from it, it was as if it had never been.

Now he was here in the Ararat, and all the people around him were his friends. They worried about what he did and didn't eat, how his relationship with Bennis was going and why it was going that way, what his work was doing to him, whether he was doing too much of it, whether he was doing too little of it. It would have shocked the hell out of most of them to be told that he was a "closed-off" kind of person, but he thought he was. He was just better at hiding it, or better at hiding the defense mechanisms that could signal its existence.

He felt a tug on his sleeve and looked around. Father Tibor was looking worried, which might or might not have meant anything in particular. Father Tibor was five years younger than Gregor and looked at least a decade older. He'd spent most of his youth and middle age in Soviet prisons of one kind or another.

"Krekor?"

"I'm okay. Kind of tired, that's all."

"Are you upset about the ceremony?" Tibor asked. "I'm not sure what to do about it. On the one hand, you and Bennis are my closest friends, and I am certified by the Commonwealth of Pennsylvania to perform marriages. On the other hand—" He threw his hands in the air. "I am not an unsophisticated man, Krekor. I know that not everyone who comes to the altar truly believes, and the world is full of hypocrites. But."

"Yes," Gregor said. "But."

"She is not the sort of woman who thrives on compromise, is she, Krekor? It's really all we need here, a little compromise. A little pro forma. I do not pretend that the questions involved are not serious. They're very serious. But in this case, for the purposes of a wedding, maybe not so much. I don't understand why I can't make her see that."

"Don't look at me," Gregor said. "I can't make her see anything. I've been trying for years."

"It is just a matter of pro forma," Tibor said again. "It is a matter of satisfying the forms when you cannot satisfy the substance. If we don't do that, I will have a problem with the archdiocese. I might be able to get away with it if the whole thing could be done in privacy, but you know there will be no privacy. You are not a private person. She is not a private person."

"Also, she can't sit back and shut up to save her life," Donna said.

The two of them turned around and looked at her, a little surprised to find that she was still there. Donna Moradanyan Donahue was as tall and fair as Bennis should have been, as if the two of them had been switched at birth, except that Donna was fifteen years younger. Having been released from the dietary strictures of pregnancy, she seemed to be mainlining caffeine in the form of thick Armenian coffee, right through the middle of the day. She drained the cup she had now and pushed it away from her, beginning to gather up her things.

"Look," she said, "this is just not going to work. If you sit around here for the next five months doing nothing but worrying at all this stuff, there isn't going to be any wedding, and then the women on this street are going to form a posse and kill both of you. You and Bennis, I mean, not you, Father. Never mind. Gregor, just make some sense, will you please? Go find yourself some work to do. Get yourself off the street for a while. Bennis has a book tour in February and early March—you can come back then. Then Russ and I can put her up for April and the first part of May, and—"

"You do realize how ridiculous it is," Gregor said. "Bennis going to stay with you as if we hadn't been living together for years."

"Just get out of here," Donna said. "You're twitchier than she is, and she's twitchy enough for an overpopulated séance. There's got to be some police force in the country that has a murder they don't know what to do with. Maybe the Bureau has a convention or something that you could go to."

"The Federal Bureau of Investigation does not hold conventions."

"Whatever. Get out of here. Do something sensible. Let us take care of all the arrangements."

"With you taking care of the arrangements, this is going to resemble a story out of the *Arabian Nights*."

Donna had all her stuff in her bag, sort of. She'd left the top unzipped and things that looked like black ribbons spilling out. She slung it over her shoulder and reached for her coat on the coatrack next to the booth. "Do something with yourself," she said. And then she stomped her way out of the plate glass front door and onto the street.

Everybody seemed to be stomping today. Gregor thought that that must mean something, but he wasn't sure what. Tibor was sitting quietly over an empty plate that had once had big piles of lamb casserole on it, and the other diners, almost all of them people Gregor knew, were paying no attention to him. Everybody was stomping, and he was stomping too, and the reason was nowhere near as simple as "getting cold feet" about the wedding or being put off because, as things stood now, it looked as if they wouldn't be able to hold it in church.

"You know," he said to Tibor, "I'm really not getting cold feet about the wedding. Sometimes I worry that Bennis might be, but I'm not."

"I didn't think you were," Tibor said.

"I've wanted this wedding since the year I met her," Gregor said. "I didn't even realize it, in the beginning. She was, I don't know, not the sort of person I thought that sort of thing about, if there was any sort of person I thought that sort of thing about with Elizabeth dead just a year. But I did think it, unconsciously, if that makes sense."

"Of course it makes sense."

"I just wish it wasn't such an enormous event. There's something about the fuss that's making me crazy. I tell myself I'm worried that it's making her crazy, and that it's going to make her back off, but I know that's not the truth. She thrives on this stuff. I had no idea she could get this involved in planning something."

"Most women like to plan their weddings, Krekor. It's normal."

"I know it's normal. She isn't normal. She's never been normal."

"Tcha. You're playing with words."

"I need to take a walk," Gregor said. "Is that rude? I don't want to be rude to you. I just need to take a walk."

"Take your walk," Tibor said.

Gregor had no idea if he was offended or not. He had no idea what the population of the Ararat would think about him going off

59

and leaving Tibor alone at the table. He had only the vaguest idea what he wanted to do. Still, walking was a good idea, and he knew where he could walk to.

2

It wasn't really a walk Gregor needed to go on. Even when he'd been much younger, it would have taken him hours to walk where he wanted to go. It helped, of course, that he was not admitting that there was somewhere he did want to go. It had been on his mind for days; he just hadn't brought it to the surface. It was odd how things worked out sometimes. When he had first left Philadelphia, he had never expected to come back, or at least never expected to come back to Cavanaugh Street. But it wasn't just the street. D.C. was a different place, a better place, as he saw it then. It was the place where he had built a reputation and a career among people whose opinions mattered in more than a local sense. Gregor was not a sentimentalist. He was not a fan of movies like *It's a Wonderful Life* that pushed the line that the great wide world was nothing but flash and ashes, and everything meaningful was to be found at home. It had been good for him to get out of what Cavanaugh Street had been when he was living there. It had been good for him to get away from family and the familiar. There was a big world out there and people made contributions in it, contributions that helped everyone everywhere. He was, he thought, making a hash of it in his own head, but the basic meaning of it all was perfectly clear to him. He liked Cavanaugh Street. He liked the people he knew there, and he liked the fact that he had known many of them for so long that they shared history in a way that would never be possible with new acquaintances. There was something to be said for having someone for whom the assassination of John F. Kennedy was the thing that happened the day after old Father Mardun Destinian had been discovered half naked with Mrs. Machanian. There was also something to be said for having someone for whom the assassination of John F. Kennedy was just the assassination of John F. Kennedy, one of those things that linked a generation, like 9/11 would link the one coming up through the public schools now.

Gregor stopped, and looked around, and realized that he was a good five blocks away from home, and not on a straight line, either. If he had been investigating his own behavior, he would have surmised that he was deliberately attempting to hide his activities from the people he lived with. Maybe that was true. He couldn't stop himself from feeling relieved that no one from Cavanaugh Street would see him hailing this cab, or hear where he asked it to go. There was something else he missed, more than a little, about his life in Washington. There was no privacy on Cavanaugh Street. There never had been. There never would be. It went against the grain of the kind of place it was.

The first cab that deigned to notice him pulled up to the curb in front of him with a squeal of tires: not a good sign. Gregor swallowed the urge to tell the cabbie he'd changed his mind and got into the backseat, folding himself up like an oversized Murphy bed. Cabs always made him feel the full extent of his height. He slammed the door after him and double-checked to make sure he hadn't forgotten his wallet, or had it lifted while he'd been walking and paying no attention to anything around him. Then he leaned forward and told the driver, "Christ the Redeemer Armenian Cemetery."

The driver made no comment. There was no reason for him to, even though the cemetery was on the very outskirts of the city and the chances of picking up a fare to return were very small. Gregor could think of no reason at all why Donna Moradanyan or Father Tibor— or even Bennis—shouldn't know that he was going out to the cemetery where his late wife was buried. He went there three times a year as a kind of ritual, to bring flowers and make sure the grave was being taken care of. Bennis didn't think he'd hatched from an egg an hour and a half ago, which was a good thing, because she certainly hadn't. Donna and Father Tibor would probably think it was very sweet that he still cared to go and visit this particular grave. When he'd first come out to Philadelphia, he'd visited it all the time, often as much as twice a week. He'd come out and stood at the foot of the plot and talked in his head to her, playing and replaying all the things that had hurt him so much in that last awful year, eventually asking her about the next few decisions he'd had to make, to find new work for himself, to settle down on Cavanaugh Street. At the time, he'd thought he'd had her approval—good, wonderful, go back to your roots, it will make you whole again. Now he wondered if he'd imagined all that. Would Elizabeth really have approved of his coming back home to Cavanaugh Street? Would she have wanted to come herself? She'd been almost as desperate to get out of the place as he had been.

The city was doing odd and twisty things outside the windows of the cab. Gregor had seen a fair percentage of it in the last few years, but in a way it had never been a city he really lived in. Even when he was going to the University of Pennsylvania, the university had been nothing more than a destination and a point of departure. He went there in the mornings, spent his time in classrooms and libraries, and came back to Cavanaugh Street as soon as it started to get dark. There was a fad these days for making movies about the wonders and warmth of insular little communities. There was that silly thing Donna and Bennis had made him see, about a big fat Greek wedding, and a hundred others about small towns and the emotional superiority of ordinary ways of life. *Family Man.* That kind of thing. The truth of it was, insular little communities were just that, insular. That was true if they were poor and struggling, as Cavanaugh Street had been, or rich and self-congratulatory, as Cavanaugh Street was now.

"It makes you feel as if you're suffocating," he said out loud.

The cabbie looked up into the rearview mirror and said, "Pardon me? Is there something you need?"

"No," Gregor said. "Sorry. I was just thinking to myself."

Actually, he'd been talking to himself, but he wasn't going to admit that, and the cabbie wasn't going to make an issue of it. They were nearly where he wanted to go anyway. He had no idea how long they'd been driving around, which meant he had no idea how long it would take him to get home when he finally wanted to go. Did he want to move away from Cavanaugh Street, was that it? Would Bennis want to move with him if he wanted to go? Bennis was Bennis. She came from a wider world. Cavanaugh Street was almost a hobby for her. She flitted in and out of it like a hummingbird flitted among the flowers.

"That was a god-awful image," Gregor said, out loud again, but this time the cabbie didn't appear to notice. They were almost at their destination. Gregor could see the great arched cast-iron gateway just ahead, the cross crowning the center of it, the letters fashioned to be something like Gothic without actually being that.

The cabbie turned left and pulled into the cemetery's broad entranceway. Gregor reached into his pocket for his wallet.

"I could drive you in, if you wanted," the cabbie said. "I could wait. It's going to be hard finding a cab to take you back if I don't."

"I know," Gregor said, getting out into the cold January air. "I don't know how long I'm going to be. Why don't you take that and keep the change."

The cabbie put the small wad of bills into his breast pocket without counting them. "It's good to see these old cemeteries kept up like this," he said. "You'd be surprised how many I see that are falling apart. Families die out, maybe, or move away. Or maybe it's just that it's not a custom anymore, visiting a grave."

"People do seem to do less of it," Gregor said.

Then he turned away and began to walk slowly through the gates, past the small guardhouse with nobody in it. It was not a quiet cemetery. The stones were very close together, and some of them were so large that they oppressed the landscape, big statues of angels and eagles, big slabs of marble with the Ten Commandments carved into them. He wondered what it cost to buy a monument like that, and why anybody would do it. He could almost understand it for the death of a child. He found it hard to comprehend that a family would go to that expense for an older member, somebody they had been expecting to die forever. Maybe families felt guilty. Maybe they just felt scared.

He made his way through along the curving asphalt drive that would have taken him to every corner of the cemetery and then out again at the front if he'd followed it that far. The wind was stiff and cold, but not as cold as it had been only a few days before. The day was grayish, as if suspended in time, neither morning nor evening, neither fully day nor approaching night. He found the lot section where he had laid Elizabeth to rest in the oddest ceremony he could remember. Father Tibor had performed it, and a dozen people from Cavanaugh Street had come, but he had known none of them at the time, not even the ones he'd grown up with. Maybe that was the problem. Maybe there was something in his mind that said that Cavanaugh Street was a grave he'd escaped from, and only returned to bury his dead, and that by staying he had buried himself as well. The idea made him impatient with himself. Had he really been unhappy all these years? Had he really gotten nothing more from the time he'd spent there than to be buried alive? He was behaving like an adolescent ass, imagining that nobody would ever understand him until he shook off the dust of his provincial home and made his way to the Great Big City.

Philadelphia was a Great Big City. Elizabeth's grave was on a small knoll right next to an expansive family plot for some people named Haladanian. Next to Elizabeth's grave there was space for only one more, and the reason for that was obvious. When he'd buried Elizabeth, he'd never expected to have anyone else in his life. He and Elizabeth had had no children. What would have been the point of buying a bigger space, to put down bodies that did not and could not even exist?

"You'd probably kick me silly if you saw me behaving like this," he said, out loud, to Elizabeth. There had been a time when he would have heard Elizabeth answering, but he didn't now. The stone he had selected for her sat in the ground, just slightly settled, the rose tint of its polished marble almost exactly the color that had been her favorite in life. He had not done that thing people did, where he forgot what she looked like. He remembered exactly. He could even hear the memory of the sound of her voice in his head. That was not the same as actually hearing the sound of her voice in his head, and it unsettled him.

Deep in the pocket of his trousers, his cell phone went off. This was a new one, called a Razr, that Bennis had bought him for his birthday. He wasn't sure why it was important to buy a new cell phone every other year or so, but she thought it was, and she bought them for him, so he took them.

He pulled it out and checked the caller ID. It was Father Tibor. He almost let the call go to voice mail, even though he wasn't entirely sure how to operate the voice mail. Hadn't he come out here to get away from Cavanaugh Street, at least for a while?

He couldn't help himself. He'd never been able to ignore a ringing phone. He flipped the thing open and said, "Tibor?"

"Krekor," Tibor said, sounding frantic. "You have to come back, right now. Wherever you are, you have to come back. There is somebody who has come here to see you."

"Somebody threatening?" Gregor thought Tibor sounded threatened.

There were sounds in the background, including something that was best identified as a roar. Tibor cleared his throat. "There is somebody to see you," he said. "I can't remember the name. He is a big man with an accent, also a bald head, nearly as big as you, and Donna has wrapped ribbons around his head."

TWO

1

Gregor Demarkian would have gone a long way to see Stewart Gordon with ribbons on his head. As it was, he had only to go back to Philadelphia proper, and the only problem with that was finding a cab. His first driver had been right. It was nearly impossible to get back once you'd let your ride go on. The cemetery was too far out to be an ordinary cruising area. If he'd been on the other side of the city, he could have gone into the Carmelite monastery and asked Sister Beata for her help, but she would only have told him to use his cell phone, and he would have been embarrassed to have forgotten about it.

He was embarrassed now, but there was nobody to catch him at it, so he just got the damned thing out of his pocket, flipped through the phone book Bennis had made up for him—very carefully removing Susan's number, or putting it someplace he'd never think to look—and tried only two companies before one agreed to send out a car for him. Then he had to stand in the cold, watching as the very few people who came here on a weekday made their way to the graves that were familiar to them. The very few people were almost universally old women in the solid black of traditional village mourning. Gregor found himself wondering if there were really that many old women in America who had come over on the boat instead of being born on the spot. It seemed to him the timing was wrong. That was his parents' generation, not his own. His parents were buried in this cemetery too, and his brother, who had not been bright enough for scholarships to Penn and student deferments from the draft. Sometimes he thought they'd gotten it all wrong. The best idea was not to have only one or two children and husband your resources so that you and they could have all the best in clothes and education. The best idea was to have as many children as possible so that you didn't end up standing in the wind on a cold January afternoon, wondering how all your family had disappeared.

Of course, Bennis was still young enough to have children, and she was one of seven, which meant she had to be not completely alien to the concept of large families. Gregor tried to envision Bennis as a mother and couldn't. Her children would all have papier mâché in their hair, and quote Tolkein at three.

The cab finally showed up. Gregor got in and gave the address of Holy Trinity Church because it was easier than the explanations he would have to give if he gave the address of any other building on the street. A couple of years ago somebody had blown the hell out of Holy Trinity, and the story had made the news as far away as Djakarta. Gregor had a suspicion that tourists had come to look at the rubble for a while, if only to give themselves a thrill about the dangers of terrorism. For whatever reason, the cabbies all knew how to get to Holy Trinity without having to have the route explained to them, and Gregor was grateful.

They had turned onto Cavanaugh Street from Gregor's least favorite cross street when he realized that he should have anticipated the problem. Stewart Gordon was no longer some guy he had known when they'd both been in the armies of their respective countries, training in intelligence and complaining about it. Stewart Gordon was now a Star, especially to small boys, and the small boys of Cavanaugh Street were lined up on the steps of Donna Moradanyan Donahue's town house in the hopes of getting a look at him.

Gregor got out of the cab and contemplated the clutch of preadolescent maleness barring his way to Donna's door. Then he got out his cell phone again and called.

"Use the alley and go around the back," Donna said. "You can use the kitchen door."

Gregor did as he was told. The alleys on Cavanaugh Street were like no other alleys he had ever seen anywhere, and the alley between Donna's house and the house next door was the most spectacular in the neighborhood. People cleaned them, and not just the people from the city, either. When Donna wasn't pregnant, she got out there with a broom and a bucket and a mop and washed the alley down at least once a month, no matter the weather.

Bennis was waiting for him at the kitchen door when he got there, a big mug of coffee in her hand. "This is interesting," she said. "He says he'll go out and sign things for people as soon as he's talked to you, but I don't think they trust him."

"They've got to trust me," Stewart bellowed from down the hall in Donna's living room. "I'm Commander Rees. Everybody trusts me."

Stewart Gordon could bellow better than anybody Gregor had ever met.

He shrugged off his coat and left it over the back of one of the chairs at Donna's kitchen table and then went down the hall to the living room. Tibor had been telling the exact truth. Donna was, indeed, fixing ribbons to Stewart Gordon's head. She was then draping them down his back and measuring them.

"What is it you think you're doing?" Gregor asked her.

"Ah," Stewart said. "It's you. Damned bloody time. Excuse me, Mrs. Donahue."

"I've heard worse," Donna said. Then she turned to Gregor.

"You'd disappeared. And he's the right size. The right height, even the right build."

"Congratulations, by the way," Stewart said. "For all the usual reasons, but also because I'm impressed with your intestinal fortitude."

"Do you know Bennis?"

"Only by reputation," Stewart said. "And, of course, because I've just met her, here. She's a very beautiful woman, in person."

"That's a nice way of getting around saying you think she's crazy."

"Everybody knows Bennis is crazy," Donna said. "Even Bennis knows it. If you wouldn't mind, Mr. Gordon, I just want to do a drape across your back and see how it falls on the shoulders. If I don't get these measurements done, I'm never going to be on time for the wedding, and then what are you going to do? Postpone it until I'm ready?"

Gregor was ready to say that he and Bennis could always elope, but he didn't, because he knew they couldn't. Bennis didn't want to elope. Donna had a long, thick length of ice blue satin ribbon in her hands and had started to pin it to Stewart Gordon's back. Gregor sat down to watch the operation. It had occurred to him that now that he was here, she could make her measurements directly instead of using a substitute, but he wasn't going to point it out to her.

"So," he said, "I take it you didn't just drop in. Didn't I hear that you were in Scotland these days, teaching?"

"At St. Andrew's, yes, on and off. It's off, at the moment. I'm in a place called Margaret's Harbor, making a movie."

"Margaret's Harbor," Gregor said. "I'm impressed. Have you met any presidents lately?"

"This president of yours doesn't go there," Stewart said, "which is a damned good thing, considering. I'm making a silly movie, but they're paying me a lot of money. Don't you pay any attention to the news at all? It's been on the news. It's been all over the news."

"That you're in a movie on Margaret's Harbor? I didn't realize you'd gotten that important."

"Be serious. The murder. The murder has been all over the news."

69

Donna stopped with pins in her mouth. Even Bennis came in from the kitchen, as if she'd magically been able to hear the word. Gregor put the coffee mug Bennis had handed him on the small table next to his chair, then thought better of it, picked it up, got a coaster from the little stack next to the lamp, and put the mug down on that.

"Well," Bennis said. "We've all been saying you need something to do."

"Okay," Gregor said. "I do think I've heard something about a murder, one of those girl singers killed her boyfriend, right, she's—"

"She's a first-class twit," Stewart said, "but I'd be willing to bet nearly anything that she didn't pull this off. Normand, by the way. Arrow Normand. That's her name."

"People in Khartoum know who she is," Bennis said blandly.

"It's to his credit that he doesn't," Stewart said. "She's a twit. They're all twits. The whole lot of them I'm working with. Well, you know, not the crew, those people. Those people are very competent. I like American film crews. They're always very professional. Which is a lot more than you can say for American actresses, if that's what you want to call this lot, which I don't, as a matter of fact, but there's nothing I can do about it. They're all first-class twits, and if it hadn't been for the money, I'd have walked out months ago. The money and Kendra Rhode. I found the body."

It was liked being in a tornado. Gregor felt a little breathless. It didn't help that Donna had gone back to draping her ribbon, openly listening, but diligently plying pins.

Gregor tried to piece it together. "I know who Kendra Rhode is. You can't be romantically involved with her, can you? She isn't the sort of person I'd expect you to be romantically involved with."

"Be serious," Stewart said. "I've got better taste and a better mind, and Kendra Rhode doesn't get romantically involved with anybody, any more than she drinks and drugs like the people she clubs around with. But she's there. On Margaret's Harbor. She came out about a week and a half ago and opened this big house her family has there so that she could give a New Year's Eve party. That's when the murder happened. On the afternoon of New Year's Eve. There was a big storm."

"A nor'easter," Bennis said. "I heard about it. Boston was closed."

"Damned near all of New England was closed," Stewart said. "I'd never seen anything like it, not even in Scotland, and it snows in Scotland. That's how we found the body. We weren't looking for a body. We thought there'd been an accident in that ridiculous purple truck of his. Why is it that so many Americans seem to work at looking like bad jokes from the *Daily Mirror*? At any rate, we went looking for the truck, and we found it, and there he was—"

"Who's we?" Gregor asked.

"Dr. Falmer. Annabeth Falmer. She—"

"She's a historian, I know," Gregor said. "Tibor gave me a book of hers about the abolitionist movement. So, let's see, we've got you, this Arrow whoever person—"

"Normand," Donna said.

"Kendra Rhode. Annabeth Falmer. Anybody else I should be worried about?"

"There are the rest of the twits," Stewart said. "Marcey Mandret. Oh, and this real estate woman who's making a completely nuisance of herself, named, I kid you not, Bitsy Winthorp. But they don't matter. That's not what I want from you. I want you to come up to Margaret's Harbor and prove that Kendra Rhode did it."

"Kendra Rhode," Gregor said.

"Maybe not directly, because she'd never get her hands dirty," Stewart said, "but she did it. I have no idea how to explain this to anybody who hasn't met her, but she did it. I've got pictures."

"You've got pictures of Kendra Rhode committing a murder?"

"Be serious," Stewart Gordon said. "As soon as this nice woman takes the pins out of me, I'll show you. I need you to come up to

71

Margaret's Harbor and do something about what's going on, or she's going to get away with it, and she gets away with too bloody much."

2

Stewart Gordon didn't have proof that Kendra Rhode had murdered somebody, or had somebody murdered, but Gregor wasn't expecting that. In a lot of ways, Stewart was the simplest man he had ever known, even simpler than Father Tibor, for whom simplicity was a religious necessity. Stewart was not religious to the point of being antireligious, but he was also a moralist of the straightforward and uncompromising kind. Intelligent and Educated people may have given up the idea of good and evil—or, at least, of evil—but Stewart Gordon never had. It shone out of him like a beacon from an old-fashioned lighthouse. He was no more able to suppress it than he was able to sing soprano.

The small boys weren't going to go away until they got what they wanted, so Donna invited them to sit in her living room and be quiet while "Commander Rees talks to Mr. Demarkian." Gregor waited for the lecture about the bloody boneheaded ignorance of American television producers to hire a Scot to play a Welshman, but it didn't come. Stewart was looming over Donna's kitchen table, pulling flat color photographs out of a big manila envelope. The envelope must have been there all along, lying on a table somewhere or stuffed into Stewart's coat, but Gregor hadn't noticed, and now he sat, fascinated, wondering how it hadn't burst. How many rolls of film had Stewart had with him? How many would he have needed? The last photograph was clearly the picture of a man who had been shot in the head. The color was so brilliant it was nearly gaudy.

Gregor leaned forward, picked it up, and turned it over in his hand. "This is the victim, I take it," he said. "And he was—?"

"Mark Anderman," Stewart said. "Not a bad kid, really. Worked as a grip. Didn't get paid much. The girls liked him, though. He was what's known these days as 'hot.'"

"You can't tell from this."

"Well, no, you couldn't, could you?" Stewart looked at the huge pile of photographs and sat down. "I shot everything my cell phone camera would let me, then I shot everything her cell phone camera would let me. She thought I was crazy."

"Who's she?"

"Dr. Falmer. Annabeth Falmer."

Gregor heard the tone so clearly, it could have been a dinner gong going off in his ear. "What's that?" he said.

"Don't be ridiculous." Stewart looked uncomfortable. "She's not a twit, you know. She's a lady. She's a very intelligent and graceful lady."

"Uh-huh."

"There's also the fact that she doesn't seem to be open to that kind of suggestion at the moment," Stewart said. "She's, uh, she's devoted to her family. She's got a grandchild on the way. She's a little young for it, but she's very excited about it. She hasn't got any of the attitude. I don't think she even knew the attitude existed before we came to the island, and I've had to work overtime to prove I don't have it in me."

"I don't think that should have been hard," Gregor said blandly. "You were with her when you found the body."

Stewart nodded. "It's something of a long story. Filming shut down early that day because of the storm. If these people had had any sense, there would have been no filming at all that day. The weather reports had been full of it for a week. But they're from Los Angeles, these people. They think they know everything."

"They probably just don't understand snow."

"Filming shut down early," Stewart said, "and I went over to this place they've got on Main Street, this sort of pub, except it's rich people on this island so the place is all tarted up. I went to have a pint or whatever you call it over here, and Marcey Mandret was there, and she was drinking some kind of champagne cocktail. You ever had a champagne cocktail? The stuff tastes like rat piss."

"I think we're having some at my wedding."

"Yes, well. That happens. So, Marcy Mandret was drinking these things, one after the other, and she was obviously completely gone. She had this little dress on that wasn't suitable for the weather, straps and no sleeves, cut high on the thigh, and it kept slipping half off and exposing her breasts. She would get up and stagger around and the dress would fall half off and it was getting out of hand. So I went up to talk to her, to tell her to get her act together and get herself home, and she threw up on the bartender and more or less passed out."

"She did this on Margaret's Harbor?" Bennis chimed in from the sidelines.

Stewart turned around. "I know. Bloody the worst place. I thought the golf ladies were going to have aneurysms. So. She passed out, and I wrapped my coat around her so that her private parts wouldn't be swinging in the wind—did I mention that these women never wear underwear?"

"No," Gregor said.

"Well, they don't, and she wasn't this time. I wrapped my coat around her and threw her over my shoulder and got out of there, and fortunately the only photographer on the premises was the guy from the *Home News,* which up until this acted like we weren't even on the island. I got out on Main Street and then I decided not to use the regular route, because there have been photographers on the island, the nasty ones, and I didn't want what was definitely going to happen if they got sight of us the way we were. So I went around to the back, but the snow was coming down very fast and I got disoriented. I knew I had to head to the sea, because that's where the house Marcey and Arrow rented was, and I followed the sounds of the water, but I got turned around. I was hopelessly lost. Then I saw this one place, way out on the beach, and it had all its lights on. So I went there."

"Annabeth Falmer can afford a house directly on the water on

Margaret's Harbor?" Gregor asked. "That can't be history, no matter how popular. Does she have family money?"

"Not the way you mean," Stewart says. "She's got grown sons, a cardiologist and a litigator, as she puts it. They think she walks on water."

"Ah."

"Here's the thing," Stewart said. "She let me in. She offered me a cup of tea with brandy in it. And she already had Arrow Normand in the house. Arrow had shown up about twenty minutes before we did, staggering around, with her hair soaked in blood and, again, no underwear. Annabeth thought there had been a rape."

"That's logical," Gregor said. "I probably would have too. Did you say her hair soaked in blood?"

"By the time I got there, the blood was close to drying and the hair was caked, but it would have been soaked. And it's longish hair. Thin, but longish."

Gregor picked up the picture again. "He was shot by someone on the driver's side. The blood went back, not out. She couldn't have had her hair soaked with it unless she was standing behind him when it happened."

"There," Stewart said. "You see? That's the kind of thing I need. The whole setup is just wrong. And the police aren't listening."

"I doubt that the police aren't listening to that sort of thing," Gregor said. "When they don't, the prosecutors go fairly nuts because they end up looking foolish. Why couldn't she have been standing behind him when it happened?"

"I don't know that she couldn't have," Stewart said, "but when we found him, when Annabeth and I found him, he was in the passenger's-side seat of the truck, lying against the side window, because the truck had gone down the slope to the beach and rolled onto its side. There was beach and rock behind him, and if a person had been there, she'd have been crushed."

Gregor considered it. "All right," he said. "Then the question becomes when he was killed, before or after the truck rolled onto the beach. Why were you and Annabeth Falmer on the beach?"

"We were looking for the truck," Stewart said. "Arrow had shown up at Annabeth's door a mess and babbling about how she was in the truck with Mark and there'd been an accident on the beach, and Annabeth got fairly convinced that Mark was still in the truck. She tried calling the emergency services to go out and find him, but we were in the middle of a major storm and she couldn't actually confirm any of what she'd heard and Arrow was in no shape to talk, so they put her off. So, when I showed up, she was thinking of walking out that way herself and seeing if Mark was there, maybe still alive, maybe dying in the weather. It made sense, you know."

"It made sense for somebody to go out there," Gregor agreed. "I'm not so sure that it made sense for a woman to go out there accompanied by a geriatric old fart like you. Is she athletic?"

"Annabeth? Not really. She looks like—she looks like Judi Dench at fifty. Do you remember Judi Dench at the start of that television series, *As Time Goes By*? It's that kind of look. Not blond, you know, but that kind of look."

"Hmm," Gregor said. The only reason he didn't have to bite his lip until it bled to keep himself from laughing was that he had had many years of training with the Federal Bureau of Investigation. He moved a few more of the pictures around. "So," he said. "You and Annabeth Falmer went out into the storm, and found this truck lying on its side on the beach. Was it easy to find?"

"Here's another thing," Stewart said. He pawed through the pile of photographs himself, found the one he wanted, and handed it across. "Look at this. What do you see?"

"The most violently purple vehicle that ever moved on wheels. Did you brush the snow off it?"

"Some. On the windshield."

"The snow was coming down at the rate of what exactly?"

"Two inches an hour."

Gregor looked at the picture again. He handed it back. "Do you have another one, close to the same shot but at a wider angle?"

"I've got two more."

Stewart found them and handed them over. Gregor looked through them, but he wasn't finding what he wanted. They'd been shot from too close in. "I don't suppose that you took pictures of the area around the truck," he said.

"No, I didn't," Stewart said.

"Or that you noticed anything?" Gregor prodded. "Say, for instance, footprints?"

"No," Stewart said. "The police were going on about footprints too. Arrow's footprints, I think. They couldn't find them. Although, you know, I understand that there's been a lot of technological progress in forensics, but I don't see that not finding footprints tells you much of anything in a situation like this. The snow was coming down, the wind was fierce, and the ocean was no joke."

"Assuming you've been accurate," Gregor said, "and Arrow Normand showed up at Annabeth Falmer's house about twenty minutes before you did, and it took you a while, say at least two or three minutes, to find the truck—"

"It was more like ten."

"So we're talking about half an hour. The only way the truck could have been clean of snow on its exposed side and part of the hood would have been if somebody had cleaned it off pretty close to the time that you arrived. There must have been somebody there. Right there. You must have just missed him. Or her."

"There," Stewart said. "You see? And whoever it was who did that couldn't have been Arrow Normand, because she was passed out at Annabeth's house. Although not as passed out as she was pretending to be, if you catch my drift. They're not actresses, these girls, but they do know how to play dead."

Gregor looked through the pictures again. Whoever had shot Mark Anderman had put the bullet in the side of his head, and that was not the safest way to shoot someone. It was better than a direct hit to the forehead, but it still risked the chance that the victim would survive.

"How many shots were there?" Gregor asked. "I can only see one probably."

"There was only one."

"He was killed with a single gunshot to the head?"

"That's what the police say."

"What happened to the bullet?"

"It exited the head on the other side. That's why there's so much blood on the window and the passenger-side door."

"Did it go through the window?"

"Yes," Stewart said. "Clean. When we got to the truck and I started taking pictures, I couldn't even see something that looked like a crack. Not that the visibility was ideal, mind you. It was the middle of the afternoon, but it was dark."

"Did they find the bullet?" Gregor asked.

"What do you mean, find it?"

"Well," Gregor said, "if he was shot in the truck, which he seems to have been, and the bullet went through his head and then through the glass of the window, it has to be somewhere. If he was shot where you found him, it should be somewhere on the ground underneath the truck. I take it the police didn't find it."

"Not that I've heard."

"Interesting."

"So it's interesting," Stewart said. "So you'll do it. You'll come to Margaret's Harbor and do something about that bloody cow and the games she's playing."

"I can't just come to Margaret's Harbor and interfere with a police investigation," Gregor said. "Cold cases, yes, those I can take on, but an ongoing police investigation is sacrosanct. I get involved in those only when the police themselves ask me in."

Stewart Gordon's face lit up. "That's what she said. That's exactly what she said. I take everything back about how stupid the police up there can be, I mean they all are pretty stupid, except for this one." He reached under his sweater and came out with an envelope that had started out clean and white and straight but was now a wrinkled, squashed mess. "She gave me this. She said it was what you needed."

Gregor took the envelope and opened it. It was not from a policeman. It was from the Margaret's Harbor Public Prosecutor, and it was about as clear an invitation as it was possible to get. She'd even italicized the word "desperate," and offered a fee she must have known was twice what he usually charged.

Gregor looked up at Stewart. Stewart shrugged. "Commander Rees of the Starfleet Cruiser *Intrepid*. You've got no idea how useful that television series has been in my life."

Gregor thought he did have an idea of just that, and also of how useless it must have been on occasion, because the small boys had reached the limit of their patience. There was a groundswell of noise from the living room, and then they all came marching down the hall, led by Tommy Moradanyan Donahue himself.

Half of them were carrying little plastic action figures that were supposed to look just like Stewart Gordon, and did.

THREE

1

Before All the Trouble Started—as that silly real estate woman put it, as if what they were going through were a neighborhood feud or a bad divorce—Annabeth Falmer had heard a lot of the women on the island complain about the publicity "the Hollywood people" brought with them. She had even sympathized. Margaret's Harbor was the kind of place, after all, where people who really wanted their privacy went to get it. In the rare cases where one of those people had become too famous, or infamous, to escape the relentless eye of public scrutiny, a silent bargain was struck, without anybody having to say anything, and that person either limited his visits or left the island altogether. This was something else, different not only from old-style infamy but from civilization as Annabeth understood it. It was as if, during all those years when she had concentrated on her work and her children and the unending bills, something had happened to the world that she had known nothing about.

Now it was ten o'clock on the morning of January 3rd, and Annabeth was standing on Main Street in Oscartown, making her way through the camera crews and television vans toward the grocery store. She was feeling a little better. Stewart had called last evening to tell her that Gregor Demarkian had agreed to come to the island to help with the investigation of the death of Mark Anderman. He had called her again, an hour ago, to tell her they had left Philadelphia for Boston, by plane, and would be in this afternoon. Annabeth had very carefully sat down at the computer and looked for everything she could find on Gregor Demarkian, and she had found enough to feel reassured. He seemed like a very sensible man. He also seemed to be a good friend of Father Tibor Kasparian, who had to be the same Father Tibor Kasparian who wrote about the Nestorians and the end of the Byzantine Empire and the demise of Greek learning in the Eastern churches. Annabeth was fairly certain there couldn't be two Armenian priests named Tibor Kasparian living in Philadelphia at the same time.

She had been less reassured by the other searches she had done. She had searched for Arrow Normand and for Mark Anderman, as a matter of course. She had searched for Kendra Rhode, who was somebody she had thought she knew something about. Finally, she had given up searching for any one of the young women who were involved in this thing and just let herself be washed by the tidal wave of items spilling across the screen. The items went on endlessly. As far as she could tell, there were dozens of people in places like Los Angeles and New York who were very young, very rich, and very stupid and who spent all their time getting their pictures taken by tabloid photographers. There were also dozens of other people—tabloid photographers and "entertainment reporters"—who spent all their time writing and illustrating articles about the first set of people. But that was not what was bothering her. She had actually known about all that, if only by rumor, and without understanding the breathtaking scope of it. There was something else going on here that made her uneasy at the base of her spine. There was something wrong, really wrong. She kept going around and around it without being able to put a name to it. It was more than outside her experience. It was outside the experience of decent people.

Her sons hadn't cared what it was; they had only wanted her to leave the island. John, who was the cardiologist, had been merely frantic. He seemed to think that Margaret's Harbor had suddenly become a hotbed of crime.

"You're not going off to lend your talents to the poor," he said. "You're not volunteering to teach history to inner-city high school students. You're stuck up there with a bunch of psychopaths. And don't think they're less dangerous just because they've got money."

Annabeth had wanted to tell him that she understood they were very dangerous indeed, but she hadn't been able to find the words for it, because she still hadn't known (and didn't know now) how to define the danger. It hadn't mattered to Robbie, who was the lawyer, because the danger he saw was entirely different.

"Murder investigations are funny things," he'd said when he called. "Not funny ha-ha. Funny peculiar. You never know where they're going to go. I don't like it that you found the body, and I don't trust this guy—"

"Stewart Gordon? You don't trust Stewart Gordon? You used to idolize Stewart Gordon."

"I used to idolize Commander Rees," Robbie said, "and I'm not twelve years old anymore. I don't know the district attorney up there, or is it the public prosecutor? It doesn't matter. I know some good people in Boston. I'll send you a lawyer."

"Robbie, for goodness' sake. I don't need a lawyer. Nobody is going to arrest me for anything."

"You don't know that for certain. You can't. You found the body. The woman they've arrested for the murder was in your living room. You're in this up to your neck. I'll send you a lawyer. I'll clear my desk and come up myself in a couple of days."

Annabeth had gotten the impression that John was going to "clear his desk" and come up in a couple of days too, but she deliberately did not press him to make that explicit. At least Robbie understood why she couldn't just up and leave the place right now in the middle of everything. Even Kendra Rhode had been told to stick around for a while.

She looked up and down Main Street. The camera trucks and the people made an almost solid line, so that it was close to impossible to cross from one side of the street to the other without weaving through equipment trucks. Every once in a while she saw a man or woman standing in the middle of the street with a microphone in his hand, filming a "report" that at this point had to be about nothing. There had been news in the first twenty-four hours. Now there was just gossip and innuendo, and lots of people who wanted to see if Marcey Mandret would come spilling out of a bar somewhere, just as drunk as she'd been the night it happened.

"I wouldn't hang around in the middle of the road like this if I were you," a man said.

Annabeth turned around and saw that she was facing a thin, driven, intelligent man of medium height, incongruously dressed in a very good suit and a Baxter State Parker. He had no hat on his head and no gloves. She thought he must be freezing. He held out his hand to her, formal and polite.

"I'm Carl Frank," he said. "We haven't met. I do public relations for the movie."

"Ah," Annabeth said.

"And I was telling you the truth. You shouldn't hang around in the middle of the road like that. They have to eat to live, those people. They don't know who you are at the moment, but they will, especially with Gordon off somewhere. You're news, you know. You found the body."

"Ah," Annabeth said again, surprised. "I think that's amazing."

"What?"

"That you knew who I was."

"We're not all Marcey Mandret," Carl Frank said. "Some of us actually finished our educations. I went to the University of Texas, myself.

I once managed to have *American Revolutions* assigned to me twice in a single year, once for a history course and once for a course in political science."

"I'm surprised they were willing to use a popular book. University departments usually prefer academic scholarship."

"They were courses for nonmajors, and I was in marketing. I think the professors were hoping to hell they could get us interested somehow. You got me interested. I've become one of those old farts who sit around reenacting the battles of the Civil War."

"From the Union side or the Confederate?"

"I try not to take sides. It's good practice for my work. If you take sides in the celebrity wars, you get squashed flat by rampaging egos. Except it isn't really ego. They've got no sense of self, most of these people. They're all flash and dash and surface. Before I got into the work I do, I used to think that was an illusion, that if you got to know them you'd find they were real people inside. And that's true for some of them, of course. Stewart Gordon, for instance. But for most of them?" Carl shrugged.

Annabeth looked up and down the street. Nobody was paying any attention to them, but it occurred to her that if this man was right, if she was considered to be "news" when Stewart was away, the quickest way to get their attention would be to stand here talking to a man they probably all knew.

The same thing seemed to have occurred to Carl Frank. "Well," he said. "I don't want to keep you. I'll get you into a lot of trouble. Do you think you could do something for me?"

"Oh," Annabeth said. "Well—"

"It's nothing huge. It's just that I'd appreciate it if you told our Mr. Gordon that I was asking about him, and mentioned that it might not be outside the bounds of reasonableness for me to wonder if he could bother to check in every once in a while. I am still responsible for the publicity on this thing, as long as it lasts, which may not be very long. But until the brass pulls the plug, here we are."

"Oh," Annabeth said. "All right. Yes, of course I could do that for you."

"They blame you for it, you know," Carl said. "When there's bad publicity on a picture, they blame you for it. I don't know how they're going to find a way to blame me for the fact that Arrow Normand decided to kill her latest toy boy, but they will. You'd better get going. It was very nice talking to you."

"It was very nice talking to you, too," Annabeth said. Then she watched him walk quickly down the street in the direction that led away from the center of town, his shoulders hunched, his hands in his pockets.

The news crews and equipment vans were still where they had been when she had stopped to talk, and the wind was worse. Annabeth pulled her coat collar high on her neck over the cashmere scarf from Harbor Halls that Robbie had bought her at Thanksgiving and headed for the supermarket again. She supposed that Gregor Demarkian would stay at Stewart's house, or at the inn if there was any room, which there probably wasn't. Still, she needed coffee and cream and a lot of other things men liked that she didn't keep around anymore unless the boys were home, and then the boys would probably be coming too.

In all the strangeness of this situation, the very most strange was this: the longer it went on, the more it felt as if she were preparing for a family holiday.

2

If Linda Beecham had had someone around that she could talk to— if she had had the kind of friends most people have—they would have known that she found everything surrounding the murder of Mark Anderman to be oddly satisfying. It wasn't the murder itself that made her feel almost triumphant in self-satisfaction. She knew nothing at all about the young man who was dead, but she had no reason to think he was any better or worse than anybody else. She supposed he had family somewhere, and people who cared for him, but maybe not. She hadn't realized until she was closing in on middle age just how alone most people were. Still, she had no reason to think badly of him, and no reason to wish him dead. She could be sorry enough about that without being a hypocrite.

What struck Linda Beecham was what had happened because the murder had happened, and what was happening still. It had infected everybody. The movie people were behaving the way they had to behave. They put on brave faces for the cameras and spoke earnestly into microphones about how they were sure Arrow Normand had had nothing at all to do with killing their dear friend, this nice boy who had had everything to live for. Then they went back to their rented houses and made phone calls to California. The filming had been stopped dead in its tracks. Linda wasn't even sure it could resume with Arrow Normand in jail, since she was playing a part in it. That thin, nervous man who did the public relations spent all his time in the bar at the Oscartown Inn, not always drinking. Linda had always been sure, deep down inside herself, that this movie would never come off. It was just the kind of harebrained silliness Bitsy Winthorp was prone to. Margaret's Harbor was never going to be a haven for movie people. The weather was bad, and the natives didn't like the intrusion.

If it had been just the movie people, though, Linda wouldn't have been feeling half as smug. The police also were acting just the way she'd expected them to, and so was the new public prosecutor, Clara Walsh. There was something about the sight of multitudes of television cameras that made everybody crazy. These days, Main Street in Oscartown was packed with them, and so were some of the side streets. There were usually cameras on the beach now, too. The island police were all walking very much more upright than they usually did. The state police were putting on their best New Jersey swagger. Clara Walsh spent her time giving press conferences from her office or the Oscartown Inn, saying not much of anything and looking absolutely ridiculous. Somebody ought to tell that woman that she was much too short to wear magenta suits.

"It's television," Linda said. "They all want to be on television. Everybody wants to be on television. It's as if they don't think they exist if they aren't on television."

Across the room, Jack Bullard grunted. He had the television on, the small one Linda kept in her office for breaking news. It was tuned to a Clara Walsh press conference.

"So," he said. "Do you know anything about this guy they're bringing in? This Gregor Demarkian?"

"I've heard of him," Linda said. "He's been on some of those true-crime shows. *American Justice. City Confidential.* He was in the papers a few months ago for something down in Philadelphia."

"Why would Clara Walsh want to bring in a private detective? Why would the police want to let her?"

Linda snorted. "For God's sake," she said. "It's all about the publicity. This has ceased to be a crime investigation. It's ceased to be about anything except the media coverage. Why not bring in a celebrity detective? It guarantees you more print. It guarantees you more airtime. And you look like you're doing something, when you're not."

"I wouldn't think Clara Walsh would want any more media than she's already got," Jack said. "I mean, look at it around here lately. They're everywhere. And they're not all Walter Cronkite, either."

"I think Walter Cronkite is dead."

"I don't, but what does it matter?" Jack said. "You must see what I mean. This is completely insane as it is. There are news reports three or four times a day. Yesterday I heard from Kevin Kelly at the morgue, and he said they've had to post guards at the laundry chutes because he's got photographers trying to get in that way. And other ways."

"And these are the people you wanted us to hook up with," Linda said. "I told you what they were like."

"All I wanted to do was sell a few pictures at a price that could help the paper out and help me out in the meantime," Jack said. "I was just trying to cut you in on what I was going to do anyway."

"And did you? Sell some of those photographs?"

"One or two. But what about the *Home News*? This is a murder. You can't say it's not really news. We come out in two days. We are going to cover this, right?"

"I suppose we're going to have to, if we don't want to look like idiots," Linda said. "Don't worry. I put Dina Coleman on it. We'll give it the entire page above the fold and say all the usual things. Not that there's anything much to say that hasn't been said forty times already. We'll use your picture of the ambulance taking the body away, unless you've sold that already to somebody else."

"I've been waiting very patiently for you."

"Thank you, I think. You are going to sell some of those, aren't you?"

"Absolutely," Jack said. "I'll let you pick what you want, and then I'm going to sell the rest to the highest bidder. I was in the right place at the right time, and I was the only one there. I'm the only one with the stills and the only one with the footage."

"You took video?"

"For a while. When I got bored. It's not the most exciting thing in the world to stand out in the middle of a nor'easter waiting for the EMTs to get over having to handle a bloody corpse. I was freezing my ass off and thinking that this is the most remarkable place. Most EMTs are used to handling bloody corpses."

"I don't think it was the blood," Linda said. "We have our share of traffic fatalities."

"Well, whatever. They were lame. And so were the local police on the scene, from what I've heard. They weren't used to handling a homicide. They screwed things up."

"That's probably just Clara Walsh's office talking," Linda said.

Jack sighed. "It's everybody talking," he said. "The first really significant thing that's happened on Margaret's Harbor in forty years, and we're all acting like a bunch of buffoons. They say the police told Kendra Rhode she'd have to stay put for the rest of the week. Do you think she'll listen?"

"I don't think it matters what she does," Linda said.

Jack turned off the television and stood up. "Maybe it doesn't," he said. "But it would be good, this setup, if I wanted to write a *Columbo* episode. It's got a kind of fairy-tale quality to it. Maybe everything on Margaret's Harbor does. You're wrong not to recognize the mystique of it. Everybody else does."

"It's not mystique," Linda said drily, "it's stupefaction. I don't care how much money you have. How big an idiot do you have to be to pay sixty-five dollars for a polo shirt?"

"It's not about the money," Jack said.

For a moment, Linda felt ashamed of herself. Jack was young. He still believed in possibility, and hope, and the future. He still thought they were all in control of their own destinies. She always made him depressed.

"Listen," she said. "I'm sorry. I've lived here too long. I don't have the—I don't know what to call it. The thing you all have. I don't see the magic in it."

"It's not that," Jack said. He had gone to the table near the window and started to pack up his professional gear, the cameras, the lenses, the film, everything in black leather carrying cases that had probably been as ridiculously priced as those polo shirts. Every once in a while he turned his head and looked out the big plate glass window onto Main Street. "You'd think you could do something with this," he said. "Here they are, all these people that you never have any access to at all. Important people. People who report the real news."

"In the real world, there really is real news," Linda said. "But no matter what you think, stories about Arrow Normand and Marcey Mandret and Kendra Rhode going to parties and getting drunk and disorderly aren't real news."

"These people report on other things," Jack said. "They go to wars.

They cover peace accords. They do special reports on epidemics. And they're here. Where I can get to them. You'd think I'd be able to make something of that."

"Maybe you will," Linda said. "Maybe you'll get to them with all those photographs you took. Maybe you'll get offered a job that will take you out of here, if that's what you want."

"I think that when this is all over, I'm just going to go," Jack said. "It's not that I don't like you. I do like you. It's just that—I could sit here forever. I could still be here when I'm fifty. And I really don't want to be."

Linda hadn't wanted to be either, but here she was, and here she was going to stay. She looked down at her desk and saw the spreadsheets from the last quarter of last year, freshly arrived. She had a new person in accounting who understood computers and liked to use them. She knew what it was to be so desperate to get out of here that you would do anything—swallow razor blades, expose yourself in Times Square—for a ticket to somewhere else, to somewhere real. She knew what it was to feel that Margaret's Harbor wasn't real.

"Hey," she said. "Here's the thing. I'll take one picture of the crime scene, and one each of Arrow Normand and Mark Anderman, if you've got them, and you can sell the rest for yourself. Go show what you've got to CBS and see if you can get them to take you seriously."

"Thanks. Thank you very much."

"It's nothing," Linda said.

It really was nothing, but Linda understood that it would be something to Jack. He had been distracted ever since the murder happened, as if Mark Anderman's bloody wound had really driven home the fact that he wasn't getting any younger, and he wasn't where he wanted to be. He would go on being distracted until he'd had a chance to give it a shot.

Linda turned back to her spreadsheets and found herself hoping that he would be luckier than she had been, that he would not end up still on the Harbor thirty years from now, with nothing to take comfort in but the uncompromising solidity of his isolation.

3

Marcey Mandret believed the world was an equitable place—or would have, if she'd known what the word "equitable" meant. The way she put it inside her own head was to say the world was "fair," and then she tried very hard not to spell out the ways in which it was that. Here was the problem, the one she could never get out from under, no matter what she did: if the world was fair, then she deserved to have more money than other people, and more publicity; but if the world was fair, and she didn't deserve to have these things, then she would eventually lose them. It went around and around and around. If the world was fair, she couldn't have gotten these things if she didn't deserve them. On the other hand, fair or not, it was possible she had cheated, maybe without meaning to, and then she would be—something. She was having that thing in her stomach again. People thought she was anorexic or bulimic, but she didn't have to be. She only had to let her stomach get like this, knotted up, and in pain, so that it felt as if she had a knife sticking into her intestines. It was impossible to eat, and if she did try to eat anything, she threw it up. She even threw up some of what she drank.

At the moment, she was drinking tea, although she hated it. She couldn't drink alcohol with the way things were right now, and she couldn't drink coffee, either, because coffee made her jumpy. It was very important that she not get jumpy at this stage of the game. It was like an obstacle course with live land mines. She had to get from here to the other side without getting hurt. It was almost impossible.

Kendra Rhode did not look like she was jumpy. She looked bored. Marcey was in awe of Kendra Rhode. She never had to wonder for a moment if she deserved the things she had. She was born with them.

She never had to worry that she would lose everything she'd worked for. She didn't work for anything, and she couldn't lose it, because she had family lawyers and family bankers and family accountants making sure it was safe, and she would inherit even more when her parents died.

Kendra was sitting in the big wingback chair next to the fireplace, the only chair in this rental that wasn't very low to the ground. Marcey and Arrow used to joke that they'd rented the place from an aging hippie. There were even beanbag chairs in some places. Kendra would never sit in a beanbag chair. Marcey thought about Arrow and took a long drink of tea. It didn't help a bit.

"So," she said, thinking that they had to talk about something. You couldn't sit for hours in the same room with a person and not say anything. Except that Kendra could sit like that. Marcey tried again. "So," she said. "I'm getting a little crazy. They keep saying we shouldn't go out and get into the papers with, you know, all that other thing going on."

"Do they have the death penalty in Massachusetts?" Kendra asked.

Marcey blinked. This was something that hadn't occurred to her. She usually didn't think much of what was going to happen in the future, even if the future was only a year or two. She tried to think it through.

"Well," she said, "California has the death penalty, doesn't it?"

"I suppose," Kendra said.

"Well," Marcey said again, "California has the death penalty, and being for the death penalty isn't hip, and California is hipper than Massachusetts. So if California has the death penalty, Massachusetts must have it too."

Kendra got that little smile on her face that Marcey had always laughed at when it was aimed at other people. When Kendra aimed it at her, it wasn't funny at all. "Think of that," Kendra said. "Using that logic, since California is the hippest state in the Union, every state must have the death penalty. But they don't. Only thirty-eight states have the death penalty."

"That leaves how many without it?"

"Twelve," Kendra said. The smile was back.

Marcey made herself take a deep, long, endless breath. It wasn't as if she'd dropped out of high school to hang around on street corners. She'd been working, and working very hard. She couldn't help it if she had missed some of the things other people might have gotten by sitting in classrooms. Arrow hadn't graduated from high school either, and neither had Kendra. It was just that Kendra didn't seem to have missed as much.

"If they have the death penalty in Massachusetts, I wonder what kind it is," Kendra said. "It's probably lethal injection. Most places have lethal injection now. It's too bad. I think it would be really interesting to watch somebody die in the electric chair."

"I don't think you can watch," Marcey said carefully. "I think they do it in private. At least, I've never seen pictures, and I think I would have."

"They don't let just anybody watch," Kendra said. "And they don't let cameras in. They just allow a few people in a kind of audience, like a theater. I've seen it in movies. They allow the victim's family if they want to come. And the person being executed gets to invite witnesses. Do you think Arrow would do that, if they decided to execute her? Do you think she'd invite us as witnesses?"

Marcey was finding it impossible to take any more deep breaths. She was finding it close to impossible to take any breaths at all. "You can't really think they're going to execute Arrow Normand," she said. "How can you think that? She didn't kill that idiot."

"Are you sure?"

"Yes, I'm sure," Marcey said. "And you are too. You know she couldn't have been the one who shot Mark. You know it."

"I don't know anything," Kendra said. "And besides, I've got a terrible memory. I can barely remember where I put my car keys."

This room was a very odd place. Marcey didn't think she had ever really looked at it before. You didn't look at rentals, really, unless there was something spectacular about them. This place was just "nice." It was the best they could get, because the people who had the spectacular houses on Margaret's Harbor didn't rent them. Kendra should have had them to stay at the Point, but she hadn't.

This room had a lot of framed posters on the walls. The posters were all of old paintings, the kind they sometimes used to frontpiece a movie or do the cover on the kind of book she always passed by without checking into. Marcey didn't know if the people who owned this house had put up posters because they couldn't afford real paintings, or if they just didn't like real paintings. These were not the kinds of paintings she would have wanted in her house in any case. They showed things that were ugly, like people dying.

Marcey bit her lip and then instantly stuck out her tongue to wet it. She tried another deep breath. She was making herself dizzy.

"You can't do this," she said finally. "This isn't like leaving her passed out in a bar somewhere and then laughing at the pictures afterward. They've arrested her. She's in jail. The judge wouldn't even set bail."

"I know. That happens in murder cases," Kendra said. "But they'll set bail eventually. Just watch. They can't keep somebody that famous in jail when she hasn't been convicted yet. It was the same with Robert Blake and O.J."

"This isn't O.J."

"It's pretty close," Kendra said. "It's close to Robert Blake, too. Washed-up has-been who used to be famous goes on trial for murder. They don't convict those people. Do you even remember why anybody would think Robert Blake was a celebrity? Had you ever heard of him?"

"He was in *In Cold Blood*," Marcey said automatically. "The first one, from the 1960s. It was in black and white. Kendra, seriously. She's in jail. And she didn't kill anybody. And you know it. You were there."

"Was I?"

"Yes, you were. I saw you there. I was there."

"You haven't said anything about it," Kendra said.

"No, I haven't said, because—because you said not to. We talked about it. You said that nothing would happen, and it would only be the wrong kind of publicity. And that's true. It is the wrong kind of publicity. But we can't just not say anything if Arrow is going to go to jail unless we tell."

"I can," Kendra said. "Besides, what would you say when they wanted to know why you hadn't said anything up to now? You'd end up sounding like an idiot, and then they could charge you with one of those things. Accessory before the fact. Accessory after the fact. I don't know. There are things."

"Things as bad as sending Arrow to the electric chair?"

"She won't have a career after this, you know," Kendra said. "She barely had one before it. She'd been going completely to hell, and it was getting so boring I could barely stand it. But after this, she'll be nowhere."

"She doesn't have to be dead. Or locked up."

"It would come to the same thing," Kendra said. "She won't be able to go clubbing anymore. The clubs won't let her in. Quite frankly, they were iffy even before this, but she was with us, so they let it pass. She won't be invited to openings. I can't imagine what that would be like. It would be like being wiped out, don't you think?"

"Wiped out?"

"As if you didn't exist anymore," Kendra said. "You know what I mean. You said it to me. She'd gotten to be a terrible bore before this and now with this it will all be over. And if you get yourself charged with something, it will be over for you, too. Can't you feel it? This is the first movie you've done in two years, and it isn't exactly the kind of thing that wins an Oscar."

"You don't have a career to worry about," Marcey said. "And nobody is going to stop you from going clubbing. Your family has money in half the clubs in L.A. There'd be no reason for you not to tell."

"Except that I don't want to," Kendra said, "and I'm not sure I have anything to say. It's ridiculous the kind of fuss they make about these things. He wasn't anybody. Why should anybody care?"

One of the posters on the wall the fireplace was on seemed to be a painting that was two paintings in one. In the front there were a lot of young men dressed up in old-fashioned clothes, all in bright colors, and with things in their hair. In the back, almost in black and white, there was a man in nothing but a rag around his waist tied against a pillar, and another man was beating him, and other men were around them both, watching. The juxtaposition of the two scenes made Marcey feel a little dizzy.

Kendra turned around to see what Marcey was looking at, and made a face. "It's by Piero della Francesca," she said. "It's called *The Flagellation*. I never liked it much. Bondage and discipline were never my thing."

Marcey looked back at the picture again. She was fairly sure that it wasn't about bondage and discipline, but she didn't know what it was about, and it made her sick to look at it.

"You just can't not say anything," she said. "You just can't."

Kendra Rhode looked into the fireplace and smiled.

FOUR

1

It was possible to get from Philadelphia to Boston by Amtrak, going through New York. It was possible to get from Boston to Cape Cod by car, which was helpfully supplied by the Massachusetts State Police, complete with flashing lights and wailing siren.

"The governor is very concerned that you get all the help you need while you concern yourself in this matter," the officer who had been sent to drive them told Gregor as he first got into the car—and Gregor was careful not to ask who'd taught him to use exactly that phraseology, or why anybody would think it would be a help to sit in the back of a police car behind the metal mesh caging meant to keep violent prisoners from strangling their captors. It didn't matter. Gregor had sat in the backs of police cars often in his career. He understood that most policemen didn't understand how disorienting they were.

It was when they got to the Cape that Gregor began to feel unhappy, and then he wondered how he couldn't have guessed. He'd been to Margaret's Harbor before. He'd been on detail for presidential visits back when he was first in the FBI and the president in the White House had liked to spend his vacations here. Margaret's Harbor was one of those places, like Mackinac Island in Michigan and Fishers Island in Long Island Sound, where rich people went to pretend they were roughing it, or at least getting back to simplicity. Comfort, convenience, and common sense were dispensable when you had enough money to do what you wanted.

"You'd have thought they'd have put in a bridge by now," Gregor said as the police car eased up to the curb near a large wharf with a solid-looking ferryboat docked at the end of it. Gregor got out and looked around. "At least I don't see any icebergs," he said.

"Well, now," Stewart said. "You can see for yourself. All that bloody stupid nonsense about the Russians. They just wanted a warm-water port, that's all. There was never any reason for you people to go off half cocked and practically start World War III over that."

"You people?"

"Americans."

"Do you talk like this in Margaret's Harbor?" Gregor asked. "Do they try to lynch you?"

"I talk like this on CNN," Stewart said. "And they're fine with it. Of course, I've got a lot of other things to say about America, and a lot of them are complimentary. So that helps. But not about American actresses. With the exception of Meryl Streep. She's a fine actress, and very professional. There's Clara. I've got a lot to say about Clara, too. I like her."

Gregor looked up and saw that there was a very small woman waiting for them on the deck of the ferry. He hadn't noticed her before because she was, really, very small, and it was easy to lose her among the ropes and life preservers. He followed Stewart onto the wharf itself and tried to make out something about the woman that wasn't related to size. There wasn't anything. She was bundled into a gigantic quilted down coat that went down past the boat's side, so that she looked like an ice blue Popsicle with red sprinkles unaccountably scattered near the front of it.

Stewart jumped from the wharf into the boat. He would. He always liked to show off just how vigorous he was at whatever age he was claiming these days. Gregor got into the boat the civilized way. The woman in the down coat hurried toward them, visibly shivering.

"It's impossible out here," she said, bringing out a gloved hand for Gregor to shake. The gloves were good leather, and the impression of red sprinkles turned out to be wisps of her hair, which was very red indeed. It was red of a shade nobody on earth had ever had naturally, and it was a good ten years too young for her face.

"I'm Clara Walsh," she said, putting her hand back into her pocket. "I'm glad to meet you, Mr. Demarkian. Mr. Gordon has been talking about you endlessly ever since we first met, but of course I knew you by reputation before that. Couldn't we all get inside and out of this wind? It's six degrees today. It's in the minus numbers with the wind chill."

"That's six degrees Fahrenheit," Stewart said. "If you people used the metric system like sensible countries, six degrees would at least be above freezing."

Gregor let this go. They had had the metric-system-versus-English-system argument before, and Celsius wasn't even the metric system. The boat turned out to have a large upper deck cabin filled with seats in two sets of orderly rows, like a movie theater. There were also benches along the walls, and a bar that was obviously set up to serve drinks and coffee.

"So this is the regular ferryboat," Gregor said. "I've never been on it before."

"You've never been to the Harbor before?" Clara asked.

"No, I've been to the Harbor," Gregor said, "but it was when I was still with the FBI. We went out in our own launch, I think. If this is the regular ferry, shouldn't it be ferrying? Won't people be wanting to go back and forth?"

"They may want to," Clara said, "but during the winter, if you don't have your own boat, you only get to go back and forth at seven in the morning and six at night. That's as often as the ferry operates. They did schedule extra runs on New Year's Eve because Kendra Rhode was having a large party, and the Rhode family got in touch with the ferry authority. But as it turned out, the extra runs didn't run anyway, because of the storm."

"I've told Gregor about the storm," Stewart said. He was pacing back and forth, as if he couldn't stop moving. "Of course, the news about the storm was in all the papers, and on television, but Gregor never notices anything unless he's looking for it."

"You said people have private boats," Gregor said, thinking that he ought to sit down before the boat started to move. "Did they have private boats that night?"

"I suppose they could have had," Clara said, "but I can't imagine anybody being able to manage it and coming out of it alive. Maybe if they were expert boatmen, and I don't mean 'expert' the way people on the Harbor think of themselves as experts. I mean if they were professional fishermen or something, the guys who go out into the Atlantic in all weathers. And even some of them don't come back when the weather is bad enough, and none of them I know of would have risked his neck just to get from the mainland to the Harbor. Well, I mean, maybe if his wife or his mother were dying and that was the only way he could get to see her. But to take somebody in, to make money on the fare? Not a chance."

"All right," Gregor said. He went to one of the cabin's small windows to look out. He could see the waters of the Cape again, and some men on the deck doing he didn't know what. He supposed it was important in getting the boat to go. He hated boats.

"So," he said. "We can be fairly sure that the people we know of who were on the island at the time of the murder were the only people on the island at the time of the murder. Nobody could have come in and then gone out by boat."

"No," Clara Walsh said. She had thrown back the hood of her dark coat. Her hair was as red as Rudolph's nose, and she had to be over fifty. "But you have to understand something. We don't think we've got the wrong person. I've looked at the evidence. The local police have looked at the evidence. The state police have looked at the evidence. We've thrown jurisdiction to the winds and let everybody and his brother see the evidence. And we've all come to pretty much the same conclusion. Arrow Normand shot Mark Anderman in the head. We don't know why. We do know she did it."

"So why am I here?" Gregor asked.

Stewart cleared his throat. "Ah," he said.

Clara Walsh ignored him. "Mr. Gordon made a fuss. A big one. And when we sat down and thought about it, we decided he was actually making a certain amount of sense. Not sense in relation to the solution of the crime. On that one, he's talking through his hat. But the simple fact is that we have to be careful here. Everybody involved here is either a high-profile personality or a person of serious influence, and I do mean everybody. It's bad enough that we're dealing with teen queen actresses and movie people, and the Harbor is now inundated with media. We've even got the BBC camped out on Oscartown's main street."

"And Al Jazeera," Stewart said blandly. "Great story about the decadence of the West with a great excuse to run pictures of girls in their underwear."

"Yes," Clara said. "The fact is that we're under a microscope, and we don't want to be perceived as being amateurish, or stupid, or hasty. The local police have cause to worry about being charged with inexperience. I looked it up. The last murder on the Harbor was in 1932, and it didn't require much of an investigation. There used to be lobstermen on the island. They couldn't afford to live there now. Anyway, one of them killed his wife's lover with a hatchet in full view of half a dozen people on the very dock we're going to now. So you see, bringing in somebody who does know something about investigating a murder, and especially someone who has investigated murders with high-profile people involved in them, made a good deal of sense on a number of accounts. And, of course, we have to worry about the lawyers."

"The lawyers?" Gregor said.

Clara Walsh shrugged. "It's every prosecutor's nightmare, another O. J. Simpson case. This young woman is not bright, but the people around her are bright, and she's got the money to hire the best legal representation out there. And she will. She's in the process of doing it as we speak. We need somebody who can think the way those lawyers think. I know a number of people who say that somebody is you."

The boat lurched underneath them. Clara Walsh and Stewart Gordon didn't seem to notice. Gregor sat down abruptly sideways on the nearest chair.

"So," Stewart said. "Don't listen to her. I've told you why I think Arrow Normand couldn't possibly have done it. And that's the way to go about it, isn't it, if you want to help the prosecution? Do your damnedest to prove the case wrong, and then if you can't, you know they're on solid ground."

Gregor sighed. "Stewart said you'd managed to keep Arrow Normand in jail. Have you still?"

"Yes," Clara Walsh said. The boat was lurching some more. "For the moment, we've been able to get away with a judge who doesn't want to grant bail. And he really doesn't. He doesn't trust those people, and I don't blame him. But we're at the lawyers again. Once her criminal team gets here, that won't last too long. They'll have her out sooner rather than later. You have no idea how I miss the days when we could just say that we don't grant bail in murder cases and let it go at that."

"Can you keep her on the island?" Gregor asked.

"Probably not," Clara said, "although we had thought of that, and we're going to try. For our purposes, though, it's not enough just to keep her on the island. This is a complicated case in some ways, if not in others. For one thing, we've got no idea at all why she'd want to kill this man. We've gone through all the usual explanations. There's no sign she was paying him blackmail, and whatever would he blackmail her about? All her dirty laundry is public anyway. She practically throws it onto the world stage to be photographed. There's no indication from anybody who knew them that he was about to leave her, and why would he? She was the one with the money and the fame and the things a partner wants to hang on to, and they hadn't been seeing each other long enough to make a Grand Passion credible. Sex and money, lust and lucre. All the usual explanations fall flat."

"So why be so sure she committed the murder?" Gregor asked.

"Well," Clara said, "let's see. First, she had his blood in her hair. A lot of it. Her hair was soaked with it. Then, he died in the truck—it was a purple pickup truck, did Mr. Gordon tell you that?—and her fingerprints were all over it, and so were his."

"Everybody's fingerprints were all over it," Stewart said. "So were mine. We'd all been in that truck."

"Her fingerprints were in the blood in the truck," Clara said. "Which is somewhat more incriminating. Then there's the way she's been behaving since, which has been, let's say, less than cooperative."

"Has she offered an explanation for any of it?" Gregor asked.

"No," Clara Walsh said. "It seems that no matter how stupid she is, she's seen enough true-crime documentaries to know she doesn't have to talk to the police without a lawyer present, and as soon as the lawyer showed up, she refused to say anything at all. And this wasn't a good lawyer. It was one of the entertainment lawyers the movie people have on tap for things like disputes over permits. When we try to ask her questions, all Arrow Normand says is 'I don't have to talk to you,' and then she completely shuts up. She's very good at shutting up."

Gregor thought about this. "What about the rest of them?" he asked finally. "You must have talked to other people, even other people who are part of this movie. Would they talk to you? At all?"

Clara Walsh shrugged. "Marcey Mandret ran off at the mouth for a bit, but none of it made any sense. I've seen the tapes. I think she was high as a kite at the time. We talked to Kendra Rhode. She didn't say much of anything and looked bored. We talked to Mr. Gordon here, and to Dr. Falmer, because Arrow Normand went to her house. We talked to some people on the set, including the guy who does public relations for the movie. He's the one I feel sorry for. Anyway, nobody has said much of anything. And it was the day of the storm. Nobody was doing much of anything. It was hard to get around."

"Yes," Gregor said.

The boat made a sudden, dramatic lurch and then seemed to glide, so slowly Gregor thought he could have walked faster.

Clara Walsh came to the windows and looked out. "Oh, good," she said. "We're on the water."

2

Gregor would have said they'd been on the water the whole time, but he knew what Clara Walsh meant, and he distrusted himself when he began to be fussy over trivialities. Still, he found himself thinking that television had done a great disservice to real detectives in real police departments all across America. Television detectives were always strong and resolute and dedicated and clearsighted. When they weren't, there was always some good reason why they were having a bad day, or something particularly spectacular to compensate. That was why Gregor truly hated the show *Monk,* even though he was forced to sit through it several times a week, since Tibor and Bennis and Donna loved it. He especially didn't like it because they kept asking him whether it was anything at all like real homicide detective work in a real police department, and of course it was nothing like it at all.

It was not a long passage from the mainland of Cape Cod to Margaret's Harbor. Gregor could see the shore of the island almost as soon as they set off, and the closer they got the clearer it was that their dock would be deserted when they reached it. Gregor found this very interesting, in a case in which everybody went out of his way to tell him just how much press there would be watching his every move. Apparently, they weren't watching it yet. He paced back and forth in front of the line of windows. He wondered what people usually used the ferry for, when it was running on full schedule.

"It can't be a commuter route," he said.

Stewart Gordon and Clara Walsh looked up. They had been talking about something else near the bar. They hadn't expected him to speak.

"It can't be a commuter route," Gregor said again. "This ferry, I mean. If it were a commuter route, it would have to be operating pretty close to full schedule even in the winter."

"Oh," Clara said. "Well, it is a commuter route in the summer, when there are a lot of people on the island. There's no point in making it a commuter route at this time of year, though, because nobody lives on Margaret's Harbor year-round and commutes to work in the city."

"Why not?" Gregor asked.

"It's too long a way, I suppose," Clara said. "It's about ten to twelve minutes on the ferry to the mainland, and then it's another hour into Boston at least, even with perfect traffic conditions, and traffic conditions are seldom perfect in Boston. Add that to the increased possibility of bad weather conditions during the winter and early spring, and I suppose most people find the idea just too much trouble. They come up for the summer though, and commute from the Harbor then."

"But there are people who live full-time on the Harbor," Gregor said.

"Of course there are," Clara said.

"What do they do to make a living? The Harbor doesn't have industry, from what I understand. There's no manufacturing, or anything like that."

"No," Clara said. "Most of the people who live on the island work for the tourist trade. They run hotels or bed-and-breakfasts, they have lawn services and cleaning services, that kind of thing. And a lot of that runs year-round. You need your house looked after if you're not going to be in it for several months at a time."

"All right," Gregor said. "But there must be other things, things that people would do on the island even if no tourists had ever appeared. There were people on the island before there were tourists, weren't there?"

"There were people on the island all the way back to the American Revolutionary War, and before," Clara said. "Fishermen, mostly. There are still a fair number of fishermen. There were farmers here once, but I don't think that there are any real working farms here anymore. We've got a couple of Potemkin farms, if you get my drift, the sort of thing rich men like to buy and have somebody else run for them, but not anything a real farmer could make a living at. And there are stores, of course, like groceries, that operate all year round. Body shops. But everybody makes more money when the tourists are here."

Gregor looked out at the shore again. There really wasn't anybody there. "So," he said, "everybody is better off when there are tourists on the island, and in the winter there aren't any tourists on the island, or not many. So this was a good thing, the movie coming to Margaret's Harbor. It meant more people on the island in the winter, and that meant more money for everybody concerned."

"Hah," Stewart Gordon said. "You've got to ask yourself whether it was enough money for the trouble. It wouldn't have been enough money for my trouble."

Clara Walsh ignored him. "The movie is fairly contained," she said. "Mostly, it was good business for the people in Oscartown, but not really elsewhere on the island. Everybody seems to have packed right into Oscartown and just stayed put most of the time, except for the drinking."

"They drink like fish, these girls," Stewart Gordon said, "except why we should say that, I don't know. I mean, fish don't drink, do they? But they do. Marcey and Arrow and the rest of them. There are roadhouses all over the place up here, and they've hit most of them."

"They have been seen in quite a few," Clara said. "We do have local police, and by and large they have not been happy. You always get a lot of drunk driving in a resort area, but in the past few months it's been excessive."

"And ask yourself why it's been excessive," Stewart Gordon said. "Kendra Rhode doesn't drink. Well, she does, but barely. I've never seen her drunk, or high, to the point where it could impair her driving, and she's been on these road trips more than once, and she's never the designated driver. Never."

"Kendra Rhode has been up here for the entire time the movie has been here?" Gregor asked. "That's been—how long?"

"About six weeks," Clara Walsh said. "And no, she hasn't been. She's been in and out. They've all been in and out, except for some of the technical people, and the director, and like that. Most of them have been here for the last couple of weeks, though. I think it depends on when they're needed for filming."

"I've been here the whole time," Stewart Gordon said. "Didn't make any sense to me to go running off to wherever the hell just because they didn't need me for a couple of days."

"This Mark Anderman, the man who died," Gregor said. "Was he here the whole time?"

"Yes," Stewart Gordon said.

"I think so," Clara Walsh said. "He was definitely one of the technical people. Unlike Mr. Gordon here, I'd have to check."

"Thank you," Gregor said. "But I'm still not getting a picture here. For the past six weeks or so, the technical people have been here, some of the actors have been here, and the local people have been here. The local people include fishermen, and people who run grocery stores and that kind of thing—what about nonessential retail? Clothing stores, that kind of thing."

"Most of it's shut up for the winter," Clara said. "There are several stores here that have winter branches in Boca Raton and Palm Beach. The owners do the season here, then pack up and open down there."

"You say there's a lot of national press here. What about local press? Are there local newspapers on Margaret's Harbor? A local television station?"

"The television stations are out of Boston," Clara said, "but there is a local newspaper. It's called the *Home News*. It comes out weekly."

"And a wonderful paper it is, too," Stewart said. "Down-to-earth. Sensible. Intelligent."

"Printing almost nothing about the movie people," Clara Walsh said.

"Printing absolutely nothing," Stewart said. "At least as long as I've been reading it. Oh, except for traffic advice. Don't use Main Street Tuesday morning, it's going to be closed for filming."

"You'd have to know Linda Beecham," Clara said, "which almost nobody does. We went to high school together, but I think that's the last time I ever really had a chance to talk to her. She's not—I don't know how to put it. Social. And, of course, she's had a very hard life. But she either isn't interested in the movie people, or positively dislikes them, because she's run nothing at all on them. Jack Bullard is ready to kill her."

"Who's Jack Bullard?"

"Her one full-time reporter," Clara said. "She's also got one technical person, and that's it. It's not a big project. Jack's young, and he's her photographer as well as her reporter, and he's taken plenty of photographs of the movie people and sold several of them to the tabloids, which is good for him. But I've talked to him. He tries every time to get her to run them in the *Home News* first, and she isn't having any."

"Does the *Home News* make money?" Gregor asked.

"It makes enough to do a little more than break even," Clara said, "but it doesn't have to make a mint. Linda actually managed to get lucky about ten years ago or so and hit a small jackpot in the Big Bucks game. I don't think it came to more than five million or so after taxes, but that's not negligible, and in Linda's case it made all the difference in the world. Like I said, she's had a hard life."

"From a poor family?" Gregor asked.

"From a middle-class family," Clara said, "but then there were terrible things that happened. Her mother and her sister both died of some kind of god-awful cancer that took forever to take its course, and Linda had to leave school to take care of them. Then, when that was over, Linda was stuck with the bills. It just sort of went on and on for decades, and then one morning there was this. The next thing we knew, she'd bought the *Home News,* and she's been there ever since."

"Interesting," Gregor said. "You'd think she'd be interested in maximizing her income. There's money to be made covering the film people, isn't there?"

"A ton of it," Stewart Gordon said. "I don't know what's wrong with Americans, and it isn't just Americans. Think of Diana Spencer. People lose their minds. They can't get enough of it. They can't get enough of this lot, and that's worse than mystifying."

"You'd have to know Linda," Clara Walsh said again. "She's a very unusual person. She doesn't have enthusiasms, and she doesn't get excited about things. She'd be a good person to talk to, though. She might not have run any stories about the film people, but I'll guarantee she knew all about them, and more than anybody else. Linda's like that. And what she doesn't know, Jack probably will."

"I haven't met her," Stewart said. "At least, not that I know of."

"Mr. Gordon likes to run around Oscartown doing his own shopping," Clara Walsh said. "He startles the hell out of practically everybody. But he's very polite. If they say hello, he always says hello back."

"Well, it's nonsense, isn't it?" Stewart said. "The way these people behave. Entourages. Bodyguards. They create their own problems, don't they? I've never in my life had to worry about being hounded by paparazzi, and do you know why? Because I don't live like a Latin American dictator who's made too many enemies. Never mind that it's expensive, living the way they do. Forty thousand dollars a night for a hotel room, for God's sake. And then who knows how much more for the entire crew she had with her."

"What?" Gregor asked.

"That's the answer to Mr. Demarkian's question," Clara Walsh said. "No, Mark Anderman wasn't on the island without a break during the entire time of the filming. About three weeks ago, he went off with Arrow Normand and the entire rest of that group to Las Vegas for the weekend, and they rented something called the Hugh Hefner Suite at the Palms Hotel. I've never been to Las Vegas, and I don't have any idea what this means, but it was on CNN. They were gone for the weekend and came back."

"A nine-thousand-square-foot hotel suite," Stewart Gordon said. "Think about it. The house I grew up in wasn't a third that size. I bet the house you were brought up in wasn't either."

"I was brought up in an apartment," Gregor said. "You said they had people with them?"

"Oh, yes," Clara said. "There was the whole crew, really. Kendra Rhode and that odious boy who doesn't seem to do anything but be vulgar. Marcey Mandret. Another film crew person, Steve something— I can't remember how this went. I think Arrow Normand went out with Steve whoever he was, but came back with Mark Anderman. They met some people from Los Angeles, I think. It really was on CNN. We can look it up on the Internet if you're interested."

Gregor didn't know if he was interested or not, but the dock was coming up fast, and they could all talk about it later. They were approaching land, and out there, waiting for them, was—nothing at all. Gregor had the feeling that he had stepped into the kind of movie he would have refused to watch if Bennis had wanted to stay up late to do it.

FIVE

1

Carl Frank understood the attractions of café society. He had understood them as a child, when he had watched his mother sitting over the social pages morning after morning in their kitchen in Saddle Ridge, New Jersey. He had understood them in college, when it seemed as if every rich girl with a recognizable Old Money name had wanted nothing more than to see a photo spread of herself in *Life,* milking cows on a commune in California. He even understood them now, although, being older, his understanding was more multifaceted. The advertising agencies only cared about reaching a great honking chunk of the eighteen-to-thirty-five year-old demographic, and the closer the skew was to the eighteen, the better. It was one of the things that left him faintly baffled. When he was eighteen, nobody he knew would have admitted to a fascination with society. Most of them wouldn't even admit to a fascination with being part of the popular crowd in high school. Now it was as if the whole world were a high school, the kind of high school where lots of rich kids dominated the sports teams and the cheerleading squad, and the smart kids went unnoticed by anybody at all.

Until they founded Microsoft and become the richest people on the planet, Carl thought—and then brushed that away. Nobody ever saw Bill Gates on the red carpet, except maybe at the White House, and probably not even then. The White House probably didn't even have a red carpet. His mind had turned into some kind of mush. He was sweaty, in spite of the cold, and he was frustrated as hell.

"No," he had told Michael Bardman earlier, using every ounce of sanity he had not to hang up the phone in the idiot's ear, "it is not possible to spin a murder in a way that will have positive results for the movie, assuming there ever is a movie, since Arrow Normand is unavailable to work at the moment. And maybe, for a good long time."

This was not entirely fair. From what Carl understood about celebrity murder cases, he was fairly sure that some judge somewhere would make it possible for Arrow to finish her work on the movie, if only so that she could make enough money to pay her legal bills. Even so, the whole thing was a mess, and it didn't look likely to clean up anytime soon. What was worse, he was having an unusually difficult time getting information. He had approached Annabeth Falmer this morning, thinking that she would be the best bet. Arrow Normand had been in her house on the afternoon in question, after all, and Marcey Mandret had too, and so had Stewart Gordon. It was practically a little Court TV true-crime documentary right there on her living room rug. At the last minute, he hadn't been able to go through with any of the things he had been thinking of. Dr. Falmer was just as clueless as he'd hoped she would be, but it wasn't the right kind of clueless. She wasn't a snob, intellectual or social. She wasn't a fool, or an airhead like Marcey and Arrow. She was just a pleasant, well-meaning, quietly dressed woman who probably didn't have the faintest idea what she'd gotten herself into. Carl Frank hadn't wanted to be the one to let her in on the secret.

The problem was, there weren't a whole lot of sources of information on Margaret's Harbor. The local police weren't talking to him, and the state police weren't talking to him either. Eventually, down the line somewhere, some secretary in a back office would pick up the phone and spill to the nearest reporter, just to make herself feel important, but it hadn't gotten to that point yet. The police had called in this outside consultant, this Gregor Demarkian, and that was all they would tell anybody for the time being. Carl had looked up Gregor Demarkian on the Internet, and been suitably impressed. God only knew what this guy charged. Considering his reputation, it was probably a lot. Whatever it was, he wouldn't be talking to Carl Frank, unless it was to get information instead of give it.

Of course, there were all those professional sources of information, meaning the press. Carl was no more of a snob than Annabeth Falmer was. He didn't turn up his nose at the paparazzi. They often knew things nobody else did, because they were practically as good as spies. Hell, the best of them, if they didn't have cameras in their hands, would have been charged as stalkers. They were stalkers. They went everywhere, and they thought nothing of breaking into somebody's house or climbing a tree outside a bedroom window to get a few money shots of the stuff going on inside. Practically the first thing Carl did when he took over publicity for a movie was to sit down with the principal actors and try to get them to deal with the reality of the attention they were getting. He almost never succeeded. There was something about actors—about "celebrities" of every stripe—that needed to believe that the paparazzi would never turn on them, that needed to forget that the point was not to make them famous but to make them pay.

"Bad news sells newspapers," he would tell them. He would look straight into their eyes and know they weren't hearing a word he was saying. He would try anyway. "From their point of view," he would say, "watching you screw up, watching you crash and burn and destroy yourself, is by far the better story. There are more people out there who are willing to pay to see that than are willing to pay to see you succeed. Hell, practically nobody is willing to pay to see you succeed."

Right now, of course, they would pay for anything, because there was nothing. He had managed to get Marcey out of the public eye for the next half second, and Arrow was where they couldn't get to her. But the paparazzi didn't have access to the local police or the state police or that prosecutor, Clara Walsh, and neither did the "legitimate" reporters now camped out on Main Street in Oscartown. He could see ABC, CBS, MSNBC, CNN, and Fox from the window of this silly upscale diner. They would hang around here until it was time for the press conference Clara Walsh had promised to give as soon as Gregor Demarkian arrived. Then they would cover that. Then they would come back here. There was nothing to do in Oscartown in the winter. There was barely anything to do in Oscartown in the summer, but then, at least, the local celebrities would be more to the liking of the national press. Katie Couric wasn't impressed with Arrow Normand. She was impressed with nearly any Kennedy.

The young woman who had taken his order for coffee had come back with his cup. She put it down on the table just as the front door opened and the man Carl was sure he was supposed to meet came in from outside. The blast of cold that came in with him made Carl's spine creak. The storm had been over for days, but it often felt as if it were still with them. The weather in California got better after storms. Out here, it just seemed to get worse.

The man was very young, so young Carl wondered for a moment if he was even of legal age. He seemed to know the waitress, which was not surprising. He came down the long line of booths and stopped next to Carl with his parka hood still pulled up over his head.

"Mr. Frank?" he said.

"Mr. Bullard?" Carl said.

Jack Bullard pulled back the parka hood, unzipped the parka, and sat down. Everything about him was not only big but outsized. His

115

feet were too big for the slenderness of his legs. His head was too big for his torso. He had to be six foot five.

The waitress came back with another cup of coffee and put it on the table. She went away without speaking, even though Jack Bullard thanked her in a voice loud enough to be heard outside on the street. Then Jack pulled over the sugar and the cream and began to load up as if he were making a milk shake.

Carl found himself wishing he still smoked cigarettes. It would at least give him something to do with his hands.

Jack Bullard had big hands, too. He finished with the cream and sugar and pushed them away. Then he shrugged the parka all the way off.

"So," he said.

"So," Carl said.

"Here's the thing," Jack said. "I'm a reporter. I may be a reporter for a little pissant paper, but I'm still a reporter. I don't get paid to withhold information."

"I understand that," Carl said. "I don't want you to withhold information. I thought you said it was your editor who doesn't want you to print any stories about the case."

"Oh, we're printing stuff about the case," Jack said. "You can't avoid it, really, it's the biggest thing to hit the Harbor in decades. She doesn't like printing stories on movie stars."

"Unusual, in this day and age."

"Yeah, well. It's the Harbor. The people here aren't much interested, if you know what I mean. The people who are usually here. But anything she doesn't want to print, I'm allowed to sell elsewhere. So."

"So." Carl looked out the window again. When he looked back, he had made up his mind for the first time since this mess had started. "I'm not asking you to withhold information. You can sell anything you've got to anybody you've got. All I'm asking is that you tell me first."

"And for that you're willing to pay me some ridiculous amount of money a week."

"A thousand dollars."

"A thousand dollars," Jack said. "It's a ridiculous amount of money. If you don't want me to withhold information, what do you want?"

"I want you to tell me before you give the information to the world so I can get a head start on spinning it. It's what I do, Mr. Bullard. I spin. That's what they pay me for."

"I don't see that there's much of anything to spin here," Jack said. "She shot him. They've arrested her. There's going to be a trial. Isn't that what usually happens?"

"Absolutely. That's what usually happens. But it occurs to me you might have heard something, or seen something, on the day in question, or since the filming has been going on here. Something somebody said, or did, or something like that. Your editor may not like to run stories about movie stars, but you've been taking pictures of them. I've seen you."

"It's like I said," Jack said. "She lets me sell what she doesn't want. I offered to cut her in on it, but she doesn't want the money."

"She's an interesting woman, your editor."

"She owns the paper," Jack said. "She's okay."

"One of the things you could do is let me see the pictures," Carl said. "Before you sell them, I mean."

"I don't take the really nasty kinds of pictures," Jack said. "I don't have pictures of people naked, or that kind of thing."

"You've got a picture of Marcey Mandret on the day of the murder, don't you? In that bar, fairly drunk off her ass."

"Sure. But I wasn't the only one. Those guys from New York and Los Angeles have been in and out for weeks. And I didn't take the kind of picture you have to fuzz parts out of before you print."

"Understood," Carl said. "But you've got others, don't you? You went to Vegas?"

"Yeah, but it doesn't matter. I got that one picture, you know, of the bunch of them together, but I sold it, and that was that. It's one of those places, you know. I don't have any advantage there. I don't know the place, or how it works. Here, I can find things nobody else can because I know things nobody else knows. At least, nobody from outside. With that one, I got a shot and that was all there was to it. They ran around town, they did things, and mostly I could never get there in time to get anything interesting. And there were always those other guys."

"Photographers."

"Paparazzi," Jack said. "I hate that name."

"Yes," Carl said.

Then he reached into the back of his pants and came out with his wallet.

2

Here was the odd thing: Arrow Normand didn't really mind being in jail. She minded not having access to her prescriptions, and not being able to get anything to drink more serious than Diet Coke, but jail itself was something she found it surprisingly easy to take. It might have been different if she had been in an actual prison, or in one of those big-city jails where she would have been locked up with a couple of dozen people. The Margaret's Harbor jail was not like any of that. There were only three serious cells, and neither of the other two was occupied. The police here didn't seem to have watched any of the shows on Court TV about life behind bars. She was never handcuffed, and the night guard had gotten so embarrassed by coming in on her at a private moment that he'd brought her a standing screen to shield herself when she was on the toilet. It was less like jail than like being involuntarily committed to rehab. She even had a pack of lawyers to talk to if she needed therapy.

Actually, Arrow had tried rehab once, years ago, and it hadn't worked out. They kept wanting her to talk about herself, which was fine—she'd probably spent more time talking about herself in the last ten years than she'd spent talking about anything else—but the things they wanted her to say didn't make any sense to her. She was supposed to have "insight." She didn't know what that meant. When other people in group had "insight," they talked about Their Addiction and Their Cycle of Codependency. Or something. Arrow had never been able to figure it all out. In the end, she had just let herself drift through a couple of weeks of beautiful sunsets and group meals in the big cafeteria that seemed to serve nothing but seafood and fruit, and then one morning she'd woken up and decided to leave. People said they were changed in rehab, but Arrow had not been. She still wasn't able to see the point.

You were supposed to talk about the really important things, she thought now, but she brushed that away. Jail made her calm, and part of the reason it made her calm was that she never had to face the public. Photographers were not allowed in this place. Neither were reporters, although she could talk to one of them if she wanted to meet him in the visitors' area. She could also get visits from friends, and for the first day or two she had expected those. Every time the door at the end of the hall had opened up, she'd been sure it was because Kendra was waiting in the visiting area, or Marcey was, or . . . She couldn't think of who else would come. Her mother might, although she barely spoke to her mother anymore. Her father might come, but she didn't "barely" speak to him, she didn't speak to him at all. Her brothers might come, and probably would, because they were still hoping she would set them up with something they'd like better than the jobs they had at home.

The more she thought about it, the more Arrow realized that she had nobody in her life who would like her no matter what. Even Mark wouldn't have liked her no matter what. If she'd suddenly been poor or not famous anymore, he would have gone off in search of somebody who was rich and in the public eye, and if he couldn't find that he would find a girlfriend who could help him pay his rent. Stewart Gordon had told her once that she would be better off, and understand more about life, if she read books, but Arrow did read books. She read Nora Roberts, and some other people whose names she couldn't remember—not crime or horror, because it bothered her, but stories about love, and about what love was. Love in the real world, though, was nothing like love in books. Men were not strong and protective. They weren't even dedicated and faithful. Love in the real world was like buying a CD, or even clothes. You got what you paid for. When you were sick of it, you lost it in the house and never found it again.

It was the middle of the afternoon, and cold. There was a television at the end of the corridor, but she didn't like to listen to it. All the news seemed to be about her, even on the music channels. Love in the real world wasn't like love in music, either. In music, two people were compelled to have each other. They couldn't stop touching each other. They couldn't leave each other alone. Everything was obsession, and if you were in love you couldn't concentrate on anything else, like making dinner, or going to the movies. In real life, nobody was obsessed with another person unless he was a stalker, and the stalkers were all bad. Lots of them were armed.

Arrow was lying on the cot with the blankets pulled up over her. It was one of the things she missed, the good cotton sheets she had on her bed back home, and the mattress that she could sink into. Still, this was what she liked doing best. She could let herself go half to sleep, not really out of it, but not really here, either. She could remember things or not, as she wanted to. She thought about things that didn't bother her, or that did, but not in the wrong way. She thought about Stewart Gordon, who actually had come to visit her, twice, and brought oranges and chocolate bars both times. She thought about that woman whose house she had fallen into on the night . . . the night . . . she didn't have to give the night a name. The woman made her uneasy in the same way Stewart Gordon did, but she didn't know what way that was, so there was no use trying to understand it. Instead, she just remembered the house, and all the bookshelves, and all the books. There were books everywhere, and when there was music on it was classical, which Arrow didn't understand either. It didn't make sense to her that people should be different from one another. Some differences made sense—men and women were different, for instance—but others made no sense. It seemed to Arrow that things should be either Good or Bad, and not just Good or Bad for her and maybe different for somebody else. Or something. She got confused. Classical music was boring, and people didn't like it, except that that woman did, and maybe Stewart Gordon did, too. There were museums full of paintings that people went to see, and bookstores full of books, and none of it made any sense at all. Maybe it made sense when you got older.

The trick was this, very simply: she could not allow herself to talk to anybody about anything, not even her lawyers. She could smile and hesitate and make out that she didn't really know what had happened. It even helped that that was about half true. She couldn't tell them anything else, because if she did . . . if she did . . .

Nothing would connect anymore. Nothing. The night of the accident, with Mark's truck falling down the hill or whatever it was. The ocean. The woman with her books and her tea. The Other Thing. The music. The movie. The cats. The woman had a cat. Stewart Gordon had a cat. In ancient Egypt, cats were sacred. If she was ever reincarnated, she wanted to come back as a cat. She didn't know where Egypt was, exactly. She thought it must be in Europe somewhere, because everything that was really old seemed to be.

Down at the other end of the hall, the afternoon guard was playing solitaire on her computer and talking on her cell phone. Arrow's cell had a window, with steel mesh in it to keep prisoners from escaping. Since Arrow didn't want to escape, she didn't mind. She could see through the window to a patch of sky, which was bright blue and brightly lit. It was a beautiful cold day. One of these days, somebody would come and get her out and she would have to do something about things, but that day wasn't now, and she was glad it wasn't.

If she could make herself sleep for the next six months, she could avoid this whole mess altogether. Somebody would sort it out without her, and she wouldn't have to answer questions about anything at all.

3

For Jack Bullard, most of the island of Margaret's Harbor was off-limits in his spare time. He suspected that it was off-limits for most of the other year-round people, too, and for the same reason. There was too much of the island where he didn't feel he fit. In season, that meant that all the places were filled with people who talked in a way, and dressed in a way, and moved in a way that made him feel like a big ox with bad manners. Off season, the effect was a little more subtle, and a little less sane. It was as if they'd left the smell of themselves around, the summer people had. It was like they were cats marking territory, and this particular territory would be forever theirs.

Standing outside on the short stretch of pavement in front of the Oscartown Inn, Jack looked at the vans lining the other side of the street and reminded himself that this off-season, the cats' territory had been violated. There were other cats in town now, and they were nothing like the pedigreed ones that usually occupied this place. Then the metaphor seemed so trite, and so corny, that Jack felt ashamed of himself. What did it mean that you couldn't find good words to explain what you were living through?

He went down the street, looking in the windows of stores. The media people left him alone, some because they'd met him, others because he had his cameras around his neck, which marked him out as somebody not likely to be of interest. A lot of the stores were closed for the winter. Nobody who lived on the island was going to be interested in eight-hundred-dollar handbags or slinky little summer dresses at six hundred dollars a pop, and the women who owned those stores spent the winter in Palm Beach, where they had branches. The bookstore was still open, although Jack had heard the two women who owned that one complaining. It seemed that they'd expected that a raft of people from Los Angeles would mean a raft of customers for books, but maybe nobody in Los Angeles read books. At any rate, they weren't doing any business.

He got to Cuddy's Bar and stopped. There was a real bar in Oscartown, down near the ferry, but he didn't want to walk all the way over there. Cuddy's was always full of photographers these days. It had been even before the murder. Now there was something like a permanent contingent. Jack remembered coming here as a teenager, and coming in the summer, too, wanting to be around all that, wanting to be part of it. He thought most of the kids who were local here went through a phase like that. He'd been in this place a lot more often this year than he'd been in it anytime since.

He went inside and looked around. The bar was nearly deserted. The tables were nearly deserted too. He put his hand up to the chest of his jacket and felt the little wad of Carl Frank's money where it bulged. He'd been afraid to put it in his wallet. A thousand dollars. He didn't think he'd ever seen a thousand dollars in cash, although he had more than that in his account these days. He sat down at the bar and asked for a Molson. Then he waited.

It took almost three-quarters of an hour, but she showed up, just as Jack had expected she would. She was not in good shape when she came through the door, but she was in more clothes that he was used to seeing her in. Maybe murder, or the avalanche of bad publicity that had resulted from the murder, had wised her up. Whatever it was, she was wearing jeans and a big bulky parka. She even had snow boots on instead of heels. Jack watched her stride down the center of the room and take one of the small tables against the wall.

Jack got up, took his beer, and walked over. Marcey Mandret unzipped her parka and shrugged it off. Underneath, she was wearing one of those skimpy little halter tops that didn't permit a bra and didn't cover her belly button. Jack put his beer down on the table and sighed.

"Go away," Marcey said. "I'm not talking to you. None of us is talking to you. This is all your fault."

"What's all my fault? That Mark Anderman is dead?"

"You know what I mean. Get out of here."

"I think you ought to put up with me for a minute. I just had a very interesting meeting with Carl Frank."

Marcey sat down in the chair on her side of the table, hard. She had already been drinking, but this was not unusual. In Jack's experience, Marcey drank most of the day, although she usually didn't start hammering it home until after five. He sat down himself and signaled to a waitress who was clearly trying to ignore them. It was Mitsy Kline, who was somebody he had known vaguely in high school. In high school, there had been two distinct groups of people: the ones who were on their way out; and the ones who would be here forever, doing jobs like Mitsy's. Jack had been part of the group that were on their way out.

Mitsy came over. Marcey looked up and said, "I want a champagne cocktail."

Mitsy made a face and went away.

"You could say please," Jack said. "It wouldn't kill you. And people around here expect things like that."

"I don't care what people around here expect. I don't care about anything. God, I hate this place. I don't know why I ever agreed to come up here."

"You agreed because you needed the work. It was the only movie you'd been offered for two years."

"Don't be an ass."

"I'm not being an ass," Jack said. "I only know what I read in the newspapers. Especially lately. I'm a photographer, for God's sake. I sold a picture. That's what I do. And what else was I supposed to do, under the circumstances? Just get up and disappear, like Steve?"

"Steve didn't disappear," Marcey said. "He—"

"I know what happened to Steve," Jack said, "but you can't do things like that and expect to get away with them. People will notice, eventually. People have noticed."

"They wouldn't have noticed if it wasn't for you," Marcey said. "And what's that supposed to be? We all trusted you. We did. We all trusted you and then you went off and did the one thing that—"

Mitsy Kline was back. She had a single champagne cocktail in the middle of her tray, and her face looked as stiff as cardboard.

"I want three more of those," Marcey said. "Right now. I want to line them up on the table."

"Of course," Mitsy said.

Jack looked at Marcey. She hadn't noticed anything, and her face was blurred. It didn't seem possible for a face to be blurred, but Marcey's was. Here was one of the differences between Marcey and Kendra Rhode, between all those people and Kendra Rhode. Unlike Kendra, their faces lacked definition. Jack took a deep breath.

"It's not the only picture," he said.

"What?"

"It's not the only picture. Not the only one I took on the Vegas trip. In fact, I took a lot of pictures on the Vegas trip. In a lot of places. And before you give me another lecture about how I betrayed all of you, I haven't sold any but the one you're all pissed about, and some of the others are a lot more interesting."

Marcey was sitting up a little straighter. Jack could practically see her struggling to return to some kind of sobriety. He wanted to scream. She was not the person he wanted to be talking to. Carl Frank was not the person he wanted to be talking to either. He wanted to be talking to Kendra, because—because.

Mitsy came back with the three new champagne cocktails. She put them down on the table as if she wanted to break them. Then she left without saying a thing.

"Pictures of what?" Marcey said.

"You should be better to people like Mitsy," Jack said. "Waitresses. Assistants. Secretaries. They can ruin your life."

"Pictures of what?" Marcey said again.

"Pictures of everything," Jack said. "Pictures of the whole damned trip and all its works. I was taking pictures all the time. You must have noticed. I'm sure she noticed. Either that, or the whole bunch of you just pose instinctively. I've got a ton of pictures from the Vegas trip, and Carl Frank is offering to pay me a ton and a half for any information I have that might keep the pack of you in line. And there are papers. The papers pay too. So—"

"So what?" Marcey said. She had finished the first champagne cocktail in a single long drink, and it looked like she was about to do the same with the second. She had it lifted in the air, but she didn't drink it. "What do you think you're going to do? You think you're going to make us like you again by blackmailing us? That's what you think you're going to do?"

It was a good thing there was nobody much in the place. If there had been reporters, this would have been on the news channels in minutes. Marcey was not being discreet, which was not surprising, because she was never discreet. The problem was that now she was not being quiet. She was shrieking, the way Jack had heard women shriek only in the movies, and she was loud enough to be heard on the pavement.

"You're such a bastard," she said, throwing the contents of the champagne cocktail on Jack's head.

Jack let the champagne run down the sides of his face. It didn't matter. This was Marcey acting. He had seen it before. He had seen it, and he had seen Arrow, and he had seen Steve, and he had seen Mark, and he was suddenly fed up with it all.

"You'd better get the news up the hill," he said, "since I'm not welcome there anymore. If she doesn't want this stuff all over the tabloids, she's going to have to talk to me."

SIX

1

Gregor Demarkian had always thought that there was something wrong with what he had been taught about "the passage of time." In fact, the idea of time as passing was all wrong. In his experience, time didn't pass. It simply was, and then it was not. That was the way it had been with Elizabeth. Even the long year of her dying hadn't made time seem to pass. She just was, and then she was something else, and then she was not. Then there was that other one, the one that stuck in his head, because even when he'd first heard it he had thought it was both nonsensical and important: Time is the measure of change. That one would have worked better than the one about time "passing," if only he had been aware of change. He wasn't, though. Things were, and then they were something else, and then they were not. Nobody could see time passing, and nobody could see change. One day, we all just woke up and it was there.

What got him thinking about the passage of time was the newsstand at the dock, and what got him thinking about that was a fluke. When they all stepped off the ferry there was a flurry of activity. A young man from Clara Walsh's office was there with a stack of large manila envelopes. Stewart Gordon was anxious to be off somewhere, Gregor wasn't sure where, but thought it might have something to do with Dr. Annabeth Falmer. Clara Walsh herself was suddenly nervous and distracted. Gregor couldn't see why. There really was nobody at the dock to meet them. If Oscartown was full of paparazzi, those paparazzi were not interested in him, or even in the district attorney who would prosecute Arrow Normand if it ever came to that. The dock was empty and cold and in need of repair. Gregor found himself wondering if there was neglect here, or if this was the ordinary depredations of a long hard winter.

What got Gregor thinking about time was the fact that he himself was distracted. Since he had nothing in particular to do, he looked around at the ferry and the dock and the little newsstand that was just a few feet onshore near the place where passengers would have to embark. The newsstand was empty and closed up, but it was not out of date. Gregor wasn't sure why he had thought it would be. What struck him was the string of tabloid newspapers hanging from the top of what would be the open stall frame once the metal security door was pulled up. The tabloids were behind a protective length of dirty plastic that looked like it hadn't been cleaned or replaced in a long time. Almost all the tabloids had pictures of Arrow Normand on them, which is what he would have expected. What he did not expect was the picture of himself, above the title in the *National Enquirer,* next to the headline, in bold and in italics: "Police Bring In Superdetective!"

Well, Gregor thought. Being a superdetective was better than being the Armenian American Hercule Poirot. On some fundamental level, it was a lot less silly. He left Clara Walsh and her assistant and Stewart Gordon talking among themselves and went over to look at the paper more closely. The date was only the day before yesterday, and he was sure he remembered that the *Enquirer* came out once a week. He looked down the line at the other papers. All of them were current, or close to. He saw pictures of Arrow Normand drunk, Arrow Normand fat, Arrow Normand being brought into a police station between two large men. He tried to make out who the men were, not their individual identities but their institutional affiliations, and could not. Were these state police, or local police, or no police at all? Nobody had told him how Arrow Normand was arrested, or where.

Gregor turned back to see that Clara Walsh and the assistant and Stewart Gordon weren't getting very far with whatever it was they were trying to do, if they even knew what that was, and he walked back to them.

"Do you mind if I ask you people a question?" he said.

Stewart Gordon straightened up. It was hard to think of Stewart being anything else but up, but he must have been. "I've got to go," he said. "I promised Anna I'd stop in. I'll come to the press conference."

"You're having a press conference," Clara Walsh said.

Gregor let this go by. He had expected a press conference. There usually was one when he was brought in, because part of the point of bringing him in was usually to let the public know that "something" was being done in a difficult circumstance. He turned back toward the newsstand and gestured in that direction.

"They've got a copy of the *Enquirer* over there, with my picture on it," he said.

Stewart Gordon snorted. "Bet it wasn't a big picture, not yet. You'll just have to get used to it. You're part of the story now."

"I don't mind being part of the story," Gregor said patiently. "The point is that I haven't been part of the story for very long, but the *Enquirer* on that newsstand has a picture of me on it. I would have thought that that stand would be closed in the off-season, but I take it it isn't. But it's not open now either."

"That's because this isn't a regular run of the ferry," the assistant said. He was a tall, cadaverously thin young man with hair so thick it looked heavier than his frame should be able to carry. "Sorry," he said. "Bram Winder. I'm Clara's deputy. We're the whole office for the island. The stand isn't open now because the ferry isn't scheduled to go through, but he opens up for regular trips. I don't know if he finds it worthwhile, and he has to freeze to death—there's nothing for heat in that thing but a battery-powered space heater—but he does it."

"It's because he's really local," Clara Walsh said. "A lot of the people who own businesses in town are summer people. But this is Harry Carter's place. He runs this thing and he does some fishing and he works as a handyman in town when there's nothing else to do."

"And he cuts cordwood," Bram Winder said. "A lot of people on the island cut cordwood, although I don't know who they sell it to. Well, to the Point, this year. Kendra Rhode has been burning cordwood up there like—I don't know like what."

"I've got to be out of here," Stewart Gordon said. "Gregor, I really will be back for the press conference, but I've got to go. I'll see everybody later."

"We could give you a ride in," Bram Winder said. "We are going to the beach."

"Thanks very much. I like to walk," Stewart said, and then he was off, striding across the boards of the dock, looking just the way he had on that silly television show. For a moment, all three of them watched him go.

"He's the most remarkable person," Clara Walsh said finally.

Gregor tried to get them all back on track. "He opens up for regular ferry trips, and the ferry crosses, what, once a day, in the morning and in the evening? Does it get much business?"

"Practically none," Bram Winder said. "But the Commonwealth of Massachusetts insists. It doesn't want the island cut off from transportation in case there's an emergency. Although these days, you know, with medical emergencies, we've got the helicopters."

Helicopters can't fly in all weathers, Gregor thought. Or maybe he had that wrong. Once, Bennis had taken him to a movie called *The Perfect Storm,* and in that movie a helicopter rescued two people off a boat in the Atlantic during a major hurricane. Gregor had really hated that movie. It had primed him to expect a heroic last-minute survival victory, and instead, everybody died.

"Okay," he said. "What about times when there are likely to be lots of people on the ferry even on a not regularly scheduled trip. Isn't that what was supposed to happen on the day of the storm? Kendra Rhode was having a party, and she got extra ferry trips to bring guests in from Boston. Would Harry Carter have opened the newsstand then?"

"I don't know," Clara said. "But even if he'd intended to, I'd be willing to bet he didn't on the actual day. He is from around here. He'd know what a major nor'easter means. And nobody who knows would stand on the edge of the water with nothing but a space heater to keep him company."

"I'm not too sure he'd have had any customers if he had," Bram Winder said. "I mean, Kendra Rhode's guests wouldn't be the people who buy the tabloids, they'd be the people who are in them. Right?"

Gregor looked at the stand, and at the dock, and at the ferry. "What about people leaving the island?" he said. "These extra ferries that were put on for the party, would they have carried people away from the island and not just onto it?"

"Do you mean you think somebody left the island that afternoon on one of the extra ferry runs?" Clara Walsh said. Then she shook her head. "No, that's not right. I told you. The ferry runs didn't happen. The storm was too bad."

"Did Harry Carter know they weren't happening?" Gregor asked.

Clara Walsh looked nonplussed. "We can ask him," she said. "But you know, I think you're barking up the wrong tree here. This was a major storm. The sea was horrific. There were no extra ferry runs, in or out. It doesn't matter if Harry Carter was here that afternoon, because nobody else would have been. He'd have had nobody to see coming in or going out."

"Mmm," Gregor said. He went all the way back to the newsstand and looked it over, front and back. It was nothing much more than a tallish wooden box. The paint was peeling on its sides and the wood was so dry and brittle Gregor could have smashed through it with his fist without seriously hurting himself, and at his time of life there wasn't much he could do that with. The fragility of the structure made the metal pull-down security window look almost poignant. Gregor wondered if Harry Carter had really had a problem with theft. What would a thief steal, and who would be that thief? If Harry Carter was leaving his cash in there—and Gregor was willing to bet he wasn't—he was an idiot.

Gregor came away from the newsstand and went back to Clara Walsh and Bram Winder. "All right," he said. "I'd still like to know. If you wouldn't mind. Are all those manila envelopes for me?"

Bram Winder looked down at the envelopes in his hands. "Yes," he said, thrusting them forward at Gregor. "Yes, they are. They're the stuff. You know, forensics. The crime-scene report. The depositions. There are a lot of depositions."

"And not much of anything else," Clara Walsh said. "The Oscartown Police Department consists of Jerry Young and whatever two locals he can pick up and deputize for the season, and this isn't the season. There was some talk in town about beefing up the force with the film people in town, but it was the oddest thing. We couldn't get anybody to take us seriously. It's almost as if they think these people are cartoons. As if they're not real people. At any rate, the town declined to spend the money, and now they're spending only enough to keep a couple of extra guards at the jail, to take the shifts, you know. I mean, you can leave the town drunk alone overnight in a place like that, but you can't leave Arrow Normand."

"Some of it's Linda Beecham's fault," Bram Winder said. "You wouldn't think a little weekly paper like the *Home News* would have much impact, especially since everybody here takes the *Boston Globe,* but it does. And she's been treating this whole thing, the film thing, I mean, as if it doesn't exist. If she'd run a few articles about the dangers posed by the island being full of strangers and, you know, that kind of thing, we'd probably have gotten them to put on a few guys and we wouldn't be in this mess now."

"He means in the mess of not having enough in the way of manpower to handle a murder investigation," Clara Walsh said. She pointed to the manila envelopes in Gregor's hands. "That's the best we could do, and it isn't very good."

"But the state police are helping, aren't they?" Gregor said. "I'm sure Stewart said something about that."

"The state police have a charter," Clara Walsh said carefully, "and that charter specifically forbids them from interfering in what should be a municipality's jurisdiction. But yes, they're helping, they just have to be careful. And of course the commonwealth has crime labs that we can use, and we have used them. It's just—not adequate, if you see what I mean. It's not what I'd like it to be."

Gregor made a noncommittal noise. Bram Winder gestured down the dock. "I've got a car waiting," he said. "I can take you to the inn to clean up before the press conference, but I was thinking, Clara and I were thinking, that since it's on the way, you might want to stop at the beach and look at the crime scene. Not really investigate it or anything, you know. I know you'd need to come back and be more thorough. But we thought, ah, to—"

"To get the lay of the land," Clara Walsh said helpfully.

Gregor had a feeling that the "lay of the land" was going to be nothing but snow, but he also thought that getting a look at it might be a good idea. He didn't know why, but he felt more than a little reluctant to go to the Oscartown Inn and check in. For one thing, he would have to call Bennis, and he wasn't ready to call Bennis yet.

"All right," he said. "You drive, I'll get the lay of the land."

2

Jerry Young was waiting for them on the side of the road that ran along the beach on the other side of Oscartown from the place where the ferry docked, dressed in a high-waisted dark blue police uniform that looked as if it had been copied from a television show. If Gregor had had to guess, he would have said that Jerry Young was not much more than just past his twenty-first birthday. The only reason he wouldn't have guessed much younger than that was because of the badge. Gregor didn't think that even in as casual a place as Margaret's Harbor they would hire a police officer too young to buy the drinks he'd have to take away from the kids he caught with fake IDs. The beach road was actually named Holcomb Avenue, and it wasn't anything like on the way from the ferry to the Oscartown inn. Gregor was fairly sure they had passed the inn as they came across town, but they'd never gotten to Main Street, so he wasn't sure. He had seen not much of anything but stretch after stretch of New Englandy clapboard and shingle houses, packed as closely together as they would have been in the cheapest suburbs of Cleveland or Detroit. Some of the houses on those tiny lots were huge, filling their limited spaces as compactly as if they'd oozed in and then hardened. Margaret's Harbor might be a vacation enclave for Old Money, but unlike some of the other enclaves Gregor could think of—say, for instance, Newport—this one was an enclave for Old Money that didn't mind living as if it were in Levittown. Clara Walsh saw the expression on his face and coughed.

"It's Oscartown," she said. "Everybody wants to be in Oscartown. Presidents have been here. Kennedys have been here."

Gregor looked up and saw a towering Victorian pile rising up at the end of the beach. "What's that?" he asked.

Bram Winder laughed. "That's the Point. It's the Rhode family house on the island. They got here before all these other people did."

The ferry. The beach. The Point. Gregor was fairly sure that they were stretched out along a single line, albeit a snaky one. He didn't think it was possible that Oscartown had two ocean frontages. The island was bigger than that. There would be other towns. He looked straight ahead as they began to pull in next to Jerry Young. There was a lot of wind. It was making the policeman's cap jiggle up and down.

Clara Walsh pulled the car to a halt at the curb and got out. Bram Winder got out too, and a moment later he was holding open Gregor's door, trying to be polite and professional without doing an imitation of a chauffeur. Gregor got out too, and looked around. There really was a wind, a good hard one. It was freezing.

"Mr. Demarkian," Clara Walsh said. "This is Jerry Young. He's the Oscartown Police Department."

"Not all of it," Jerry Young said, grabbing Gregor's hand and pumping it. "I'm glad to meet you, Mr. Demarkian. We've heard a lot about you. I'm hoping you can do something about this mess before we all go crazy."

"Jerry doesn't like having Arrow Normand in his jail," Clara said. "It upsets his equilibrium."

"It upsets everything," Jerry Young said. "You don't know what it's like. We've got photographers staking us out every hour of the day, trying to get in side doors, climbing through drains. They're crazy, all these people. And then there she is. She won't talk. She won't even talk to her lawyers. She won't talk to us. She just sits there, under a blanket, sacked out."

"Shock," Clara Walsh said solemnly.

"Oh, for God's sake," Jerry Young said. "She was treated for shock. And it's been days. She can't still be in shock after all these days. I'll tell you what I think. I think she's some kind of mental defective. I think she never could talk except for what they wrote down for her. And now there's nobody to write things down for her, so here we are."

Gregor was turning into an icicle. He thought about Bennis and Donna and the wedding arrangements back home. He thought about Tibor. He thought about Lida and how she had probably packed food into his suitcases somewhere. Then he looked down off the road onto the beach. They were standing just above an outcropping of rocks, deep and tall and solid looking, but with rounded edges, because they were so close to the sea. He looked beyond the rocks to the beach itself, and then to the ocean, which seemed to be very far out.

"Close to low tide," Jerry Young said helpfully. "High tide, it comes all the way up to those rocks, and in a bad summer storm it will come up to the sidewalk. There aren't too many summer storms that bad, fortunately."

"Huh," Gregor said. He looked around again. "This is where it happened? This is where you found the body?"

"And the truck," Jerry Young said. "Yes, sir. I'm not sure we can say that it happened here, though. I mean, I'd have assumed it did, but one of the guys from the state police said that since we didn't find the bullet, it might have been done somewhere else. The bullet went through his head, you know, and out the other side, and then through the window over on that side—there was a hole. But we looked for the bullet, all over here. And we didn't find it."

"Huh," Gregor said again. He went as close to the edge of the sidewalk as he dared. He was wearing good city shoes. It hadn't occurred to him to wear anything else. He didn't like the idea of stepping off into the snow, which looked like it was at least ankle deep. "Did you just look," he asked Jerry Young, "or did you get some equipment out here and clear the area and sift through it?"

Jerry Young looked surprised, but what bothered Gregor was that Clara Walsh looked surprised too. "Do you mean to say you want us to dredge the place?" she asked. "The way we'd, I don't know, the way we'd search a lake?"

"I'm saying that there's a lot of snow," Gregor said, "and a bullet is a small thing. Granted, you'd think there ought to have been some sign of it, a hole, some melted place that shouldn't have been, but it seems like a lot of people were walking around here that night—"

"It wasn't really the night," Jerry Young said. "By the time I got here, it was maybe four or four thirty in the afternoon. People just think of it as night because it was so dark. The storm, you know, was blocking out everything, and so the streetlights were on, and people thought—"

"Yes, I see," Gregor said. "But I'm right, aren't I? There were a lot of people here."

"Yeah, sure," Jerry Young said. "Even before I got here. And then after I got here, I called the state police, and they came, you know, and then there were more of us. But we really did look. We looked hard. We looked right at the time, and then we looked later, when the wrecker came to take the truck away. We got down on our hands and knees and sifted through snow until we were blue."

Gregor walked back and forth along the sidewalk. One of the pictures Stewart had shown him on Cavanaugh Street was of the truck on these rocks, on its side. The good thing about cell phone photographs was that they were available in an emergency. The bad thing was that the image quality often sucked, and Gregor hadn't realized, from that particular photograph, just how steep and ragged the outcropping was. It didn't matter that it had no sharp edges. There were so many thrusts of rock going in so many different directions, any vehicle that landed on them would be totaled by definition.

"He was lying against the door, wasn't he," Gregor said. "I'm trying to remember this from Stewart's photographs. He was lying against the door, and the door must have been lying against the rocks. He was in the front passenger seat."

"Right," Jerry Young said.

"Was he wearing a seat belt?" Gregor asked.

"No, I don't think he was," Jerry Young said. "But does that matter? He didn't die in the crash. He died of a gunshot wound. Why would you care if he was wearing one or not?"

"I don't care if he wasn't wearing one," Gregor said. "It doesn't mean anything. Lots of people don't wear seat belts when they should. If he was wearing one, though, it would mean he'd gotten into the car intending to go somewhere. Which would have been useful information."

"Ah," Jerry Young said, but he still looked confused.

"Okay," Gregor said. "Let's see if I can get this straight. He was in the truck, and the truck was coming from the center of town when it went off the road. Is there any way you can know if he was in the passenger seat when the truck left town? I assume it had to have been coming from there, right, because he was with Arrow Normand and she would have been on the set of this movie they're making."

"I don't think so," Clara Walsh said. "I mean, they don't always shoot everybody every day, but Mark Anderman would have had to be on the set that morning because he had some kind of technical job."

"And they did film that morning?" Gregor asked.

"Oh, yes, in the beginning," Clara Walsh said. "We checked into that. It made the people in town laugh their heads off, but what are you going to do? If we'd said there was a good chance of a major earthquake, they probably would have taken us seriously. But nobody knows what a nor'easter is really like unless they live here."

"So," Gregor said. "Mark Anderman was at work, and then work stopped sometime that morning—"

"About one in the afternoon," Jerry Young said. "I was sitting in Cuddy's when Marcey Mandret came in and started drinking champagne cocktails like they were water. I guess by then the snow had gotten so bad they'd just given up."

"Huh," Gregor said again. He walked back and forth, back and forth, but there was nothing to see, and he had never understood fictional detectives who seemed to be able to bring insights out of obsessive behavior. There were the rocks, and the sea, and the picture in his mind of the truck crashed on them. He wanted to establish a sequence. His major problem was that he wasn't sure a sequence of what.

He tried one more time. "Mark Anderman was riding in the passenger seat," he said, "and who was driving? Arrow Normand was driving?"

"She told Dr. Falmer she was," Jerry Young said. "At least, that's what Dr. Falmer reported. Arrow Normand came to her door and started babbling about how there had been an accident, and it was her fault. I figure she wouldn't have said it was her fault if she hadn't been driving."

"All right," Gregor said. "Let's assume that for the moment, for the sake of argument. They came along this road. Arrow Normand was driving. Mark Anderman was in the passenger seat. The truck went off the road. Here's the first question: why did the truck go off the road? Yes, I know there was a nor'easter. I know a lot of vehicles were going off the road. But why did this one go off the road? The first possibility is that somebody shot Mark Anderman in the head. Assuming he was shot in the car, it would have to have been somebody sitting next to him, not behind him. Again, assuming Stewart's pictures are correct—"

"Do you mean you think he doctored them?" Clara Walsh said.

"No," Gregor said. "I don't. So it would have to have been somebody in the car, and then the chances are good that the person who did shoot him was not Arrow Normand."

Now all three of them looked surprised. "How could you know that?" Bram Winder demanded. "If she was driving the car, and he was in the car—"

"Stewart Gordon got a picture of her, too," Gregor said. "She wasn't just covered with blood, she'd been sprayed with it. Look at the photographs. The blood didn't spray toward the driver's side. It wouldn't have, but it's clear in the photographs that it didn't. It didn't spray to the passenger side, either, although there was blood there because the bullet seems to have gone through that window. It sprayed back. In order to get sprayed with blood, Arrow Normand would have to have been behind the passenger seat and sitting pushed forward toward the open area in the center."

"She could have been doing that," Jerry Young said automatically. "It was a pickup truck, but it was a fancy pickup truck. There was a backseat."

"I wonder if somebody was following it on the road," Gregor said. "Or if somebody was following on foot, or watching on foot."

"You mean you think it's for sure that she didn't commit the murder?" Jerry Young said. "Just like that? You haven't been here, what, an hour? And you just know?"

"All I know is that logic is always right, even if you can't make yourself believe it," Gregor said. "And right now, I have a set of facts that would make more sense if there were a third person involved. Of course, if there is a third person involved, there's the big question. Arrow Normand must have some idea who that person is. She must have seen the murder happen, or somehow been out of the way and then come back right after it happened, or at least been on the scene— knocked out, maybe, by the accident—and that means that she must either know who did it, or suspect who did it. So, why isn't she telling anybody?"

SEVEN

1

Stewart Gordon liked to think of himself as a straightforward man, and in most areas of his life this was absolutely true. It was simply easier to speak his mind than to remember what it was that would offend somebody this week, especially since the definition of "offensive" seemed to change on a daily basis, and in ways he could never anticipate. Hell, even the words you were allowed to use changed on a daily basis, and it didn't help much if you were known to be an outspoken Man of the Left, as he had always been. The trouble was that he was a Man of Another Left, not the Marxist one that saw all the events of history through the distorting lens of socialist inevitability. You had to be an idiot if you thought socialism was inevitable, and Stewart was no idiot. But he wasn't a man of the New Left, either. He had no stomach for the romance of the primitive. He didn't think that Western civilization was the most corrupt, the most racist, the most sexist, the most oppressive civilization in the world. He'd seen a lot of the world, and he'd had a decent education. He had no illusions about Nature, either, or primitive peoples. The Noble Savage was the pipe dream of all left-wing movements. The only way you could believe it is if you had never really met a savage—or if you had, and you were as accomplished at self-delusion as Michelangelo was at sculpture. He'd never understood all of that, that screaming need so many people had to declare that having to live in a world with Fox News was much more oppressive than living under a government that would execute you for sleeping with your boyfriend, especially if you also happened to be a boy. Stewart was a Man of the Left in the sense of being in favor of a welfare state that really provided things for people, like food and shelter, when they had no other way of getting them. He believed not only in safety nets, but in thick safety nets, and in never trusting anything said by any large organization. That took care of both corporations and government bureaus, and Stewart thought that was exactly where his suspicions ought to be.

The other thing Stewart was sure of was that he did not like drama and fuss, and speaking his mind saved him from both. Almost all the drama and fuss in the world came from either trying to hide something, or trying to pretend you hadn't really meant to do something you had really meant to do. Stewart had always thought that Don Imus was a pompous jerk, but if he'd been Don Imus he wouldn't have apologized no matter what he'd said, and he wouldn't have ended up out of a job. If you were honest, you stood by what you believed, even if other people didn't like it, and you were open about who you were. That was why he was always very clear about the fact that he did not believe in God and did not approve of religion, and the fact that he thought the American government was in thrall to the most vicious kinds of capitalists, and the fact that he was not interesting in shacking up with some woman without benefit of matrimony. Back in the days when he was playing Commander Rees, the network had truly hated it whenever he gave interviews. At one point, they had even threatened to fire him if he did any more.

The one problem with this, the one thing that didn't fit, was the simple fact that there was a part of his life he was hiding. He'd been hiding it for many years, and he'd never had a problem with it until now. Well, he thought, as he strode back across town past the huge houses on their tiny lots, maybe "hiding" was the wrong word. He wasn't actively hiding it as much as he was just not talking about it. He wasn't ashamed of it. He wouldn't have been embarrassed if his secret had become public. These days, there wouldn't even be any real consequences if it did. It was just that he had spent so long—nearly thirty years now—saying nothing on this particular subject, it no longer occurred to him to mention it even when he should.

He had told Gregor Demarkian that he was going to check up on Annabeth, and he was, eventually, but right now he was heading for his own rented house. It was a very nice house, since the production was renting it for him, and he didn't need to spend his own money. It was not, however, on the beach, because Stewart didn't like the number of hurricanes that hit the Atlantic coast of America during the season, and when they had first begun filming it was still the middle of hurricane season. This was a little overcautious. Hurricanes rarely came this far up. The ones that made it north of North Carolina tended to peter out in Connecticut. Still, he hadn't liked the idea of them. He'd asked for an interior house and gotten one, on a good acre plot, so that he didn't have to know what his neighbors were watching on television every single night.

He let himself in through his back door, took off his watch cap and threw it over one of the coat pegs in the back hall, and headed to the back of the house and his bedroom. It was too hot in here. Central heating in America was so good that it was impossible to find a decent temperature to live at. You were either freezing or boiling, and he preferred to be boiling. He took off his peacoat and dumped it on the bed. Then he took off his gloves and sat down.

The pictures were in the drawer of the little table with the lamp on it. He kept them there so that he could take them out and look at them, which he liked to do. Someday this whole thing was going to come out and people were going to say that he had abandoned his

143

children, that he had erased them from his life and pretended they didn't exist. This was not true. He had three children, all of them by the same woman, the first woman he had ever slept with and the only woman he had ever married. He had been seventeen when he'd gotten her pregnant, and due to start at university. They had married quietly and spent the next three years trying to negotiate his life as a student and hers as an almost-single mother. He would pack up his books and notes and go to the house she had rented in the nearest town and sit with Colin while she went to work as a barmaid. Then Andrew had come along, and Caroline, and the next thing he'd known, they were all living in London, in the worst sort of area, and he was trying to find his way as an actor.

It was the first American offer that had made him think about the name, and made Connie think about it too. They were divorced by then, but Stewart was anything but an absentee father. They lived only a few streets away from each other, and he came to play with the children three or four times a week. He also paid for things, because by then his acting career was actually getting off the ground. He had something significant to do in the West End almost every season, and enough television work to make him think about buying a house for Connie and the children. It didn't occur to him to want a house for himself. It would have seemed like too much space. Then the offer had come, and he had sat at Connie's kitchen table for an hour, turning over its ramifications as if he were studying it for a laboratory. The money had been terrific, and not for a starring role, but it wasn't the money that had bothered him.

He got the pictures out and spread them across the bed. There were three of each of the children, the first ones as children, the second at the age when they had left secondary school, the third more recent. They were all grown now, with families and professions, and they all liked him, as far as he could tell. He had nothing to be ashamed of in his children, except maybe that nobody on earth knew they were his children, outside the very restricted circle of themselves.

144

Hell, every once in a while he indulged in that thing where he looked himself up on celebrity "info" sites, and most of them didn't even register the fact that he had once been married.

He thought about using the cell phone and decided against it. International calls were not always clear on cell phones. He picked up the landline and then had to go to his cell to find the number. These digital storage devices were hell on the memory. You didn't have to remember, so you didn't bother. He got the number and punched it into the landline and waited. The phone rang three times before it was picked up, and then Caroline sounded wary. She was a psychologist. God only knew what might have gone wrong with her day today.

"Caroline," Stewart said. "It's your father."

"I know it's my father." Caroline sounded relieved. "I'd recognize your voice anywhere. Anybody would recognize your voice anywhere. How are you? I was thinking about calling last week, when the news hit the papers here, but Colin said he'd called, and you sounded busy. Are you all right? Are they going to arrest you for murder?"

"No, they are not going to arrest me for murder," Stewart said. "And I'm fine. There's a friend of mine they're bringing in up here to help with the investigation. It's not about that, though. That really doesn't matter. It's, ah. Well. Do you hear from Andrew?"

"He's in the Amazon basin," Caroline said. "He'll check in in a day or two and we'll tell him all about it, but he probably hasn't heard any news for a week. They're doing—I don't know what they're doing. Some kind of lemur, I think. Is that what you called about? You wanted to find out about Andrew?"

"No," Stewart said. He was finding it unbelievably hard to say what he wanted to say. He never found anything hard to say. He was proud of his children, though. Caroline was not only a psychologist but married with a child on the way. Colin was a barrister in a first-rate firm in London. Andrew was a zoologist who studied—well, Stewart wasn't sure what he studied. Nobody was ever sure with Andrew, but Cambridge had taken him on, and some American foundation kept giving him lots of money to mount expeditions to the Amazon, so Stewart assumed that Andrew was well respected in his field. He found it interesting that none of his children had been interested in being an actor.

Caroline was getting concerned. "Dad? Are you all right? Colin said when he called your house, a woman answered. Is it something about that? I talked to Mum about it. I hope you don't mind."

"No," Stewart said. "No, I don't mind. And it's, well, yes, it is in a way about her, but not exactly. I mean, not directly."

"So is she somebody important? Is she somebody we should know about? It's been a while since you've hung around with one of those six-foot Amazons with the hot and cold running neuroses."

"She's not six feet tall," Stewart said. "And she's not neurotic that I know of. Her name is Annabeth Falmer. Dr. Annabeth Falmer. She—"

"The historian," Caroline said. "Really? This is serious. She's got to be almost as old as you are."

"Caroline," Stewart said. It wasn't true that all his girlfriends since his marriage had been six feet tall. It was true that they had all been neurotic. He tried again. "I called because I wanted to know if you resented it. The name. If you wish your mother and I hadn't changed your name to keep you away from my publicity."

There was a short silence on the line. "What an odd thing to say," Caroline said finally. "Especially after all these years. And no, if you want to know, I didn't resent it, and I don't think Colin and Andrew did either. Especially not after you became Commander Rees, and it was all over everywhere. You were. I mean by then we were, what, in our teens? We weren't stupid. We could read the tabloids. I don't think any of us was interested in having that kind of publicity in our lives."

"Some people like it," Stewart said. "In Los Angeles, there are some people, girls especially, who, ah—"

"Who become celebrities by proxy?" Caroline said. "Do you really think I'd want to do that? Or that Colin would? Or Andrew? God, can't you just imagine Andrew in a tabloid, siccing a python on the photographers?"

"Yes," Stewart said. "Well. You were always very sensible children."

"We're not children anymore, Dad. Colin is forty-five."

"I know that." He looked at the pictures on the bed again. Then he gathered them up and put them back in the drawer. Maybe the time had come to keep them out and around and not care if people saw them. There was no chance anymore that any of the three of them would be plagued by schoolyard bullies because he had his picture all over American television.

He had one of those rare but desperate moments when he wished he still smoked cigarettes. It passed. "I did something stupid," he said. "Not deliberately, you understand, but it was stupid. And now I'm not entirely sure what to do to make it right."

"Whatever did you do?"

"It's what I didn't do. I didn't tell Annabeth about the three of you."

"You never tell any of your girlfriends about the three of us. I think the last one I met, I was introduced as your niece. And I was fourteen."

"Yes," Stewart said. "Well."

The pause on Caroline's end of the line was longer this time, and when it was broken it was broken with an explosion of laughter. "Good grief," she said. "You're serious. You're serious this time."

"Possibly," Stewart said.

"Well, but, how long have you known her? What's she like? Is she gorgeous—but she couldn't be as gorgeous as the girlfriends, could she, because she must be in her fifties. Have you asked her to marry you? Are you going to?"

"I've known her for a week," Stewart said, "and I'm not going to ask her to marry me before I ask her to, ah, yes, that's none of your business."

Caroline was giggling helplessly. Stewart could hear her.

"It really isn't that funny, you know. And I have to somehow explain why I didn't mention the three of you, never mind your mother."

"Oh, I've got to tell Mum. This is wonderful. And Andrew. He'll laugh for a week. We're all grown now, though, so we expect to be invited to the wedding, especially if you're telling her anyway. And you'd better tell her. If she finds out after you're married, she'll have your head, and quite rightly, too."

"Caroline," Stewart said.

But it was no use. Caroline couldn't stop laughing, and Stewart couldn't stop feeling that he had, in his old age, become a figure of fun to his own children.

2

For Kendra Rhode, the days since the murder of Mark Anderman had been a raging annoyance, of a kind and duration she hadn't been required to suffer through since she'd been in high school. Today alone, a day on which nothing much was happening, she had had to take two telephone calls from family lawyers, one from the firm in New York, which was furious at her, and one from the firm in Los Angeles, which was ready to chew her head off. The consensus was complete. Nobody understood what she was still doing on Margaret's Harbor. She had nothing to hold her there, no obligations she was required to meet, and by staying where she was she was putting herself and possibly other members of the family in jeopardy. Kendra had been told all about the police when she was very young, and about "ordinary people," who were not so much ordinary as full of resentment against people like the Rhodes.

"You must never forget," one of her aunts had told her, at one of those insufferable family "receptions" her father was always making her mother put on, "no member of the public understands who you are, or what you are, or what you're going through. They think you have an easy life."

"Of course we have an easy life," Kendra's sister Cordelia had said later, up in her bedroom, where she and Kendra had both gone to hide from the aunts. "What does that woman think? That it isn't easy not to ever have to worry about paying the bills?"

Kendra had been about nine at the time, and she had found it difficult to know where her sympathies should lie. She hadn't much liked that aunt—she didn't like any of her aunts; her aunts were all "horse people," which Cordelia said meant they looked like their horses, and sounded like them too—but she hadn't liked Cordelia, either, and still didn't. If anything, she found her aunts easier to understand. The ordinary members of the public didn't know what she was going through. They thought she was brainless and spoiled and shallow, and she was really none of those things. She had emotions like anybody else. Some of them ran very deep. Some of them were painful. She had insecurities. Then there was the simple fact of her career, which had not gotten off the ground, and was having a hard time getting, because nobody would take her seriously. When you were born with money, people treated anything you wanted to do as if it were a hobby. You didn't need the money, so you didn't need the career. They believed that, and then they laughed at you.

Cordelia was one of the people who had called over the last few days, and she had not been happy.

"I don't know what it is you think you're doing," she'd said, her sharp-edged caw bouncing through the ether like a weapon, "but you're putting yourself in a position to get arrested, whether you had anything to do with the murder or not. You had something to do with him. You know you did. And a piece of utter brainless crap that episode was. I don't even want to think about."

Cordelia was in Palo Alto, California, at Stanford, getting a doctorate in microbiology. It occurred to Kendra that nobody ever failed to take Cordelia's career seriously. Even their father and the lawyers took it seriously. The people Cordelia worked with sounded like they adored her, on those few occasions when they were required to sound like anything. The occasions were a matter of some animosity between Cordelia and her, because she was always the cause of them.

"What the hell do you think it makes me look like," Cordelia would say, "when my dissertation adviser is woken up at four o'clock in the morning so that a reporter can ask him how he thinks Kendra Rhode's sister is going to respond to her latest arrest for DUI? Or the thing with the underwear, which is, believe me, beyond utter crap."

"Crap" was Cordelia's favorite word, and she used it in every other sentence when she was talking to Kendra. It didn't help that Cordelia was everything the lawyers and their father wanted a Rhode to be, even more so than their sister Melissandra. Melissandra just did all the things that were expected of her, like graduating from high school, and going on to Mount Holyoke for a couple of years. That wasn't as good as Cordelia's Yale, or graduating magna cum laude, or getting a doctorate, but it was something, it showed "seriousness," as their father always liked to put it. Kendra knew they were all missing something. She was serious. She was deadly serious. She just didn't see the point of trivialities like diplomas and college degrees, when they didn't matter to anybody who didn't need them to get ahead in the first place. Kendra was already ahead, and she had every damned intention of staying that way.

The call from her father had come in just after she'd managed to get Marcey Mandret out the door, which meant she was already past the point her patience could stand. Marcey Mandret had seemed like a good idea back in California, and Arrow had too, but the longer Kendra had known both of them the more she had realized that there would be no point in keeping them around for the long haul. People said that Kendra Rhode never faced up to her mistakes, but this was not true. She'd been very young when she'd first come out to California, only just eighteen and fresh from one of those East Coast debuts that make the guest of honor feel like she's about to die of boredom or commit mass murder. She hadn't understood then that there are different kinds of fame, and that some kinds are better than others. Or rather, she had understood that, but she hadn't know which was which. Marcey Mandret and Arrow Normand had looked, then, like the hottest things out there, the real players in a world where being a player was the only thing that mattered. Now Kendra understood that they were only "pop tarts," and "pop tarts" were, by definition, ephemeral.

Besides, they had both been too easy. Arrow had been easier than Marcey, but Marcey was no pillar of integrity and common sense either. If there was one thing Kendra couldn't stand, it was people who let themselves get plowed under when they didn't have to. She also thought it was never the case that anyone "had to."

The housekeeper who came to the door to tell her that her father was on the phone was diffident. Kendra did not have rages at servants, but she did have looks, and most of the people working at the Point were a little afraid of her. This was something Kendra did not notice. She expected people to be afraid of her. That was part of being a Rhode.

She told the housekeeper that she would take the call in her bedroom and went upstairs. She was glad her mother had gone back to New York, or wherever she had gone. Her parents were not on good terms with each other, and her mother wasn't on good terms with anybody else in the family. Kendra was fairly sure her mother had been a "pop tart" once, but a smart one, the kind who did not let herself get plowed under.

She let herself into her room and locked the door behind her. She didn't like being walked in on when she was making a phone call. This did not apply to cell phones, where she was required to talk in public all the time, because people always called her when she was walking to her car or in the middle of a designer boutique.

She stretched out on her bed and picked up the phone. "I'm here," she said, and waited to hear the click on the other end of the line. Her father waited to hear it too. There was still no guarantee that one of the servants wasn't listening in, but you did what you could do, and you suffered through the tell-all memoir later.

"Daddy?" she said.

Kendra hated talking on landlines. They always felt to her as if the person she was talking to was much farther away than he would be on a cell. This made no sense, and she knew it, so she let it go. You had to be very careful what you said in public. The media would make you sound like an idiot even if you weren't one. It was so easy to take a sound bite out of context.

"Daddy?" she said again.

"I've been talking to Tom Marquand in New York," Kenneth Rhode said. "He says you're refusing to leave the Point?"

"I'm not refusing to leave it," Kendra said. "I'm just not leaving it at the moment. I will in a couple of weeks."

"A couple of weeks could be too late. You know, nobody is trying to scare you here. We're being absolutely honest with you. Local prosecutors have reputations to make, and prosecuting a Rhode for murder would make a reputation."

"They're not going to prosecute me for murder," Kendra said. "They've got Arrow in jail. I asked Tom about it and he said it really was odd that she was still in there. He said any decent lawyer could have gotten her bail in a couple of hours. He said—"

"I know what he said. He said it to me, too. That doesn't change the fact that you're sitting there in the middle of everything, reminding people that you're a part of that mess. That's what I don't like. Granted, given the way you live, you can't seem to stop reminding people that you exist, although that would be the better course of action. Go out to Hawaii and stay at the place there. It's the most secure one we've got; we can keep the reporters away indefinitely. Drop out of sight for a while and let events take their course."

"I don't want to drop out of sight for a while," Kendra said. "I don't want to drop out of sight at all. I know you're not interested in taking me seriously, Daddy, but I really do want a career. A real career. And dropping out of sight won't get me that."

"No," Kenneth said. Kendra made a face. She could practically see him rolling his eyes. "If you can't drop out of sight, and I admit I didn't expect you to, the least you could do is change the context. You're just sitting out there, right where that man was killed, and people not only

notice you, they put two and two together. Pack up your stuff and go
back to California. Get your picture taken at clubs. Do whatever it is
you have to do so that people will stop connecting you to—"

"They don't connect me to it, Daddy," Kendra said. "They don't
connect me to Arrow anymore. They know we had a falling-out,
ago. It was in all the papers, and on MTV."

district attorney may not read those particular papers," Ken-
"And I'll bet you anything she doesn't watch MTV. If you
'm going to order the Point closed so that you have to

ıı you do that, I'll move into the Oscartown Inn, or rent a house.
Or move in with Marcey. There's always going to be something I can
do. I'm not going to leave here until the movie is finished filming."

"Why? You're not in the movie."

"I've been in movies," Kendra said.

"You've been in two," Kenneth said. "In one you had one line, in
the other you had none. Oh, and that doesn't count the tape,
which—"

"Which was not my fault," Kendra said, "and you know it. That
was a private tape, it was just between the two of us—"

"Well, it's not between the two of you anymore," Kenneth said.
"And how you failed to anticipate that would happen is beyond me.
What was that guy anyway? He makes sex tapes. He calls them something else, but that's what he does. Your tape was just a little harder
core than his usual. You're not in this movie. There's no reason why
you should hang around a murder scene until the movie is finished
shooting, which I understand is a bit iffy anyway. With Arrow Normand in jail, they're going to have a hard time getting it into the can."

Kendra hated it when her father tried to use media slang. He got it
wrong. He always got it wrong. She looked down at her bare feet. She
had had little American flags painted on her toenails, she couldn't remember why. American flags were for the Fourth of July. Usually, she
was very careful about these things.

"If you close the Point, I'll move into town," she said again, because the easiest way out of any conversation with her father was to repeat things until he couldn't stand to hear them anymore. "And I have to go. I've got things I've got to do."

"What things?"

"Things," Kendra said.

Then she put the phone back on the receiver and lay back across the bed, staring at the underside of her canopy. When she was growing up, all the girls at school had had canopies on their beds, and one or two of them had had bed curtains. Kendra hadn't understood the idea of bed curtains at all. You closed them and then you were in a small space with no air where nobody could see you. Why was that supposed to be a good idea? Kendra had had the same problem with English literature, and biology, and especially mathematics. She hadn't understood why anybody would want to know anything about them, never mind why she should be required to. She still didn't understand why most people wanted the things they wanted, unless they were also the things she wanted.

What her father didn't understand was that the things she wanted were not optional. They were like oxygen. They were the only way it would be possible for her to survive.

EIGHT

1

Gregor Demarkian did not think of himself as old in any absolute sense. He thought of himself as older—older than Tommy Moradanyan Donahue, for instance, who had more energy than Gregor ever remembered having, and older than Bennis, as a matter of principle. He even thought of himself as "old-fashioned," by which he meant that he respected education and patience more than brilliance and speed. "Old" was a word for people who were failing, and not even all of them. Elizabeth, struck down by cancer when she was only forty-three, had never been old. She had only been in the wrong place at the wrong time, with the wrong genes, in a world where education and patience had yet to find the answers to the questions she needed to ask. Old George Tekemanian was failing from sense to sense and year to year, but somehow he managed to live in the present. Maybe that was the definition he wanted. Maybe "old" was a word for people who lived in the past, and Gregor Demarkian had never allowed himself to live in the past.

He had allowed himself to think about the past, often, and it was the past that slapped him in the face as Clara Walsh's car pulled up to the curb next to the small, neat form of a woman who seemed to be waiting for them. For a moment, he thought she was someone he had known in some other part of his life. There were a lot of those people scattered across the landscape: witnesses in investigations so old he had to look at his notes to remember what the crime was; victims and the family members of victims; peripheral characters whose backgrounds had to be checked and rechecked, just in case, because not to check was to risk disaster. Clara Walsh seemed to be taking forever to get the car parked. The wind was rising all around them, and the street on which they sat looked like the stage set for a movie about New England. There was too much white clapboard, everywhere. The Oscartown Inn had a big, deep porch with tall columns all around it. Up at the end of the street, Gregor could see what he thought was the start of a town green, with a big gazebo for band concerts. He turned his attention back to the woman at the curb. The more he thought of it, the more he was sure that this woman was none of those things. It wasn't the woman herself he recognized. It was the—it was the aura she seemed to carry around her.

Gregor brushed away the very accurate image he had of the glee Bennis and Donna would display if they ever found out he'd even considered the word "aura," and tried to give his full attention to the woman on the curb. She was middle aged, middle height, middle weight, not striking in any way at all, except that she was. Gregor thought again about those people you just had to look at whenever they were in the room, the "people who glowed in the dark," as somebody in his childhood used to say. This woman was one of those, and like so many of them, there was nothing objective he could find to explain it. She had dark hair going to gray that she had pushed up under a navy blue snow hat. She was wearing one of those quilted down coats that made anybody who wore one look like a mushroom in heat. The coat was navy blue, like the hat. Her hands were stuffed into the pockets of it.

Clara Walsh had finished her seesaw parking maneuver. "Oh, my God," she said. "That's the woman I was telling you about. Linda Beecham. The woman who owns the *Home News*." Then she saw the look on Gregor's face and coughed a little. "Linda is a little disconcerting," she said. "In person, if you know what I mean."

Gregor did not know what she meant, but he was willing to wait and see. He had been a little worried that he would find a circus when he arrived. He'd been on high-profile cases before, and cases that involved celebrities, and those tended to bring with them all kinds of crazy media attention. Still, there was nobody on the curb but Linda Beecham, and although there were media vans along the street, nobody seemed to be in them. If Gregor hadn't already seen this story a hundred million times on CNN and Fox, he'd have wondered if Clara Walsh had managed to keep a lid on it. That would have made Clara Walsh not just a genius, but something on the order of the Angel of Everything.

"I wish she had more expression in her face," Clara Walsh said suddenly. "I really do. It's the eeriest thing. It's like a machine that's talking to you. Or a corpse. It's as if one day when nobody was looking, she had all the emotion drained out of her."

Clara bumped the car one more time, as if she were docking a boat instead of parking, or as if she had no trust at all in her ability to line up at the curb. Then she turned the engine off. Gregor looked back at Linda Beecham and thought that he had it, finally, the thing that compelled him to look at her, the thing that would compel everybody to look at her. Then he wondered if she had been one of the people who glow in the dark before whatever had happened to her to cause her to go blank like this. Maybe she had been, or maybe she hadn't been. It didn't matter. Blank people always made the people around them want to look at them.

"She's a perfectly nice woman," Bram Winder said. He was really talking to Clara Walsh, but it was a small car, and everybody had to listen. "I've spoken to her dozens of times. She's very pleasant. She's just not all touchy-feely like some encounter-group twit trying to express her feelings."

"I didn't say she wasn't pleasant," Clara Walsh said.

Clara was gathering up her things, checking through her purse, pulling out her black leather briefcase. Gregor still had the manila envelopes he'd been handed, some of them already opened. Clara opened the driver's-side door and got out, and when she did, the rest of them got out too. That was when the wind hit them in the face. Gregor wondered just how bad the wind chill was, since the tip of his nose had gone numb. On the curb, Linda Beecham backed up a step and waited, patiently.

"If I hadn't know her all my life," Clara said, "I'd think she was autistic. Not the way autistic people actually are, but the way they used to be described in my psychology textbooks. People without affect. She wasn't always like this. She used to be a very happy person. Or she seemed to be."

"You didn't know her that well?" Gregor asked.

"No," Clara Walsh said. Then she bit her lip, and there was nothing left to stop them all from going ahead with whatever was about to happen.

Gregor took a last long-range view of Linda Beecham, then followed Clara and Bram into the wind. There were flags along the street, an American one on a tall pole, several others attached to the facades of some of the little stores. All of them were whipping around as if they were in a hurricane, and yet Gregor was sure there was no bad weather predicted for Margaret's Harbor for a week, and that hurricanes didn't come this far north this deep into the winter season. He looked from one side to the other, at those empty vans that said CNN and Fox News on their sides, at the little stores, at the inn. Linda Beecham was definitely looking at them, and Gregor was willing to bet anything that she was definitely waiting for them, but she was not moving in their direction. She was just standing still.

"It's not where the fishermen go," Clara Walsh said, leaning back to be sure Gregor heard her. "Where we came in by the ferry. There's a different wharf for fishermen. Twenty years ago or so there was a big problem out here, with the fishermen, because the pleasure boats use up a lot of space, and they pollute the water. So there was a compromise."

"I know what kind of compromise it was, too," Bram Winder said. "The fishermen got shoved off into some makeshift hellhole, and the yachtsmen took over all the good berths. Money is always louder than tradition."

Gregor thought this was probably true, but it wasn't something he could think of an answer to. They were walking carefully up the sidewalk. The Oscartown Inn, unlike the other businesses on the street, was set a little back from the road itself. There was a patch of something that would be lawn when the green came back. Up close, Linda Beecham looked even more average and middle-of-the-road than she had from afar, and if anything with even less outwardly expressed emotion. Blank people, Gregor thought, and then she was holding out her hand to him.

"I'm very glad to meet you, Mr. Demarkian," Linda Beecham said. "You're the first interesting news we've had here in weeks. I'm glad to see you, Clara. They said you'd be here. I figured you had to be the person I had to talk to."

"I thought you were here meeting Mr. Demarkian for the paper," Clara Walsh said.

Linda Beecham did not look surprised. "It was Jack who was supposed to meet Mr. Demarkian for the paper," she said. "I don't do the reporting. I wouldn't know how. He was going to meet the boat, in case you were wondering. The *Home News* does cover murder investigations. Or we would, if we ever had any. But that's the trouble. Jack, I mean."

"Has he gone missing?" Clara said. "Has he run off with a movie star, or taken a job with the *Weekly World News*?"

"I wish he would take a job with somebody," Linda said. "He's not going to get anywhere hanging around here. He even knows he isn't going to get anywhere hanging around here. I tell him and I tell him, but he doesn't listen to me."

"So where is he, when he's supposed to be here?" Clara asked.

Gregor watched as Linda Beecham looked Clara very carefully in the face, as if she were looking for something in particular. He wondered what.

"Jack," Linda said, "is out cold at Oscartown Hospital."

"What?" Clara said. "Why? For God's sake, don't tell me somebody shot him."

"Nobody shot him," Linda Beecham said, and Gregor realized she was still studying Clara Walsh's face, as if it were a cryptogram she was going to have to solve. "And I thought about it, and of course we did call the police, but you know what Jerry Young is like. It's Margaret's Harbor. Nothing ever happens here. He doesn't have the experience. And besides, I couldn't find him. So I thought I'd come get you, and maybe Mr. Demarkian here."

"For God's sake," Clara said. "What happened? Is he all right? Is he dead? Don't you ever just let yourself go long enough to show a little emotion?"

Linda Beecham ran her eyes up and down Clara Walsh's face, but there was still almost no expression on hers. "He's not dead," she said. "If he was I'd have said so. I don't know about all right. Somebody went after his right hand with a small, very sharp little ax."

2

Linda Beecham didn't really know that Jack Bullard had been attacked with "a small, very sharp little ax." That was one of the first things Gregor found out on the way to the Oscartown Hospital, along with Jack's last name and the fact that Clara Walsh didn't trust Bram Winder to drive a car.

"At least not a car with me in it," Clara said, staring straight ahead as she sat at the wheel. Bram was in front with her. Gregor was in back with Linda Beecham, who seemed not to have any other form of transportation. Gregor found it hard to orient himself geographically. Oscartown was small and on the ocean. Beyond that, he remembered almost nothing else about it. The very little he did remember belonged to another era, with other people in it.

Clara drove on what seemed to Gregor to be side streets and secondary roads. She did not head down toward the glimpse of town green he had seen. She did not head into built-up residential areas. Clara drove past houses that seemed to have been planted in the sand on their own, without a single consideration being given to convenience, or civilization.

They drove and drove, so long Gregor wondered if they would come out on the other end of the island and take another ferry. Instead, after a while, civilization began to creep up on them, in the form of architecture, most of it precious. There were more enormous houses on very small lots. Oscartown seemed to specialize in those. Most of these houses were new. All of them had gates and multiple announcements of security systems. There were no people on the street, anywhere. It was like traveling through a Stephen King novel.

"It's the summer people," Linda Beecham said, beside him. Her voice was so unexpected, Gregor experienced it as sudden, although it wasn't really. It was just flat. He turned to look at her and saw that she was looking out at the houses, not at him. "Nobody who lives in this neighborhood really lives here," she said. "They live in Boston, or New York. They come up for the summer and drive the prices of everything right through the roof."

"There were always summer people," Clara said firmly. "Even when we were children."

"There were fewer of them then," Linda said. Then she turned slightly in Gregor's direction. "There were a lot fewer of them. And they were a different kind of person. Without this mania for display. The old summer people had money. The new summer people have money and want to make sure you know about it."

"The film people aren't summer people," Bram Winder said. "They're not even winter people. Nobody knows what they are."

They were pulling up to the back of a large, low brick building. Just past it, Gregor could see the beginnings of what might be another town, including the green with the flagpole, straight along the street. Just past the green he could see cars and vans parked every which way, as if there were a parking lot there, although he was sure there couldn't be. He thought they might just have come out on the other side of Oscartown.

"Welcome to my world," Clara said, pulling into a parking space at the side of the brick building. She had followed the line of Gregor's sight. "There are probably a thousand people up there, but with any luck they don't know there's any reason to be here. Do they know, Linda?"

"I don't see that there is any reason," Linda said. "It's not about the movie people. It's about Jack."

"Right," Clara said.

She got out of the car, and the rest of them got out of the car with her. Gregor looked around. If this was the hospital, it was very small. He had no idea how well equipped it was.

"It's very good with heart attacks," Linda Beecham said, as if she knew what he was thinking. "Other than that, you could die here."

"It's not bad for delivering babies, either," Clara said. "For God's sake, Linda. You turn me into a tour guide. You're so damned negative."

"I'm not negative," Linda said, but it was automatic.

They had been walking along the side of the building all the time they were talking. Now they turned a sharp corner and Gregor found himself looking at what had to be the front of the hospital. There were columns, the kind of columns that appeared at the front of stately brick houses meant to be Old, and Greek Revival, but the columns weren't holding anything up but a little triangular facade. There was a curving drive, wider than the usual, that was meant to allow more than one car at a time to have access. There was a little offshoot of the drive marked EMERGENCY, with one ambulance parked in the three-space section right before the door.

"If you need serious medical attention, you go to Boston," Linda Beecham said.

Then she strode past them and walked through the hospital's plate glass front doors, a compact, solid little figure in sensible shoes and that ridiculous coat.

Gregor followed Clara and Bram because that was what gave him the most time to look around. The front foyer was clean enough. In fact, it was almost too clean. It was also very empty. The little gift stand was closed. The woman at the reception desk was reading a paperback romance novel with a picture of a boat on the cover.

Clara went up to the reception desk and cleared her throat. "Elyse? Linda came to get us at the ferry."

Elyse put down her romance novel. She had to be well into her seventies. "Oh," she said. "Miss Walsh. He's up on the third floor. It's awful, if you ask me. I mean, there isn't anybody at all on the third floor. But Dr. Ingleford said the second floor had all those flu cases, and flu was catching. So there he is."

"That's fine," Clara said. "He can't be all alone, though, can he? There must be a nurse up there."

Elyse considered this. "I think Sheri may be up there with him. One of the aides, at any rate. I don't know if they mean to keep him or not, but if they do, they're going to have to move him off that floor. It's creepy up there. It's too quiet."

"Does he have a television?" Clara asked.

"He may have, but he can't watch it, can he, when he's not awake?" Elyse looked indignant. "But Dr. Ingleford said I wasn't to say it was a coma, because it isn't one. It's just something in his system. It's just hypnotol. Or something like that."

Gregor had not been paying much attention to this particular exchange. He had been looking at the out-of-date magazines in the window of the gift shop, and at the way the chairs set out in a square

163

in the waiting area looked as if nobody had ever sat in them. Now he looked up and gave Elyse his full attention. She was not playing around. If anything, she was working very hard to give Clara Walsh her full attention.

Clara looked mildly annoyed, and nothing else. Gregor came closer to the reception desk. "Just a minute," he said. "Do you mind if I ask you something? Could you by any chance have gotten the name of that drug wrong?"

"Oh, honey," Elyse said, "I get everything wrong. It's a good thing I'm just the receptionist. It would be dangerous having me work in a hospital if I was doing anything else."

"Would you know the name of the drug if you heard it again?"

"You could try me," Elyse said. "I couldn't promise you anything. I hate to be around sick people. Did I tell you that? Doctors and hospitals. They do good work, but I hate to be around sick people."

"How about Rohypnol?" Gregor asked. "Could it have been Rohypnol?"

"Don't be ridiculous," Clara said. "They wouldn't have given him Rohypnol. Nobody would have given him Rohypnol."

Elyse brightened. "That's right. They didn't. That's what Dr. Ingleford said. They didn't give him hypnohol, or whatever it was, they gave him some cereal, and the cereal made him pass out, and now it's going to be hours before he's up and around again. I remember because I thought it was so odd, that cereal could make you pass out. But there he is, you know, up there, and his hand is a mess. Isn't it terrible what goes on these days? Here's Jack that everybody's known forever and somebody cuts up his hand. And he's not awake, so nobody knows why."

3

Dr. Ingleford was not exasperated, although Gregor would never understand why. He was sitting at the nurse's desk at the end of the

small ward on the third floor, looking through papers and not seem-
ing much interested in moving. Gregor had expected an older man,
retired now, and happy to put his hand in on the very few cases that
were likely to come his way in Oscartown—or a young one, with a
distinct air of incompetence. Instead, Michael Ingleford looked and
acted like a big-city surgeon with an operating schedule the length of
Orlando Furioso, and he couldn't have been more than fifty-two.

Dr. Ingleford looked up when Clara, Bram, Linda, and Gregor got
off the elevator, and put down the folder he'd been holding. "Ah," he
said. "The cavalry has arrived. Linda said she'd gone to get you out of
the ocean."

"Just from the Oscartown Inn," Clara Walsh said. "For goodness'
sake. What the hell is going on around here? Mr. Demarkian didn't
even get to register and park his suitcases."

"Tim Haling said that to me not an hour and a half ago," Dr. In-
gleford said. "I think that's why Linda went to get you." He turned to
Gregor and held out his hand. "You must be Mr. Demarkian. I'm
Mike Ingleford. Tim Haling is our guy in the emergency room today.
You can't blame him, you know. He knows he's out of his depth.
What we get mostly up here are drunks, heart attacks, and kids on
dope. And the kids bring the dope from Boston."

Gregor raised an eyebrow, but he didn't go any further than that.
The ward was like the lobby had been: almost too clean, and almost
deserted. He saw no sign of the nurse or nurse's aide that Elyse had
spoken of downstairs.

Linda Beecham had started to pace, back and forth in front of the
tiny nurses' station. It was the first sign of emotion Gregor had seen
in her. "You know as well as I do that kids have drugs up here even in
the off-season," she said, "and they don't go to Boston to get them.
Elyse said you said somebody gave Jack a drug, which I find interesting, because you didn't say it to me."

"You'd have probably gone storming off before I knew," Mike Ingleford said. "But to make you feel better, I'm getting ready to send

samples of blood out to Boston as we speak. Stan Miltern is going to run them over to the mainland on his boat. Which is what we have to do, since we don't have the ferry much this time of year."

"They came over on the ferry this time of year," Linda Beecham said, but her heart wasn't in it. Her voice had gone flat again. She had even stopped pacing.

Gregor watched Mike Ingleford give Linda Beecham a long, steady look, then turn his eyes on the rest of them. "Well," he said. "We got this far, anyway. Not that I didn't know what it probably was when he came in, but then we've gotten some experience over the past few months. It's interesting, really. It's what I came up here from New York to get away from."

"You're from New York?" Gregor asked.

"I'm from Oscartown," Mike Ingleford said. "But I went to Yale to college and then to medical school at NYU, and I just stayed in the city. And then I got tired of it, and tired of the way my children were turning out, so I came back here. I know you think I'm an idiot to think the kids here go to Boston for their drugs, but by and large it's true. And that means that drugs can be hard to come by during the winter."

"But not this winter," Clara said.

"We've got movie stars," Mike Ingleford said. "I've been running this hospital for a decade, and the first time I ever saw Special K, it was after the barbarians invaded. Lucy Guthorn showed up at two in the morning, a complete mess, and Sheri had to wake me up out of a sound sleep to come and fix it. Which I did, barely."

"And you're sure that was the fault of the . . . barbarians?" Gregor said.

"Of a guy named Steve Becker, yeah. I don't know if you've picked up on him yet. He's not actually part of the movie anymore. I think he got canned. He used to work on the crew, same as the guy who was murdered."

"Jerry Young tried to find a way for me to charge Steve Becker with rape," Clara said, "but it was too late. Sheri had never had a rape case before. She didn't know what to do. And Lucy, of course, Lucy just wanted to clean up. They all do."

"Ah," Gregor said.

Mike Ingleford shrugged. "It's one of those things. You don't know where the better part of valor actually was. Maybe Lucy was better off with it turning out the way it did. This way, there was no publicity. She didn't have to get hammered by that asshole's lawyers. She didn't have to have her face splattered all over the news—"

"I wouldn't have done that," Linda said.

"You wouldn't have, but plenty of other papers would have," Mike Ingleford said. "Steve Becker might not have been important in himself, but he was part of the movie and it happened here when the movie was filming, and all the rest of them were probably somewhere in the vicinity when the rape happened. It would have been absolutely lovely."

"Wouldn't you like to see Steve Becker convicted of something?" Clara said. "I would. I'd like to see any of them convicted of something."

"Everybody would," Mike Ingleford said, "but I don't think much would come of it. Not on a first conviction, assuming you even got one. Rape isn't an easy crime to prosecute, and it's harder when the alleged rapist is young and white instead of some scruffy old guy with a sex-offender record. Still, it's worthwhile in this case to remember that the only time we've ever seen the drug before is when Lucy showed up after being with Steve Becker, because here we are."

"I thought one of you told me that Steve Becker wasn't still on the island," Gregor said.

"He's not," Mike Ingleford said, "but the rest of them are. And they all hang out together."

Gregor looked up at the ceiling. It was a modern ceiling, and clean. It was as if the Oscartown Hospital kept itself always at the ready in case any patients decided to visit it, but they almost never did.

"So," Gregor said, glancing at Bram Winder, who had gone over to the window to lean against the sill. "Let me get this straight. This photographer, this Jack—"

"Bullard," Linda Beecham said.

"Bullard," Gregor repeated. "What is he? Young? Old? Experienced or not?"

"He can't be all of thirty," Linda said. "He grew up here, I should know, but I get a little hazy about ages. He's only been out of college a couple of years. This is his first job."

"All right," Gregor said. "Young. In good shape? Fat and ungainly?"

"In good shape," Mike Ingleford said. "Very athletic, in a lot of ways."

"Good," Gregor said. "So that means that it's unlikely that anybody could have attacked him without his fighting back."

"Well, unless he'd been drugged to the gills," Mike Ingleford said, "which he was. Is, really. We got as much of it out of him as we could, but he's going to have to sleep the rest of it off, and there's a lot of the rest of it."

"What did he take it with?" Gregor asked.

Mike Ingleford looked nonplussed. "I'm sorry," he said. "We're not really equipped to do that kind of analysis. I feel like an absolute idiot, because we could have been, but—"

"The Department of Homeland Security was handing out money like candy after 9/11," Clara Walsh said. "One of the things they were handing out money for was updating crime labs and crime-analysis facilities. We got offered some money, but—"

"But we thought it was stupid," Linda said, "and it was. This isn't a terrorist attack. There aren't going to be any terrorists on Margaret's Harbor. Not unless one of the summer people has a son who decides to convert to Islam and go fight with al Qaeda, which is the sort of stupid thing those people do. What's Special K?"

"Ketamine hydrochloride," Mike Ingleford said. "It's one of the drugs sometimes called date rape drugs."

"But it doesn't usually knock you out, does it?" Gregor asked. "I thought it was a dissociative drug. It makes the user floaty, and compliant, and not aware of pain."

"Yeah," Mike Ingleford said. "They use it as anesthesia for some things, both for humans and for some of the larger animals in a veterinary practice. But Special K will knock you out if you've had enough of it."

"It will also kill you if you've had enough of it," Gregor said.

"I know," Mike Ingleford said. "In higher doses, it has a tendency to induce coma. It doesn't seem to have this time, and if it's any consolation, which I don't suppose it is, I don't think whoever gave it to Jack Bullard meant to kill him. If he had, he would have killed him. I think it was just a case of double dosing to make sure the job got done right."

"And what job was that?" Gregor asked.

"The destruction of Jack's hand," Mike Ingleford said. "His right hand, by the way, the one he actually needs. Somebody went at it—"

"With a small sharp hatchet," Gregor said. "At least, that's what Ms. Beecham told us."

"I said that was the right kind of thing," Mike Ingleford said, "but since we don't have it with us, we can't know. My best guesses would be a small hatchet or a medium-sized meat cleaver. Went at his hand over and over again. Broke virtually all the bones and came close to severing his fourth finger and his pinkie. It was a sloppy job, by somebody without finesse or patience. If whoever it was had kept his nerve, he could have taken off Jack's hand and been done with it."

"And the weapon wasn't found on or near the body?" Gregor asked.

"Nothing was found on or near the body," Mike Ingleford said. "The only reason we found Jack is that he stumbled into the Home News Building and Linda found him. She called us as soon as she did."

Gregor turned to Linda Beecham. "He was conscious when you first saw him?"

"He passed out in front of my eyes," Linda said.

169

"You'd better do something about security for this place as quick as you can," Bram Winder said. He was still standing at the window, but he was no longer leaning against it. He had his back turned to them and was looking out. "This is it," he said. "The rampaging hordes have arrived."

PART II

ONE

1

It was this—the arrival of the rampaging hordes—that finally made Gregor Demarkian feel old, and then only after he realized that Bram Winder had not meant to be sarcastic. Bram hadn't even meant to be metaphoric, but there was no time to think about that while the crisis was in progress, and the fact that it was a crisis became clear in no time at all. At first, all Gregor saw out the window where Bram stood pointing was a crowd of people, almost all male, near the hospital's front portico. Then he realized that the people he could see were visible only because all the space under the portico was already taken. He pressed his face more closely against the glass and tried to see out onto the street beyond. It was difficult. The hospital was set back a little from the road. The best Gregor could get was the edge of a van here and there, and a street where the snow hadn't been adequately cleared. Maybe snow on Margaret's Harbor was like street signs in northern Connecticut. Only the people who didn't belong here worried about it.

Gregor stepped back a little. "Press," he said. "National press. I take it they've decided that Jack here is connected with the murder of Mark Anderman."

"I don't think so," Bram said. "They'd never show up here like this for Jack Bullard, not unless he'd been arrested, and even then you wouldn't get most of that crowd. It has to be something else. Something must have happened to one of the twits."

Clara Walsh was at the window now too. "I didn't hear any sirens. It couldn't have been an emergency."

"There aren't always sirens in an emergency." Bram turned to Mike Ingleford. "Are you the only doctor here? Is there somebody else on call?"

"I'm the only doctor," Mike Ingleford said, "but there's a nurse practitioner in the emergency room. Leslie O'Neal. She doesn't usually have anything to do. And Tim is on call if we need him."

Somebody's cell phone went off. Everybody checked his pocket, automatically, even Gregor. He had no idea why. Bennis had "downloaded" a "ring tone" for him. When his cell phone went off, he got the first few notes of Beethoven's Fifth. When Bennis's cell phone went off, it played the first few notes of "Eine Kleine Nachtmusik."

The sound stopped. Mike Ingleford was staring at his phone. "You were right," he said. "Somebody's been admitted to emergency. Leslie wants me down there right away."

Bram Winder was pacing back and forth in front of Jack Bullard's hospital bed. "It'll be Marcey Mandret. It would have to be. There are only three people the nutcases would come out for, and those are Marcey Mandret, Arrow Normand, and Kendra Rhode. And Arrow Normand is still locked up, as far as I know."

"But it could be Kendra Rhode," Gregor suggested.

Bram shook his head. "Do you pay any attention to celebrity news? No, I don't suppose you do. I don't. The whole thing is stupid beyond belief. But here's the thing about Kendra Rhode, the one thing

I think makes her an interesting person. You've never seen a picture of Kendra Rhode drunk, or stoned out of her gourd, or sloppy in public. Never. And do you know why?"

"Why?" Gregor had barely been aware of the fact that there was somebody named Kendra Rhode until Stewart Gordon had brought his attention to her.

"Because she doesn't get plastered," Bram said triumphantly. "She gets other people plastered. She loves to watch them make idiots of themselves. She loves to watch them crash and burn. But she's not stupid, and she's not some nobody out of Arkansas who's impressed as hell at herself for having all this money. She's always had it, and she's always had influence. The secretary-general of the UN came to her fourth birthday party."

Gregor found himself wondering who had been the secretary-general then, but it was the kind of thought he had when the back of his mind was working on something else. Mike Ingleford was packing things into his pockets, getting ready to go downstairs, and Bram and Clara Walsh obviously expected to go with him.

"Dr. Ingleford," Gregor said. "Is it Marcey Mandret down there?"

Mike Ingleford looked up. "Leslie didn't say. She did say female, red hair, and overdose."

"Oh, good Lord," Clara said.

"Leslie will get the stomach pump going," Mike Ingleford said. "I'd better get moving."

"I think we'll all get moving with you," Clara Walsh said. "For God's sake, what's going on around here? I feel like Jessica Fletcher."

Gregor stayed at the window for a moment more. The crowd was dissipating, but he was sure that was only because they had managed to get inside the building. The town beyond looked as deserted as it had when they'd been driving through it. He thought he'd seen paparazzi before. He'd had cases where the press was a constant and unyielding presence. There was something about the crowd downstairs that was new. It pulsed. He ran the word around in his head. It fit, but he didn't know why it fit.

He walked away from the window, preparing to follow Mike Ingleford, Bram Winder, and Clara Walsh out of the room, and found himself face-to-face with Linda Beecham.

"It's just Jack," she said. "Up here, I mean. Date rape drug. Hand useless probably forever. But it's just Jack."

"I think Dr. Ingleford said he'd be all right, in the long run," Gregor said. When his voice came out of his mouth, it was unbelievably gentle. He didn't know why.

Linda Beecham had turned away while he'd been thinking of his voice. Now he saw only the side of her face as she stared toward the window. She wasn't actually looking at anything. She was only not looking at him.

"It's only Jack," she said again. "And the funny thing is, Jack used to talk about it. About how people aren't real anymore if they're not on television, if the photographers don't follow them around. He had all these ideas—has them, I suppose. He's not dead yet. About how there's a fundamental injustice to it, about how there's a corporate plot. Something. I didn't listen much."

"I think he'll be all right," Gregor said again. "I think the general consensus is—"

"When I was growing up," Linda said, as if she hadn't heard, "people had to do something to be famous, and people had to do something really important to be really famous. People paid attention to Marilyn Monroe, but they didn't take her seriously. Einstein was really famous. Albert Schweitzer was really famous. Presidents were really famous."

"I wouldn't have thought you were old enough to remember Albert Schweitzer."

"I think he died before I was born," Linda said, "but he was really famous. I remember hearing about him. The Mother Teresa of our time. Did you know she wrote a book?"

"Who?"

"Kendra Rhode," Linda said. "Or rather, her dog wrote a book, theoretically. My guess is that some ghostwriter wrote the book, and got badly paid for it, and then the family had connections with some publisher. Like that record album she put out. She paid for it herself. Jack thought it had to be deliberate, the things that are going on, but I don't think so. I don't think life is deliberate. I think it's all chance and circumstance."

"All of it?" Gregor said.

"All of it," Linda Beecham said, and now, suddenly, there was emotion in her voice, a lot of it, and none of it pleasant. "I think we invent things, religions, and philosophies, and problems, we invent them to make it seem like it all makes sense, but nothing does. It's just chaos. We're all like bowling pins on a big hardwood floor and the bowling balls come flying at us for no reason at all and some of us fall over and some of us don't, and none of it means anything at all. None of it makes sense."

"We can make sense of some of it," Gregor said. "I can make sense of what happened to your friend Jack, if I look at the problem long enough. I can make sense of what happened to this man Mark Anderman. Crimes get solved. Crimes are deliberate."

"They've all gone," Linda Beecham said. "You'd better go after them, or you'll get left behind."

2

What was downstairs was not "the press" as Gregor had known it. It wasn't even "the celebrity press" as Gregor had known it. Apparently, the kind of reporters and photographers who followed heavyweight personalities like national news anchors and presidents of the United States were different from the ones who followed people like Marcey Mandret and Arrow Normand—which made a lot of sense, but Gregor had never had a reason to consider it before. He wondered if he should have taken Stewart Gordon more seriously than he had. Stewart fulminated. He did it a lot. He was doing it even when they were both twenty-two-year-old nobodies in army uniforms. Gregor tended to take the fulminating in the same spirit he took old George Tekemanian's head shaking about the younger generation. It began to occur to him he might have been wrong.

Leslie O'Neal turned out to be a young and ferociously competent-looking woman in an old-fashioned nurse's cap, as if she'd stepped out full-blown from a movie about Cherry Ames. Gregor saw her for the first time as he came through the fire doors at the bottom of the stairs he had taken to get to the emergency room, and with her he saw Stewart Gordon, his peacoat unbuttoned, looking frazzled. Gregor assumed that Clara, Stewart, and Dr. Ingleford had taken the elevator, since he hadn't heard them on the stairs, but when he pressed the button for the elevator himself it seemed to be stuck on the ground floor. Once he got through the fire doors he saw what might have been the reason. There was another set of fire doors on the opposite end of the hall he stepped into. They were being held shut by a plank of wood threaded through their handles, and the woman in the nurse's cap was Scotch-taping thick blue paper across the small windows near the top center of each one.

"It won't do any good," Stewart said, seeing Gregor come through. "They'll just find a heating duct to crawl through. It's worth a small fortune to get a picture of the body."

"Body?" Gregor asked. "Is she—?"

"Of course she's not dead," Leslie O'Neal said. "She's not even OD'd, not really. She's just a silly girl who took a bunch of crap and passed out, and now we have to stop everything and deal with it. Honestly. These people. You two look big enough, though. You can hold the fort while I go help Dr. Ingleford."

"I called nine-one-one," Stewart said. "I had to call nine-one-one. I couldn't get her to talk to me."

Leslie O'Neal turned her back on all of them and hurried away down yet another corridor. Gregor looked around. There was a lot back here, more than you would think there could be given what the lobby looked like. What there wasn't was any sign of people.

Stewart was looking at the fire doors Gregor had come through. "We'd better secure those," he said. "They'll figure it out sooner rather than later. There's got to be another piece of that wood around here somewhere."

"Is it always this deserted?" Gregor asked. "It's the oddest thing. It's like a ghost town."

"It is, really, during the winter," Clara Walsh said. "I remember it growing up here. There are all these houses and stores and restaurants and I don't know what, and not a tenth of them can operate without the summer people. I suppose it would be sad, except that it's always been this way as long as I've been alive. You'd have to go back to the nineteenth century to find a Margaret's Harbor that was mostly about the people who actually lived on it."

"They're in the stairwell," Stewart said. "I can hear them. We'd better do something before this gets very bad."

They did something, Stewart directing. Gregor did not mind that. Stewart had always been good at directing, and good at doing the sensible, straightforward thing. They found another plank of wood in a room that seemed to have been given over to the collection of junk. Stewart pawed through piles of boxed paper and old molded plastic until he came up with something suitable, and then said something under his breath about what the hell anybody had ever wanted it for. They got the door secured just as the first of the photographers came down the stairs from the second floor. Gregor found himself wondering if there were patients up there, or staff, or anyone, that these people might be disturbing. Stewart had a handful of printout paper. He slammed it against the windows in the door and began to Scotch-tape it up.

"This is ridiculous," he said. "They'll be in here in twenty minutes."

"I've called the state police," Clara Walsh said. "I don't know what else I can do. Jerry can't handle something like this on his own."

"Don't presidents of the United States vacation here?" Stewart said. "You've got to have something to take care of one of them."

"We don't take care of them," Clara Walsh said. "The Secret Service takes care of them."

The doors to the landing were bulging. Literally. They were pushing in like the ones from that old horror movie, *The Haunting*. Gregor looked at the other doors and saw that they, too, were bulging. In fact, they were bulging even more dangerously because there were more people on that side trying to push in. This was insane.

"There've got to be laws," Gregor said. "It can't be legal to do something like this. What if they compromise treatment? Couldn't they get sued?"

Stewart sighed. "They could, but it's worth the risk. The tabloids pay big for photographs of the right people, and even bigger for photographs of the right people in—what will we call it?—compromised circumstances. Dead. Dead drunk. Half undressed. Shoplifting."

"And these are the right people," Gregor said. "Marcey Mandret. What does Marcey Mandret do? I mean, she's in this movie with you, I know, but what else does she do?"

"She's been in a couple of movies," Stewart said, "all minor, mostly aimed at teenagers."

"And that's enough to cause that?" Gregor asked.

"No," Stewart said. "There are lots of young, pretty actresses with more substantive careers than that, and they're not being followed around by a crowd of photographers who'd just as soon see them dead as alive. It's what I've been trying to tell you. They do it. The people like Marcey do it. They do it on purpose."

"Do what on purpose?" Clara Walsh asked.

"Become targets of the paparazzi on purpose," Stewart said. "Look. Be sensible, all right? There really are some people with enormous careers who become targeted against their will, but it's actually very rare. I was on the most popular science fiction program in the history of television. It's got a cult following. I saw somebody dressed

180

up as me on line for voir dire at the O. J. Simpson trial. With a mask of my face, yet. But those idiots are not following me. They don't care what I do or where I am. Why?"

"I don't know," Clara Walsh said. "I've spent the last several days wondering why they aren't following you. You seem like a better candidate than, well, the girls. If I may be so politically incorrect."

"I think the phrase going around town is a lot more politically incorrect than calling them girls," Stewart said. "But here's the thing. I don't ride around in limousines. I walk. I do my own shopping. I go out to ordinary pubs and a few restaurants on my own or with friends. I go to the bookstore. If somebody says hello, I'm polite and I keep on walking, because it's really incredible what kind of nuts there are out there, but I don't make a fetish of my 'privacy' or my 'safety.' I just live like a human being. I'm boring. You can't do anything with me. I don't even show up for openings except every once in a while when I've got a friend I want to support. And it's not just me. Think about Julia Stiles."

"Who?" Gregor asked.

"Lovely young woman," Stewart said. "American actress. Very beautiful. Better looking than this lot. Very intelligent. Studied at Columbia. Been in a few serious movies. *Mona Lisa Smile,* for instance. But you never see her in the tabloids. And you never see her on the red carpet, as they all like to put it. Do you know what the 'red carpet' actually is? It's a device for letting the lunatic press know that you're fair game. Everybody talks about how crazy these people are, and what scum, and they are scum, they're the embodiment of the decadence of late capitalism, but the thing is, they're not stupid. They know it's easier to make a living with people who are cooperating. They get into these symbiotic relationships with the twits who want the publicity, and then they ride the pony until it collapses. And it does collapse. It has to collapse. You can't run a career the way Marcey Mandret is running hers, or Arrow Normand used to be running hers, and I say 'used to be' deliberately. She isn't going to have one left when this is over. You can't run a career like that and have it last. You can't run a life like that and have it last. Los Angeles is littered with people in their thirties who used to be famous and now show up only when they get hit with a drunk-driving hit-and-run, or overdose in an alley. I hate Los Angeles."

"There's somebody at the window," Clara Walsh said, pointing toward the ceiling.

Stewart and Gregor turned to look. The window was a very small one, not meant to open, almost exactly where the ceiling met the wall, and there was indeed somebody in it, hitting against it in a way that was sure to break it eventually.

Stewart shrugged. "It's got wire. They can break through it, but they can't get in."

"However did they get up there?" Clara Walsh said. "What do they think they're doing? What does anybody around here think they're doing?"

"It's like Anna Nicole Smith," Stewart said, turning his attention to Gregor again. "You have to ask yourself, I have to ask myself, if what you're dealing with is a form of mental retardation. Or ignorance so profound that it becomes impenetrable. They don't understand, do you know that? They don't understand that people are making fun of them, that they're not famous in a way anybody would want to be. They don't know the rules."

There was yet another set of fire doors in the center of the block, but it was surrounded entirely by emergency room cubicles, and there were no photographers pushing to come through. Leslie O'Neal came through this set and looked around until she found Stewart Gordon. She did not look at the doors secured with boards or at the window near the ceiling, even though the glass broke over her head.

"Mr. Gordon," she said. "Miss Mandret is asking to speak to you. Dr. Ingleford doesn't approve, but Miss Mandret is staging a fit, so come along."

3

If Marcey Mandret was really having a fit, it couldn't have been much of one. It was only a minute or two before Stewart Gordon was back in the emergency room's tiny central core, looking bemused and more than a little flustered. In the meantime, Gregor Demarkian and Clara Walsh tried to talk to each other, hampered by the fact that they really had nothing to talk about. Clara Walsh was the public prosecutor, not the chief of police or the head of the homicide investigation— assuming there even was a head of the homicide investigation. Gregor had no idea what the chain of command was here, or even who was responsible for seeing that the police work got done. There had been some talk about the state police, but Gregor didn't think that was the direction to look. The only time he had ever heard of the state police taking charge of a municipal homicide was in those small towns in Connecticut that had what they called a "resident trooper," a statie who lived in town and acted as a one-man police department. Oscartown was small, but not that small, and in season it probably needed a force of at least three or four. Somewhere there had to be police, and forensics, and all the other things he had come to count on in both his long careers. The forensics were never as good as television cop shows made them look like they were, but they at least gave you something.

Once or twice, Gregor tried to get a look out of one of the fire doors. He peeled back a corner of Scotch tape and lifted the heavy wad of printout paper to look out, but all he saw was people looking back in, dozens of them, their faces pressed to the glass. There were even dozens of them now in the back landing, which was not good news. All of them seemed to have cameras. None of them seemed to be going away. He wondered where the state police were, the ones who were supposed to come in and break this up. Then it occurred to him that if Oscartown didn't have enough police to break up a riot, they might not have enough to conduct a homicide investigation.

Clara Walsh peered into his face. She looked concerned, but Gregor thought she might be one of those women who always look at least a little concerned. "Are you all right?" she asked him.

He shrugged and looked back toward one of the sets of fire doors. "I was wondering who had jurisdiction. Who was actually investigating this homicide."

"Ah," Clara Walsh said. "That bothers you, too. Well, it's Jerry, of course, even though he's not really set up for it. We can get the state police to help, but they don't have jurisdiction. Which leaves Jerry up a creek. I don't think there's ever been a homicide in Oscartown before, at least not one where the perpetrator was in any way in doubt."

"Domestics," Gregor said.

"Exactly," Clara Walsh said. "Or else somebody gets high as a kite and into a fight, as we used to say when I was growing up. There isn't a lot to do on the island during the off-season. People get cabin fever."

Gregor was going to say that cabin fever was unlikely when there were ferries to the mainland available, even if they didn't run very often, but Stewart Gordon was emerging from the bowels of the emergency room, his jacket off and on his arm, as if he were a butler bringing it in to a guest in a hurry to be gone.

He started to put it on as soon as he saw Gregor and Clara. "Well," he said. "That was interesting."

"Was it interesting?" Clara asked. "Was it something I should know about? Or something somebody should know about? Mr. Demarkian here has just reminded me that the line of command in this case is, ah, fuddled."

"I don't think it has anything to do with the case," Stewart said. "She says she took a 'little too much Valium,' which sounds about right. I don't see why she'd lie about it. Although, if you ask me, the problem isn't the Valium, it's the drinking on top of the Valium, and she's been at it. Am I the only person left in the universe these day who knows what the signs of alcoholism are? It's the middle of the day."

Clara Walsh shook her head. "And that's all she had to say? That she'd taken too much Valium? Did she mention if she took too much on purpose? Was she trying to commit suicide?"

"I don't think so," Stewart said. "You'd better ask Dr. Ingleford about that. No, that wasn't what she wanted to say. She wanted to say that she wanted me to know that she hadn't stayed in the Hugh Hefner Suite in Vegas."

"What?" Gregor said.

Clara Walsh just blinked, but it had the same effect.

For once, Stewart Gordon looked surprised. "I've mentioned this, I know I have. The trip to Vegas a couple of weeks ago. More than that. Four or five. We had a break in the shooting schedule and they all took off there overnight, on a whim or something, I think it was. You must have seen it in the papers. It made every tabloid from here to Guam. Because of the Hugh Hefner Suite."

"You haven't mentioned it," Gregor said carefully, "but—"

"Of course I mentioned it," Stewart said. "It's high on my list of absolute stupidities. Nine thousand square feet. Its own indoor pool. I've got no idea what else. Forty thousand dollars a night. Arrow wanted to stay in the Hugh Hefner Suite because Britney Spears had stayed there. So she did. Or something. I don't know. They took off for the night. Arrow checked into the Hugh Hefner Suite. And then, you know, somebody sold the story to the tabloids, which was inevitable."

"Who sold the story to the tabloids—Mark Anderman? The one who died?" Gregor asked.

"Oh, hell no," Stewart said. "They don't stay in relationships that long, these girls. Arrow was going out with Steve Becker at the time of the Vegas trip. He worked as a grip. Arrow dumped his ass either on the trip or just after it. I don't know. And I don't know if he sold the story to the tabloids. I don't remember seeing one of those front-page things with a little thumbnail picture of him on it. But somebody did. The story was everywhere before they'd even got back here. And there were pictures."

"Ah," Gregor said.

"There's no ah about it," Stewart said. "That's another thing about them, these girls, I mean. The men are awful. I mean awful. Chorus boys. Grips. Minor-league hangers-on. The relationships last a couple of months and then the men disappear, because they weren't visible to begin with. If that makes any sense. If any of it does."

"It makes sense," Gregor said. "In a odd sort of way."

The door to the waiting room was now bulged out far enough that Gregor was half afraid it would crack into pieces, in spite of being made of metal.

Clara Walsh gave it a long hard look, and took out her cell phone.

TWO

1

By this time in her life, Annabeth Falmer had a long list of things she knew to be true, and one of the most important was this: it is not the case that every action produces an equal and opposite reaction. In fact, in Annabeth's experience, actions produced overreactions, or no reactions at all, but almost never the sort of reasoned, proportionate response that took into account the mitigating circumstances in whatever it was that had happened. Mitigating circumstances and proportionate responses were for other people's problems, not your own. It was easy to keep your head when at the very base of it you didn't care. When you did care, there was too much at stake for "rational" to be something you were interested in pursuing. When you cared because you were in pain, very little would do as a response short of a total annihilating blast. Annabeth didn't like to admit it, but she had been thinking about annihilating blasts now for the better part of two months.

Actually, she was only thinking about annihilating blasts in that not-quite-subconscious substratum of her mind, the one that played the background music to everything else she did. In the foreground, at the moment, was the fact that she had become increasingly afraid of her telephone. Lately, there was always something coming over it that she didn't want to hear. That designation applied especially to her sons, who seemed to be coming apart at the seams. From the way they were behaving, you would have thought Margaret's Harbor was a crack-infested inner-city hood, complete with vacant lots, burned-out buildings, and drive-by shootings.

"You can be out of there in a day and you wouldn't have to do a thing," John had said, only an hour ago, for what had to be the fortieth time. "You'll like Chicago. You'll be close. We can visit. At least you'll be away from all that craziness with the movie people."

"I can send somebody to pack," Robbie had said, not ten minutes later, and also for the fortieth time. "You've got no idea what's going on out there. It could be a serial killer. It could be a stalker. You had two of those women in your house."

Annabeth had wanted to say that she had also had Stewart Gordon in her house, but she had a feeling that that would be something she would find hard to explain. It hadn't occurred to her until now that she and her sons had always had an unspoken agreement. It was so unspoken, she had never really agreed to it. It was odd the way it happened between parents and children, and maybe between parents and grown children most of all.

"You become an icon," she said to the air while pretending to talk to Creamsicle. "You become a picture in a book. You have no movement."

She heard the tap at the back door—she was standing in the kitchen waiting to hear it; she wasn't an idiot—and went to let Stewart in from what looked like the beginning of another windstorm. She'd forgotten how much she hated the cold when she'd decided to come up here. She'd always hated the cold. Even as a child, she had liked snow only when she could look at it from the safety of inside. She had hated it when her mother had bundled her up and shoved her out the door, with the admonition that she needed to "play in the fresh air."

"I've always hated the fresh air," she said to Stewart as she watched him stamp snow off his boots in her tiny mudroom. "I don't know if I've ever told you that about myself. I don't know if I've ever told myself that about myself."

Stewart took off his navy watch cap and his scarf and threw them both over the hook next to the door. "Are you all right? You sound flustered. You haven't been bothered by the vermin, have you?"

"No," Annabeth said. "There were some people taking pictures of the house before, but they didn't come to the door, and I can't stop them from taking pictures of the house. No, it's just my children. They're being—something."

"Protective." Stewart had his peacoat off. Annabeth found herself marveling at how incredibly careful he was to stay true to type. "If it was my gray-haired old mother in the middle of a murder investigation, I'd want to get her out of here too."

"Remind me to dye my hair as soon as I can buy some L'Oréal at the drugstore."

"I was being figurative," Stewart said. He came through into the kitchen and let Creamsicle jump down onto his shoulders. Creamsicle liked him, although it might be mostly that he had his own cat and probably smelled like it. He pulled out a chair at the kitchen table and sat down. His face was flushed and shiny under the thin layer of stubble that seemed to have sprouted from everywhere. It was a little disconcerting. Annabeth was used to seeing him as hairless as a baby.

"So," Stewart said, "as I said on the phone, I've got Gregor Demarkian here, and Marcey's had another of her half-fake overdoses. And that's where things stand. Not much, I suppose, but better than we were."

"And you're glad to have Gregor Demarkian here."

"I am. Mostly I am because I know he won't jump to conclusions. He won't decide that Arrow must have killed Mark Anderman somehow, because she was there, or seems to have been, or—you know the thing. The thing the police do."

"The police don't seem to be doing much of anything," Annabeth said. "And I thought you liked the district attorney, or the public prosecutor, or whatever she's called."

"Clara Walsh. I do like her. She's a smart woman. But with official authorities, the temptation is always there. Go for the easy target. And God only knows Arrow is an easy target. The girl stupefies me. I can't figure out how she got into the position she's in. She's got nothing at all in the usual way of qualifications for it, and considering how low the qualifications are, that's really saying something."

"Go into the living room and I'll make some tea," Annabeth said.

"I can make us tea," Stewart said. "You do too much work. You don't know how to relax."

"Go sit somewhere," Annabeth said.

Stewart got up and headed for the living room, a big lumbering figure with a bald head and a spine far too straight for the twenty-first century. Annabeth picked up the kettle to be sure it was full—which it was, which wasn't surprising, since she'd filled it as soon as he'd called to say he was coming—and reached for the tea canisters on the shelf. Stewart liked Darjeeling better than Earl Grey. He never put anything in his tea, not even sugar.

She took down a tray and put two tea mugs and two spoons on it. Then she took down a tea ball and filled it full of loose Darjeeling. She'd never been able to handle the British habit of chucking loose tea into the bottom of a teapot and letting the grinds fall where they might. The kettle went off. She poured hot water into the teapot and then picked up the tray and headed for the living room. It was the kind of moment she hadn't expected to have again in all of her life, and she wasn't sure she was having it now. It had been a long time since she'd had a man her own age around who wasn't married to somebody else or somebody she wouldn't consider in her worst night-mares. She didn't understand the drill anymore. She was probably

190

misreading all the signals, or misreading the fact that there were signals at all.

She brought the tea into the living room. Stewart was half stretched out on the couch with Creamsicle on his chest. She put the tray on the coffee table and headed for the wing chair.

"Here's the thing," she said as Stewart sat upright and reached for the teapot. "I've got a problem, and I'm not sure what to do about it. I'd know if there was any sense that the police were on hand, anybody in particular to talk to, but there doesn't seem to be. So I thought, you know, we could talk to your Mr. Demarkian, and he'd know what to do next."

"What to do about what? Has somebody been bothering you? I know a certain amount of bother is inevitable, but that doesn't mean—"

"Nobody's been bothering me," Annabeth said. "It's just that my cleaning service isn't coming in this week. The storm caused a lot of problems, so they can't get anybody here until Monday at the earliest, and probably not until after that. So I cleaned up some on my own."

"You'd think there'd be somebody on the island who wouldn't mind having the work," Stewart said. "You'd have to pay them under the table, but it would be worth it not to be held up by the ferry service."

"Yes," Annabeth said, "I know. But I've got this service, and they aren't coming in, so I cleaned up a little. And I found something."

"Found what?"

Annabeth bit her lip. "You're practically sitting on it. I didn't want to touch it, you see. I mean, I watch as much true crime as anybody, and I know there are all kinds of things that matter, fingerprints, and fibers, and things like that. But I've been sitting on it for days, and now you are, so I'm not sure how much all of that matters. Oh, for goodness' sake. You've got to stand up. And look between the cushions."

Stewart still had the teapot in his hand. He put it down, stood up, and turned around. By now Annabeth was biting her lip so hard she could taste blood. She hated this feeling she had that she was being puerile and hyperfeminine, that she was behaving like those women in the Miss Marple mysteries she'd been thinking about on the night of the storm.

Stewart bent over and pulled apart the cushions he'd been sitting on. Then he stepped back and said, "Christ on a crutch."

"Exactly," Annabeth said.

"How did that get there?"

"Well," Annabeth said, "I don't know, and that's the problem, isn't it? I mean, I suppose it could be the murder weapon, but that doesn't make any sense. Why would it be here? But it's a gun, and a big one, and I think it's the right kind. I'm not sure. I don't know about guns. But it's not mine, and it doesn't go with the house. And there it is. And on the night of the storm, Arrow Normand was lying right there on that couch all bundled up in one of my blankets."

"Did she have a gun on her when she came in?"

"I don't know, Stewart, I really don't. I just found it a few hours ago. And then I just left it there and walked around it because I really didn't know what to do next. But I've got to do something. I can't just pretend I've never seen it."

"No," Stewart said. "You really cannot."

"And my sons are going to blow gaskets over this," Annabeth said. "So I thought I'd wait until I'd had a chance to talk to you. I don't know why I thought you'd know more about this than I would, but there is your Mr. Demarkian, and he would. Wouldn't he?"

I sound like Doris Day, Annabeth thought. Next thing, I'm going to start stamping my foot when I'm angry. She reached to the tray and poured herself a cup of tea. Stewart was standing with his back to her, holding the cushions, looking at the gun. Annabeth thought it was a very big gun, maybe the size of a small cannon. Or maybe she was just losing it altogether.

Stewart let the cushions drop and turned around. "All right," he said. "We get Gregor over here and see what he can do. But in the meantime, I'm going to use your other chair. I'm not going to sit on that."

2

There were people who said that Kendra Rhode acquired friends and lost them when it served her best interests, and although that was only half true, Kendra didn't understand why it was something she should be ashamed of. There was, in reality, very little Kendra understood about the man-on-the-street understanding of a "friend," which seemed to her to be a pledge of mutual self-destruction: a friend was someone you attached yourself to, and stuck to, even if it meant chopping your own head off in full view of the American public. Did that make any sense? Why would anybody be like that, even for somebody she was married to? In Kendra's world, there were exactly three kinds of people: family, about whom you could do nothing; people you knew, about whom you could do very little; and "friends," meaning people you went to clubs with, and shopping, and got photographed with, who were important only as long as they were part of the scenery that built your image.

Arrow Normand had definitely been part of the scenery that built Kendra's image, and so had Marcey Mandret, but it had actually been months since either one of them had interested her as individuals. With Arrow, there had been very little interest to begin with. Kendra had seen what was wrong the first day they'd spent hanging out together, and she didn't believe, even now, that anybody else had ever been fooled. Kendra didn't care much for "intelligence." In her experience, "intelligent" people were either bitter and poor, or snobbish and self-important. Even the best of them took too many things too seriously, like art. That being said, Kendra saw no virtue in stupid people, either, and Arrow Normand was profoundly, almost breathtakingly stupid. She was also something worse. She was someone who could not maintain her identity, even for a second, without the help of the machinery that created it.

Kendra was smart enough to know that she did, in fact, have considerably more wattage than the people she hung out with. She had infinitely more wattage than Arrow, and enough more than people like Marcey so that if she was out with them the cameras would be on her. This was partly good luck, and partly calculation. You couldn't arrange to be born with wattage, any more than you could arrange to be born a Rhode, but she'd been born with both advantages, and at the very core of her soul she believed she had deserved them. It was silly what people said to her sometimes, what people called out to her as she was walking into clubs or premieres or wherever it was everybody was being photographed. It would not have been a better thing to have started poor and worked her way up. The people who did that kind of thing were not interesting. They weren't admirable. They were just the grown-up version of the kids they'd all called "grungies" in school, the ones who spent all their time trying desperately to qualify for the Ivy League.

The calculation part was trickier, and this afternoon Kendra was aware that she was taking a risk. She didn't like risks, except for the kind that made people call you "daring," meaning the silly kind, like taking off your clothes and jumping into the fountain at the Plaza. Zelda Fitzgerald was one of Kendra's icons, and also one of her cautionary tales, the first in a long line of celebrity debutantes gone bad. Brenda Frazier, Gamble Benedict, Cornelia Guest. Kendra could come up with half a dozen names, girls who had come out and then blown out, or disappeared, after they'd gotten the reputation for being entirely crazy. It was why she was careful about what she drank and what she put up her nose, but it was also the reason she had days like this one. The trick to longevity was taking care about the things that should be taken care of, and never forgetting which those were.

If she had wanted to make a splash right off the bat, she could have gone right out her front door. There were no photographers at that door, but that was only because the door was set back from the road, and there was a gate. Robber barons knew a thing or two about maintaining their privacy and managing their publicity, although not enough not to get tagged with a name like "robber barons." At any rate, there was a gate, and the photographers were camped out there, and she could have gone straight through in her car and gotten her picture taken just as much as she wanted.

Calculation really was tricky, however, and this afternoon Kendra had a lot of it to consider. There were things that could kill you in this business—which was the way she thought of it, her life, her career, this business, although she never did spell out, even to herself, what any of those things meant. Getting sloppy drunk and ending up in rehab, or, worse, in jail, was one of those things. She had actually been arrested once, for driving without a license, and the pictures in the papers the next day had scared the hell out of her. Drugs and liquor were only cool so long as it looked as if you and your friends could indulge in them without having to worry about the grubby little details, like federal laws. They were fun only as long as it looked as if you were in control of them and not them in control of you. There was nothing more pathetic than a celebrity who weaved and bobbed and made a fool of herself on camera, like Danny DeVito on that talk show. As soon as a celebrity appeared on camera obviously out of control of himself and his environment, you knew it was the beginning of the end. Or, worse, it was the beginning of the beginning, the beginning of the endless rounds of stories about epic drunks and bar fights and getting refused entry by clubs.

Still, drunk and disorderly was bad, but it wasn't fatal. People came back from that. They went to rehab. They rebuilt careers. They took on the coloration of people who had had religious conversions, and went on *Larry King Live* to talk about how terrible they had been before they'd confronted their addiction. No, the thing that really killed you, the thing that colored you so that you could never get clean again, was the legal system.

She had gone out the back door, toward the ocean, and walked along the little stone path that skirted the edge of their private beach. On another day, one of the photographers might have been walking back and forth along the fence and seen her, but today she was fairly safe. Not only was just about everybody staking out the little jail where the police were still keeping Arrow Normand, but the last thing Kendra had seen on television before she came out was a report that Marcey had ended up in the emergency room with some kind of overdose. Then there was that Gregor Demarkian person, whom the police were bringing in to help with the investigation. There were a lot of diversions, in other words. She would be able to get where she was going with the minimum amount of fuss, and only be photographed after, when she was ready.

The easiest way into town from the Point was the footpath they'd used to call the Road to Oz because it was made of sort-of yellow bricks. Kendra had dressed up like an Eskimo in a parka and high shearling-lined boots, and she imagined that she looked like anybody else would look, walking into town, except that she was taller. Town seemed to be deserted when she got to it too, which was both satisfying and a little annoying. There was nobody from the media hanging out on the porch of the Oscartown Inn, and nobody at the door of that little bar everybody went to because there was nowhere else to go. It occurred to Kendra that Marcey Mandret might have died, which was more interesting than it might have been under other circumstances.

Carl Frank was waiting at a table in the main dining room. It was not a private table, in a private room, but there was no help for that. The only private rooms at the Oscartown Inn were the bedrooms upstairs, and the last thing Kendra needed at this point was a rash of stories about how she'd gone to some PR person's room. PR people were people you hired, and when they screwed up and you had to fire them, you gave interviews where you said things like, "Suzi wasn't just my PR person, she was my friend, and as a friend the best thing I can do is urge her to go to rehab."

Everybody went to rehab these days. It was like everybody going to church when she was a child.

She made her way to Carl Frank's table and sat down. He had carefully positioned himself facing the doors to the room, so that if any photographers did arrive looking for something to shoot, they'd get the back of Kendra's head and maybe a few minutes of confusion before they knew what they were about. Kendra sat down and gave the waitress who came over a faint, meant-to-be-self-deprecating smile. It didn't quite come off, because the waitress was somebody she recognized. That was one of the odd things about Margaret's Harbor. Kendra didn't know the names of practically anybody who lived here, but she knew most of them by sight because she'd spent every summer of her childhood on the island. Unlike some of the other people who grew up summering here, though, Kendra had never wondered what became of the children who stayed behind for winter when all the real people went back to the city. She'd known from the beginning what happened to them. They grew up to be waitresses at the Oscartown Inn.

The waitress came back with an ordinary cup of coffee. The Oscartown Inn served cappuccino, but it was really awful cappuccino, and Kendra wasn't in the mood. She got her compact out of her purse and checked her hair. It looked the way it always looked. She looked the way she always looked, except that in better weather she wore fewer clothes.

Carl Frank was looking at her the way people did when they wanted her to talk first. It was the kind of thing that annoyed the hell out of her.

"So," he said, finally, when he realized it wasn't going to happen. "You do understand that I'm not the right person to talk to about this."

Kendra shrugged. "You're the only person I can talk to about this. The film's on its third director. The producer is nowhere to be found, and hasn't been for weeks. Besides, my father says that you're

Michael Bardman's spy on this movie, and Michael Bardman definitely is the right person to talk to."

"You could probably talk to him by going through your father."

"Not really. The Rhodes don't do much with entertainment, and my father wouldn't help me with this in any case. He thinks I should find somebody he knows and settle down."

"You will, eventually."

"Maybe," Kendra said. "Maybe I'll have a glorious great flaming flash out and become a legend. You know this idea isn't stupid. She hasn't done more than a fifth of what she was hired to do out here, and from what I've heard she's done nothing at all otherwise. She can't continue with the film now—"

"You're making a lot of assumptions here, aren't you?"

"No," Kendra said. "You know and I know that they're going to charge her with murder, even if they can't make it stick. If they weren't going to do that, they would never have held her so long in jail. And then there's that, too. She can't come back now. She's been in jail long enough so that if she does come back, that will be the story, and the only story, about this movie, ever. You'd be throwing good money after bad."

"Maybe we should just shut down the production," Carl said. "I've been suggesting that for a while now."

"It doesn't make any sense to shut down the production for Arrow Normand," Kendra said. "The part she had was small anyway. You'd have used a filler if you hadn't wanted a name for the publicity value. And these days, my name has a lot more publicity value. Arrow used to be famous, but I don't think that's going to last very much longer. If people know who she is next year, it will just be because she's going on trial. And nobody will care."

Kendra Rhode disliked Carl Frank almost as much as she disliked Stewart Gordon, but where she never knew what Stewart was thinking, she always knew what Carl was. That was how she knew that she was about to get what she wanted, or at least the beginning of what she wanted. Calculation was tricky, yes, yes, but it was almost always worth it.

She felt a brush of air behind her and thought that somebody must have come into the dining room from the outside. She reached for her bag again. She had hidden it under her down coat on the way here, but now she saw no reason why she shouldn't leave it out in full view of the public, just in case the person who had come in was somebody who might recognize her.

The best way to make sure that you didn't get tainted when one of your friends screwed up was to give people something else to say about you, and Kendra was fairly sure she just had.

3

Back on the third floor of the hospital, Linda Beecham was waiting. She was waiting for Jack to wake up, and she was waiting for the photographers to be gone from the lobby and drive. It wasn't that she thought anybody was interested in her—nobody ever was—but that she didn't want the kind of trouble she could get into by not paying attention. It was one thing to say that nothing touched you anymore. She didn't think it did, and on most days she found herself wondering how anybody could be bothered by anything, anywhere. The world was an empty place. That was how she thought of it. She was sure there had been substance to it once. She was even sure she had noticed it. She remembered long summer afternoons when she was in junior high school, sitting on the broad front lawn of her parents' house with the spring's crop of kittens in her lap, watching older girls drive by in their own cars and wondering what it would be like to be like them. At that point, it had never occurred to her that she would not be like them. Her life seemed to stretch out in front of her in an orderly and pleasant way: a few years in college; a job in Boston or New York; a man to marry; children. It was the life of everybody she knew, practically. It was what had happened to her own mother, and to the mothers of most of her friends. They came back to Margaret's Harbor, eventually, because it was a good place to bring up children. Sometimes she tried to remember when she had first known that her life was not going to be like that at all, but she always came to the same conclusion: there had never been such a time. It was just that one day she woke up, and all that was gone, and it didn't even occur to her to think about getting it back.

She looked down at Jack for a moment and then wandered over to the window where she had last seen Gregor Demarkian standing, to see what the world was like outside. The drive was still full of cars and vans. There were still men with cameras everywhere, including the kind of cameras that made film for television stations. She remembered the morning she'd realized she'd won the MegaMillions jackpot, the cold morning of a day very much like this one, with snow on the ground and clouds in the sky. Maybe it would have been different—maybe she would have been different—if it had been one of those absolutely enormous jackpots, hundreds of millions of dollars instead of just sixteen, the kind of money that not only changes your life but your very soul. As it was, she had just sat there at her kitchen table with the *Boston Globe* laid out against the vinyl of the tabletop, thinking that she was going to have to hurry if she was going to get in to work on time. The numbers were there, staring at her, and in the back of her mind there was a calculation going on. She would have to take her ticket over to Braintree in order to get it cashed, and she had no time to do it in. She worked six days a week. She worked as many hours as she could get anyone to give her, because that was the only way she could meet her bills, and half the time she didn't meet them. She couldn't take time off to go to Braintree. She'd end up getting fired.

Every once in a while, she caught a show on cable called *Jackpot Diaries*. People from around the country talked about winning whatever it was they had won. They talked about elation, and the way their lives were changed, and how happy they were now that they didn't have to worry about money. What happened to her was nothing like that. She did finally figure out that she could take the day to go to Braintree and not worry about getting fired, but she felt no elation, and no sense that her life was changing in any meaningful way. What happened was that something inside her stopped. All of a sudden, she wasn't afraid anymore, she wasn't panicked, she didn't wake up in the middle of the night with her mind racing, wondering how she was going to solve this or that or the other financial crisis in a sea of financial crises that would never end. All of that came to an end, and what was left was what she was now, this eerily calm person, this person for whom any emotion at all was an event. Maybe she should have packed up and moved someplace else, just to put her life back on whatever track she'd thought it was on when she was fourteen. Maybe she should have done something spectacularly stupid to bring herself to her senses. She could have bought herself a fur coat, or jewelry, or something she didn't need.

The problem was that money was not the issue; money could not fix what had really been broken. She was glad she didn't have to worry anymore. She was even glad to own the *Home News,* because it structured her life and gave her a place to go every day. Other than that, she was neither sad nor glad about anything. When she woke up in the morning she only cared to note that she was still alive, and that that would have to be enough.

She went back to Jack's bedside and picked up his left hand to look at it. It was covered in bandages, but she knew where all the wounds were: the ones on the fingertips; the ones on the palms; the thick sticky gash at the very center. It was wrong for things to happen the way things had happened to her. It was wrong for things to happen to ordinary people in the world like Jack.

Suddenly she felt very cold, and very tired. It seemed to her that she had been awake for hours and hours, maybe even days. She would have hated winter and everything that went with it if she could have worked up the energy, but all she could do was want desperately to be away from here. She hated hospital rooms. She hated hospitals. She especially hated the sense of inevitability that went with them, the sense that you were going to die, we were all going to die, no matter how much we didn't want to, no matter how hard we tried not to. That was the thing she had hated most about her mother's dying, that sense that failure was assured, that failure was the only option.

She walked out into the hall and looked down in the direction of the nurses' station. Leslie would be there, at the desk, reading a book or tidying up files. She couldn't leave the ward empty while Jack was still on it. Even so, the ward felt empty. The whole hospital did. Around her and around Jack there was nothing but empty rooms, bed after bed carefully made up with fitted dust covers that would have to be taken off and replaced by real sheets if the time ever came to admit somebody. She walked into the room across the hall and looked around. Her mother hadn't been in this hospital when she died. She had been in a hospital in Boston, where the real doctors were, and the real medical services. Margaret's Harbor was a place for housewives' knees and golfers' elbows, and the stray heart attack, the one that came in the night after the day you'd spent on your boat, the day that had been perfect in every particular. Failure was the only option. Once you knew that, you had nothing left to do in your life.

Linda went back into the hall again, and then back into Jack's room. He was fine. He was breathing normally, in spite of all the drugs he had in him. She went to the window and looked out again. She was aware that she was only pretending to have something to do. She was really only pacing, back and forth, marking time. She had done a lot of pacing in her time.

She had left her down coat on the visitor's chair, a green plastic and pressed-wood thing somebody had shoved into a corner where nobody would ever want to sit. She got the coat on and went back to Jack's bedside. His eyes were closed. His hair was dark and damp and matted with sweat. He did not seem to be sweating now. It was just his hand that was damaged. Nobody had taken a knife or an ax to his throat.

Linda buttoned up her coat and went into the hall again. If she was careful, she could get to the elevators and outside without having to stop and talk to Leslie. She hated to stop and talk to people. She never had anything to say, and they always seemed to be expecting something she couldn't give them. She didn't want to talk about Jack, or what she would do without him at the paper for the next few days. Or few weeks. She wondered about those drugs. They weren't supposed to do any permanent damage. They were only supposed to make you forget. Then again, you weren't supposed to take enough of them to pass out cold.

She got lucky. Leslie was not at the nurses' station. Maybe she'd gone down the hall to the bathroom. There were things at the nurses' station. There were folders left out on the desk, and what was probably Jack's file, open, with a pen lying across it. Linda didn't stop to look. She was going to press the button for the elevator. She decided against it. Leslie could come back at any time. Linda went through the fire doors to the stairs instead. She could go down two flights of stairs, for God's sake. She wasn't an invalid.

In the stairwell, the hospital seemed more than deserted. It seemed like a ghost place. There were no sounds at all, anywhere, that she could hear. She wondered where this stairwell was, where she would come out when she got to the bottom. It wouldn't be the lobby or the emergency room. If she'd been anywhere near either one, she would have heard noises.

Once when she was very small, her parents had taken her on a trip to Maine. She didn't know why they had wanted to go to Maine, or what they had actually been doing there, but she remembered being taken to this big shack on the ocean where you were supposed to sit at a trough and eat clams out of their shells. The clams were in ice, and people reached into the ice to pull them out and open them up and swallow them down. This was not what her parents had expected her to do for her own dinner. They had gotten her a little cardboard dish of French fries to eat instead. She hadn't been able to eat, because she was sure that there was murder going on all around her. They were killing the clams. They were murdering the clams. The clams were being slaughtered and she could do nothing at all to stop them.

It was odd, she thought now. There was a time when she had cried for the murder of clams, and now she could work up no emotion at all for the murder of an actual human being. Of course, she hadn't known Mark Anderman—but then, she hadn't known the clams.

THREE

1

What Gregor Demarkian needed was an oasis of calm, a place where nothing was happening, and where he did not have to feel confused. That was the problem with Margaret's Harbor as he had so far experienced it. It was a mass of confusion, complete with events that came out of nowhere and went nowhere, and a Greek chorus made up of howling idiots lit up like saints in halos of flashbulb bursts. It was all well and good to tell him he needed to do something about "the case," but there was no case. There was no real police investigation. There were no real suspects. Everything in Margaret's Harbor was in a state of suspended animation except for the photographers, and they were perpetual-motion machines.

He had demanded that Stewart Gordon take him to the Oscartown Inn and his own things, and Stewart had, without complaint. That was about an hour ago, Gregor thought, but he wasn't sure, because he had done a very odd thing. Instead of going straight up to his room after he'd checked in, he'd gone to the little pub and ordered himself a cup of coffee. The pub was almost empty, except for a well-dressed but not particularly impressive middle-aged man sitting against the long wall. The man had a copy of the newspaper, and was paying no attention to anything else. The coffee came and was good. Gregor sat staring into the distance, thinking about what it was these people wanted him to solve. It made him uncomfortable to think that none of them were really concerned with finding out who had killed this young man. Solving the murder was a side issue. Solving the publicity problem was the real issue, and it was in nobody's control and never would be.

Gregor drank his coffee and tried to think. He thought about Stewart Gordon. He thought about Clara Walsh. He thought about what little he knew about the people involved in this. Arrow Normand and Marcey Mandret and Kendra Rhode were on television. He'd seen them there, if not often. Annabeth Falmer was a writer Tibor talked about. It was just the murdered man, this Mark Anderman, who was a complete and utter blank.

He had just finished his coffee when a woman walked in, dressed elaborately in overbulky outerwear, and went to sit down with the middle-aged man. She started to unwind herself from her clothes, and Gregor realized that this was the infamous Kendra Rhode, right down to the thick and oddly hooded eyes that had become her trademark everywhere. If she was supposed to be incognito, she was doing it badly—but then, if reports about her were true, she never did anything incognito. The point of her life was making sure that none of it was ever lived unobserved.

Under other circumstances, with a different person, he would have gone up and introduced himself. He was probably going to have to talk to her eventually, and it was always best to talk to suspects and witnesses before they'd had time to get ready for you. In these circumstances, Gregor knew it wasn't possible. This was a woman who talked to no one when she didn't want to. She even had a plausible reason to refuse.

Gregor finished his coffee, got out of his chair, and went back to the lobby. Then he finally went up to his room and let himself in. He found his bags already in place, his big suitcase laid out open on the bed. He went across the room and sat down in a big wing chair to look inside it.

Father Tibor Kasparian was in the habit of giving Gregor a lot of books, most of which Gregor had no idea what to do with. Sometimes there were popular novels, meant to help Gregor relax, which did nothing of the kind, because Gregor didn't understand them. There was Harry Potter, for instance, which Tibor loved, and a little collection called *A Series of Unfortunate Events. A Series of Unfortunate Events* seemed to be a detective story that never came to a definitive end, which Gregor found annoying, and Harry Potter seemed to spend his time riding around on broomsticks and casting spells to turn people into hot fudge sundaes. Gregor just found that stupefying. Did even children want to read about magic anymore? Did anybody care that witches had never ridden around on broomsticks, that there were no magic spells, that the whole thing was just pretend? Apparently not, because in the two weeks after Father Tibor gave Gregor *Harry Potter and the Sorcerer's Stone,* some police department in rural Pennsylvania refused to provide security for the public library on the night they did a reading for children from the Harry Potter books. The police department didn't want to encourage children to engage in devil worship and witchcraft.

Sometimes, Tibor gave Gregor histories of one place or time or the other, although Gregor could never figure out just what it was Tibor wanted him to learn. There were American histories, usually of the period of the Founding, as if Gregor wouldn't have gotten enough of that in elementary school. There were histories of the Soviet Union, including a very disturbing one from France, called *The Black Book of Soviet Communism.* Gregor didn't think he needed that, either. He'd never been one of those idiots who went around talking about how the Soviet Union was a workers' paradise. There had even been one history of the House of Tudor, and what that was in aid of, Gregor would never know. He did think it was interesting that Tibor never gave him histories of Armenia. Gregor knew nothing about Armenian history, and didn't want to. He was not one of those people who needed to create a fantasy nostalgia "background," where his immigrant ancestors were Hardworking, Good, and Honest People with Hearts of Gold. Gregor had grown up with those immigrant ancestors. He'd gotten out as fast as he could.

Sometimes, Tibor gave Gregor books that seemed to have been chosen at random. That was what had happened this time, at the last minute, when Gregor's suitcase was open on his bed and Tibor was in a hurry to drop off the book and get to a meeting.

"It's the Philadelphia Improvement Society," Tibor had said, dropping the thick oversized paperback down onto a carefully folded stack of ties. The ties were not carefully folded, because Gregor had folded them. Gregor had never folded a tie in his life. Bennis had folded them, and then Donna had come in, decided they were done all wrong—they would have to be as Bennis had grown up in a house with staff—and done it again. Gregor was wondering if he was going to wear a tie at all, or if Margaret's Harbor was one of those places where everybody pretended to be casual in $150 polo shirts.

"They're going to regret that name," Tibor said, looking down at the book. "It's a nineteenth-century name. It's the kind of thing people named things before the days of television."

Father Tibor was an immigrant from Armenia, but even Armenia hadn't been without televisions in his lifetime. Gregor thanked him for the book, then stood back while Bennis and Donna came in and out, making sure he had things he hadn't even known he'd owned.

"This is the Web address," Bennis had said at the very end, handing him a three-by-five card to stuff into the book, so he wouldn't lose it. "There's also the snail mail address. See if you can't actually go up there when the case is over. That would be best. You could pick up the order yourself. I've written the order on the back of the card. Call first."

Now Gregor sat down in the big wing chair next to the bed and looked into the open suitcase at the book and the three-by-five card sticking out of it. The Oscartown Inn was a "nice" place, in the way that word was defined by women who had gone to Seven Sisters colleges. It was old, and well cared for, and impeccably clean. His bed was a four-poster and there was a fireplace on the opposite wall. The management would probably refuse to light it even if he asked them to—there had to be fire code considerations, even here—but it was the fact of the thing that counted. Gregor turned off the ringer on his cell phone. Then he turned off the ringer on the phone next to his bed. He wanted to sit in this room for an hour without talking to anybody about anything, and certainly without talking to Stewart Gordon or Clara Walsh about the Case.

He reached into the suitcase. The book was called *Lost in the Cosmos: The Last Self-Help Book*, by somebody named Walker Percy. This was more than a little confusing. Tibor did not ordinary give him self-help books, and did not ordinary read them except to complain about them. Gregor pulled out the three-by-five card. On one side there was the Web address, written out carefully by a woman who assumed that Gregor would be absolutely clueless when it came to the computer:

www.boxhillconfections.com

On the other side was the order, sort of. It seemed to be in code. Gregor looked it over for a minute and decided that Bennis was ordering wedding favors, and that the wedding favors would be chocolates, and that the company that made these chocolates was in Maine. Did Bennis really expect him to get all the way from Margaret's Harbor to Maine, in a little side trip? Apparently, she did. At the bottom of that side of the three-by-five card was a little note, carefully written out in minuscule handwriting in red pen:

I need 750 of the chocolate yaprak sarma.
Janet will know what I mean.

Yaprak sarma was an Armenian dinner dish that consisted of meatballs encased in a bulgur crust. This was going to be chocolate encased in what?

Gregor got out of the chair, got the laptop out of the suitcase, and set it up on the desk. He took off his tie and his shoes and his socks. There was an Internet connection here someplace. He'd look for it after he had his shower. He wondered if Janet, whoever she was, would have a picture of chocolate yaprak sarma on the Web site of Box Hill Confections. He wondered if he would ever get used to the idea that he was going to have another wedding, and not another wedding of the kind he had sometimes imagined in the years since he and Bennis had met.

There, he'd admitted it to himself, the thing he'd been keeping in the back of his mind for months: over the course of all these years, even before he and Bennis became any kind of official couple, he had imagined them one day married. For some reason, though, he had seen them in a registry office someplace, or eloping to Las Vegas to get married in an Elvis chapel. He hadn't envisioned a Bennis as completely wrapped up in the preparations for a formal wedding as Donna Moradanyan Donahue would be in decorating the street for Christmas. It had thrown him off balance. It had been a good part of the reason why he had not been interested in taking a case for months, and a good part of the reason why he had taken this one.

It all seemed to come together, but he couldn't say how. He was tired. He had a headache. He needed a shower.

He would take the shower and then sleep for a while, and after that was over he would be ready to talk to Stewart Gordon and Clara

Walsh again, and to finally figure out what it was he was supposed to be doing here.

2

Gregor took a long time in the shower, long enough so that his skin began to look pickled, and by the time he was done he thought he had the claims on his attention at least tentatively organized. The trick was to separate the case and Bennis, and then to let Bennis take care of Bennis. Bennis and Donna didn't really want his input on the wedding, no matter how much they said they did. They wanted to stage a spectacle, and he knew from experience that they were very good at it. His one hope was that they would be limited by their audience. This was a wedding they expected to hold on Cavanaugh Street, with the residents of Cavanaugh Street in attendance. That meant it would have to take place in Father Tibor's church, which held only about four hundred people at capacity, and which Father Tibor would not suffer to be turned into an Egyptian pyramid or a seventeenth-century pirate ship. Then there would be the reception. They were counting on good weather so that they could hold it outside. They'd applied to the city for the permits they needed to block off the street the way you would for a block party. This meant accepting certain limitations—they would have to admit anybody who came along and wanted to attend—but these were not the kinds of limitations that bothered them. Gregor had wondered, on and off, what would happen if one of the people he had been instrumental in putting behind bars got out on parole and decided to attend for reasons having less to do with congratulations than with revenge, but when he had broached this possibility to Bennis, she had brushed it off.

"The people you put behind bars stay there," she said. "Some of them just die. I'm not going to worry about some serial killer from your past deciding to sneak into the reception and start killing off little old ladies. You might worry about me starting to kill off little old ladies, because I've had it with some of them. If what's-her-name Vardanian says one more thing under her breath about cows and milk, I'm going to strangle her."

"Stella Vardanian barely speaks a word of English."

"She says it in Armenian, Gregor, but trust me. I can understand."

The bathroom was big and elegant, but not silly. Gregor dried himself off and got on the clean boxer shorts and T-shirt he had brought in with him. Then he looked at his hair in the mirror as if there were something he could do about it. Bennis was probably right. In spite of the fact that she was a complete Anglo, the kind who could trace her ancestors back to England for four hundred years, she probably did know enough Armenian by now to get the reference to cows and milk. Gregor just barely believed that old women still talked about cows and milk, or that virginity was still an issue, for anybody, anywhere. Especially for him. He was, after all, fifty-six. Bennis had to be close to forty. What did Stella Vardanian think they'd been doing with their lives up to the point where they'd met each other, or at least up to the point where Bennis had met him?

He went out of the bathroom into the room itself. The suitcase was still on the bed. The laptop was set up on the desk. The laptop's screen showed the home page for Box Hill Confections. Gregor didn't remember plugging the laptop into the Internet connection or bringing up Box Hill, but he'd been distracted. He still was. He sat down at the desk and looked for a minute through Box Hill's pages: chocolates, confections, wedding and event favors. There was nothing to tell him whether or not the company made chocolate yaprak sarma as a matter of course, but he did find pictures of all kinds of truffles and crèmes, and he thought Bennis and Donna had probably come close to passing out cold from ecstasy. This was just what they needed, a specialty gourmet chocolate place that treated cacao content like the Holy Grail.

He collapsed the Box Hill page and called up Google instead. Then he typed in "Arrow Normand" and waited to see what would happen.

He should have known better. The first page took forever to load, and then it announced that there were a total of 329,224,544 results. Gregor had a feeling that this was actually an understatement. He looked at the results on the first page. They were mostly about the murder of Mark Anderman, and Arrow Normand's address. That made sense. Results would be sorted by starting with the most recent, and this was the most recent thing that had happened to Arrow Normand. It was not, however, what Gregor wanted to know about right now.

He thought about it for a minute, and tried "Arrow Normand" and "Hugh Hefner Suite." This was better. The page that came up declared that there were only 12,224,488 results. He looked through the ones on the first page and decided to try CNN first. He got five short paragraphs announcing that "it had been reported" that Arrow Normand and her friends had spent a "wild weekend" in the "very expensive Hugh Hefner Suite" at the Palms Hotel in Las Vegas, along with five or six photographs of Arrow Normand with various people, or in the vicinity of various people. He recognized Marcey Mandret from the hospital, and both of the people he had just seen in the restaurant downstairs, although the man was in the background and fuzzy. This was not helping. Gregor hit the Back button and looked through the rest of the results on the page.

The one he wanted was almost at the end. It was from something called SarahSurveysSociety, which seemed to be some kind of blog. The headline was: "Has Arrow Normand Lost Her Mind?"

For half a minute, but no longer, Gregor wished he'd already met Arrow Normand. Stewart could give all the lectures he wanted about how incredibly stupid the woman was, but Stewart thought everybody was stupid. Gregor dismissed the qualm and concentrated on the blog entry, which was immensely long for that kind of thing, and illustrated. He saw pictures of Arrow Normand at parties, and the beach. He saw pictures of Arrow Normand in shorts and halter tops, in bikinis, in ball gowns. He saw pictures of Arrow Normand happy, and sad, and wasted, and crying, and angry. He even saw one picture of Arrow Normand trying to fill her own gas tank.

In the beginning, the pictures bothered him, and he couldn't put his finger on why. Then it hit him. Arrow Normand was not beautiful. She wasn't even especially pretty. She didn't have that thing that some actresses and models have, where their looks are not conventionally attractive but are at least compelling. Arrow Normand looked like every high school cheerleader from the small towns of the Midwest, "cute" in that way high school girls are because they're very young, but also "cute" in that way that disappears as soon as they get older. And Arrow Normand's "cute" was definitely disappearing. He could see it in the progression of the pictures. The older she got, the pudgier she got. She never got pudgy enough to be fat, but she no longer had clear physical definition, and her face had gone almost completely slack. There was no significant bone structure to hold it together. Even her hair got flatter and more colorless the closer to the present the pictures were taken. What was worse, she looked out of place. When she appeared in pictures next to other "celebrities"—and next to Kendra Rhode especially—she looked like that very same small-town ex-cheerleader, getting her picture taken with her favorite star. She did not look like a star herself, or like anybody who could ever be a star.

Gregor scrolled to the beginning of the blog's entry, which took a while.

"Everybody knows that celebrities are about excess," the blog began,

> and everybody knows that Arrow Normand is dumb, but this latest trip to Las Vegas really takes the cake. It's not just the fact that we've got one more piece of evidence that the woman can't count. The Hugh Hefner Suite is rumored to cost $40,000 a night, which is more than a lot of people make in a year, and Normand is rich, but not that rich, and she won't be rich for long if she goes on spending it like water. We've been through

things like this with Arrow before, though, and you can't make people wise up. What with having her favorite latte flown in every morning from L.A. while she's location filming in Milan, by private jet yet, to the tune of $20,000 a flight, never mind the waste of fossil fuels, and the nearly daily shopping trips to Chez Guitarra at $6,000 a pop, we figure Arrow is going to end up flipping burgers in Cincinnati by the time she's thirty anyway. God only knows nobody is buying her records anymore, and her label is set to drop her, and money doesn't last forever.

But people can be stupid about money without being stupid about everything else, and Arrow Normand's problem is that she's stupid about everything else, and especially about her image. Kendra Rhode and Marcey Mandret can afford to get drunk as skunks in public every night, but Arrow is supposed to be America's Little Girl, and when America's Little Girl goes to bed in an expensive hotel suite with one guy and wakes up with another, people start to wonder if she's worth the attention she's getting. And the men. For God's sake. Can't the woman find a decently employed guy to take her out once in a while? The one she checked in with was Steve Becker, who gets some minor pickup crew work on movies, and the one she checked out with was Mark Anderman, who does the same. Neither one of them is bringing home enough to afford the coffee at the Palms, never mind the suite, and you gotta know that when they go out to dinner, it's Arrow who's picking up the checks. Arrow flew back to her New England movie set with Anderman, but Sarah's ready to predict it won't last long. Sarah's ready to predict that Arrow won't either, either on that movie or in the universe of celebrities.

Arrow Normand hasn't lost her mind. She never had one.

Gregor sat back. That was something. He went back to the Google results page, then on to the second page. Arrow Normand seemed to inspire a lot of blogs. He wondered if she read these things. It couldn't be easy to read about yourself over and over again in entries like Sarah's. It was hard enough to read about yourself in ordinary news reports, which almost never got things entirely right. He went back to Sarah's page and bookmarked it. He would rather have had a printer and a hard copy. He hated reading things on a computer screen. At the moment, this was the best he could do.

He was just thinking he ought to get the dates worked out in his head when there was a thunderous pounding on his door, and the even more thunderous voice of Stewart Gordon said, "Gregor? Are you in there? Are you dead?"

3

If Gregor Demarkian had not met Stewart Gordon before Stewart Gordon was famous, he would have thought that the man was a prime ass. As it was, he had, from the beginning, thought that the man was crazy. Sometimes it was as if they were in some odd World War II movie, with their roles reversed: Gregor was the shy reserved one; Stewart was the confident energetic one; the Yanks and the Brits had changed personalities when nobody was looking. Gregor couldn't even blame it on Stewart's size. The man was tall, and broad, and not likely to fade into the background in any room, but neither was Gregor. It was more a matter of attitude, and Gregor had never been able to figure out how it worked.

When Gregor opened the door to the corridor, Stewart was not there alone. He had yet another small, neat middle-aged woman with him, so that Gregor found himself wondering if this had become a hobby. This woman was retiring rather than brisk, and not inclined to makeup, but she had that indefinable something that Gregor recognized in Clara Walsh and Bennis, that something you got from living all your life among the WASP establishment.

Stewart had her by the hand, and dragged her in past Gregor as if she were a small child needing to be led to a waiting train.

"This is Anna," he said. "Annabeth. Annabeth Falmer. I knew her as Anna before I knew her as Annabeth. That's the trouble."

"It doesn't matter," Annabeth Falmer said desperately. "It's just that—it's just—Anna sounded better than Annabeth professionally."

"She writes books," Stewart said. "I told you about her. Father Tibor has heard of her. Everybody has heard of her. She's writing a book now, when she's not being invaded by drunken twits and finding firearms in her sofa. Here, sit down. Take the thing out and show him."

Gregor was still standing at the door. With Stewart, everything went by quickly. Gregor closed the door to the corridor and came back into the center of the large room. Stewart had practically pushed Annabeth Falmer into the wing chair, and now she was sitting in it with her feet flat on the floor and a large tote bag in her lap. She looked confused.

"How do you do," Gregor said, holding out his hand. "I'm Gregor Demarkian."

"How do you do," Annabeth Falmer said. "I've seen you on television. And Stewart has, you know, told me a lot about you."

"About you in the army," Stewart said. "Those are the best stories about you, whether you know it or not. There he was, from one of the greatest cities in the world, with no more of a clue than the most mold-besotted hayseed. And they put him in intelligence. Intelligence."

Annabeth put the tote bag on the floor and shrugged out of her coat, which was not the standard quilted thing Gregor had gotten used to seeing since he'd come off the ferry, but a good black wool that must once have been expensive and that seemed to have gotten only more so with age. She picked the tote bag up and looked inside it.

"Well," she said.

217

"Yes," Stewart said. "You have to tell him. There isn't anybody else to tell, and he'd be the best person anyway."

Gregor gave a glance at the computer screen, still full of images of Arrow Normand, and came around to sit down on the edge of the bed. It was always awkward talking to people in hotel rooms, especially women.

Annabeth reached into the tote bag and came out with a big, see-throw, self-closing plastic bag, the kind used to put things away in freezers. Gregor stared at it for a moment without realizing what he was seeing. Maybe it was because he was used to seeing those bags hauled out so that somebody could feed him, but for a split second he thought he was looking at an enormous pork chop that had been burned into an unyielding solid hunk. Then his brain adjusted to the situation he was in, and he saw it was a gun.

"Ah," he said.

"I wish you'd stop saying 'ah,'" Stewart said. "This is serious. Annabeth found this in her couch, the same couch she put Arrow Normand to sleep on the night we found the body. And we thought it might be the gun used in the killing, but maybe not. Why would it be in Annabeth's house?"

"We did try to be careful," Annabeth said. "I mean, I did, and then later Stewart did. Neither one of us touched it with our hands. We used a handkerchief to pick it up."

"Yes," Gregor said. "Well. Let's think. This is at your house? Have you owned it long?"

"Oh," Annabeth said. "No. No. I've only been there since the end of the summer. It was to write a book, you see, and the boys found me this place, and I don't know what kind of deal they got, but it was fully furnished and I could bring Creamsicle—"

"The cat," Stewart said helpfully. "It's a little orange cat."

"I'd guessed that," Gregor said. "So, it came fully furnished. That means the couch where you found the gun was there before you got there?"

"Yes. Yes, it was," Annabeth said.

"And was this the first time you'd gone rooting around in it?" Gregor asked.

Annabeth looked confused for a moment, then brightened. "Oh, no. I clean as a hobby, or something. I've pulled the cushions several times and vacuumed out underneath them. If you don't do that, couches get really foul. I've taken the whole thing apart several times before this."

"And that's what you were doing this time, taking the couch apart to clean it?" Gregor asked.

"Not really," Annabeth said. "I sat down on it, which I don't usually do, but I was setting up to give Stewart some tea when he came and I was arranging some things on the coffee table, and I sat down to do it, and I sat down on something hard. So I went looking, and that was what I found. It was just there. Between the cushions and a little underneath."

"And it's not yours?"

"Of course it's not hers," Stewart said.

"No it isn't," Annabeth said, "although you should hear my sons on the phone these days. They want me to get one. They both live in suburbs, you see, and there are burglaries. But this is Margaret's Harbor. Nothing ever happens on Margaret's Harbor."

"Somebody just got murdered here," Stewart pointed out.

Annabeth ignored him. Gregor ignored him too. The gun in the plastic bag was large and heavy, not a "ladies' gun" as some of them were called, not small so that it could fit into a purse. He looked up instinctively and checked the pictures of Arrow Normand on his laptop screen. She was a very small woman, tiny, not much taller than five feet. She didn't look strong, and she didn't look athletic. Even in the pictures where she was supposed to be performing, the illusion of a toned and trained body was just that, an illusion. She faked it with spandex and Lycra.

Stewart turned his head to see what Gregor was looking at. "Aha," he said. "You've looked her up. Our Arrow."

"She's very small."

"And?"

"And this is a big gun," Gregor said. "It's a heavy gun. It's heavy even for Ms. Falmer there—"

"Dr. Falmer," Stewart said automatically.

"Annabeth," Annabeth said.

"It's heavy even for Annabeth," Gregor corrected himself, "and she's not only larger in terms of height and body build, but she's got more muscle on her. At least, as far as I can tell from photographs. Has it been fired recently?"

"We didn't fire it, if that's what you mean," Annabeth said. "We only picked it up with a handkerchief, like I told you. I'm not sure I'd know how to fire it."

"It's simple to fire a gun," Stewart said. "You make sure it's loaded, you make sure the safety is off, and then you pull the trigger."

Gregor opened the plastic bag. Then he reached behind him into his suitcase, took the first tie that was handy, and took the gun out with that. Then he smelled the barrel. There was nothing. He dropped the gun back into the bag.

"Well?" Stewart said.

"It smells new," Gregor said, trying to be cautious. Trying to be cautious around Stewart was like trying to be—Gregor stopped. He didn't know what it was like. He had no metaphor. "It smells new," he said again, "as if it has never been fired at all. Ever. Which I can't vouch for until we get it tested. Try to get that through your head."

"What would Arrow have been doing carrying around a gun that had never been fired?" Stewart asked.

"Are you sure she was carrying it around?" Gregor said. "There was somebody else there that night, wasn't there? You said you carried Marcey Mandret to Dr.—Annabeth's house, and that's how the two of you ended up finding the body of Mark Anderman."

"Marcey Mandret wasn't carrying a gun," Stewart said. "I know. I had her over my shoulder. She wasn't even carrying underwear."

"In her purse?" Gregor suggested.

"Didn't have one," Stewart said. "I mean, I suppose she did have one, earlier in the day, but by the time I was wiping her up off the floor it had disappeared somewhere. Well, all right. I mean it didn't occur to me she should have it. I was busy trying to get her out of that place before she landed on the front page of the *Enquirer*. Again. But she couldn't have been carrying anything, and especially not anything that heavy. She was wearing so little, I would have noticed."

"They were both wearing practically nothing," Annabeth said. "When Miss Normand came to my door, I thought there must have been a rape, because she wasn't wearing any underwear. Stewart explained it to me later, and it made sense, because of the shoes. You should have seen the shoes. There was nothing to them. They were just straps. And in that storm."

Gregor looked down at the gun again. Arrow Normand shows up at Annabeth Falmer's door wearing practically no clothes, no underwear and strappy sandals in the middle of a raging nor'easter. Stewart Gordon shows up at Annabeth Falmer's door properly dressed for the occasion, but carrying Marcey Mandret, who is also wearing practically no clothes, no underwear and strappy sandals, over his shoulder. Arrow Normand is in shock. Marcey Mandret is dead drunk. There's a body in a pickup truck down on the beach, and somebody has shot him through the head. Now there's a gun in Annabeth Falmer's couch, and nobody knows how it got there.

Gregor looked up. "When Arrow Normand got to your door, was she wearing a coat?"

"No," Annabeth said, "why?"

"Was she carrying a purse?"

"No," Annabeth said again.

"Was her dress long, to the floor or at least below the knee?"

"It was cut practically up to her—" Annabeth stopped. "Um. You know. Is this something I should be figuring out for myself?"

"Well," Gregor said, "if she wasn't wearing a coat, and she wasn't carrying a purse, and she was dressed in practically nothing and wearing strappy sandals, I don't see how she was any more capable than Marcey Mandret was of carrying around a whacking huge firearm like that without any of you noticing."

FOUR

1

Arrow Normand understood that the time had come to do something about her situation, and she understood this most clearly because her mother was waiting for her in an interview room down the hall. That was how the guard had put it when he came to bring her the news, "Your mother is waiting for you in the interview room down the hall," as if she ought to know about interview rooms, and halls, and everything else that happened in this place. The news made her dig even deeper under the pile of rough gray blankets they had given her. It was up to four now, and lying underneath their weight she sometimes thought she was back at home on one of those days when it snowed so hard that there wasn't any school. That was real home, not home as she was supposed to think of it now. Los Angeles never felt like home to her. There was too much sunlight, and too many people who looked as if they weren't entirely real.

After a while, the woman guard came down to see her, standing just outside the bars as if she were waiting for a dog to do its business. Arrow didn't understand why she had to make so many decisions. It was nice here, with the blankets, and thinking about things she hadn't really brought to mind in years. She missed Halloween, with candied apples and cider in pumpkin shells and kids running around in costumes knee deep in leaves. She missed sitting at the kitchen table in their old house with her paper dolls stretched out all along the surface, trying to decide if Sophisticated Suzy or Marvelous Melanie should wear the Dutch dress with its little wooden shoes. On the other hand, that last memory wasn't as good as it should have been, since it always included the sound of her parents fighting. Her parents had fought nonstop when she was a child, but it wasn't until after her mother had taken her to L.A. that they had ended up divorced.

The woman guard's name was Marcia, or maybe Marsha. Arrow hadn't asked her how it was spelled. She stood at the bars and waited, patiently, as if she had all the time in the world.

"Your mother is here," she said finally. "Don't you want to talk to her?"

Arrow closed her eyes and wished that the blankets on top of her were heavier. If they were heavy enough, nobody would be able to get them off, and she'd be able to stay put until she wanted to come out and eat some food. She didn't mind the food. They brought her whatever she asked for. Marcia had even brought her a latte that had been flown in especially from her favorite place in L.A. The truth was, though, that Arrow didn't like lattes all that much either. She only knew she had to drink them. Milk shakes made you fat and, even worse, made you look like a dork.

She turned around on the narrow little cot and sat up, still keeping the blankets clutched against her chest. People thought she had killed Mark Anderman, and she knew it, but she didn't think Marcia did. She didn't think the other guard did either, the male one. She wondered if her mother did. It was one of those things she had been working very hard not to know.

"I'm tired," she said, looking at Marcia, square and solid in her dark blue uniform. "I just want to sleep."

"But it's your mother," Marcia said. "And it's perfectly safe. There aren't any photographers here. I can get you all the way down to the interview room and back without your having to see anybody at all."

"Is my mother by herself?" Arrow asked. Her mother was almost never by herself, but there were different kinds and different degrees of having someone with her.

"She's by herself," Marcia said. "I heard the sergeant say that they think you feel overwhelmed by the lawyers, and that's why you're acting the way you are. Most people don't want to stay in jail for days at a time. They want to go back to their own homes if the police will let them."

"It's not like real jail here," Arrow said. "It's not like on television."

"That's true," Marcia agreed. "It never is like television here, and you're all we've got at the moment, so we can be even more accommodating, but it's still jail. I read about you in *People* where it said you love to take hot baths. You aren't going to get a hot bath here."

Part of the problem was that she was very cold. She was cold even under the blankets, but she didn't want to say so, because whenever she did, they brought in a doctor to look at her. She didn't think she was sick. She didn't think she was going to run a fever or fall over or do any of the things that got you hospitalized for exhaustion in L.A. She just thought she needed more blankets, all the blankets that they had in the world.

"Okay," she said finally. She swung her legs off the cot and stood up. They had given her a jail jumpsuit to wear, and that was like television. It was orange. She actually liked wearing it. It was loose, and soft, almost like wearing nothing at all, but at the same time it covered her up entirely. That was another difference between real home and Los Angeles. In Los Angeles, she wore things that showed a lot of skin, halter tops, dresses and skirts cut way up high. At home, she wore things that kept her warm, like corduroy jeans and big, thick sweaters that had belonged to her older brothers and fell down halfway to her knees. She wished it wasn't the case that people wouldn't like her if she did the things she wanted to do. She wished she could dress in big thick sweaters without having stories about it written up in all the papers.

She shook out the folds of the jumpsuit. It never seemed to wrinkle. Everything Arrow owned wrinkled on sight, unless it was sparkly and had a lot of metal.

"Okay," she said again.

Marcia was giving her one of those long looks people gave her a lot these days, as if by staring at her long enough they could reveal all her secrets. She didn't have many secrets, though. It was hard to have secrets when people were photographing her all the time. She had just the one thing, or maybe two, and those weren't secrets as much as they were things she just couldn't talk about. There were a lot of things she couldn't talk about, because it was very important not to get people angry with her.

"Life is like high school," her mother had said once, before they had gone to L.A. "Everything is a popularity contest."

Marcia had swung open the barred doors of the cell. Arrow looked around and wondered what real jail would be like. Everybody said she was going to go to jail, that she would be convicted of murder and sent to a penitentiary. She wasn't supposed to hear the news, but she did. There was a little television set up at the guards' desk at the end of the hall, and the guards always seemed to have it on blasting. She couldn't imagine going to jail, but she couldn't imagine singing in front of millions of people, and she'd done that dozens of times.

Marcia was waiting. Arrow went through into the corridor. Marcia started down the hall. Arrow followed her. Secretaries stood up from behind their desks, officers stood up in their cubicles. There weren't very many people here, but all of them wanted to see Arrow pass. She tried to stand up very straight while she walked.

The interview room was a small place with a regular door and no windows, not 150 feet from where Arrow had been. There was a big conference table inside, surrounded by chairs. The conference table was made out of cheap pressed wood. It was peeling in the corners. The chairs were armless and had plastic pads on the backs and seats. Arrow's mother was a violently blond woman with too much hair and too much jewelry. She had been like that even before they'd moved to California, but back at (real) home the jewelry had been fake.

Arrow suddenly wished that there were pockets in the jumpsuit. She couldn't think of what she was supposed to do with her hands. Marcia gave her a little push in the small of her back, and she stumbled forward.

"I'll leave you two alone for a while," Marcia said, stepping back into the hall.

Arrow heard the door close behind her. Her mouth was dry. Her throat was dry. She was sure that if she tried to talk, the words would come out in a squeak.

"I don't know what you think you're doing," her mother said. "But you've got to stop doing it. You've got to let us get you out of here."

The walls in this room were gray. Arrow seemed to remember being in another room where the walls were dingy white. She had no idea how big this building was, or how many people worked in it. When she was a child, her father used to take her to work every once in a while, holding her hand and leading her through threading corridors that were like avenues in a maze. He worked in a company that did something with insurance, Arrow wasn't sure what. She only knew it was a dead end, and then only because her mother had told her so.

"Arrow," her mother said. "You have to listen to me."

"I am listening to you," Arrow said. Then she came forward and sat down in one of the chairs.

"Whether you realize it or not," her mother said, plowing on determinedly, as if Arrow had done something wrong and she was ignoring it, "this sort of publicity is an absolute disaster. Nobody recovers from something like this. Not if they go on trial, and not if they don't go on trial and the police don't have anybody else to charge. Even if they just let you walk away, if they don't have anybody else to charge, everybody will just assume you did it. And that will be it. It will be over. You might as well pack up and go back to Ohio."

One of the things Arrow could not ever say to her mother was that she liked Ohio, never mind that she wouldn't mind going back there. That was a wrong thing to say on almost every level. She folded her hands on the table in front of her. That reminded her of real home too. It reminded her of school, where they would be told to fold their hands on their desks whenever the teacher thought they were getting too rowdy.

"Listen," Arrow's mother said, raking her long, thin fingers with their even longer, thinner nails through her thick hair, "they've brought this man out here, this Gregor Demarkian. I want you to talk to him."

2

Marcey Mandret knew that it was not okay to get drunk and stay drunk, even in an emergency, but her problem was this: in an emergency, she often couldn't think of anything else to do. At the moment, she was in the biggest emergency of her life, in spite of the fact that she was still part of the inner circle. That was very important. Being part of the inner circle meant you were protected, and being protected meant that nothing really awful could happen to you. Or something. It was hard to work out. Marcey found most things hard to work out. Mark Anderman had been part of the inner circle, at least on the night he died, and what had happened to him?

Marcey was lying on a bed in the emergency room, and she knew that if she started thinking about Mark Anderman, she would start to shake. It was dangerous to show emotion if it was real emotion. Camera emotions were all right because that was your job. That was why the paparazzi took pictures of you. People thought they took pictures of you because you were famous, but that wasn't true. There were a lot of famous people who never got their pictures taken. They never appeared in the newspapers. They never saw their lives covered on

CNN. Every once in a while you would see them, on a talk show or on that silly *Inside the Actors Studio* thing, and realize you knew nothing about them. They weren't really famous anymore. You only said they were out of politeness.

No, what the paparazzi wanted—what everyone wanted—was acting. These people had to make a living. The money was in the drama, the breakups and meltdowns, the blood feuds, the disasters. It was as if the whole world were your own personal high school, and you were part of the popular crowd. Everybody wanted to talk about the popular crowd. Everybody wanted to gossip about interesting people, and people became interesting when they became popular. At least, that was what Kendra had told her. She might be mixing it up. She was very tired, and beyond being tired she was scared to death. Still.

Marcey thought about Stewart Gordon for a minute, but only for a minute. He had come in here and given her his usual advice, and she was glad of that. That was what she had called him in for. But she hadn't actually intended to take his advice. His advice was always wrong because he didn't understand how things were supposed to be. He was old, and he had been to college for years and years, and he read books. He was content to be only sort of famous. People recognized him from television, but they didn't follow him around to stores or try to sit at his table in restaurants. Marcey wondered what that was like. It wasn't like being invisible, or nonexistent, or whatever it was nonfamous people were. She didn't think about those people much, because there didn't seem to be a point. Their existence was hypothetical, as Kendra put it. Marcey had had to look up "hypothetical," and then it had taken her forever because it didn't occur to her it was spelled with a *y*. Sometimes she thought Stewart Gordon might have a point, if only a very little one, about education. It was embarrassing to get into things like that. It made you look like a rube.

She tried sitting up in the bed, and it worked. She had no idea how long she'd been lying in it, but she thought it was a long time, long enough so that they should already have found her a bed in the regular hospital. Unless they didn't mean to admit her to the regular hospital. In L.A., it would have been automatic. She'd have passed out dead drunk and had her stomach pumped for alcohol and then they would have put her in a room and kept everybody in the world out except the people she wanted to see. Maybe this was not the way they did things in Margaret's Harbor. If it wasn't, she would have to insist. She couldn't go walking out the hospital's front door into the waiting flashbulbs of the press, not when she was looking like this, and didn't have a chance in hell of looking any better anytime soon.

She swung her legs over the side of the bed. The sudden movement made her heave. She sat very still until her stomach settled. Her head did not settle. She was very dizzy. She pushed herself forward and slid slowly toward the floor. For a split second, she thought she wasn't going to get it done. She thought her legs were going to collapse in front of her and the nurse was going to find her in a puddle on the linoleum. That would be an interesting headline: "Marcey Mandret Hospital Collapse!" Or however they would put it. Everything that happened to her seemed to come with exclamation points. She wondered why that was. Kendra said that it was very important to stay in the public eye all the time. It wasn't success that brought fame. It was fame that brought success. People would pay to see famous people even if the famous people had done nothing at all.

There was a little table on rollers right next to the bed. Marcey braced herself on it, very carefully, so that it did not roll out from under her. Then she braced herself on the bed. She stood up. Her back hurt. She stopped leaning against the bed and stood up absolutely straight. Her back still hurt. Her stomach was still rolling. She was still dizzy. Nothing much had changed from an hour ago, except that she thought she was pretty close to sober.

Sometimes she thought Kendra might be wrong about things, especially about publicity. It did not seem to Marcey that Kendra was becoming successful. In fact, everything Kendra did fell apart. On the other hand, Kendra did not have to be successful if she didn't want to, because she already had money. Real money. Money made Marcey's mouth go dry. She spent so much of it all the time. She spent it and spent it, and it was always there, but she wasn't sure how that happened. The movies paid her. The taxes were enormous. There had to be some explanation for this.

She was wearing a hospital gown. The only clothes in the room were the ones she'd been wearing when she'd been brought in, and they were no help. They were her going-out-in-public clothes. There was practically nothing to them. Marcey could feel the cool breeze on her bare behind, which meant she was in this hospital gown without underwear, and it felt awful, even though she almost never wore underwear. It was one thing to go commando because you were being daring and naughty and hoping to get a little attention, and another to have your bare rear end exposed because you'd gotten too drunk to stand up and they took your clothes. She looked around the room for anything that would suit, but all that there was were sheets and pillowcases. She tried to strip the sheet off the bed and it wouldn't come. She saw the visitor's chair and sat down in it. She wanted to throw up again. She wanted to pass out.

She looked around the room one more time. In the beginning, the hospital had seemed to be full of people. There was the doctor, and a nurse, and Stewart Gordon, and some people he had with him. Now she couldn't hear anybody at all, at least anybody close, but that didn't mean there wasn't anybody. She got onto her feet again, and this time it was better. Here was something she was good at. She could negotiate a space when she was dizzy and unsteady on her feet. She couldn't go out with the gown like that. She couldn't get the sheet off the bed. She looked around again and realized that there was not just a sheet, but a blanket. The blanket was folded at the foot of the bed. She didn't have to rip out hospital corners to get it.

The blanket was heavy. It was impossible to tie around her waist like a sarong. Marcey had no idea how people managed to do that in movies. She tried tying it in a knot in front of her, which left her legs exposed in the front, but at least covered her backside, and the front of the hospital gown went down almost to her knees. She wished she had something she could use to cover up completely, like one of those things Muslim women wore. It would be the perfect disguise, if she ever decided she needed a disguise. She could go anywhere she wanted and nobody would know who she was.

She looked down at her feet, and it was just then that she realized she had no shoes. That was when all the resentment and anger and annoyance she had been feeling since they'd first gotten here finally took her over, and she admitted to herself that she didn't just hate Margaret's Harbor in the usual way. She hated Barbie dolls and tacos, too, but that was normal hate. It was the kind of hate you were supposed to have. She hated Margaret's Harbor with an emotion so deep it split her in half. She hated the twin sets and the A-line skirts and the books that were absolutely everywhere. She hated the weather. She hated the women with their snow boots and espadrilles and faces that had never seen a face-lift. What was wrong with all these people here? Who did they think they were? She didn't care if presidents of the United States had vacationed here. Presidents of the United States were boring.

She hobbled over to the side table, where somebody had left her clothes, folded, and got her shoes. They weren't much better than going barefoot, but they would have to do. They were all she had. If this were a movie, she would be able to go through the rooms without being seen and find something to wear. She would never get away with that on her own.

It didn't matter. What did matter was getting out of here, and she was going to get.

3

Stewart Gordon knew that there were times, these days, when he was just a cartoon of himself, but he also knew that he had tried and failed to find any other way to handle the changes in the world he had to live in. He was very careful never to tell anyone that he wished he had not taken that part in that "damned science fiction television show," as one of his fellow cast members had put in, in the London *Guardian,* in the middle of a rant about the tyranny of middlebrow. He wasn't sorry he'd taken that part. It had made him financially independent even without the residuals, and with them it had made him more than comfortable. These days, he got the work he wanted, just because he wanted it. He never had to take work just to work. He took vacations when he wanted to take them. He bought the books he wanted to read. He went to the theater when he felt like it. There was a lot to be said for financial independence, and he didn't mind saying it, no matter what sort of effect it had on his standing as an unrepentant socialist of the sixties generation.

The problem was that it wasn't only money that made Stewart Gordon decide to accept film roles, and the other thing—that ingrained Scottish need to work and go on working, that Calvinist charge to never be idle on pain of hellfire and eternal death—was not as easily satisfied as the need for money was. *Nightmare Island,* the thing was called, last time he checked, but the name had already been changed so often he might be getting it wrong, and the title was so silly it made him want to cringe. The plot had possibilities, because all plots had possibilities. What made the work was not the plot but what you did with it. Unfortunately, they were doing absolutely nothing with this one. Bunch of teenage girls going to high school on this tiny island, their big evil principal, the arrival in the middle of the night by a mysterious man, in a boat—good grief, Stewart thought, you could do an enormous amount with that setup. You could rival Edgar Allan Poe, or Henry James. Unfortunately, all anybody wanted to do with it here was the obvious: give Marcey Mandret a chance to wear very little in the way of clothes; give Arrow Normand a way to sing; film Stewart himself looking menacing for no good reason. That was the problem with the Scottish thing. It made him accept work he shouldn't have touched with a ten-foot pole. It also made him stick with it. It was enough to make a sane man British.

Now he paused at the door to the dining room of the Oscartown Inn and looked around. Carl Frank was definitely there, along the wall at the back, at one of those ridiculously small tables for two. Weren't Americans all supposed to be fat as elephants? How did they fit at those little tiny tables for two? He had to watch himself. He'd turn himself into an ass. He should have walked Anna home, even if it would have attracted the photographers, a large contingent of which were wandering through the corridors of this very hotel. They weren't used to these people here. The hotels in Los Angeles made the paparazzi stay outside.

Somebody exploded a flashbulb in his face, and he pretended not to notice it. They weren't really interested in him. They were just bored. Of their three prime targets, one was in jail, one was in the emergency room, and the last was hiding out in her palace fortress. Palace fortresses should have gone out with the Blitz. It really was enough to make a sane man British.

Stewart made his way to the back, stopping politely to tell the seating hostess that he was meeting someone who was already here. She seemed relieved. Stewart thought she was probably having a bad month. You had no idea how rude people like Marcey Mandret, or the press that followed them, could be, until you'd met them, and then you were often left breathless. He got to Frank's table and pulled out a chair. It was a ridiculously small chair. Those elephantine Americans would probably fall right through it to the floor.

Carl Frank was getting up, but only halfway. It was one of those Los Angeles things, a nod in the direction of etiquette while still being entirely, offensively dismissive. Stewart sat down. A waitress rushed over, and he asked her for coffee.

"So," he said. "There's some reason for us to be meeting in public? I'd think you'd want to keep the papers from plastering a photograph of us in the middle of some big interior spread full of rumors about the ultimate demise of the movie."

"I always meet in public," Carl said, unperturbed. "I'm a lot less worried about rumors of the ultimate demise of the movie than I am about people saying I've been engaged in some kind of secret, under-handed scheme to—I don't know to do what. But I do know Michael Bardman. Whatever it was, he'd believe it."

"Ah," Stewart said. "This is about Michael Bardman. How is the old bastard? I hope he's got ulcerative colitis."

"If you could get ulcerative colitis by being an asshole and an idiot at the same time, he'd have it," Carl said. "And that will tell you how he is: being an asshole and an idiot. But I got an interesting proposi-tion today, and I don't dare not take it to him. So I thought I'd run it by you first."

"Run away."

"Kendra Rhode came to see me," Carl said. "Actually, she called, and I had her meet me here. She actually made some attempt to get here without anybody seeing her. It even mostly worked, until the end, when she wasn't trying anymore. Do you want to know what she asked me about?"

"Do I have to know?"

"Well, Stewart, if we take her up on it, you'll have to live with it, so you should know. She came here to suggest to me that now that Arrow Normand is out of the picture, she should take over the part. Herself. Kendra Rhode wanted the part for herself."

"I got that bit," Stewart said. The waitress had come with the cof-fee. He thanked her for it and gave it a go. It wasn't bad. He'd spent a lot of his youth being forced to eat in the little convenience areas for British Rail, and almost any other coffee wasn't bad. He homed in on what seemed to be the issue. "Is that true?" he asked. "Is Arrow Nor-mand out of the picture?"

"Not officially, no," Carl said. "And I'll have to admit, until

Kendra came to see me, I'd been operating under the assumption that we'd find some way to pull it out of our asses. It's a small part. She spends the only significant time she has in the movie singing, and Kendra Rhode can sing well enough to handle that particular scene. And I've got to at least contemplate the possibility that Arrow won't be available for any further filming."

"You mean because she'll be in jail?" Stewart said. "There's no chance of that. Even if they charge her, they'll never keep her locked up until the trial. It wouldn't be worth the trouble, and what would be the point?"

"It used to be standard operating procedure before the seventies," Carl said. "You always kept people charged with murder locked up."

"That was because they never had people who brought paparazzi with them when they got locked up," Stewart said. "It was hassle enough when the accused was Robert Blake, for God's sake, and he was pretty much washed up. The only interest the press had in him was that he was charged and he used to be famous. And Phil Spector. Legendary to people who know the business, but nobody in particular to the man in the street. But you're talking about Arrow Normand here. She'll slide into oblivion in another five years or so, but at the moment she's the biggest thing in Manolo Blahniks."

"Used to be," Carl said.

Stewart shook his head. "It will be used to be when the slide is over. But they like the slide, those people. They like to watch people fall on their asses, or worse. There's no point in holding Arrow. It's not like she can disappear. She'll be hounded anywhere she goes. I can't even figure out why she's still locked up. It's been days. Clara Walsh says it's because she's been clever—that Clara has been clever, not Arrow Normand; Arrow Normand is never clever—but my best guess is that for some reason, Arrow doesn't want to leave. Considering what's waiting for her on the outside, I don't blame her."

"Well, there's something else to think of," Carl said. "Maybe we shouldn't want her on the movie anymore. She'll bring bad publicity.

Or maybe she'll just be so stressed she won't be able to work. There are reasons why we might want to replace her, Stewart. The question becomes whether we should replace her with Kendra Rhode."

"No."

"It's not as stupid an idea as it sounds," Carl said. "She's well known. A lot of people love to hate her. She'll be at least something of a draw for those reasons alone. And this picture might need the help, if it ever gets done."

"No," Stewart said again. "And what's more, you agree with me. You can't stand the woman. So what's this about?"

Carl Frank sat far back in his chair, smiling slightly. "Do you think Arrow Normand killed Mark Anderman?"

"No."

"Why not?"

"Because she's not, because she's not—" Stewart didn't know how to put it. "She wouldn't blast somebody in the head at close range. She wouldn't be able to stand the noise and she'd go completely crazy with the blood, but in the end she'd probably miss because she'd be closing her eyes as she went along. The whole scenario is wrong. It doesn't fit her. And I don't think she gave a damn about Mark Anderman, any more than she gave a damn about Steve Becker, or the six or seven others before that. She had no reason to kill him. And no capacity."

"Do the police think Arrow Normand killed Mark Anderman? And don't look like that, Stewart. You're in contact with the police. You've got a lot more contact with them than I do."

"It's not a matter of the police," Stewart said. "It's the crown prosecutor, or whatever you call them here, that seems to be in charge. And I don't know what she thinks. I think she thinks that she doesn't have any other explanation. That's why I called Gregor Demarkian."

"Exactly," Carl said. "But if they don't come up with any other explanation, Arrow Normand will be assumed to have committed murder, whether they try her or not, and whether she did or not. And then the movie is left with a hole because we couldn't put it out with her in it under the circumstances. So I'll ask you straight-out. Would you have any objection to Kendra Rhode taking over Arrow's part in this movie?"

"Yes," Stewart said. "Of course I would."

Carl Frank allowed himself a full, unrestrained smile. Then he said, "Good."

FIVE

1

Gregor Demarkian needed to think, and the last thing he needed when he needed to think was something to think about. He realized that this sounded contradictory, put the way he'd put it, but he knew what he meant. The world was full of distractions. It contained more distractions than information. You had to be careful about what you allowed to grab your attention, or you'd find yourself spinning your wheels about nothing at all.

The first call he made was to Clara Walsh, and he made it on the hotel's landline. He didn't care about what Bennis said about the expense—and she didn't have to worry about expenses, and he had enough to use a hotel landline if he wanted—but cell phones still made him nervous, and he was under the impression that they were easy to intercept. He had no idea why somebody would want to intercept his calls at this point in the proceedings, but he was dealing with people who risked death to get photographs of other people nobody could figure out what they were famous for. He didn't think he was dealing with rationality.

He put the call in to Clara Walsh and looked at the gun in the clear plastic freezer bag while he did it. It sat there like a child's version of major military artillery, too big to have been anything but— but what? What was the point of this, after all? Did somebody think he was going to start suspecting Annabeth Falmer of killing Mark Anderman? Or maybe it was Stewart he was supposed to suspect. At least Stewart had a hope in hell of actually being connected to the dead man. Gregor hated gestures. He especially hated gestures that were made gratuitously, by adolescents who thought they were smarter than everybody else.

It took Clara Walsh eight rings before she picked up. Gregor was surprised that he hadn't been routed to her voice mail.

"Yes?" she said, sounding distracted.

Gregor realized that she probably had call waiting, and that she hadn't recognized the number that had shown up on it. He made a mental note about one more thing to hate in modern technology. Then he said, "It's Gregor Demarkian. I need to ask you to do something for me."

"Oh." Clara Walsh sounded confused. "I'm sorry, I didn't—we're supposed to meet in three-quarters of an hour, right before the press conference. Can it wait until then?"

"I'd rather it didn't. Jerry Young is handling the details of this case, isn't he?"

"More or less," Clara Walsh said, "but there are things, you know. Forensics. The state has had to handle the forensics because we don't have anything like the facilities for that here."

"Somebody has to be coordinating the details," Gregor said. "The forensics. The background checks. Who would that be?"

"I really don't think there's any one person," Clara Walsh said. "I could check if you want me to."

"I'd like you to check, and then I'd like you to get whoever that is over here in the next ten to fifteen minutes. Before the press conference. I need to know something about Mark Anderman. You know,

Mark Anderman. The man who died. The guy nobody ever talks about."

Clara Walsh let a long stretch of silence go by on her end of the line. "Mark Anderman," she said. "It's not that we never talk about him. It's that there isn't much to say."

"There has to be something to say," Gregor said. "Somebody killed him, and he didn't die in a mugging or an attempted robbery. At least I assume that's been fairly well established."

"It has been," Clara said. "But—"

"Somebody who has been murdered deliberately," Gregor plowed on, "is somebody with something about him that made somebody want to kill him. That may seem simplistic to you, but it's an important point. I can't believe it was blackmail. I can't believe it, for one, because there's nothing to blackmail these people about. I've been on the Internet. They live their lives in public, and the more public the better. Besides, hangers-on in this group don't blackmail their celebrity friends, they take the information to the tabloids and get paid for it. That makes them more money, and it has the added advantage of being legal. So there must be some reason why somebody wanted this man dead. The best way to find out what that was is to find out something about him. Do you think we could do that?"

"I," Clara Walsh said. "Well. All right. Yes. We could do that. You said in fifteen minutes?"

"At least half an hour before the press conference. I want time to ask some questions."

"All right," Clara Walsh said. "I'll—let me get on the phone. Do you want us to meet you over there? The press conference is there, so it would be—"

"Here will be fine. Come up to the room. I'll get it straightened up before you arrive."

He'd also get dressed before they arrived, but he saw no point in saying so. He hung up, then reached into his suitcase for a clean pair of pants. He pulled them on and went across to the desk to look at the computer. He typed in "Mark Anderman," but all that came up were stories about the murder, which wasn't surprising. He tried "Steve Becker," but all that came up that time were stories of the murder too, and one or two about the Hugh Hefner Suite. He looked at the screen for a moment and got up again.

Here was what these people did, the way they lived, in a universe of publicity, a universe where nobody was really real unless he was very well known. It didn't matter among whom he was well known, or what he was well known for. It only mattered that he was front and center, that his name was in papers and magazines and on television, that people he didn't know had heard of him. There was no shame, in anything. Men of Gregor's generation would have been ashamed to be thought of as living on a woman's money. These men did not care, and some of them actively sought out women to take care of them. The public did not reject them for it. It laughed sometimes, but it didn't reject them, and when they got dumped it sometimes found itself sympathetic. Men and women both, in Bennis's generation, would have been ashamed to be seen living off family money. There was something snobbish about inheriting a pile of cash, and parasitic, and it had to be atoned for by good works. People like Kendra Rhode didn't mind being known for living off family money at all, and didn't see a reason why she should be expected to do anything. Doing was for people who absolutely had to, and boring. It wasn't "hot," and it wasn't "fun," and it wasn't anything to worry about. Family money, unlike the kind you had to earn, lasted forever.

Gregor looked back at the computer. Then he got a clean shirt out of the suitcase. Then he sat down on the side of the bed again and picked up the phone. He knew Bennis's cell phone number by heart, but he was hoping to get her at the apartment. More and more, he liked the entire idea of landlines.

Bennis picked up, saying "Hello" against a chorus of voices elsewhere in the apartment. It hadn't occurred to Gregor that she might have company.

"It's me," Gregor said. "What's going on over there? It sounds like you're holding a convention."

"I'm in the bedroom. There's a bunch of people in the living room. And some in the kitchen. Donna is throwing me a shower."

"You're having a party?"

"Sort of," Bennis said. "What about you? Where are you? Did you get in touch with Janet? They said on the news that you were going to give a press conference, and we thought we'd settle down and watch you."

"I have not gotten in touch with Janet," Gregor said, "but I did look up Box Hill Confections on the Internet. I'll get around to the other stuff you wanted me to do. Right now, I want you to do something for me. You're pretty good at searching for things on the Internet, right?"

"I'm good enough," Bennis said. "Donna's better."

"Fine, if Donna has time, get her to help you. I need you to find everything you can on a man named Steve Becker. I don't know if it's Stephen with a *ph* or with a *v*."

"Who is he? Or is the point that you don't know?"

"I'm not entirely sure who he is, in the ordinary way," Gregor said. "He was some kind of minor functionary on the film out here, and for a while he was Arrow Normand's boyfriend. Or something. I don't know what you call it in circumstances like these. Anyway, she went to Las Vegas with him and a group of other people, and they stayed in this ridiculously expensive—"

"Oh, I know," Bennis said. "The Hugh Hefner Suite at the Palms. I heard about that. It's nine thousand square feet and has its own pool, and it costs forty thousand dollars a night. Do you really mean you hadn't heard about that before you went out there?"

"It's not the kind of news I tend to pay attention to," Gregor said drily. "The thing is, Arrow Normand went out to Las Vegas with Steve Becker, but she came back with Mark Anderman—"

"The guy who was murdered," Bennis said.

"Right. Who was also a minor functionary on the movie. Arrow

Normand seems to have a habit of dating minor functionaries. Anyway, Steve Becker didn't return to the film, from what I can understand because he'd been fired. I think the idea is that you don't keep the toy boys around after they've outlived their usefulness, because they upset the stars, or something. My guess is that he's either sold his story to a tabloid or is in the process of negotiation to sell it, hopefully the former, except that I can't find it. There are stories with him in them, but nothing of him, you know, the way those stories are. 'I Spent a Night with Arrow Normand!' Nothing like that, that looks like he sold it himself. So maybe not. But I want to find him. I think it would be interesting to find out something about this situation from somebody with an ax to grind."

"Those guys usually disappear when they lose their famous friends," Bennis said. "There's not much else for them to do, Gregor. They aren't anybody."

"I know," Gregor said, "but it's been one of those things I've been thinking about. The toy boys aren't anybody, but neither is anybody else involved in this thing. There's enormous publicity, and apparently enormous public interest, and yet most of these people have minimal if any claims to prominence. They're not great singers or actors. They haven't invented anything. They don't run governments or corporations. The most diligent of them are like the teen idols of the fifties, except that they've taken on the kind of significance that used to be reserved for—I don't know whom it used to be reserved for. I've never seen anything like this before. Do you know that a horde of photographers tried to break down a door in the emergency room this afternoon to get pictures of Marcey Mandret lying in a hospital bed. Who the hell is Marcey Mandret?"

"She's an actress. She's been in a couple of movies."

"Not any of the movies I've ever seen," Gregor said. "It's almost a form of mass hysteria."

"Maybe it is," Bennis said. "I don't think you're going to save the soul of popular culture from the Oscartown Inn, though."

"I don't want to save the soul of popular culture," Gregor said. "I just want to find out enough about Mark Anderman to discover why somebody would want to risk virtually everything to kill him. Not that murderers are great at risk assessment, but you know what I mean."

"You mean you want me to find Steve Becker," Bennis said. "Not just stories about him, or even by him, but him."

"It does occur to me that if I had to have a suspect for the killing of Mark Anderman, Steve Becker, or somebody in Steve Becker's position, would be the most likely one."

"I've got to go get a tail pinned on me," Bennis said. "It's a game Donna thought up. I'll get Donna when this is over and we'll take a whack at it."

"A tail pinned on you with what?" Gregor asked.

Bennis had already hung up in his ear. Gregor put the phone back into the cradle and looked around the room. It was a very nice room, but he had to do something serious about getting dressed, and then he had to do something serious.

2

Gregor didn't know what he'd expected to find when he finally got Clara Walsh to let him talk to a real, live policeman, but it wasn't what he found when he made his way downstairs and was shown to "the Ivory Room" by one of the young men who manned the desk. He tried not to be too judgmental about the naming of the room. He hated it when hotels named rooms. He even hated it that the White House named rooms. He had expected, when he'd asked Clara Walsh to bring him somebody in law enforcement, that they'd meet in his own room, which would be cramped but private, and he really didn't care what a mess it was. Instead, exactly sixteen minutes after he'd hung up on Clara Walsh, there was a phone call from the desk and a request that he meet Clara in "the Ivory Room."

In his mind, men who served as the single law enforcement officer

245

in small towns were older, and balding, and running to fat. They were also not very bright. He had no idea where he had come up with that image. It didn't even fit Andy Taylor, and that was the single most famous image of a small-town sheriff in American popular culture. Still, it was the image he had, and when he walked through the door of the Ivory Room—which was being held open, politely, by the young man from the desk—he at first didn't realize what he was seeing. He saw Clara Walsh, looking like herself, and Bram Winder and Jerry Young, and a young man standing beside them, looking like a marine out of uniform.

A second later, Gregor realized that the young man who looked like a marine was a cop, and a second after that he was sure that the cop had once actually been a marine. He looked very young, barely out of high school, in fact, but Gregor guessed he was probably closer to thirty. He had the kind of posture that made you wonder if he had swallowed a flagpole.

The cop came forward and held out his hand. "Mr. Demarkian?" he said. "I'm Don Hecklewhite. I'm with the state police. I'm sorry to be out of uniform. It's my day off."

"Marines?" Gregor said.

"Yes, sir. Six years."

Clara Walsh cleared her throat. "It's no time to be talking about the military," she said. "If you were both marines, you can go someplace and get some beers and talk about it later. I have a press conference due to start in ten minutes, and we can hold them up for a while, but they're going to get restless. Could we get this done, whatever this is?"

"I was in the army," Gregor said. Then he let himself look around the Ivory Room. There was some real ivory in it, which surprised him. It was illegal to trade in ivory, and Oscartown was the kind of place where the guests would care. The ivory was in the form of carved pieces, many of them very elaborate, all of them looking a little yellow with age. Maybe ivory was morally all right if it was old enough. Maybe the guests had pieces at home, brought back from tours of India by grandparents in the days when killing elephants was just as natural as having champagne at debutante parties.

Gregor pushed all these images out of his head and concentrated on Don Hecklewhite. "You're on your own? You don't have a partner?"

"No, sir," Don Hecklewhite said. "We don't usually ride together. It's not efficient. And in this part of Massachusetts"—he shrugged—"there's not much call for us. It's like Oscartown. They take on some extra people in the season, but for the winter, Jerry here is it." Don Hecklewhite hesitated, then looked apologetically at Jerry. "I did talk to the town council about taking on at least one other man while the filming was going on. It's not as crowded as it is when the summer people are here, but at least in Oscartown itself there's been a significant uptick in the population. And an uptick in the population usually means trouble of one kind or another."

"And has there been that?" Gregor asked. "Trouble?"

On the other side of Clara Walsh, Jerry Young snorted. "Sort of. Nothing serious. A real rash of drug-related crap, the drugs they use for date rapes, and now there's Jack, and I haven't talked to him yet. And a lot of drinking and driving, which we get here in the winter in any case. Mostly the big problem has been the photographers. They camp."

"They camp?" Gregor asked.

"They don't put up at hotels," Clara Walsh put in. "Not that there'd be enough room for all of them anyway. But it's the middle of the winter. You'd think they'd want somewhere warm to go. Instead, most of them sleep in their cars, right outside the houses where the girls live. Young women. Whatever. They camp."

"Ah," Gregor said. "And these photographers, they're around all the time?"

"They came in when the film people did," Jerry Young said, "and they've been in ever since. Hordes of them. They camp out in front of the inn here, and at the houses where Marcey Mandret and Arrow Normand live, and outside where the filming is going on, and in the bars and places like that, anywhere they think they'll be able to get a photograph. We're falling over them all the time. They're falling all over each other. It's insane. And I think it's catching. Jack was getting like that for a while there."

"Jack, the man who just got drugged and hacked at?" Gregor asked.

"Yes, sir," Jerry Young said. "Jack's a photographer too, he's just local. He was chasing after them for a while there. He said he got good money for the pictures when Linda didn't want them. I used to have such a crush on Arrow Normand when I was in high school. Now she's in our jail, and nobody can figure out why. I thought these people had lawyers that got them out no matter what."

"Jack Bullard got attacked?" Don Hecklewhite said. "Why didn't anybody tell me that?"

"He got drugged and beat up," Jerry Young said. "I'll fill you in after all this. Somebody went at his hands and cut them up. No, not true. Just one hand. The right hand."

"Linda must be close to losing it," Don Hecklewhite said.

Clara Walsh looked exasperated. "O.J. had to stay in jail awaiting trial," she said. "It makes me crazy, this idea that the justice system stops dead just because the defendants are rich and famous."

"Well, it works for the rich," Jerry Young said. "Sorry, Ms. Walsh, but you know it's true." He turned to Gregor. "Do you know why I'm the only cop in town? Do you know why we take on a couple of extra men in the season, but we never really man up to a full complement? It's because nobody wants to arrest anybody here. These people who come in the summer, they're the heads of corporations, they're the heads of foundations and museums, we even get congressmen and senators and sometimes presidents. They get drunk and drive. Their kids get drunk and drive. We aren't really supposed to arrest anybody. We just pour them into the back of the cruiser and drop them at home, and if we pick up any one somebody too often, we suggest that maybe it might be a good idea to do a stint in rehab."

"And there aren't any real crimes?" Gregor asked. "At all?"

"Burglaries," Jerry Young said. "We get a fair amount of those, and I've gotten pretty good at handling them. And we get what are probably rapes, but nobody calls them that. And nobody will."

Gregor thought about it. In a way, this made perfect sense. The FBI and the Secret Service operated on similar principles when it came to guarding high-ranking government officials or their children. If a senator got nailed for driving drunk, it was almost always by the regular D.C. police or the police of some town where he wasn't known and nobody cared. He shifted focus.

"So," he said. "I asked for some information about Mark Anderman."

Don Hecklewhite leaned over Clara Walsh's shoulder and took a thick manila envelope off the lamp table at her side. "This is it," he said. "Everything we know about the man. Everything Jerry knows, and everything I know, plus a summary of the forensic report. It looks like a lot, but it isn't much. The bulk is mostly pictures of him with Arrow Normand. He was twenty-four. He graduated from some high school in California, not a place I'd ever heard of. He had a little string of minor arrests, disorderly conduct, public drunkenness, that sort of thing. Nothing much."

"And family?"

"None that we could find," Jerry Young said. "The stuff we got faxed from California mentioned a younger sister, but we weren't able to track her down. His father seems to have been long gone. His mother died about three years ago. He had a job, you know, that wasn't a very good one, except it let him hang around with Arrow Normand."

There was a knock on the door. Clara Walsh got up to see what it was about, and came back looking agitated. "That was the management," she said. "The Versailles Room is full of reporters and they're not being well behaved. The inn wants us to get in there and get this over with."

"In a second," Gregor said. "Something just occurred to me. You said the photographers were everywhere, all the time. They always

249

hung out where they thought they could get pictures of Marcey Mandret and Arrow Normand."

"That's right," Jerry said. "Leeches have a less firm grip, if you ask me."

"Where were they the night of the murder?" Gregor asked. "I don't remember seeing anything about them being near the truck when it crashed, or after the crash. And I've talked to Stewart, at length. He brought Marcey Mandret to Annabeth Falmer's house over his shoulder, and Arrow Normand showed up at Annabeth Falmer's door dead drunk, and yet nobody has mentioned anything about photographers being there at any time."

"It was the storm," Jerry Young said. "You weren't here when it happened, and you're not from around here, so I don't know if you understand just how bad a nor'easter like that can get. It doesn't usually, this early in the season, but this was a kicker. Most of these guys are from California. They're not used to that kind of weather."

Gregor thought about it some more. "Stewart showed me photographs taken at the scene that he took with his cell phone camera. I've got those photographs upstairs in my things somewhere, and I can show you later, but what I remember was that the hood, windshield, and the driver's-side door of the car were almost entirely cleaned off. This was before you got there, and before the state police got there. Was that a function of the truck being on and running warm?"

"I'll check," Jerry Young said, "but I don't think so. By the time I got there there was snow all over the truck and it wasn't running, but I don't know if it was running when Mr. Gordon got there and he turned it off, or what."

"No," Gregor said. "He would have known better than to turn it off."

"We really have to go," Clara Walsh said. "If this press conference turns into a brawl, we're going to be in more trouble than we are now."

Gregor reached into the inside pocket of his jacket and came up with Stewart Gordon's surprise, still in its clear plastic freezer bag.

Jerry Young blinked. Don Hecklewhite leaned forward. Clara Walsh blanched. Only Bram Winder had no reaction at all, and he wasn't paying attention.

Gregor handed the gun to Jerry Young, since he was technically the man in charge of the investigation. "Annabeth Falmer found that in her couch this afternoon," he said. "You'd better get it checked out. It was the same couch Arrow Normand was collapsed onto the day Mark Anderman was murdered, but I'd be willing to bet it wasn't Arrow Normand who brought it into the house."

SIX

1

In the first few moments after waking up, Jack Bullard thought he was in his bed at home. Then, when that didn't work—the light was all wrong; the windows were too large and horizontally rectangular; the colors were sickly and green—he wondered if he had ended up in the bed of some girl. There used to be a lot of girls when Jack was younger. That was especially true in high school. Margaret's Harbor was like a lot of places where the local community lived hand in glove with people much richer and more sophisticated than they were themselves. Advancement fever had infected it, and that meant that the local high schools were full of year-round kids with dreams of going off to the Ivy League, or something close. It was not "cool" to be stupid at Margaret's Harbor High School, even though the school served the whole island instead of any one town, and it was full of fishermen's children who resented the hell out of the entire system. No, the biggest status symbol at MHHS was an acceptance letter to someplace "good," and until you were in your senior year and had one, the assumption was that you were "smart" enough to get one.

Jack had always been smart enough. He had always had a place at the best table in the lunchroom, and the attention of the best girls, who were all "smart" enough too. There were dumb blondes at MHHS, and even cheerleaders, but nobody ever took them seriously.

One of the reasons Jack thought he might be waking up with a girl was that there was a girl in the room, over by the windows, standing with her back to him, looking out. Jack wished that he could concentrate, or even make himself sit up. He had what felt like the mother of all hangovers. It had even invaded his limbs. They all felt weak. He wasn't certain, because he was numb all across his torso, but he was pretty sure his penis was weak too, and just lying there, which might explain why the girl was fully dressed and at the window while he was here in bed and definitely not. It had been a while since there had been hot and cold running girls in his life. College was not everything he had expected it to be. There, everybody had been "smart," and a lot of people were smarter than he was, and a lot of them were richer, too. It was hard to compete when the girls thought it was sweet but kind of pathetic that he had never been to Europe. Jack thought that it might have been in college when he first began to realize that life was more complicated than he had expected it to be, and that he did not want to be the kind of corporation lawyer his education would best suit him for. Corporation lawyers made lots of money, but they weren't anybody. They were as invisible as he had been most of his life, and the money did not make up for it.

He was blithering in his head. Maybe he had blithered to this girl, and that was why she had gotten out of bed and left him alone in it. He wished he could think. He wished his head weren't pounding. He wished a lot of things, the most urgent of which seemed to be that he had been able to explain it all to his mother before she died. His mother had not approved of any of the girls he had gone out with in high school. She was always afraid he would get one of them pregnant and ruin everything.

The girl at the window turned, and Jack noticed a number of

things at once. First, he was in a hospital room. It was a bare, blank hospital room, and from the silence all around him it seemed as if the rest of the hospital was empty. He tried to remember everything he could about the hospital in Oscartown, but there was nothing to remember. He'd spent almost no time there. He had no idea if it did a lot of business or not, if it was normal or odd that the place should be dead silent and cavernously empty. Then there was his right hand. It was bandaged up like something in an Abbott and Costello movie, into a wad that looked almost like a fighter's glove. When he tried to move his fingers, they hurt badly enough so that he wanted to cry out in pain. He didn't. He wasn't entirely sure why. He felt as if he were in an episode of *The Twilight Zone,* so that he knew that making noise would be bad for him, but he didn't know why.

The third thing he noticed was that the girl was not just a girl. It was Kendra Rhode.

If he could have sat up or reached for anything in any way, he would have grabbed the white styrofoam cup that was sitting next to a can of ginger ale on a flat, high table next to his bed. Ginger ale would be good. Anything would be good. His mouth was dry. His head still hurt. He wanted to reach out and touch Kendra's arm, that perfect arm. In a world of ghosts, of outlines of people without substance, Kendra was one of the very few whose outlines had been all filled in.

She was leaning against the heating register under the windows, looking at him. She knew he was awake. Jack stuck the tip of his tongue out and tried to lick his lips, but his tongue was dry. He was lucky it didn't stick out there, making him look like a retarded person.

"Kendra," he said. It came out, but only barely. He made another effort. "I thought you. Weren't. Weren't. Talking."

Kendra came over and looked down at him in the bed. It wouldn't occur to her to offer to get him ginger ale, but he didn't mind that. He was a ghost. She had no reason to think he needed ginger ale. He really was blithering. He was. How close to the sun did you have to get before you got warm? How close to the sun did you have to get to burn yourself dead? Was heat better than light? Would light illuminate you if you were only an outline of a person, if there was nothing really real about you?

He put out his hand, and she got the idea. She picked up the cup and looked inside it. Then she popped the top on the can of ginger ale and poured some of it in. Jack's hand was still out. She put the styrofoam cup full of ginger ale in his hand. It was his left hand. It didn't work that well. He spilled more ginger ale down the side of his face than he got into his mouth.

Still, it worked. It worked well enough. "I thought," he said, and this time the words came out the way they should have, although he sounded hoarse, "I thought you weren't talking to me."

"I'm not talking to you," Kendra said. "Why should I talk to you? You betrayed me."

"I didn't betray you. I sold one picture. I have to sell pictures. That's how I make a living."

"You sold the wrong picture."

"No," Jack said. And this was true. He remembered the pictures. He remembered the one he sold, and he remembered the ones he still had back at the house. "There were other pictures," he said. "There were worse pictures."

Kendra turned away, back to the window again. Jack hated this. He hated it. When she was not looking at him, he felt as if he weren't really real. It was as if she took some part of him with her. This was an important point. Before the movie people had come to Margaret's Harbor, Jack had spent most of his time feeling not really real, feeling as if he were a ghost, but he hadn't been able to pin it down to something specific. Now he thought he had, and it was only this terrific dryness in his mouth and throat that was keeping him from articulating it.

He tried to drink more ginger ale. He got some. He got more down his face and neck. There was a point here. There really was. He only had to grasp it.

"Why am I here?" he said.

Kendra turned around again. Jack felt warm. "You're in the hospital," she said. "Something happened to your hand."

"What?"

"I don't know," Kendra said. "I didn't even know you were in the hospital. Marcey's downstairs. With alcohol poisoning, the silly cunt. I was walking back to the Point from the inn and there were all these paparazzi, trying to get a picture of Marcey on her ass, so I ducked in a door. It's not true that I always want my picture taken."

"I know," Jack said.

"I don't know what I'm going to do about Marcey," Kendra said. "It's bad enough with Arrow. Not that I think she killed anyone. But the police do. Maybe they're going to give her the electric chair. Do they have the electric chair in Massachusetts? Maybe it's all lethal injection now. I don't like lethal injection. It lacks drama. It lacks everything, really. People go to be witnesses at executions, but with lethal injection there isn't anything they can see that they wouldn't be able to see anytime. The electric chair would be better. People would jump."

Jack wanted to put the styrofoam cup back on the table, but he didn't know how to do it. He was suddenly infinitely, inconsolably depressed. He had no idea why Kendra had come into this room, or why she would have been going back to the Point on the back streets she would have had to use to end up at the hospital, but he did know that she had done none of those things out of a desire to see him. It should have been enough that she still recognized him, but it wasn't. And that was in spite of the fact that he knew she was perfectly capable of treating people as if they had never existed, even after she'd known them for years.

"I want to know what happened to me," he said.

Kendra turned away from the window. "I think I can get out now, if I go out this end. They're all over there. They don't seem to be moving. Marcey's such an ass. She's always flashing around making an idiot of herself."

"I want to know what happened to me," Jack said again.

"I don't know what happened to you," Kendra said. "Maybe it will be on the news, and you can find out that way. There's going to be something about me on the news in a day or two. You should watch for it. That is, if Marcey and Arrow haven't done some other stupid stuff and everybody is watching that."

Jack wanted to say that Kendra was always on the news. She was even on the real news, like CNN. Instead, he watched her check through her purse for he didn't know what and then send him the kind of little smile and wave she gave to photographers when she wasn't feeling antagonistic about being photographed. Then she was gone, out in the hallway, out of sight. He couldn't even hear her footsteps walking away.

He was still lying in bed with the styrofoam cup in his left hand. The cup was still half full of ginger ale. He still couldn't put it down.

This was a metaphor for something, and as soon as his head cleared up, he would figure out for what. At the moment, he was only angry, as angry as he had ever been in his life, the kind of angry that makes some people rise up like rockets and lay waste the landscape, and in no time at all he was actually sitting all the way up.

2

If Linda Beecham had stayed just five more minutes in Jack Bullard's room, she would have seen Kendra Rhode coming in, but she didn't. Instead, she left while there was nobody else there, and not much of anybody on the floor. She walked down the long empty hall to the elevators, looking into empty rooms to the right and left of her. She wondered why nobody in Oscartown ever seemed to be sick in the winter, and then reminded herself that most of the residents who really were residents probably lacked health insurance. Health insurance was one of those things she had been careful to provide for all her employees at the *Home News.* She even provided it for part-time people and the cleaning staff. It was one of the things she remembered best about the years of having no money at all, and one of the things she resented most. If the *Home News* had had a political ideology, it would have been solidly liberal in most ways, but it would have been downright socialist on the subject of health insurance. If Linda Beecham got to run the country, health care would be universal, government-provided, and without limits. It would be like the best of the policies afforded to multimillion-dollar-earning CEOs, but for everybody.

There was a lot of commotion on the ground floor at the front, and Linda stopped for a minute to watch it. There was an assault going on, against the emergency room. Linda recognized the signs of what she had come over the last few months to think of as "the barbarian hordes," and she wondered which of the women they followed had managed to get herself into a state this time. There was too much of everything wandering around Oscartown these days. The film people brought in everything bad the summer people did, but they brought in more. They brought in this mania for public display. Linda thought there was something profoundly wrong with anybody who wanted to have her picture in the papers. Publicity meant exposure, and exposure turned you into a target. Linda knew all about being a target.

She stood on the pavement near the hospital's front door, watching the door a few yards down where the emergency room was. She thought that if there was a real emergency anywhere on the island, the ambulance wouldn't be able to get out of its stall to get to it, and wouldn't be able to get up to the emergency room door to bring the patient in. She thought about Jack upstairs in that empty room on that empty corridor, the nurse by herself at the station, reading through a magazine, noticing nothing that was going on. Lately, it was brought home to her again and again just how uninhabited Margaret's Harbor really was. They were all out here, wandering around on their own. What they had once stood for didn't matter to anybody, and most of them couldn't remember what it had been. There was a Fox News van jammed right up onto the sidewalk in front, and Linda suddenly realized that its presence so far up on the pavement made the emergency room's sliding glass doors stay permanently open, in the middle of winter, with temperatures below freezing and heading to something dangerous the closer it got to night. They had a different set of priorities, these people. They cared about things that were—

But Linda didn't know what they were, and finally she turned away from the scene and began to make her way toward the center of town. Nobody was interested in her anyway. She wasn't a recognizable face, and she was middle-aged and tired. These days you had to sparkle and shine to get noticed, and sometimes even that didn't work.

When she got out onto Main Street, she looked up at the Congregational church and the clock on its spire, and realized she'd spent more time than she'd thought she had watching the news vans. She'd left Jack's room at one—she knew because she'd checked her watch while she was waiting for the elevator—and it was now almost quarter to two. Main Street was as deserted as it would have been if this were an ordinary winter. She passed Cuddy's, looking through its tinted-glass windows while she walked. It was dead empty. Only Dora Malvern, who worked the afternoons as a waitress, and Chuck Verle, who did the same as a bartender, were inside. In a way, that was surprising. There were "real people" bars in Oscartown, on the back streets and down near the ferry, but during the off-season the fishermen took possession of the places the summer people liked to go. It was a matter of pride.

She passed the front of the Oscartown Inn, which was also deserted. She supposed Mr. Demarkian must be inside, doing whatever consultants did when they were called in to a crime the police couldn't solve. She didn't see the point of it. The police had Arrow Normand under arrest. If Arrow Normand had been any ordinary girl from the island, she'd have been locked up for serious and on her way to a trial without calling in consultants from as far away as

Philadelphia. Linda had an editorial about it, set and ready to go in the next issue of the *Home News.* It was taxpayer money Clara Walsh was wasting on this Gregor Demarkian, and taxpayer money she was wasting on her attempts to tie herself into a pretzel so that the world wouldn't think she was being unduly harsh to Little Miss Pantyless Wonder. Or something. It was so very cold now. The wind was coming in off the ocean. It chased down Main Street and made the signs shudder and sway. Jack was up there at the hospital. He might never be able to use his right hand again. He would almost certainly never be able to feel anything with his fingertips.

She got to the *Home News* and let herself in the front door. This was not something she usually did. She usually used the side entrance, which had stairs directly up to her office. She stopped in the big front room and looked at displays of last week's edition. The lead story was about the proposed new system of charging for sewer services. It was the kind of thing people who lived on the island really needed to know. The story of the murder was below the fold. There were no pictures of Arrow Normand or Marcey Mandret or any of the rest of them, and the headline said: "Crime Scene on Beach." There was a picture of Mark Anderman, lifted from a wire-service story, but it was tiny, so tiny you'd need a magnifying glass to make out the features. Linda suddenly felt enormously satisfied by the whole thing.

She was just about to go upstairs when the door to the street opened, and instead of her usual customers—somebody from the IGA with this week's ad; somebody who wanted to advertise a used lawn mower for sale or a litter of puppies in need of a home—a too-well-dressed middle-aged man came in, wearing a serious city coat instead of a parka. It took her a moment to recognize him. It was obvious to her, from the way he looked at her, that he didn't expect her to recognize him at all.

"Carl Frank," he said, holding out his hand. "I'm—"

"I know who you are," Linda Beecham said. "You're Michael Bardman's hit man."

"I'm the publicity director for the movie," Carl Frank said.

Linda turned away from him. It was time to go upstairs and get some work done. Without Jack here, there was a lot of work to do, a lot of work she had forgotten had to be done. It was odd how you got used to things like that.

"I came to see you," Carl Frank said. "If you wouldn't mind. We could talk."

Linda turned back. "I do mind," she said. "I don't see what we have to talk about. I don't print stories about the movie. I don't even print stories about the people who are in the movie. Except for the one about the murder, and that was only because it was inevitable."

"I know," Carl Frank said. He looked around the big front room, at the two young women taking telephone calls, at the blown-up covers of old editions of the *Home News* in their stainless-steel frames. The covers were from before Linda's time, but she had kept them because she remembered them. The time JFK and Jackie had come to Oscartown. The time Amanda Kay Adams had made it all the way to the U.S. Olympic figure-skating team. Carl Frank didn't seem to be impressed. "Couldn't we talk," he said, "somewhere out of the way?"

Linda turned her back on him and headed upstairs, but she didn't tell him he couldn't come, and she didn't protest when she heard him behind her. She let herself into her big second-floor office. This was still her favorite place in town. She could see everything from here, or at least everything on Main Street. She took off her parka and put it on the coat tree. She pulled out the chair behind her desk and sat down. Time seemed to be oddly warped. The clock on the Congregational church now said two fifteen.

Carl Frank closed the door to the stairs and looked around for a chair. There was one, but not a comfortable one, because Linda didn't like people to stay too long in her office.

Carl Frank took the chair anyway and brought it as close to Linda's desk as he dared. Then he sat down in it. "I know you don't run stories about the movie," he said. "I know you didn't run much of one on the murder. But you're not the only one here. You have a full-time photographer, and he takes a lot of pictures. I've seen one of them."

"He won't be taking any more pictures anytime soon," Linda said flatly. "He's in the hospital. He's going to be there for a while."

"In the hospital for what?"

Linda almost said it was none of his business. "He was attacked by somebody who mangled his hand," she said. "He was drugged, with one of those date rape drugs. Drugged enough to get knocked out cold."

"Really? You can die that way, taking that much of those things."

"I know."

"Do the police know who did it?"

Linda treated this with the contempt it deserved. By now, Carl Frank had to know that Jerry Young was the only policeman in town, and that he'd hardly be in a position to "know who did it" almost as soon as it was done. Except, of course, that in other circumstances, in the normal way of life, he would know. That was part of what it meant to live in a small town. You got to know people too well. You got to understand them.

"I'm sorry about your photographer," Carl Frank said, "but it's you I wanted to talk to. He takes pictures. I understand he takes pictures for you."

"He takes pictures for himself," Linda said, "and I get first crack at them. I don't publish stories on the movie, Mr. Frank, and I'm not interested in using those pictures. Jack sells them where he can for the extra money, and I'm happy to let him."

"He took pictures on the Vegas trip," Carl Frank said. "Did you see those pictures?"

"I saw the one everyone's seen," Linda said. "It's impossible to avoid it, especially since the murder."

"He took other pictures."

"I'm sure he did," Linda said, "but he wouldn't have bothered to

262

show them to me. If I'm not going to be interested in pictures of Arrow Normand and Marcey Mandret and Kendra Rhode right here on the island, I'm not going to be interested in them in Las Vegas. It's beyond my comprehension why anybody's interested in them."

Carl Frank stared at her for a long moment, long enough to make her uncomfortable, and Linda Beecham was never uncomfortable. Then he turned around and looked out the big plate glass window onto Main Street.

"You can see everything from here," he said, turning back. "I envy you. Almost everything I need to keep track of is just out of sight. Is your photographer hurt too badly to talk to me about a proposition?"

"When I left him, he wasn't even awake."

"All right. Then I'll wait a few days," Carl Frank said. "But I'll be back. And I've got the impression that you have some influence here, so I'll leave the message with you. He did take other pictures on the Vegas trip. Do you know why he hasn't sold any of them to the tabloids?"

"No," Linda said. "Do you?"

"No," Carl Frank said. "And I have to admit, I think it's odd. But odd or not, it's the fact, and I can work with the fact. I want to buy the pictures. Negatives, digital memory resources, whatever. I want them all, and I want all the possible avenues of reproducing them, and I'm willing to pay a lot to get them. Say, something on the order of one hundred thousand dollars."

"What?"

Carl Frank stood up. "I told you I was serious," he said. "One hundred thousand dollars. But I've got to have them all, and I've got to have a signed contract attesting to the fact that I have them all, because if one of them surfaces after I've paid for them, I have every intention of filing the world's biggest bitch of a lawsuit. I don't know what he's saving them for. I don't care. I'm pretty sure he'll never do any better than what I'm offering. I'll make the offer to him myself in a couple of days, when he's feeling better. In the meantime, it would be good of you to mention my offer to him when you've got a chance."

Linda Beecham rubbed her hands together. Carl Frank was taller than she'd originally thought. Either that, or he had the ability to loom when he wanted to. She felt as if she were standing under a vulture. She was also suddenly cold again, although she shouldn't be. Jack was always warning her that windows provided no insulation.

"Well," Carl Frank said. "I'll go. Have a good day."

3

Over at the Oscartown Memorial Hospital, Jack Bullard was considering the possibility that he had just made the biggest mistake of his life—except that he really couldn't be said to be considering anything, because that would have taken too much energy. He was out of bed. He had been out of bed for minutes, or maybe hours. He didn't know. He was out, and on his feet, and he should never have done it. Never. He thought he was going to throw up.

The bed was a long way away. It was across the floor, on the other side of the world. He was in the hallway. He couldn't remember exactly how he had gotten there. He was just so angry at being confined, so angry at his body for not working, and in the end he couldn't just lie where he was and not move. His hand hurt. Both of them did, but the right hand, the one with the bandage on it, was killing him. It was not a pain he felt directly. If he had felt it directly, he would have died. Instead, the pain was out there somewhere, wandering around, teasing him. His head hurt too. His right hand was bleeding. He thought he might have stitches. He thought he might have ripped them open. There was blood everywhere.

It was lying there holding the styrofoam cup of ginger ale that had done it. He remembered looking at the cup and the way it seemed to float above him, the way his own left hand seemed to float there too, but weigh a million pounds, and then the silence of the corridor, the silence that should have had footsteps in it.

And then the silence wasn't the silence. There was noise. He could hear it. There was noise from downstairs and noise in the stairwell and everything, nothing, it didn't matter. He could hear himself calling out. His voice sounded like it belonged to somebody else. He wondered where the nurse was. He wondered why nobody had seen him. He thought he had been moving very fast, moving against the pain, moving and moving and moving until it was all over, and now the stitches on his hand were torn and there was blood and he was passing out in the middle of the empty corridor, with the emptiness and the ghosts all around him.

SEVEN

1

Gregor Demarkian had been to press conferences before, more than he could count. He had even been to press conferences where there was a certain amount of fame involved. What he hadn't done, and what he hadn't had time to consider the ramifications of, was to be at a press conference where the object of interest was himself. Even now, checking his tie in a mirror in the men's dressing room off the Ivory Room of the Oscartown Inn, he was thinking more of Arrow Normand than he was of Gregor Demarkian. He had noticed the crowd of people making its way into the Versailles Room—what did it mean, that an inn in one of the oldest parts of New England, an inn that could trace its continuous operation to before the American Revolution, named its largest and most prestigious ballroom after a palace of decadence in pre-Revolutionary France? The crowd looked as if it had blood on its hands, and there were too many photographers, but Gregor chalked it up to the level of competition involved in this thing. For reasons he would never fully understand, news outlets around the world would pay thousands of dollars for the right kind of pictures of people who had done little or nothing in their lives. Arrow Normand, Marcey Mandret, Kendra Rhode, even that silly woman Anna Nicole Smith, who was constructing her life as a parody, could make a man a quarter of a million dollars in a single day if only he could get them where he wanted them and get them alone. It was the alone that mattered. It was exclusivity that brought in the real cash. It was something that made Gregor Demarkian wonder why these people wanted to pay any attention to him at all.

"It's the dead-air problem," Bram Winder said helpfully while he waited for Gregor to stop fussing with himself and let them all get on with it. "In a story like this, there are a hundred different important things that happen, but they happen in clumps. The rest of the time, there's nothing, there's no news. But these people can't handle the prospect of no news. They've got to have something. So they take whatever they can get."

"Can they always get something?" Gregor asked. "Isn't there ever a point where there's just no news at all?"

"All the time," Bram said. "Then they just blither. They get up there on television and talk about what happened, then they talk about why they're so obsessed with it happening, then they talk about why the public is so obsessed with it happening, which is a little off if you ask me, because the public wouldn't be so obsessed with it happening if the news media wasn't obsessed with it happening. If you know what I mean."

Gregor considered it. His tie was straight, but for some reason he still wasn't ready to go out and face questions, and that in spite of the fact that he had no real answers to give anybody. "Do you really think that's true?" he asked. "That people only care because the media cares? I'll admit, this isn't my sort of thing—well, I mean people like Arrow Normand aren't my sort of thing—but I've seen this material. I go to newsstands. I channel surf every once in a while. Somebody must be interested. The news is everywhere."

"It's like a gigantic national high school," Bram Winder said. He sounded sour. "And not a good high school, either. Not a New England high school. Like one of those high schools you see in the teen movies where everything depends on sports and the popular crowd. These people are the popular crowd. Nobody knows why. Nobody ever knows why. But they are."

The door to the dressing room popped open and Clara Walsh stuck her head in. "You can't just stand around fidgeting," she said. "This thing is due to start any minute—"

Gregor checked his watch. "Five minutes," he said.

"Whatever," Clara said. "We really can't afford to be late. They're in a very ugly mood, and the thing with Marcey Mandret this afternoon hasn't made them any better. It's useless trying to explain to people that a woman can't grant interviews when she's passed out cold, and it's less than useless to explain why the hospital would be legally liable if it let you take a picture of the woman that way, and so now they're all snarling, and blaming it on me. I wish you'd hurry up."

"What about Jerry Young and Don Hecklewhite?" Gregor said. "It would be something if we could announce that we'd found the gun, or something that could be the gun. They don't need complete forensics for that. They only need to check the raw facts against—"

Clara White made a face. "Honestly," she said. "We can't announce that now. We really can't announce where we found it. I want to keep my job, and I'll agree that looking like I'm doing something in this case would help with that, but I think Annabeth Falmer would probably have grounds to sue if I let it out like that. Or if you did. Jerry and Don will do what they can. Just hurry up."

Gregor was hurrying. He watched Clara Walsh disappear through the swinging door and fixed his tie again, unnecessarily. Then he looked at Bram Winder, up and down.

"Are you worried about that?" he asked. "Losing your job?"

"No," Bram said. "I don't think Clara is either, not really. She's just worried she's going to screw this up."

"Do you think that gun was the one used in the murder of Mark Anderman?"

"I think only the forensics could tell us for sure," Bram said, "but you've got all the information right there. You've got manila envelopes full of it. You could make that call just as well as I could. Maybe better."

"All right," Gregor said. "Then I will. I do think it's going to turn out to be the gun. It smelled new, but that may only mean that it was fired just the one time, and then cleaned. In the short run, though, in the absence of a bullet, it's going to be very hard to tell. It's possible that it's going to be too hard to tell even to bring it into a courtroom. Which leaves a couple of interesting questions."

"Like what?"

"Well," Gregor said, "like how it got into Annabeth Falmer's couch. I think the idea is that we're supposed to believe Arrow Normand left it there when she was at Annabeth's house on the night Mark Anderman was murdered. But that's got two problems. First is that, from all accounts, Arrow Normand was wearing so little in the way of clothes it would have been impossible for her to conceal a large, heavy gun of that kind on her person. But you know, that's not really a deal breaker. Stranger things have happened. The deal breaker is something else."

"What?"

"The fact that the gun smells new," Gregor said. "If it's ever been fired, it must have been cleaned. So either the gun is new, and it isn't the gun used in the murder, or the gun is the one that was used in the murder, but it's been cleaned. But Arrow Normand has been in jail more or less continuously since New Year's Eve."

"New Year's Day," Bram Winder said. "Jerry Young didn't. Well, he wouldn't. Right on the spot like that, if you see what I mean. He had to—"

"He had to be reasonably sure, yes," Gregor said. "Still, there isn't enough time for her to have taken the gun, cleaned it, and then put it in the couch, and why would she want to put it in the couch anyway? She'd only be implicating herself."

"Maybe she thought she would be implicating Marcey instead," Bram suggested. "Marcey was there that day too."

"I know," Gregor said. "And I know everybody assumes that Arrow Normand is too stupid to walk and talk at the same time, but that's a little far-fetched. I'd say that she just got a break. If that's the gun that was used in the murder, and it's been cleaned, then that fact and the fact that it would have to have been put in the couch well after Arrow Normand was on it pretty much get Arrow Normand off the hook here. It does make it a little more difficult for me. I could have sworn, looking at this material, that there was only one possible solution to any of this, but—"

"Wait," Bram Winder said. "You think you know who committed this murder? Already?"

"I think there's only one person where the psychology will fit," Gregor said. "Although I'll admit that I'm guessing, since I haven't really talked to much of anybody yet. If I was constructing this as the plot of a novel, or a television show, or a film—"

"But this isn't a novel or a television show or a film," Bram Winder protested. "God, I hate this. The world isn't a movie. No matter what anybody thinks. In real life, in real crimes, things don't turn out the way they do on *CSI: Miami.* Never mind the fact that real-life forensics are not nearly that good. In real life, crimes are messy, and they don't make much sense."

"I'm not saying this crime makes sense," Gregor said. "I'm saying that murders usually have motives. And in this case, there's only one person for whom there is a motive that makes any sense at all. Even though, as I said, I'm guessing, because I haven't talked to much of anybody yet. And then there is the problem that although my guess can certainly have committed the murder of Mark Anderman, there are a few other things connected to this case that—well. . . ."

"That what?" Bram Winder said. "That he couldn't have done? Or she? What other things are connected to this case anyway? I can't believe you're doing this. I think you're crazy. You're going to get us all killed."

The room was suddenly filled with the opening bars of Beethoven's Fifth Symphony. Gregor got the cell phone Bennis had given him out of his pocket and checked the caller ID. It was Bennis, not Tibor, which probably meant that the call was more than side issues, and he ought to take it. Of course, it could be about the wedding, and then he would have wasted his time.

"Could you give me a second?" he said. "I've got to take this call."

"I think you're crazy," Bram Winder said. "I think you're so crazy, you're going to be the worst idea Clara ever had, and I'm going to go down with her."

Then he stalked out of the men's sitting room with all the dignity of the hero of an Oscar Wilde farce.

2

Gregor Demarkian didn't really need to take this call right this minute. In fact, in spite of the excuses he made in his own head, he was fairly sure that this could be nothing but Bennis hyperventilating about the wedding again, or, worse, Donna on Bennis's phone, demanding answers to questions he didn't begin to understand. Did he want silk or organdy for the bows on the pews at church? Did he prefer gold charms with Jordan almonds for reception favors, or something more modern, but bulkier? He was sure grooms did not have to make these decisions in most weddings. He knew he had never had to make them for his wedding to Elizabeth. Of course, Elizabeth's mother had been alive, and very active, when that had happened. Maybe Bennis's problem was that she didn't have her mother to arrange her wedding.

On the other hand, Bennis's mother had been a Day, a real

daughter of the old Main Line, and having that woman arrange his wedding would probably have been even worse than having Donna arrange it. And he would have liked the people less.

He fiddled with the buttons he got wrong half the time and said, "Hello," as he put the phone to his ear, hoping. It worked. Bennis's voice came bouncing at him, a little hiccough-y the way voices on cell phones got.

"You're supposed to say 'Demarkian here,' or something like that," she said. "Not just 'Hello.'"

" 'Hello' is what I always say when I pick up the phone. I'm trying to avoid the imminent start of a press conference here, so I'd appreciate it if you'd talk to me a little. I take it this is about the wedding."

"No," Bennis said. "Actually, not, although if you've gotten in touch with Janet, I'd appreciate it. I mean, really, Gregor, hand made chocolates, and all she wants is to sound you out about it. She's trying to be conscientious here. She is being conscientious here. And they're very good chocolates. So cooperate."

"I thought you said this wasn't about the wedding," Gregor said.

There was a sigh on the other end of the line, the kind of sigh all women perfected, on the assumption that all men were inherently impossible. "I called a friend of mine," Bennis said. "I mean, I know you said to check the Internet, and I would have gotten around to it eventually, and I will if you still want me to. But I called a woman I knew at Vassar. At the moment, she's the editor in chief of *Celebrity* magazine."

Gregor thought about that for a moment. "Should I be impressed with that?" he asked.

"Well, Iris isn't," Bennis said, "but for your purposes at the moment, she's perfect. *Celebrity* magazine is about celebrities, which Iris defines as 'people who are famous who haven't actually done anything.' I thought that was a little harsh, considering the fact that the celebrities you're interested in are all making a movie, which is doing something, if not something as important as bringing an end to the conflict in Palestine. Is Stewart Gordon going to come to our wedding?"

"If you invite him, he probably will," Gregor said. "Although I think he's falling in love, so you'd better let him bring a guest. Does this Iris person know where Steve Becker is and what's he's doing?"

"Yes, she does," Bennis said, "and she knows a lot more than that. Steve Becker is associate producer on a movie tentatively called *Nemesis Rising* that is, at the moment, filming somewhere in Canada. He started there on December fifth. Don't go looking in your notes. I have it. The Las Vegas trip was November eleventh. Anyway, it's anybody's guess how he suddenly got to be an associate producer when all he was on that movie of yours was a grip, but the general feeling seems to be that Michael Bardman paid him off."

"All right," Gregor said. "Even I've heard of Michael Bardman. Isn't he the head of some studio or the other?"

"Of Archer Entertainment, yes, which is a production company, which is not exactly the same thing as a studio. But it's also Archer Entertainment that's making your movie, so you see how that could work."

"Michael Bardman is out here?" Gregor asked.

Bennis was exasperated. "Of course not. Michael Bardman doesn't go running around to location sites for minor films, even his own minor films. He's always got some guy on the production whose main job is to report to him and keep things moving and cool. On your movie, it's a guy named Carl Frank. His official title is head of public relations for the movie, or something like that. If you haven't seen him around just yet, there's this picture of all of them, well not really of him, of Arrow Normand and Steve Becker and Kendra Rhode and all of them when they first got to Vegas on that ridiculous trip—"

"I know the picture," Gregor said. "They're all standing in a line with their arms around each other's shoulders."

"That's the one. Carl Frank is just in the background to the left, practically like the devil waiting to score a soul. Or something. Ignore me. I've been talking to Tibor. They're all in that picture. Carl Frank is in the back. Mark Anderman is standing next to Kendra Rhode with his left arm around her neck, practically hanging on her, and Steve Becker is on the other side of her, with his right arm around Kendra Rhode and his left behind Arrow Normand's back. And that, you see, is the big deal. The picture."

"The picture is a big deal?" The door to the dressing room had opened and Bram Winder was standing in it, looking thunderous. Gregor waved him away and turned so that he couldn't see him. "It didn't look like a big deal," Gregor told Bennis. "It's a staged shot, from what I can see. And there's something wrong with the light."

"I know," Bennis said. "The flash glinted off somebody's jewelry and spoiled the effect. But it doesn't really matter what the effect is, because that picture is the only one. There are some other pictures, single shots here and there, a few people got with cell phone cameras, but the thing about the Vegas trip is that they managed to go out there without the usual army of photographers. According to Iris, that's because of two things. First, there weren't that many photographers hanging around the set on Margaret's Harbor before the murder. There were a few, you know, but these guys have to make a living, and there wasn't enough action on Margaret's Harbor to make it feasible for most of them to hang on full-time. Add to that the fact that Kendra Rhode had adopted some local newspaper reporter as practically her court photographer, and most of the big-time guys stayed in L.A. The other thing has to do with the posses."

Gregor sighed. "I take it we're not talking about the old West," he said.

"Don't be ridiculous," Bennis said. "No, the posses are the entourages, what these people call their entourages. Most of them travel with huge crowds of people. Assistants. Makeup artists. Hair people. Other people who just seem to be along for the ride. Iris said something about one woman who does nothing but carry water for somebody. I'm sorry, I can't remember who. Anyway, the posses are huge, usually between thirty and fifty people, and they're all paid. And they're not in Margaret's Harbor, because Michael Bardman had a full-time fit about the way they were mucking up the filming. Apparently the movie is over budget and behind schedule, and somewhere around the middle of October he told Arrow Normand and Marcey Mandret to send their people home for the duration or he'd fire both of them. And he didn't just tell them. He wrote a letter and he leaked the letter to CNN, so it was all over everywhere. Anyway, they took the hint, and the entourages dispersed to points unknown, probably back to California. So there was nobody to alert the press when Arrow and friends took off for Las Vegas. Do you see what I mean?"

"Sort of," Gregor said. "This was a stealth operation."

Bennis laughed. "Nothing with these people is really a stealth anything," she said, "but without the posses it was a lot easier for them to move around without being noticed, and they did. They were in Vegas for hours before anybody from the press realized they were there. They came in on a private jet. Kendra Rhode's private jet, by the way. They hired a car to take them to the hotel. They checked in. They got dressed up and went out. They had time to pose for that picture you saw, and probably a lot of other things, and it was nearly eleven before the regular press knew they were there. And then they weren't for much longer. They just retreated to the Hugh Hefner Suite and made like a fortress. And then, the next day, they came home."

"With somewhat more publicity?"

"A little more," Bennis said, "but it was very early in the morning, around six or seven, so not as much as you might think. And it's driving everybody crazy. Because this local guy, the one Kendra Rhode turned into something like her personal photographer on Margaret's Harbor, he was with them, and people saw him taking pictures, but the only picture that's ever come out has been that one I told you about, the one you saw, with all of them together. There are people who'd pay a lot of money for a few more of them, especially if there are any from inside the Hugh Hefner Suite. Iris said people have contacted this guy, this—"

"Jack Bullard," Gregor said.

"That's right. That's it. People have contacted him, but all he says is that he doesn't have anything to sell, which nobody on earth believes. The best guess there is that he's saving them up for a book for later, that there's something really nasty in what he's got, something unusual. But so far, not a thing. And Iris says the word around town is that Kendra Rhode has dumped him anyway—nobody will say why."

"But presumably because of something in the pictures," Gregor said.

"I told you I could do better than just look up things on the Internet," Bennis said. "Is any of this any help to you at all? Does it make any sense? None of these people make any sense to me, and I've been around famous people most of my life."

Gregor was going to tell her there was a difference between fame and celebrity—it was a lecture he'd heard more than once from Father Tibor—but Clara Walsh had slammed back the dressing room's swinging door and was marching on him, men's room atmosphere be damned.

3

When Gregor finally went into the Versailles Room, it wasn't as bad as he'd feared, although it was odd enough. The room lived up to its name in some ways. The walls were all lined with mirrors, making the space look seven or eight times as large as it was. And the space was large enough. Gregor had been to the palace at Versailles. He had seen the original Hall of Mirrors. It was, by modern standards, a rather smallish room, nothing to rival even Mrs. Astor's ballroom, never mind major public spaces like the Colosseum or Madison Square Garden. This space was twice the size of the room it was trying to imitate, yet in spite of that, and in spite of the illusion created by the mirrors, the men and women sitting in row after row of wooden folding chairs looked cramped. The cameras and the light crews just looked out of place.

Still, in spite of all Clara Walsh's talk—and Stewart Gordon's—about ravaging hordes, the crowd was polite and orderly enough, and at least the front ranks of it were filled with people Gregor recognized from news outlets he understood. CNN, ABC, NBC, MSNBC, Fox. The names were familiar and familiarly unthreatening, and for some reason all their major correspondents seemed to be in their forties or above. It was in the rows at the back that Gregor could see the trouble coming. All those were filled by people he did not know, from places he had never heard of, and most of the correspondents were young. That, he thought, would be the Internet contingent, the infamous blogs, the people he was supposed to be afraid of. He tried to concentrate on the rows in the middle, where most of the print media was. *The New York Times* was up front, but the Cleveland *Plain Dealer*—well. Gregor supposed that Cleveland was used to taking a backseat to New York.

Clara Walsh was up at the makeshift podium, introducing him. Gregor only half listened. Everybody said the same things about him when they were presenting him to an audience. They covered his career in the FBI and his time with the Behavioral Sciences Unit. They mentioned the latest case or two that had received some serious publicity. They stressed the fact that he was a consultant and not a private eye. Gregor was still fixated by the audience. The seats were in a block, without a row up the middle, even though the room had been set up horizontally, along the length instead of the width. It felt odd. He wondered why it was so.

Clara had turned to look at him, which probably meant he ought to get up. He did get up. He thanked her, although he didn't know for what, and stood at the podium, looking out. In spite of all the deference paid to the broadcast and cable media, the woman from *The New York Times* was front and center. From what he remembered, the reporter from *The New York Times* was always front and center, no matter what the story was, or where. Maybe there was some kind of protocol here, where everybody was required to acknowledge the importance of *The Times* above all other newspapers.

I'm up here blithering inside my head, Gregor thought, and then called on the woman from *The Times* because she was right there in front of him.

"Mr. Demarkian," she said, "there have been rumors for the last few days that you have been asked here by members of Arrow Normand's family because they are unsatisfied with the level of professionalism exhibited by the local police. Is there any truth to those rumors?"

"No," Gregor said, relieved beyond measure to be able to give a straight answer to the first question out of the box. "I'm sure Miss Normand has a wonderful and loving family who care deeply about her interests, but I've never met or heard from any of them as far as I know. I was asked to come here by Clara Walsh, in consultation with the Oscartown Police Department."

The woman from *The Times* sat down. There were a hundred hands in the air. Gregor knew he wasn't going to be able to get away with calling on only people in the front row. If he tried, it would be all over the Internet in seconds. He squinted into the distance and picked a young man midway into the block of seats. The young man was clean-cut and reassuringly ordinary looking. He didn't even go in for flamboyance in ties.

Gregor pointed to him. The young man stood up and said, "Tom Carlyle, *St. Louis Post-Dispatch*. Could you tell us what you're charging the Oscartown Police Department for your services? Do you think the Oscartown Police Department would be willing to pay your fee if this case had not involved celebrities?"

Gregor sighed. You couldn't trust anything these days. Back when he'd been with the FBI, "clean-cut" had almost always meant "respectful." There was a pitcher of water and an empty glass on the podium. Gregor poured himself some water and drank it. "In the first place," he said, "I'm not sure it's the Oscartown Police Department that's paying my fee. It may be Clara Walsh's office. In the second place, most of the cases I'm called in to consult on do not include celebrities. I have no particular expertise at working with celebrities, but I do have some expertise at working with the analysis and classification of evidence, which is what I'm doing here."

"Are you trying to say that the fact that the accused in this case is Arrow Normand makes no difference at all?" The question came from a very young man all the way in the back of the room, and he was nothing like clean-cut. In fact, Gregor wondered what he'd done to get that hair. It looked as if he'd been electrocuted.

Gregor cleared his throat. "You are . . . ?" he said.

The young man with the electric hair said, "I'm Bobby Gedowski, from Caught in the Crosshairs dot com. And I'll repeat. Can you really say that the fact that this case is about Arrow Normand makes no difference at all? That you and the police are handling this the same way you'd handle a domestic disturbance in a trailer park?"

"No," Gregor said, "but not necessarily for the kind of reasons you're implying. A domestic disturbance, in a trailer park or elsewhere, isn't usually a matter where it is difficult to unravel the facts of the case. The facts are presented to the officers who respond to the call. The officers may have to deal with differing claims of culpability, and who hit whom first, but almost always the universe of their investigation is right there in front of them, and there's no need to go further afield. This case, like most of the ones I'm called in to consult on, contains a high level of ambiguity. Evidence is there, but its import isn't clear. Some of the evidence is missing. What is and is not a fact is not clear. And in cases like that, whether they involve celebrities or not, it is in the interests of justice for everybody to be very careful. The system should be as good a system as we can make it. The fact that it can never be perfect, that it will convict the wrong person on occasion and release the wrong person on occasion, is no reason to stop trying to eliminate error in all its forms wherever we find it."

The man who jumped up next was pudgy, middle-aged, and smug. "Lou Bandovan, *Christian Reporter*," he said, without waiting for Gregor to call on him. "Wouldn't you say that the disgraceful acts committed in this place are the result of a popular culture steeped in obscenity and lawlessness meeting up with an elite liberal culture committed to moral relativism?"

There were groans, and not just from the front of the room. Gregor didn't know what to say. He wasn't even sure that there was anything to say.

"Well," he started, because he was sure he had to say something, "I don't know about obscenity or relativism, but I do know that crime is a constant in all human societies, and murder especially is a constant. Some of the oldest anthropological artifacts are the bodies of men and women murdered millennia ago. In fact—"

Gregor didn't have much to follow that "in fact." He was spinning words in hopes that one of the reporters he thought he could trust would raise her hand. He was almost ready to get down on his knees and plead with the gentleman from MSNBC.

Then, at the very back of the room, an odd thing happened. There were a pair of double doors there, where the reporters had been let in before the start of the conference, and for a split second they pulled back and revealed the hall outside, along with two or three men in green blazers. Then the doors closed again. There were sounds from the hall. Somebody seemed to be shouting. Then the doors opened again, and Gregor saw, framed by the light coming in behind her, a very young woman with very red hair and the oddest assortment of clothes. She was poised and still for only a moment. Then she lurched forward, almost running, and fell into the last row of chairs.

"Shit," she said, out loud, very much out loud. "Shit, shit, shit."

The reporters were no longer the least bit interested in Gregor Demarkian. They were interested only in this young woman with her red hair and her odd clothes and this flailing performance she was putting on, falling into the lap of one person and then the other, pushing her way against the chairs instead of going around the block. She seemed to be trying to get to the front of the room, but that wasn't entirely clear, because she was laughing and crying at the same time and cursing in the middle of all of it.

Finally, she got to a place in the middle of the sea of reporters, with all the cameras and their lights aimed at her face, and let out a long, piercing, wailing scream that could have broken eardrums. Gregor was sure that she'd managed to break his.

"Goddamn it!" the young woman screamed. "Will somebody around here fucking listen to me? Kendra Rhode is dead."

PART III

ONE

1

Later, Gregor Demarkian would tell Bennis Hannaford that the scene around Kendra Rhode's body had been "crazy," but that was almost as if he'd called the *Mona Lisa* "cute." Gregor had been at crazy crime scenes before. He'd been there in the dark when the Philadelphia Police Department had pulled an endless stream of bones out of a cellar, all thought to be the work of the Plate Glass Killer. He'd been in the middle of a hurricane in North Carolina when a young woman brought her smashed and bleeding baby out of the rain and blamed the death of it on witches. He'd even been on the scene at an attempted assassination of a president of the United States. He'd never seen a crime scene completely wrecked before. It was so completely wrecked that nothing and nobody could put it straight, and nothing the police managed to find would ever be credible evidence in a court of law. These were not crime reporters they were dealing with. The words "reasonable doubt" meant nothing to them, except as the hinge of suspense in a courtroom drama, which, like all dramas, they found inherently unreal. They were, however, much better at knowing where the news was than any other reporters Gregor had ever met, and they were fast.

The woman who had come careening into the Versailles Room in the middle of the press conference was Marcey Mandret, and in the beginning the photographers were concentrated on her. They should have been. She had been one of their main targets for weeks, and there she was, not exactly sober, unsteady on her feet, half undressed, hair a fright, screaming at them. It didn't take them long, however, to realize that Marcey Mandret was talking about Kendra Rhode, and Kendra Rhode was a much bigger and better target than this everyday pop tart who had been in the tabloids far too often for far too little reason. They were out the door in a shot, and Gregor found himself staring across a vast expanse of empty space with only the old-line print reporters in it, and not many of those.

It was Gregor who got to Marcey Mandret first, soon followed by one of the older women reporters.

"She's in shock," the woman said. "Did she say that Kendra Rhode was dead? How can Kendra Rhode be dead?"

Gregor could think of dozens of ways, and reasons, why Kendra Rhode could be dead, but he let it pass and tried to concentrate on this young woman. It was hard to identify what she was wearing. None of it seemed to go together, and none of it seemed to be useful to any present purpose. She was also crying, her head buried in her arms, her arms propped up against one of the folding seats.

The doors at the back opened up, and Stewart Gordon came in, striding, the way everybody remembered him striding across his space-ship on that television series that assumed that manned space flight to other galaxies would take place in vehicles large enough to stage a political convention in. Stewart saw Marcey Mandret and walked right up to her, leaned over, and sighed. Then he straightened up.

"She's supposed to be in the hospital," he said. "We left her in the hospital. I talked to the doctor. She's supposed to be there for two to three days."

Marcey jerked her head up. "Kendra's in the hospital. That's where she is. Right at the bottom of the steps. And her head is on backward."

"What?" Clara Walsh said.

Marcey had gone back to burying her head in her arms and sobbing, except that every once in a while she seemed to be giggling. It was hard to tell. All the sound coming out of her was muffled.

Stewart Gordon tapped the reporter on the shoulder to get her to move back, then gestured to Gregor, who moved back too. Clara Walsh and Bram Winder just stood there, which was all right, since there didn't seem to be anything for them to do. Stewart knelt down on the floor and pulled Marcey up just a little.

"Calm down," he said. "Take a deep breath."

Marcey looked up at him. "Kendra's dead. And if Kendra's dead, that's going to mean that Arrow's dead, because there's going to be nobody to say that Arrow couldn't have been there when Mark was killed. I can't say it, because I wasn't there."

"Wait," Clara Walsh said. "Kendra Rhode could give Arrow Normand an alibi? And she didn't? Why not?"

Stewart gestured frantically at Clara to be quiet, but Marcey was talking now, and it was obvious she had no intention of stopping. "She didn't because she wanted to see if they'd give her the death penalty. Arrow. If they'd give Arrow the death penalty. She likes to get people in trouble and watch them squirm. She does. And now she's dead, right there, I saw her. She's lying there with her head on backward and she's never going to be able to say and Arrow is going to go to the gas chamber and—"

"Lethal injection," Clara Walsh said. "And I don't think—"

"She's just lying there," Marcey said.

Stewart was more practical than any of the people who were supposed to be practical. Gregor was gratified to see it.

"Listen to me," he told Marcey again. "You saw Kendra Rhode with her head on backward, which doesn't surprise me a bit. It's like

The Exorcist. Possessed by demons seems to me to be just about right. But where did you see her? When did you see her?"

Marcey looked confused. "It was just now. I told you. I was trying to get out of the hospital without everybody seeing me, and there's a way, going down these back halls and places, locker rooms, like that, and I was going around and around and I was at the back, which was good, because there were no paparazzi around the back. I just wanted to. I want to." She looked confused.

"We'd better get over to the hospital," Clara said. "Or, better yet, we'd better get Jerry Young and go. If there's a body, or even if there isn't—"

"And I went through these doors," Marcey Mandret said, "and they were the kind they have in schools, you know, with the little window with the wire in it up near the top, and there she was, there she was, at the bottom of the stairs and she had her head on backward and she wasn't breathing. I put my ear up to her chest and she wasn't breathing."

"Call Jerry Young, but call the hospital first," Gregor said. "It sounds like Kendra Rhode fell down a flight of stairs. I don't think we can count on Miss Mandret here to be accurate about the breathing—"

"I'm going," Bram Winder said, and went.

"She's not a liar," Stewart Gordon said, more than a little indignant. "She's a twit, and she's a fool, and there are squirrels with better educations, but she's not a liar. If she says she saw Kendra Rhode at the bottom of a staircase, she saw Kendra Rhode at the bottom of a staircase."

"I'm sure she did," Gregor said. "I'm just not sure she knows how to check for breathing, especially if the breathing is faint, which it can be after a bad fall."

"Oh," Stewart said.

"There was somebody at the top of the stairs," Marcey said. "Way at the top, not just up at the next landing. And he was breathing very hard."

"Did you see who it was?" Stewart asked.

Marcey shook her head. "I didn't really look. I threw up. And then all I could think of was to find somebody, and the best place to find anybody in Oscartown is the inn, so I came here. I didn't want to go to the front of the hospital and see the photographers again. I didn't want. I didn't know what. I'm sorry. I'm so cold. I want to go home. I want to go all the way home, but I can't go there, because my father. My father doesn't talk to me. He says it's all my fault. And it is. That's the worst of it. It is."

"What's she talking about?" Clara Walsh demanded.

"We'd better get over to the hospital," Gregor said. "We'd better find Kendra Rhode before the reporters do."

2

Gregor liked to think that if he had really understood what was going on on Margaret's Harbor, he would have behaved differently, that they all would have behaved differently, in the face of what really was a stampede. As it was, only Stewart knew what was going on, and he was frantic. He was so frantic, Gregor and Clara Walsh both moved instinctively to calm him down, as if what was needed in this circumstance was patience and deliberation.

"You don't understand," Stewart kept saying. "They do know where she is. They do and we don't because it's what they are. If we don't get there immediately there's not going to be a crime scene. There's not even going to be a body."

It seemed self-evidently true that the paparazzi couldn't "know" where Kendra Rhode, or Kendra Rhode's body, was. They hadn't even stayed long enough for Marcey Mandret to give away any of the details. Bram Winder was calling for backup just in case, but Gregor thought they needed only to follow Marcey's lead to get in before most of the photographers did, if not all of them, and he said as much.

Stewart Gordon threw up his hands and threw back his head—a

classic Commander Rees gesture, if there ever was one—and took off on his own.

Clara Walsh, Bram Winder, and Gregor started in the direction of the hospital, which was less than a city block and a half away, with Marcey as their guide. They got to the intersection of Main and Bell and turned right. They got to the intersection of Bell and Chabron and—

The hospital was on Chabron, set back from the road. The front door and its curving entryway were deserted, but the sliding glass doors at the emergency room entrance to the side had been broken. Little pellets of safety glass lay all over the sidewalk and the asphalt drive. Marcey Mandret blanched.

"Oh, God," she said. "I shouldn't have done it. I shouldn't have come to the press conference, it was just that I couldn't find anybody anywhere, everybody was gone, even Stewart was gone and—"

"What in the name of God is that sound?" Clara Walsh said.

Gregor couldn't place the sound either, but it was more feral than otherwise and it seemed to be coming from the back. He stepped through the broken glass to find the emergency room's waiting area completely deserted. He followed the sound and came upon Mike Ingleford looking crazed.

"I called the state police," he said. "I told them we had a riot. It's worse than a riot. There's a woman in there. I think they killed her."

"They killed her?" Gregor said.

Gregor stepped past Mike Ingleford, turned the corner in the corridor, and stopped. There were dozens of them, at least, maybe over a hundred. He tried to remember if there had been this many at the press conference. He thought there were more here. He had no idea where they had come from. They were everywhere in the corridor, blocking the doors to the rooms, shoving equipment on wheeled carts into the walls and breaking some of it, overturning some of it. Gregor pushed his way through the crowd, inch by inch, person by person, but it was a struggle. The men around him were just as determined as he was, maybe more so, and they fought to hold their places and to get ahead into the crowd.

That was when Gregor first heard what he was sure was a woman crying, and then, a second or two later, a low scream. "Don't," the woman was saying. "Don't. Don't. Please don't."

Gregor thought the voice sounded familiar, but that was beside the point. If Marcey Mandret was right and this was Kendra Rhode, then Kendra Rhode was not dead, but in trouble. If Marcey Mandret was wrong and this was not Kendra Rhode, then somebody else was in trouble. Of course the voice sounded familiar. He must have heard Kendra Rhode's a thousand times, without being aware of it, on television.

He pushed at the crowd and made progress. Determination, concentration, and the conviction that a live person needed help ramped up his progress. He saw Stewart Gordon maybe four feet ahead of him, moving and pushing as well, that bald head bobbing and weaving among the dark-haired ones around it, tall enough to act as a beacon. Gregor pushed. Stewart pushed. Suddenly, he seemed to pop right out of existence, and the next thing Gregor heard was his deep, classically trained actor's voice saying, "Get the bloody hell away from her."

It was a deep voice, and it stopped time, if only for a moment. Gregor was just able to push through a few more layers before they started agitating again, and everybody started yelling again, but it was enough. He didn't have far to go to the front. They were crammed against a doorway; that was the problem. He could see now that what he had thought was a wall was a doorway. He grabbed at the jacket of the man immediately in front of him and pulled him back. He hooked the leg of the next man up and pulled him to the side. There was the doorway and what seemed to be a single layer of men to go, and in a second he was past it, into the stairwell, into the center of the mess.

And it was not empty. There was no space. The people here were thicker than they had been outside. Flashbulbs were going off at a rate that Gregor was sure must make it impossible for any film to come out. Stewart seemed to be in the process of socking somebody in the jaw. A small woman—Leslie? Gregor had met her before; she was a nurse—was lying on the floor near the stairs, splaying her body over something Gregor couldn't quite make out, and openly crying.

"Stop," Leslie kept saying. "You've got to stop."

Nobody was stopping, and Stewart couldn't knock out enough of them to cause any serious dent in the insanity. Gregor was pinned in place. He squirmed and kicked and tried to maneuver, but he'd gotten as far as he could get for the time being. There were so many people in the small space, it was hard to breath. There were people all around him and there were people above him, on the stairs, snaking up into the second floor. For all Gregor knew, they might have come from above.

Two pairs of hands came out of nowhere and lifted Leslie up off the floor. She was flailing and screaming, and the hands were not gentle. They tossed her to the side, into the crowd, against the wall of men stuck in that corner there, and suddenly Gregor saw what everybody was trying to get to. The body of Kendra Rhode was lying on the floor, its neck broken clean through, its head, yes, almost slightly backward. There was no way the woman was alive, but there was no way to know when or how she had died either. She could have been dead when Marcey Mandret found her or she could have died since, at the hands of these people, these people who seemed to want nothing and to care about nothing except the picture, the picture and the person who was not a person, the person who was—

Going to be torn apart, Gregor realized, with alarm. The photographers weren't just taking pictures of the body. They were grabbing at the body, tearing at it. Somebody came forward and ripped a huge length of material off the front of Kendra Rhode's dress. Somebody else pulled at the parka she was wearing until it came all the way off. Gregor was close enough to realize that Kendra Rhode had not been wearing underwear. Her legs were wide open and they were taking pictures of that, too, over and over again. Stewart Gordon was bellowing. Gregor could barely hear him over what had become the crowd's droning roar.

Somebody grabbed at Kendra Rhode's arm and pulled it. Somebody else grabbed at her leg. There was suddenly a tug of war going on, people on one side with the left arm and people on the other with the right leg. Hands kept coming out of the crowd and grabbing more and more clothing, more and more clothing, so that Gregor was sure that at any moment there would be no clothes at all. There would be just the naked body and maybe not all of that, because it wasn't impossible to pull a body apart if you had enough people and they were willing to go ahead with it. A hand came out of nowhere and went up between Kendra Rhode's legs and then up into her, all the way inside her, as if this were a snuff film and they'd gotten to the part where the actors got to sexually assault the dead body. Stewart Gordon saw it too, and lunged forward. Gregor saw the hand and arm jerk away from Kendra Rhode's body as if they were a light plug being pulled out of a socket.

"Goddamn it to bloody hell," Stewart Gordon said.

And that was when they first heard the sirens.

3

There weren't as many sirens as there had seemed to be. Gregor and Stewart would find that out in no time at all. In the circumstances, it didn't matter much, because the sirens acted like heat on ice cream. They melted the crowd away. It happened so fast, Gregor could not tell anyone, later, just what the sequence of events had been. One moment, the stairwell was crammed tight with people. Stewart was holding on to the photographer who had put his hand into Kendra Rhode's body and was getting ready to hit him. Gregor had pushed all the way to the body itself and was knocking back other people who were grabbing, poking, kicking, snatching, anything to get a piece of her, anything to touch the dead flesh, anything to take away a souvenir, although by then there were no souvenirs left. Then the sounds started

293

and suddenly, it was over. Done. Finished. The crowd had ceased to exist. There was no way to tell where it had gone. There was only Gregor, and Stewart, and Leslie on the stairs, sobbing. Kendra Rhode's body was stark naked and bent in ways no live body ever could be.

Stewart stepped forward and threw his jacket over Kendra Rhode's torso. "Don't tell me we're preserving evidence," he said. "There's no evidence to preserve."

They could hear people in the corridor beyond the stairwell. The fire door opened and Jerry Young stood there, with Don Hecklewhite behind him, and beyond them men in uniform Gregor didn't recognize. They all looked stupefied.

Clara Walsh came up behind them. Gregor could see her red hair moving among the uniforms. For some reason, it struck him as odd that both Clara Walsh and Marcey Mandret had red hair, although Marcey's actually looked red, and Clara's looked dyed red. This line of thought made no sense at all. If Gregor hadn't known himself better, he would have wondered if he was in shock. He thought the nurse named Leslie really was in shock.

Clara made it to the front of the police ranks and stepped into the stairwell. She looked down at Kendra Rhode's body. She looked up at Gregor and Stewart and Leslie. She said, "My God. What happened here?"

"She wasn't naked to begin with," Stewart said. "They pulled her clothes off. Ripped them right off of her while I was standing here and Gregor, too. They pulled the body around. They took pictures. I can't imagine what they took for pictures."

"She could be alive," Leslie said. "She could be. She fell down the stairs, I think. I came out into the stairwell because of Mr. Bullard, Mr. Bullard got out of his bed somehow and he got into the corridor and the door to the stairwell was open when I found him, so I got worried about it, and I came into the stairwell and I looked down and there she was at the bottom. I think she fell down the stairs. But people fall down the stairs all the time and they break their necks and they're still alive, so I came down here, I came down here, I did come down here and then there was noise and then people started coming in, all those people, and then—"

"Listen," Gregor said gently. "Try to think. Was she alive when you got to her?"

"I never got to her," Leslie said. "I got partway down the stairs and then they were everywhere. I couldn't check. I couldn't check. But she could still be alive. Somebody should check."

"She's not alive now," Gregor said. "I think I can guarantee that. You can check her if you want to, though."

Leslie looked up at the faces around her, police faces, Clara Walsh's face. Then she seemed to decide that she had been given some kind of permission. She went down a few more steps to the body itself and put her stethoscope in place on her ears. She put the scope under Stewart's jacket and felt around, then felt around again, then listened, then listened again. She withdrew the scope and shook her head.

"No," she said.

"Didn't you say that Mr. Bullard was out of bed?" Gregor asked. "Maybe you should make sure he gets back into bed."

"I did," Leslie said. "I put him back into bed before I came out to the stairwell. I don't even know why I did. It was just that the door was open, and that didn't make any sense, and we don't know what happened to Jack, so I thought whoever had attacked him might still be around, or something, you know, the way it is on television. Attacked him before, I mean. I don't think he was attacked this afternoon. I think the door was open and she fell down the stairs and he heard her cry out and tried to go to her. I must have been in the ladies' room or downstairs picking up lunch. It doesn't make any sense to have just one nurse on duty when there's a patient on the ward, but then there are almost never any patients on the wards during the off-season and it costs so much money to keep people on. But I should have been there. I shouldn't have left the station. I don't even know what she was doing here."

Gregor looked up and around the crowd again. Mike Ingleford was there, at the back, with his arms folded across his chest. "Dr. Ingleford," Gregor said. "Do you think it's possible to find out whether Kendra Rhode died from the fall or from the actions that took place afterward?"

Mike Ingleford looked amused. "I'm not a pathologist," he said, "but I think I can assure you that forensics has not advanced to the point where it could tell you if a woman died now or fifteen minutes from now, if that's what you're asking."

"What about what she died of?" Gregor said. "She fell down the stairs, Leslie thinks, and probably broke her neck. Could we find out if she died from the fall or from being manhandled later?"

"I doubt it," Mike Ingleford said. "I don't want to be a pessimist here, but assuming the reports are accurate and that she fell down the stairs and broke her neck, then in all likelihood that's what she died from, whether she died instantaneously or because somebody pulled at her body while it was lying there and finished the job the broken neck started. But there would be no way that I know of to distinguish between the two."

"That's what I was afraid of," Gregor said.

Jerry Young came into the now-open central area next to the body. "We ought to secure the area," he said. "This is a crime scene, no matter what the difficulties. We need to put up tape and get some people in here who can at least attempt to collect evidence."

"You should collect evidence on them," Stewart said, jerking his head in the direction of a generalized outside. "It can't be legal, what they did. It can't be legal."

"It's not legal, but my guess is it also isn't going to be possible to pin any of it on anybody in particular," Gregor said. "And I agree with Jerry. This is a crime scene and it ought to be secured. But the damage has been done now. If somebody murdered Kendra Rhode we're never going to know it and we're never going to put that person away. We'd better hope that if somebody did murder Kendra Rhode, it was the same person who murdered Mark Anderman."

"Why?" Leslie said, looking confused.

"It's because he thinks he knows who killed Mark Anderman," Bram Winder said, coming in from the rear and looking more disheveled than Gregor would have suspected he could get. "He thinks he knows right now, already. He hasn't even talked to anybody, and he thinks he knows."

"I don't just think," Gregor said. "I know, and after all this I'm positive. But for the moment we need to let Jerry Young and the people he's brought—"

"Sheriffs from the other towns on the island," Jerry said. "I just called everybody, and I called the state police, and I said emergency, and I said hurry, and here we are. We're not much, but we did some good."

"You did a lot of good," Gregor said, which was the truth. He had the horrible feeling that if the riot he'd just been involved in had gone on much longer, the rioters would have torn Kendra Rhode into pieces. "Now the rest of us should get out of your way. Stewart?"

"Christ on a crutch," Stewart said.

There was a rustle in the crowd, and Marcey Mandret came through, still looking wild, still looking not quite sober. Then she started laughing, and couldn't seem to stop.

"I told you so," she said. "I told you so. Look. She's got her head on backward."

TWO

1

Arrow Normand could not have explained how she knew the things she knew, but she knew them, and she didn't have to wait that long for her information. She knew that Kendra Rhode was dead before dinner on the night it happened, and she knew, waking up the next morning with the sun streaming in through the small window at the top of the wall of her cell, that she would be leaving jail soon. She was much calmer, if not perfectly calm. Too much of her life was about to be over for her to be perfectly calm. She kept wishing there were a way to avoid all the things she would have to go through now. It would be much better if life were more like a dotted line than like a real line, with everything all connected. She thought she wouldn't mind so much having to leave California and her house and her cars and those big blown-up pictures of herself that she had on all her walls, if she could just wake up some morning, just like this one, and be without them. It was the process she was really afraid of. People would yell at her. Her mother would yell at her, and try to fix things, which would be worse. Nothing was fixable. Then there would be the stories, the photographers in her driveway while she moved her things out, the auction—she was sure there would be an auction, because it was what people did; they didn't put all their things in the trash, they sold them—and finally all the weeks and months and years of watching people talk about her as if she weren't really there. She wondered if it was possible to have cable TV without having either MTV or VH1. She didn't want to see herself in one of those half-hour programs about "where are they now." She didn't want to think about the people she knew, the people who were really not her friends, and the things they would say about her when she was gone. Maybe they wouldn't say anything at all. Maybe, when you didn't belong in the places where she had belonged until now, maybe it was just as if you had never been.

The guard who was on this morning was named Marcella, a new one, brought in from another town on the island. Arrow didn't know if she had ever been in any of the other towns on the island. She thought she must have. They'd been filming here for months. They'd been driving around in cars. It was hard to think. She wished her usual people were here, the ones who knew her, the ones she could trust to like her, at least for the moment. When you didn't have money and you weren't famous, people had to like you "for yourself," and Arrow didn't have the faintest idea what that meant. She had a self, but it was all bound up in this, in what she was on the set of a movie or on a stage when she sang. There were people who said she didn't sing very well, and secretly, she had always known they were right. If she sang well, they wouldn't have to tech up her voice all the time, to make it stronger, to make it not so obvious when she couldn't hold a note or got the melody wrong.

Marcella was in a hurry, and she didn't understand why Arrow wasn't in a hurry too. "Come on, now," she said, checking to see if Arrow had changed into the little pile of clothes she'd brought in with breakfast. "Your mother is waiting for you, and a lawyer, and some other man, the investigator they brought in. And there's not much time to talk, because there's a hearing. You're going to walk out of here today."

"Yes," Arrow said, and then, "thank you." She had to remind herself to always say "thank you," and "please," and all those other things, because one of the biggest mistakes stars made was to think that they didn't have to say those things, that they didn't have to be polite, because they were not like other people. Stewart Gordon had told her that the first day they were on the set, when he had reamed her out about the way she'd spoken to one of the costume women, and then he'd told her she'd better call her the "costume woman" and not the "costume girl," because "girl" in a case like that was offensive. Stewart Gordon knew things like that, lots of them. Arrow could never help wondering how he had found out.

Marcella had brought her a pair of jeans and a white turtleneck and a crew-necked navy blue wool sweater. It was the kind of thing Arrow had seen pictures of students wearing on college campuses, but not the kind of thing she had ever worn herself. She wondered where the clothes had come from. She was sure the jail hadn't provided them, and she was sure her mother hadn't picked them out. If her mother had picked out something for her to wear, it would have been a designer dress of some kind, and it would have required strappy little sandals. The shoes that had come with this outfit were thick suede boots with a faux shearling lining that went halfway up her calf. They were the kind of boots that were meant to be worn in the snow.

Arrow got into the clothes. There were kneesocks to go along with the boots. Everything had come from L.L. Bean, which Arrow thought was a store in Maine. Back home, the kind of girls who hadn't liked her had all had clothes from L.L. Bean, the kind of girls whose families went white-water kayaking on vacations and who grew up to go to colleges in the East. Some of those colleges were probably right around here, if not on Margaret's Harbor then near it. Margaret's Harbor was in Massachusetts, and Arrow was sure that one of the places was in Massachusetts, the same place Hillary Clinton had gone to for college, and Hillary Clinton was married to a president. Arrow sat down on the side of the cot and looked at her feet in the big suede boots. She looked exactly like everybody else on Margaret's Harbor looked, if they actually belonged on Margaret's Harbor and weren't part of the film crew. She wondered what she would wear when she got back home and couldn't have designer dresses anymore. She wondered what she would drink instead of the coffee she had flown in every day from L.A.

Marcella came back, and looked relieved that Arrow was dressed. "I don't know what's wrong with you," she said. "I'd be ecstatic if I was getting out of jail. I'd be over the moon. And I probably wouldn't be getting out either. Not in circumstances like these."

Arrow didn't know what "circumstances like these" were, but she didn't ask, because she hated making herself look stupid. She followed Marcella down the hall to the same conference room where she had met her mother yesterday. The televisions were all off. The corridor was empty. The corridor was always empty. Arrow wondered what they were saying about Kendra now that she was dead. She didn't think it was going to be anything good.

Marcella opened the door to the conference room and shooed Arrow through it. Her mother really was there, sitting at one end of the long wooden table with her arms crossed over her chest. Standing next to her was the man who had been hired to be Arrow's attorney, not her regular attorney from Los Angeles, but a criminal defense attorney. Standing a little farther into the room was a big man Arrow recognized from television as Gregor Demarkian. She bit her lip and waited.

"Well," her mother said. "Arrow, I want to introduce Mr. Demarkian, the man I told you about. He's—"

"I really must interject here," the lawyer said. "I really must protest. I do not believe this interview is a good idea. I do not believe it is in Arrow's best interests. Arrow, I insist you do not answer any questions until I give you permission to do so. Mr. Demarkian will ask. I will consider the question. I will okay the question if I think it is proper, and then, and only then, will you answer it."

Arrow looked from the lawyer, to her mother, to Gregor Demarkian. How did you know if somebody was a friend of yours? How did you know if they even knew you, or saw you, or—Arrow had run out of categories. She thought it might have been different if she had had a different kind of growing-up. She should have gone to an ordinary school somewhere, and had slumber parties. She should have had best friends and best enemies and days when she cried because she hadn't been named to the cheerleading team.

"Arrow," her mother said, sounding cautious.

"I want everybody to leave here except Mr. Demarkian," Arrow said.

"Absolutely not," the lawyer said. "There is no way you can talk to a member of the law enforcement team without an attorney present. There is no way—"

"I want everybody to leave," Arrow said. "Right now." She swung around to Gregor Demarkian. "I can do that, can't I? I'm over twenty-one. Just over, but I'm over. I can tell them to go if I want to."

"You can," Gregor Demarkian said. "But your attorney has a point. Anything you say to me, I will report to the police and the prosecutor. It might be an intelligent thing to have a lawyer present."

"I don't care what you report to the police," Arrow said. "I want them out of here."

"Well," Arrow's mother said. "Roger, maybe, just for a minute, you could step out. I can run interference here for a minute or two—"

"I want you out too," Arrow said. "I want just me and Mr. Demarkian. That's all."

"But you can't just talk to him alone," her mother said. "He's, well, he's—"

"I've heard all about him on television," Arrow said. "I want it to be me and Mr. Demarkian and nobody else in here. And don't tell me you won't let me, because I've got the right, and you can't stop me. I'll tell the judge and he'll make you. Get out of here."

"I think we need to seriously consider the possibility that you should seek other counsel," the lawyer said.

Arrow didn't have the faintest idea what that meant, and she didn't care. She just stood where she was, staring straight into Gregor Demarkian's eyes, refusing to look at either of the other two. She had a prayer going on at the back of her head, over and over again, like a mantra. It went: Get them out get them out get them out. Her mother was trying to talk to her. She wasn't listening. Her mother was putting a hand on her arm. She didn't react. She had to stand still and concentrate. She had to focus. She had to will them out of the room.

And finally they were gone.

Arrow looked around at the empty room. She checked the door to make sure it was closed. She pulled out a chair and sat down. She felt too tired to breathe.

"Well," she said.

"Well," Gregor Demarkian said. He came down the length of the table and sat next to her. "Are you sure you know what you're doing here? Your mother has your best interests at heart. Your attorney is paid to have your best interests at heart."

"I think my mother has her own best interests at heart," Arrow said. "And I think my attorney mostly cares about how he'll look in a big famous case. Neither one of them will care about me in a week. You know I didn't kill Mark, don't you?"

"Yes," Gregor said. "I know that. If it makes you feel any better, I'm here because Stewart Gordon knows that too. He was so convinced you were being wrongly accused, he came all the way down to Philadelphia to get me."

"Was Kendra murdered?" Arrow asked. "I listened to some of the news last night, but I couldn't figure it out. Maybe she was murdered, and maybe she fell down the stairs."

"Do you want to know officially, or unofficially?"

"I want to know what's true."

"My best guess," Gregor Demarkian said, "is that she was killed, but not murdered. That she was pushed, and ended up dead, but not because the person who pushed her necessarily wanted her to end up dead. I'm fairly sure, however, that the same person pushed her that murdered Mark Anderman."

"And you know who that is?"

"Yes," Gregor said. "Or rather, I know what person, in what position in this thing, it would have to be. I've just gotten here, though. I haven't talked to everybody yet."

Arrow took a deep breath. "I didn't see who killed Mark."

"I know," Gregor Demarkian said.

"We had an accident, in the truck," Arrow said. "That was true, what I told that lady, the one whose house I ended up at. We'd had, you know, kind of a lot to drink, more than we should have, because it was the middle of the day. But it felt like night. Because it was so dark. It felt like the middle of the night. So we were drinking, and we had, you know, some, something to smoke—"

"Marijuana or cocaine?"

"Marijuana," Arrow said. "I don't. I mean. I don't know. Cocaine scares me. It does bad things to people."

"True enough."

"And we had an accident," Arrow said. "The car went off the road. It just went careening off, over the rocks, onto the beach, and it was dark and there was all this snow, and he fell on me."

"Who fell on you? Mark Anderman?"

"He fell on me," Arrow said again, "and I hit my head, and he did, and there was blood everywhere, and I couldn't get him to move. He didn't answer me. He just lay there on me, and I had to wiggle and do things to get around him, because the truck was on its side and I had to climb over him, and my hair got full of blood."

"And you walked to Annabeth Falmer's house?"

"I just walked out onto the beach," Arrow said. "And I walked around. And I was still really high, you know, but I was dizzy, too, I was so dizzy I thought I was going to pass out, but that scared me. I thought if I passed out I was going to lie down in the snow and die of the cold. That happens a lot. You hear about it on the news. So I was

304

scared and there was this house with lights on and I headed for that, and the lady was very nice. She gave me a blanket and she tried to get me to drink some tea."

"And that's it?" Gregor Demarkian said. "You didn't see anybody else near the truck? You didn't hear gunshots?"

"No," Arrow said. "I thought Mark was dead, though. I thought he was dead and I was going to die too, you know, because I'd been driving. It's one of those things, you know, that you can't do. Kill somebody when you drive drunk. Your career is over after that."

"And that's why you've sat in jail for days?" Gregor said. "Didn't anybody tell you that Mark Anderman didn't die in the accident? He died of a gunshot wound to the head."

"Yes, I know. No, that wasn't why I stayed here. I stayed here because it was quiet. I really wanted to be quiet."

"You're going to be considerably quieter at home," Gregor said. "For one thing, you're going to have better security."

"I don't think so," Arrow said. She looked around the room. It wasn't much of a room. It was less than a movie set. In the conference rooms she was used to, everything was thick and expensive, the carpets, the furniture, even the decorations on the walls. There weren't many decorations on these walls. She took a deep breath. "When I heard about the gunshot wound, I thought Kendra had done it, because she was the one who should have done it. Did you know about that? Did you know that Kendra married Mark Anderman that weekend in Vegas?"

2

The pictures were all over the Internet in no time at all. Marcey Mandret saw them first thing the next morning as she was sitting at the computer at Annabeth Falmer's house, dressed in baggy sweat clothes and drinking something called "double spice chai" tea, into which Dr. Falmer had put a ton of honey but no milk. Marcey did not know if that was because Dr. Falmer didn't know how "chai" was supposed to be made, or because she didn't have any milk, which was possible, since lots of people were lactose intolerant. The pictures made Marcey want to heave, but that wasn't difficult, since she'd been wanting to heave for hours. She had the mother of all hangovers. Her head pounded. Every single muscle in her body ached. Dr. Falmer had brandy, but Stewart Gordon had already told her she wasn't going to get any of it.

She looked at the photographs on the screen again, and again. Different Web sites had different collections of them, but every Web site she'd visited had had what she now thought of as the Picture, the one of Kendra naked and spread-eagled with somebody's hand up her . . . up her . . . Marcey didn't usually have trouble with words, not even vulgar words, but this morning she couldn't make the word for that one come into her head. There was something . . . weird about the pictures she was seeing . . . creepy . . . something. She wished she knew if there were words for the things she was thinking. It was like the pictures were a prophecy, as if she had seen her own death plain. But that wasn't quite right, because her own death could come while nobody was looking, or even wanted to look. Her own death could come after she had ceased to exist.

She heard a car outside and stiffened. Dr. Falmer came hurrying in from the living room and gave her a pat on the shoulder.

"It's quite all right, Miss Mandret, it's not the paparazzi. It's Gregor Demarkian. I think the paparazzi are all over at the jail. Arrow Normand's just been released."

Marcey relaxed. She was a bigger star than Arrow was, but business was business. Arrow coming out of jail was a money shot if there ever was one. She took a long, deep sip of tea. There was so much honey in it, it coated her throat, which actually felt good. The kitchen door opened and she heard Stewart booming on about something. The other man, the one who was Gregor Demarkian, had a softer voice. Marcey wondered, not for the first time, why the people who had built this house had put the front door where nobody would ever use it.

Dr. Falmer came into the alcove where the computer was. "Why don't you come out and sit with us in the living room," she said. "I've got more tea, if you're about to be out, and I've got cookies. Mr. Demarkian is just settling in."

Marcey looked at the screen full of pictures again. If Dr. Falmer had noticed them, she hadn't said anything. Marcey wondered if she would have. She said "just a minute" to Dr. Falmer's retreating back, deleted the Web page, and then put the computer on to CNN. It was one of those computers that stayed on almost all the time, or stayed on the Net almost all the time. Marcey wasn't sure how that worked. Back in Los Angeles, she had a tech person to do that kind of thing for her.

She got up and went down the little hall to the living room. She felt odd in the clothes she was wearing. They were warm, which was good, but they hung on her, and they covered her completely. She felt as if she were in hiding, which she possibly was. She'd forgotten the tea. She went back and got it. Then she edged into the living room and looked around.

"Splendid," Stewart Gordon said. "Why don't you sit down in the club chair, Marcey. You can balance your teacup on the arm."

"Do you need more?" Dr. Falmer said.

"This is Gregor Demarkian," Stewart Gordon said. "Gregor, this is Marcey Mandret."

Gregor Demarkian held out his hand. Marcey took it. Gregor Demarkian did not seem particularly scary close up. Stewart Gordon seemed scarier. Marcey took a long sip of her tea, so long she felt as if she were going to drown in it. Dr. Falmer saw her and took the cup away to refill it.

"The one thing I want you to understand," Gregor Demarkian said, "is that, at this point, I do not think you are a suspect in the murder of Mark Anderman, or in the murder of Kendra Rhode."

"Was she murdered?" Marcey asked. "She was at the bottom of the stairs. I thought she must have fallen, or been pushed, and it made sense to think she'd been murdered, but I didn't really know. I don't really know. You shouldn't rely on what I said, at the time, you know, because I was—"

"Right royally pissed," Stewart Gordon said helpfully.

"Oh," Marcey said. "No. I mean, I wasn't pissed at all, I was just still sort of high, you know, and things were fuzzy—"

"He meant high," Gregor Demarkian said. "It's a Britishism. Although it's usually used to mean drunk, and as I understand it you'd had rather more than alcohol yesterday."

"Yes," Marcey said. "Rather more."

"Oh, for God's sake," Stewart said. "You were high as a kite. I saw you. We all saw you. He's not a reporter. Make some sense."

"I'd had some Valium," Marcey said. "And, um, maybe some Prozac. And things. Pills I had around the house. I was nervous."

"Because of the murder of Mark Anderman?" Gregor asked.

"Sort of," Marcey said. "I was mostly nervous about Arrow. I didn't know Mark all that well. He was just one of those people, you know. He was around. He was on the set but not important. Or sometimes they were not on the set, they were local. And around and cute. And it's boring out here. There's no place to go but the Oscartown Inn or that bar, Cuddy's, the one with the dark windows. There's no music. Or. You know. Anything."

"Okay," Gregor said. "I want to talk about the afternoon that Mark Anderman died. And I'll repeat, you're not a suspect. It's marginally possible that if Kendra Rhode was murdered, you could have committed the crime, but it is not possible in any way that you could have murdered Mark Anderman. At the time he was killed, you were in full view of a few dozen people in Cuddy's, or on your way to this house with Stewart Gordon, or here, pretty much passed out. So it would be helpful if we could talk about that night, and about what led up to that night, without beating around the bush. Do you think we can do that?"

"I can try," Marcey said. She thought Gregor Demarkian was a lot like Stewart Gordon, and not just because he was also very tall and deep-voiced. There was something about both of them that just made her want to do what they told her.

"All right," Gregor Demarkian said. "You went on the trip to Las Vegas. Yes?"

"Yes," Marcey said.

"Why did you go? Why did anybody go?"

Marcey blinked. "I don't understand," she said. "What do you mean by 'why'?"

"Well," Gregor Demarkian said, "did you go because you wanted to gamble, or because there was legal prostitution in Nevada and you wanted to access some, or—"

"No," Marcey said. "No. For God's sake. No, we were just bored. The trip wasn't even planned. We just got to the end of filming in the early afternoon and we were all sitting around in Cuddy's being bored and Kendra said we should go to Vegas, and so we did."

"And you got there how?" Gregor Demarkian said.

"In Kendra's plane," Marcey said. "Kendra has her own plane. Not that she drives it herself, you know, she has a pilot, but she was keeping it at the airport in Boston, so we all went there. And we got on the plane and went to Vegas, you know."

"And you got there when?" Gregor Demarkian said.

"At four o'clock Vegas time," Marcey said, "but you have to work that out, because the time zones change."

"I know. So you got there around four o'clock and you went to the Palms. Did you have reservations?"

"Kendra and Arrow made them from the plane," Marcey said. "Arrow wanted Kendra to have the Hugh Hefner Suite, but Kendra wouldn't take it. She said it was 'ostentatious.' I had to look it up. Arrow didn't even know what it meant."

"So you got to Vegas and went to the Palms and checked in," Gregor said. "That would be you, and Kendra Rhode, and Mark Anderman, and Steve Becker."

"And Jack Bullard and that man. Carl Frank," Marcey said. "We

309

couldn't believe it when we saw him there. He didn't come with us. He's like a spy. He's around everywhere."

"And Jack Bullard?"

"Oh, he was one of those people," Marcey said. "I mean, he's a photographer, but not a real one, don't you see? And he's local, and he's cute. And Kendra liked to have him around. So he was with us that night. He took the pictures, for the, for the—"

"For the weddings?" Gregor Demarkian said.

Marcey sighed. "You know about the weddings."

"I know about the weddings," Gregor agreed. "It wasn't hard to figure out. There's that picture, with the ring on Mark Anderman's hand catching the light and spoiling the shot. Kendra Rhode got married to Mark Anderman and Arrow Normand got married to Steve Becker."

"God, you're good," Marcey said. "Carl Frank came rushing in the next morning and fixed it all, and nobody's heard a thing about it. Steve just disappeared. Mark came back with us. Well."

"Well, what?" Gregor Demarkian said.

"Well, he didn't fix it all," Marcey said. "He fixed Arrow and Steve, but not Kendra and Mark, because he said Kendra had nothing to do with him. So, you know, Mark came back with us on the plane when the weekend was over."

"And he and Kendra were still friendly?"

"Yes, of course they were," Marcey said. "Only he was paying more attention to Arrow, because Carl Frank paid him to. It was supposed to be a, you know, a diversion. He was supposed to hang out with Arrow so that nobody would ask what had happened to Steve. People would just think Arrow had dumped him and wouldn't worry about it."

"Why Mark Anderman and not Jack Bullard?"

"Carl Frank doesn't trust Jack Bullard," Marcey said. "He's a photographer even if he isn't a real photographer. Jack is. You know. And as it turned out, he was right not to trust him, because Jack Bullard sold that photograph, the one everybody sees, the one you were talking about, with the ring."

"But he could have sold a lot more photographs, isn't that right?" Gregor said. "He must have taken other pictures."

"He did take other pictures," Marcey said. "He told me about them. Later. The day you came. He wanted me to tell Kendra that he had them."

"And did you?"

"Yes," Marcey said.

"You said, when you came to the press conference, that now that Kendra was dead there was nobody to get Arrow Normand out of jail. What did you mean by that?"

Dr. Falmer had brought the new cup of tea some time ago. Marcey had noticed it but not paid attention to it. Now she picked up the cup and took a long drink, so long her throat felt as if it were melting. This was the part she was worried about. She was worried about it because she was sure she should have done something with the information days ago, and she was just as worried about it because she wasn't sure what the information was. She put the cup back on the arm of the chair and took a deep breath.

"Kendra told me a couple of days after it happened that she'd seen Mark Anderman alive after the accident."

"Seen him alive how?" Gregor said. "Do you mean she went to the scene of the accident and looked into the truck?"

"I don't know," Marcey said. "She wasn't clear about it. She said she was in her bedroom at the Point and she looked out and she could see the truck on the beach. She could see there had been an accident. And her mother was there, helping with this party she was supposed to have for New Year's Eve, except it never happened because of the storm. Anyway, she left the house and went out to the beach so that she could get away from her mother, which sounds like Kendra, the kind of thing Kendra would do. She said she went out on the beach and that the last time she saw Mark Anderman, he didn't have a bullet hole in him. But she wouldn't talk to the police about it. She said that if I told anybody she'd just say that I was lying. Or that she'd lied to me. She said she wanted to see, she wanted to see if they would give Arrow the death penalty."

"Marvelous," Stewart Gordon said.

Gregor Demarkian sat back. Marcey found him a very soothing person. Everybody in this house was soothing, except for her. She wished she understood why. Dr. Falmer had a big plate of cookies that she was passing around. Marcey took one when the plate came to her, and then wondered what she was supposed to do now.

She should have said something to the police when Kendra first told her. The only reason she hadn't was because she was afraid Kendra would be angry at her, and when Kendra got angry enough she made you disappear.

THREE

1

Marcey Mandret wanted to go back to the computer. Gregor could see that all through his conversation with her, and he thought Stewart Gordon and Annabeth Falmer could see it too. The two of them were looking the way parents would when their child was behaving oddly in a bad circumstance, and Gregor found that just a little relaxing. They were both so young, Arrow and Marcey, and they both seemed to him to be so alone. Maybe it was just the fact that he came from what had been, at least for his generation, an immigrant community, maybe it was just that he associated loneliness with middle age, but for some reason the way these girls lived looked to him to be completely unnatural, and he wasn't thinking of the money, or of the publicity. Young girls were supposed to have parents and other relatives to look after them. They were supposed to have mothers to keep them safe and to have the suspicions they were too young to have. They were supposed to have fathers to protect them from the worst in human nature. They were supposed to have anchors to the past and to the future, so that they could keep their own lives in perspective.

There was no perspective here. It was as if these girls had been born first thing in the morning and knew nothing else but the little they'd seen since.

Marcey drifted back to the computer, and Gregor followed Annabeth and Stewart into Annabeth's kitchen. It was a beautiful kitchen, large and open to the outside. There was a solid line of windows along one wall that looked out onto the boardwalk and the beach. There were open shelves, painted white, carefully filled with multicolored crockery that had been chosen with an eye to the effect it would make. There was a long table, also painted white, with chairs to match. Stewart sat down in one of them and Annabeth headed for the kettle.

"I hope you don't mind all this tea," Annabeth said. "I don't drink coffee. It's not a thing, you know, not a matter of principle or anything, I just don't like the flavor of coffee. I don't even like coffee ice cream. So I tend not to have it in the house. And when I do have it, I do it wrong. Or people say I do."

"She makes a very decent cup of tea," Stewart said.

"Tea will be fine," Gregor said. He went to the line of windows and looked out. On a clear day, like today, you could see quite a bit of the beach, but not far enough to catch the place where the truck had gone off the road. It was surprisingly noisy, too. Gregor wouldn't say the surf was pounding. This was an island off Cape Cod, after all. The Cape kept the worst of the Atlantic from hitting the shores of Margaret's Harbor. Still, the sound of the ocean was clear, as were the sounds of birds. Gregor thought the birds must be freezing to death.

Annabeth was getting tea mugs off one of the shelves and putting them down on the table. Gregor looked up and down the beach one more time, and then across, to the big house on the rocky outcropping at the end of the island.

"That's the Point?" he said. "I didn't realize you could see it from here."

"You can see it from most of the island, really," Annabeth said. "It's on very high ground. It's like the Eiffel Tower. Although it's odd

314

to think of Margaret's Harbor as having something like the Eiffel Tower."

"Margaret's Harbor doesn't want anything like the Eiffel Tower," Stewart said. "Damned ugly building, if you ask me. Just the kind of thing. Look at this, it's so modern! It's great art because you hate it! There's something the Americans get right. Won't give the time of day to that kind of bloody stupidity."

"Some of us must give the time of day to that kind of bloody stupidity," Annabeth said, putting a teapot down in the center of the table. "We've got the greatest collectors of modern art in the world in this country, and they're always lending their collections to museums for shows."

"Ever go to one of them?" Stewart said.

"No," Annabeth said.

"There then," Stewart said.

Gregor moved away from the windows. Annabeth was dumping loose tea into the teapot without benefit of a tea bell, which was the way the British did it. He made a mental note to find out later whether she had always done it that way, or if she'd begun to only recently, because of Stewart. Here was an idea: Stewart Gordon getting married again after all these years. Gregor thought it was as funny an idea as Gregor Demarkian getting married again after all these years.

Gregor took a seat at the table. The teapot was enormous, of a size to serve a small army. It had a cat on it. The real cat was sitting on a little navy blue cushion in a little wicker basket on the short counter that held the microwave.

"So," Gregor said as Annabeth poured hot water over the loose tea in the pot, "two people, two requests for impressions and general information. Jack Bullard and Carl Frank."

"Jack Bullard? Really?" Annabeth looked surprised. "I wouldn't have thought. I mean, he can't have killed Kendra Rhode, can he? I know I heard something about how he'd been found out of bed collapsed in a hallway or something, but he would have been too weak, wouldn't he have? And then there's his hand and the drugs somebody gave him. You're not saying you think he drugged himself and cut up his own hand? Or are you saying that the drugging and the hand had nothing to do with the rest of it?"

Gregor sighed. Too many people read detective novels these days. Too many people watched cop shows. "I definitely think the drugging and the attack on Jack Bullard's hand had something to do with the rest of it," he said patiently. "As to Kendra Rhode—" Gregor shrugged. "We may find out, in the end, just what happened to her, but I'm not optimistic. Maybe she was pushed down those stairs, maybe she fell, but right now the most important question has to do with what she was doing there. Why was she in the hospital at all? She couldn't have been trying to avoid the paparazzi. The paparazzi would have been there at least some of the time, and some of them would have been there all of the time. Most of them didn't attend my press conference."

"You think she went there to talk to Jack Bullard?" Stewart said.

"Either that or to find Marcey Mandret," Gregor said, "and that doesn't make much sense, because she could have seen Marcey Mandret more easily a little later. But she knew Jack Bullard, right? He was allowed to hang around the bunch of them."

"As their pet photographer," Stewart said. "Absolutely. I've seen that before. They pick someone, usually someone who's really lame and nothing like top class—"

"Jack Bullard was lame? As a photographer?" Gregor asked.

"Actually, as a photographer, he was pretty good," Stewart said, "at least if you look at his other work instead of that idiotic picture with the light contamination. It's beyond me why he bothered to sell that one. He must have had others from the Vegas trip. No, professionally, the boy has a lot going for him. Personally, though, he's way out of his league. He doesn't know squat about the kind of people he's dealing with, either the celebrities he's trying to photograph or the photographers he's trying to compete with. Which was why

Kendra and the girls were attracted to him, if you ask me. He could be manipulated. If there had to be pictures, they could make sure they were the right pictures."

"So he went on the Vegas trip," Gregor said.

"Right," Stewart said. "And he got that photograph, and he sold it, and that apparently caused some kind of falling-out. Anyway, he was around less after they all got back, and Marcey and Arrow were barely speaking to him. Kendra Rhode wasn't speaking to him at all. They were all pissed off about that picture. I don't see why. There wasn't a single one of them doing anything they could get arrested for."

Annabeth picked up the teapot and began to pour tea into mugs. "At least he came back," she said. "That other one didn't, do you remember, you were telling me? Some boy who worked on the movie that Arrow Normand had a crush on. He went to Vegas with her and now he doesn't even work on the movie anymore."

"He's got another job," Gregor said. "That's Steve Becker. Carl Frank got rid of him and packed him off to another movie. I presume because he didn't want Becker hanging around with Arrow Normand anymore. What I don't understand is this—after they all got back from Vegas, Arrow Normand was hanging around with Mark Anderman, right?"

"Right," Stewart said. "These girls have terrible taste in men, truly. They date the worst twits, you wouldn't believe it. They never get interested in somebody whose career is on their own level."

"You don't get interested in women whose career is on your level," Annabeth said. "And if you tell me that's different because you're a man, I'll hit you with this teapot."

"Seriously," Gregor said. "They were hanging around together, Arrow Normand and Mark Anderman."

"Yes, I said," Stewart said.

"He wasn't hanging around with Kendra Rhode?"

"Well, of course he was hanging around with Kendra Rhode," Stewart said. "They run in packs, these girls. They're always together."

"Okay," Gregor said. "But here's the thing. The Vegas trip was weeks ago, right?"

"Right," Stewart said. "In November."

"And in November, Carl Frank ran interference with Steve Becker, got him a job on another movie, and got him out of the way. But I can't find any indication whatsoever that Carl Frank attempted to do anything to get rid of Mark Anderman."

"Don't look at me," Stewart said. "I wasn't aware of the Steve Becker thing. But Carl Frank. Now there's an interesting case. Have you met him yet?"

"No," Gregor said. "Clara's arranged a meeting for this afternoon. Why is he an interesting case?"

"He's not what he seems, for one thing," Stewart said. "He's supposed to be head of public relations for the movie, but that's ridiculous. You don't send somebody of that caliber to be director of public relations for a movie that isn't even in the can yet, never mind park him out on location for months at a time. Granted, none of us expected to be here this long, that's a function of the twits. But you don't do that. Carl Frank is a public relations specialist like I'm Father Christmas."

"What is he then?" Gregor asked.

"Michael Bardman's hit man," Stewart said promptly. "Ask anyone. They all knew it. Even that woman, that Miss Beecham, who runs the local paper, she knew it. Bardman's a notorious control freak. He's got ten movies going at once and he hates to be out of control of any of them, so he always has somebody. On this movie, Carl Frank is that somebody."

"And what does he do as that somebody?" Gregor asked.

Stewart seemed to drain the tea in his cup in a single gulp. "He spies," he said. "He spies on all of us, but especially on the girls, because the girls are the big trouble. They get drunk. They get doped to the gills. They careen around in public making spectacles of themselves. They get the local population totally pissed, and then they're late for work. Or worse. We've had three-day stretches where nothing got done because one or the other of them was indisposed. The one truly satisfying thing about being stuck on this godforsaken rock is the fact that the local hospital doesn't deal in admissions for 'exhaustion.' I like that doctor, that Ingleford guy. They'd show up screwed up, he'd pump their stomachs and send them home."

"Did you know that Mark Anderman and Kendra Rhode were married during that trip to Vegas?" Gregor asked.

It was silly of him to care that he'd been able to cause surprise, but he did. Stewart looked so wonderfully flabbergasted.

"For God's sake," Stewart said. "What was that about?"

"I think it was proof positive that Kendra Rhode was not always in control of herself and her life," Gregor said. "My guess is a lot too much alcohol. That is, by the way, why Kendra Rhode and the other women were angry at Jack Bullard for publishing that picture. The light contamination comes from a glint off Mark Anderman's wedding ring. Once you know what it is, it's easy to see."

"But it must have been the shortest honeymoon in existence," Stewart said, "because by the time they got back here, Anderman was all over Arrow. They went everywhere together for weeks. It was worse than it had been with Steve."

"Yes," Gregor said. "I keep getting that impression. But that leaves us with a significant question. Why did Carl Frank get rid of Steve Becker but not Mark Anderman?"

"Maybe Mark Anderman refused to be got rid of," Annabeth said. "I mean, he'd gotten one to marry him, maybe he was hoping to get another one. I can't imagine that Kendra Rhode's money wasn't tied up legally six ways to Sunday. It's what you do with trust funds, because there's always the chance that the heir will be an idiot. Maybe he hadn't realized that when he married Kendra Rhode, and then, when he did realize it, he decided to go for something else. Somebody else. To stay on the gravy train."

"Nice," Gregor said. "I don't think I could have done better myself. There's only one significant problem."

"Only one?" Stewart said. "You always were a bloody genius."

"This doesn't take a genius," Gregor told him. "The problem is simple. Carl Frank went to a lot of trouble to get rid of Steve Becker. He doesn't seem to have gone to any trouble at all to get rid of Mark Anderman. And Mark Anderman might have refused to be gotten rid of, but if Carl Frank is Michael Bardman's man on this movie, he could have gotten Anderman fired. And he didn't. From what I've been able to find out, he didn't do anything at all. Why not?"

2

Of course, Gregor thought, walking back to the center of town, there was always one thing Carl Frank could have done about Mark Anderman, and that was to kill him, or to get him killed. The problem with that would be motive, and the problem with motive in this case was that all of them felt completely inadequate to Gregor. It wasn't that Gregor had illusions about murderers. He'd spent the better part of his career at the Bureau dealing with serial killers, and enough time since dealing with local police departments to understand without illusions that most people who killed did so with very little objective reason at all. Your average serial killer had a sexual itch he couldn't, or wouldn't, help scratching. Gregor would have said that half the serial killers he had known had been mentally ill in the commonsense definition of the term, delusional, haunted by voices. The rest of them lived lives so disconnected from the everyday that they might as well have been aliens, but deeply insecure aliens, always convinced that the world looked down on them for their stupidity, always desperate to prove that they were smarter than the people who rejected them. That was true even of the ones it shouldn't have been true of, which was why, when Gregor thought back on his life in behavioral sciences, the name that always came to mind was Theodore Robert Bundy. The average nondelusional serial killer was a nerdy nonentity or a pudgy loser. Ted Bundy was athletic, handsome, smooth. The average nondelusional serial killer was a constant failure in all things, large and small. Ted Bundy was an academic success, a man with a job in the governor's office, a law student. It was as if Ted Bundy had been invented for Hollywood and the best-seller lists. He was the kind of killer who interested people because he was, in fact, interesting. It made sense to most people that a loser or an ugly would give in to rage and start lashing out. Besides, they didn't have to take that sort of person seriously, because they didn't have to think of him as somebody like themselves. It made everything a lot easier for everyone if the general public could see crime as something committed by people so vastly different from themselves, so utterly unlike anybody they knew, that criminals were literally a different species.

Of course, most crime wasn't committed by serial killers. Most crime was committed by ordinary people in the day to day, and most of the murders there made absolutely no sense at all. A couple of guys get into a fight at a bar and one of them has a knife. He probably never used the knife before, and he carried it only to make himself look cool to women. A guy stays home to babysit for his girlfriend's baby and the baby cries. He can't stand it and he can't stand it and so he picks the baby up by the feet and bashes its head into the wall, and when he's done he can't even remember doing it. Real violence was not like the violence in Agatha Christie novels. It was just there, out in the middle of nowhere, with no rhyme or reason, committed in an instant, finished in an instant. People's lives changed overnight. They ended whether the person you were talking about was the victim or the perpetrator. Often it turned out that the impetus was the same as the impetus for those serial killers who did not hear voices in their heads: the gaping nothingness of being nobody in particular, of trying to exist in the world with nothing and nobody to validate you. Gregor wondered if almost all crime might be like this, or at least if almost all violence might be. Maybe there was really only one motive, and that was the need to compensate for a deep and abiding sense of failure, a failure that went all the way down. He wondered how many people there were like that out there, and what they appeared to be on the surface. He wondered if his brain was beginning to freeze in the New England weather.

I sound like one of those women who does crime analysis on television, he thought, and then, since that was the worst insult he could make about anyone, he tried not to think about it. He had been walking for only a little while, but the town was already in front of him. If he stayed on the road he was on, he would curve along the beach to the Point. If he turned inland and went right, he could make his way to the hospital, where paparazzi were still hanging out in search of . . . whatever. He turned to the left instead, and reached the beginning of actual blocks and actual town, which could be distinguished by the fact that there were sidewalks. There were not a lot of sidewalks in Oscartown. He passed a small bakery that seemed to be closed up for the winter, and two clothing stores that definitely were. He came out on Main Street and looked up and down it. He had no idea where the paparazzi were now, but they were not in front of the Oscartown Inn, and they were not in front of the little bar where everybody went when they weren't filming a movie or doing whatever else people did here. Gregor looked up at the bar's sign. It was only a few feet in front of him, much closer than the inn. He turned and looked back the way he had come. It wouldn't be that long a walk for anybody. It wouldn't be that long a drive, even in a bad snowstorm. He'd been exaggerating the difficulty of getting around. When he had tried to imagine this scene, everything had been farther apart.

He turned back to Main Street and made his way up it to Cuddy's. He looked through the windows and satisfied himself that there was not much of anybody inside. So far, he had been very lucky not to be caught up in a maelstrom of publicity, but he had no idea how long his luck would last. He went into the bar and looked around. There were two men at the bar proper, and nobody at all at any of the tables. He didn't want to sit at the bar. He always felt silly doing that, and it was too public. He found a table at the back and sat facing the bar and the bar's door to the street. He could see everything from where he was, even though there was nothing to see.

The waitress must have been bored, because she arrived almost before Gregor was all the way into his seat.

"Good morning," she said. "What can I get you? We don't do food here in the morning, but we do pretty good coffee if you don't want that mocha latte whipped cream with sprinkles stuff."

The waitress was young and bouncy and looked as if she had never had a moment's worry that she might not be the most important thing in the universe. Gregor looked at the two men at the bar. They were both nursing coffees. In New York, he had seen men sit at bars and drink at eight o'clock in the morning, drink steadily and with purpose, as if this were a job they expected to get paid for.

He turned back to the waitress and said, "Coffee would be excellent. No cream. No sugar. Just coffee."

"Great. And I'm really glad you don't want that mocha latte whipped cream stuff. I mean, really. It's dessert. It's the coffee equivalent of a drink with a little umbrella in it."

The waitress went off. Gregor tried to judge her age, and came up with "younger than Donna Moradanyan," which didn't mean much of anything. He assumed that the drinking age in Massachusetts was twenty-one. It was in most states since the federal government had started to tie transportation funding to making sure the legal age was no lower. If the waitress was twenty-one, she had to be in college, or finished with it, or one of those people who had never gone.

Gregor got out his cell phone and opened it up. He turned it on. It promised him there was service. He tried the automatic dial thing and screwed it up somehow, he wasn't sure how. He could never get the technology straight. He punched in Bennis's number and listened to the ringing, which sounded far away, although he had no idea why that would be the case. The waitress came back and put his coffee down. He thanked her and, just then, heard Bennis pick up.

"Gregor?" she said.

Gregor hated caller ID. It made everybody sound psychic, and he did not believe in psychics.

"Gregor?" Bennis said again.

"I'm here," Gregor said. "I'm sitting in a bar called Cuddy's, at ten o'clock in the morning, having coffee. I've had a very odd day."

"Already? I'm surprised there's a bar called Cuddy's that's open already. Or is it like New York, where they can open at eight and serve alcohol straight through?"

"I don't know," Gregor said. "I'm having coffee. Everybody here is having coffee. The place is absolutely pitch dark. Let me ask you something. Why have all the paparazzi disappeared?"

"What?"

"The paparazzi have disappeared," Gregor said. "Yesterday, they were everywhere, and I mean everywhere. They were crawling out of cracks in the sidewalks. We couldn't get away from them except by locking ourselves in rooms, and then they were right outside. They stormed the emergency room where Marcey Mandret was yesterday after she did something to herself, I don't know what. They were at the press conference. They were at the scene where Kendra Rhode died before we were. And now they're nowhere at all."

"Ah," Bennis said. "Did I hear something about the paparazzi ruining the crime scene? I mean, where Kendra Rhode died?"

"If there was a crime scene," Gregor said. "I don't know if we'll ever know. Yeah, they got there before anybody else did and they ripped the place apart. There's not going to be any uncontaminated evidence of what happened. It was a fair mess."

"My guess is that they're looking to stay out of trouble," Bennis said. "They do get into trouble, you know, Gregor. They get into a lot of it. After the Princess of Wales died, for instance. They get sued. They get prosecuted sometimes. There have been some pictures on the Internet this morning—"

"Yeah," Gregor said. "I've seen them. Everybody's seen them. Marcey Mandret is fascinated with them. I suppose I don't blame her."

"Yes, well, one of them shows what has to be a criminal act. I mean—"

"I know," Gregor said. "I was there. And I mean I was there when it happened. I haven't had to see a photograph of it. Stewart Gordon got the guy out of there and nearly beat him up."

"Well, he could be prosecuted for that," Bennis said. "I don't mean Stewart, I mean the guy. Well. If the prosecutor wanted to push it, he could be in a lot of trouble. So my guess is that the vast majority of these guys are just making themselves scarce for a few days until the outrage wears off. Most of them have probably already got money pictures enough to last a few weeks. And there will be time to get more. This story is going to last forever."

"I haven't seen the news. I've been afraid to look."

"They're treating it like the start of World War III," Bennis said. "Nine-eleven wasn't as huge as they're making this. It's everywhere. Are you really going to solve this murder? You'll get offered your own show on Court TV."

"I don't want my own show on Court TV. Tell me something else. People who work around people like Kendra Rhode, people who do publicity, for instance, or who work for the studios—"

"Kendra Rhode wasn't connected to a studio," Bennis said. "You know that, don't you, Gregor? She made a music CD but she had to pay to have it put out herself. She's one of those people."

"One of what people, this time?"

"For God's sake, Gregor, I grew up with girls like this. It's not true that you can't achieve anything if you're born with money, but it is true that you can't if you act like a spoiled brat. Kendra Rhode expected her name and her family and her cash to get her everything automatically, without actually having to work at it. And what happens in a situation like that is that nobody takes you seriously, and the public really doesn't like you. I saw the video of one of the singles off that album. It wasn't bad. It wasn't any worse than the stuff Arrow Normand does, or Britney Spears, or Jessica Simpson. Standard pop crap, but catchy enough. But practically nobody bought the album. It sold less than most midlist books. Which is saying something."

"Did anybody like her?" Gregor asked. "I can't seem to find anybody who did. Even the people who were supposed to be her friends don't sound very friendly. They mostly sound afraid of her, even now that she's dead."

"That, I couldn't tell you," Bennis said. "There's a reason I walked out on all that twenty years ago, and a reason I'm still out. You will notice that you're not getting married anywhere on the Main Line."

"Tell me about the people who work for these people," Gregor said. "Do they hate them too? Do they resent them? Are they celebrities manqué?"

"I'd expect it depends on the person," Bennis said. "A lot of them just have a job. Some of those can be good jobs to have. Some of them not so much. Why?"

"I've got to go see a man who's supposed to be standing in for the Man," Gregor said. "The guy who is Michael Bardman's spy on this movie. The guy who has had to deal with all the nonsense these people have put out. The guy who is most likely to have had a standard motive for wanting Mark Anderman dead, and Kendra Rhode in the bargain. And I can't get a reading on him at all."

FOUR

1

The photographers started to creep back around noon. There were only a few, and they were keeping their distance, but Annabeth Falmer could see them from her kitchen window, hiding behind cars, shoving themselves against driftwood at the start of the beach, waiting. By then she had not only Marcey Mandret but Arrow Normand in her living room, and Arrow Normand's mother, who she thought was one of the most unpleasant human beings on the planet. Annabeth understood the photographers. They were trying to make a living, and they made a better living the more aggressive they got. Only a very few of them could have "special relationships" with celebrities that would let them get exclusives just for being who they were. Annabeth wouldn't for a moment excuse their behavior just because of that. Everybody had to make a living, and most people managed to do it without being crude, rude, objectionable jerks. It was just that she understood it, and she didn't understand Arrow Normand's mother at all.

"We'd be back in Los Angeles already if it wasn't for the filming,"

Mrs. Normand said, her voice sounding like a television turned all the way up on speakers that had started to go bad. "I couldn't believe it when I heard they were going to go back to filming the day after to-morrow, but I talked to Carl Frank, that son of a bitch, and they are. Maybe Arrow could get some kind of medical exemption. You're a doctor, right? Stewart Gordon called you doctor? Maybe you could give Arrow a note and we could get out of here."

Arrow was sitting in the big club chair. Her mother was sitting at one end of the couch. Marcey Mandret was sitting at the other. Annabeth found herself wishing that Stewart had not gone off to do whatever it was he had to do, because at least he could find a way to talk to this woman. Oddly enough, Annabeth was having very little trouble talking to Marcey and Arrow, who seemed to be mostly young. Arrow was also deeply and profoundly stupid, but there was no malice in it, and she always seemed to be trying very hard. Mrs. Normand looked more like a caricature than a human being. Her hair was long and bright blond. Her makeup would have made more sense on someone fifteen years younger and several shades lighter complexioned. Her nails were several inches long and so red they would have glowed in the dark. Annabeth put the big tray of tea things and cookies and little cakes on the coffee table and then re-treated to a straight-backed chair that she didn't usually consider comfortable. Right now, its principle distinction was being on the other side of the coffee table from all the rest of them, and that was comfort enough.

"Well?" Mrs. Normand said. She sounded annoyed. "Will you give Arrow a note so that she can skip the filming this week? I mean, you do talk, don't you? A couple of minutes ago, I think I even heard you."

Deep in the club chair, Arrow stirred, looking mulish. "She isn't that kind of doctor," she said. "And Mama, I told you, I don't want to skip the filming. We only have another week before we're finished—"

"If we all show up on time all the time and we're ready," Marcey said from the couch.

"And I don't want to have to do this anymore," Arrow said. "If I skip, I'll just have to come back and do it later."

"What do you mean she's not that kind of doctor?" Mrs. Normand said. "Do you mean she's some kind of shrink?"

Annabeth Falmer had never used the "doctor" in front of her name except at academic exercises, where other people insisted, and this was why. Now she drew her chair up to the coffee table and began to pour out, starting with Marcey's cup, because she'd spent enough time with Marcey to know what she wanted. She tried to remember how Arrow Normand and her mother had ended up in her house, but it was a blur. Stewart had thought it would be best "under the circumstances," but she wasn't sure what the circumstances were, and she had no illusions about this house's security against rampaging paparazzi. For some reason, Mrs. Normand took the situation as given, so Annabeth thought that must be something, she didn't know what.

Marcey liked her tea with enough honey in it to re-create a beehive. Annabeth fixed it and handed over the cup. Marcey took it as if she were taking a life preserver, and then she drank half of it off in just one gulp. Annabeth didn't know how she did it. The water was scalding. She didn't seem to care. Annabeth looked at Mrs. Normand again. Arrow might be stupid, but her mother was something worse, ignorant and proud of it, and angry as hell.

"I don't understand," Annabeth said, without meaning to—she hadn't meant to speak aloud at all, "why all of you are so angry all the time. You'd think you'd be ecstatic. You're young. You have more money than most people will ever see. You're famous. I'd have killed for half of that at your age. But you don't seem to like it."

"Oh, God," Mrs. Normand said. "She is a shrink. That's just what we need. A shrink. Maybe we can get a psychological note. Maybe we could have you checked into the hospital for exhaustion."

"She's not that kind of doctor," Arrow said again. She sounded mulish *and* resentful. Annabeth got the impression that Arrow was mulish and resentful around her mother a lot. "She's a doctor of philosophy. She's like a college teacher. She teaches history."

"A college teacher," Mrs. Normand said.

"Well, no," Annabeth said. "I don't teach. I mean, I used to, you know, but since the books have become reasonably successful, there's been no need, so—"

"You write books," Mrs. Normand said. "What kind of books? Do you write romance books? I like those. Nora Lofts. That kind of thing. Arrow read a book once. *Chicken Soup for the Soul.*"

"Oh, for God's sake," Arrow said.

Annabeth poured her a cup of tea and handed it over, but she had no idea how Arrow liked her tea. She gestured to things on the tray and Arrow got up to fuss among them for a moment, but she had said what she had to say to her mother. It was Marcey who was leaning forward to enter the fray.

"She writes history books," Marcey said, picking up a ladyfinger and turning it over in her hand. She wasn't looking at it, though. She was looking straight at Mrs. Normand. "She writes books about women in American history, mostly, but sometimes about the founding fathers, and that kind of thing."

"You mean she writes schoolbooks?" Mrs. Normand said.

"I mean she writes real books, for real people," Marcey said. "The kind of books you see in bookstores. She writes about what history was really like instead of what we're told it's like. Stewart Gordon bought me one to read. It's about Abigail Adams. In case you're completely clueless, she was the wife of John Adams, who was the second president of the United States."

"And people read history books when they don't have to and they're not in school?" Mrs. Normand said. "Well, it can't be too many people who do that, can it? I mean, what's the point? History has already happened, hasn't it. It's not important to people the way things are that happen today. I like to read about people, that's what I like, when I read. I don't do it much. It takes too much time."

"You should read Shakespeare," Marcey Mandret said. "He knew about people."

"Nobody can read Shakespeare," Mrs. Normand said. "He doesn't make any sense. People have changed too much, that's the problem. People aren't what they used to be like. They aren't even what they used to be like when I was growing up. And the music." She stopped still, as if she had just realized there was music playing in the background, which there was. It was the first prelude of Bach's *Well-Tempered Clavier.* "Well," Mrs. Normand said. "There isn't much point to the music, either, is there? It's just depressing most of the time, and if there's one thing I know, it's that people don't like to be depressed. What are we doing here, anyway? I mean, what was the point of bringing us here? This place gives me the creeps."

"We've got to be somewhere," Arrow said. "We can't go back to the house—the paparazzi will have totally staked it out. We've got to be somewhere while Carl Frank finds us another place to stay. If Kendra was still alive, maybe we could stay at the Point."

"You couldn't stay at the Point," Marcey said, sounding sharp. "Don't you know that? She wouldn't let any of us stay at the Point. She wouldn't let any of us get in the way if there was something she wanted to do."

"I think it's a terrible thing," Mrs. Normand said. "A young girl like that, so beautiful, and so rich. I think all the flags ought to fly at half-mast for a week. After all, we fly them at half-mast for politicians nobody has heard about for years. I mean, I thought Ronald Reagan was dead long before he actually died, and then when he did die, they made all that fuss about him, and who really cared? I mean it. Who really cared? You couldn't turn on the television for days without seeing something about it, and then there was the funeral, and it was on a million stations, you couldn't get away from it. Kendra Rhode did more for America than Ronald Reagan. She was a cultural icon."

Annabeth had poured a cup of tea for Mrs. Normand. Now she

extended it across the table. Mrs. Normand looked into it and made a face.

"Tea," she said. "I never drink tea. It tastes like piss. Don't you have any coffee in this house?"

"She's already told you she doesn't have coffee," Arrow said, sounding so exasperated now she was almost crying. "She doesn't drink coffee. Why don't you ever listen to anybody?"

"Everybody drinks coffee," Mrs. Normand said. "Don't be ridiculous."

"I'm afraid I don't drink coffee," Annabeth said. She was being polite. She was being so polite it was killing her. "I have orange juice. And I think I have mineral water, in, you know, little bottles. But maybe not, because it always seems to me to be rather silly to buy water."

"God, this place gives me the creeps," Mrs. Normand said. "It really does. All these books. And what kind of books are they? *The Moral Obligation to Be Intelligent*. Who reads a book like that?"

"It's a collection of essays," Annabeth said. "By Lionel Trilling. Essays about literature, mostly."

"Oh," Mrs. Normand said. "Lit-ra-chur. Aren't we all important around here. And that painting. That awful painting. How can anybody live with a painting like that? People don't want to be reminded of death and pain and misery. People want to have fun."

"That's the point," Marcey Mandret said. She was sitting all the way up now, and Annabeth thought she looked like an entirely different person. She looked like an entirely different person from the one she'd been just this morning. It was an odd thing to see.

"It's called *The Flagellation*," Marcey said, "and I don't remember the name of the man who painted it. It was somebody from the Renaissance, in Italy. And that was his point. That people like to look at the young and the beautiful and the rich, but it's that kind of selfishness that killed Christ. It wasn't the Romans who killed Him, it was ordinary people, and ordinary people's sins, because ordinary people don't help the poor and the helpless, they only care about money and fame. They only care about celebrity."

Annabeth poured herself a cup of tea and counted to ten in her head. She had no idea what to make of this at all. She had said something to Marcey once about *The Flagellation,* but not all this. She couldn't imagine that Marcey had thought it through for herself, although she was willing to entertain the possibility that the girl was brighter than she'd thought at first. Right now, Marcey seemed both bright and desperate.

"Don't tell us you've become one of those Christians," Mrs. Normand said. "Don't tell us we're all going to have to listen to sermons from you on a regular basis."

"You don't have to be a Christian to understand it," Marcey said. "The part about torturing Christ and putting him on the cross is, it's a—"

"Metaphor?" Annabeth said helpfully.

"Yes. Thank you. It's a metaphor. Stewart told me. When we care only about money and fame and youth, we don't just hurt ourselves, we hurt all humanity everywhere, we make the world a worse place than it could be. And we make ourselves worse too. We make ourselves trivial. We make ourselves morally trivial people, and we waste the life we've got, we waste it on—oh, hell. We waste it on Kendra Rhode."

"I'd be careful what you say about Kendra Rhode," Mrs. Normand said, her face screwed into a triumph of spitefulness that seemed almost violent in its intensity. "The police haven't ruled out murder yet, you know, and you were the one who was there, weren't you? You were right there in the hospital. If you don't watch out, you'll end up in the same jail Arrow was in, and there won't be anybody to get you out."

Marcey got up off the couch, as if she didn't want to be on it while Mrs. Normand was still there, and paced across the room to the windows that looked out on the beach.

"I don't care if they do think I killed her," she said. "Somebody has to start telling the truth about Kendra Rhode."

2

From the way the light was coming through the windows, Jack Bullard thought it had to be nearly noon—and that, considering how much time had passed since he first woke up, was very disturbing. He was not the kind of mess he had been the day before. The effects of whatever the drug was that somebody had given him had worn off, and aside from that he had only the painkillers to worry about. His hand hurt, but not as much as it might have. That was the blessing of Demerol. He felt very relaxed and tired. That was the blessing of Demerol too. He did not know what he was supposed to feel about the things that were going on or the things that had happened to him, and that was something no Demerol could help. He could sit up and get himself juice and water if he wanted. It felt like too much trouble. He could go to the bathroom on his own, which he did when it was necessary. He could walk down the hall and talk to whomever had taken Leslie's place for the day. None of this felt to him as having any point at all. He had been watching television for hours, and the television said the same things over and over again, and none of it made any difference. He wondered what would happen now. Maybe there would be a big public funeral, in New York, where Kendra was from. Limousines would line up outside the church in which she had been baptized, even though she hadn't been inside it since. Men and women would walk up the church steps as if they were walking down the red carpet. Maybe that wouldn't happen at all. Maybe the family would revert to type, and the funeral would be private, and there would be no press allowed at the service or the grave. Jack knew what he would want at his own funeral. He would want the limousines, and the long procession to the cemetery, right there on CNN. He would want the commentators on Fox to talk about what a bad influence he had been, because the commentators on Fox always pretended that it was better to be obscure and prissily "moral" than to be famous and sane. He would want Katie Couric, too, if Katie Couric was still working. It was so hard to think about time. Time came and went. It slithered. In fifty or sixty years, when he was ready to die, Katie Couric would probably already be dead.

Linda was sitting in the visitor's chair on the other side of the sliding table. She had been there for fifteen minutes, but Jack hadn't said anything to her besides "Hello." He couldn't think of what to say, and there was something about the way she was sitting where she was that made him think there was more of a point to this visit than just visiting. Death bothered him, he realized, but only sometimes. The death of Mark Anderman hadn't bothered him at all. Mark was and then he was not, and in between it was as if he had never been. He'd been a blank, or a black hole, a depression in the ether. The death of Kendra Rhode bothered him very much, but not just because she was famous, or rich, or somebody who had come to talk to him only moments before she'd fallen down a flight of stairs and broken her neck. It was just that, in his head, Kendra Rhode was not supposed to die. She was supposed to be incapable of dying. He had felt that way about presidents once, when he was very small. He had imagined that there was something about being famous that made you immortal, and that being famous meant being in the encyclopedia, and that presidents were always in the encyclopedia. Something like that. It was confused. He could even remember when he'd realized, for the first time, that this was not true. He was in his seventh-grade math class, and his math teacher, Mr. Lamont, had brought in the news that—but his mind had gone blank. He couldn't remember. His body felt as if all the blood had been drained out of it. All he could see, or think about, was Kendra, on the television in still pictures and video clips, giving interviews as if nothing like death had ever occurred to her.

"Somebody died," he said out loud.

On the other side of the table, Linda stood up. "Yes," she said. "Yes, somebody did. Kendra did."

"Not now," Jack said. He knew that Linda was taking this all wrong. She was assuming that he was behaving the way he was because he was sick, because he hadn't recovered from the drugs and the things that had been done to his hand. He didn't know how to tell her the truth. He didn't know if it was important. "When I was in seventh grade," he said. "Somebody died. Somebody important. And it was a big deal at the time. And now I can't remember who it was."

"When was it?" Linda asked.

Jack thought about that. Seventh grade. Junior year. He remembered most of his time growing up with markers like that, not with real years. He had to think hard to figure out the real years. "Nineteen eighty-two," he said finally. "I think."

"Brezhnev died in 1982," Linda said.

Jack turned his head from side to side. He knew who Brezhnev was, sort of, but he wouldn't have known in 1982. He tried to think about it. He thought about Kendra instead, looking so real up there, looking as if she really existed.

"John Belushi," he said finally. "It was John Belushi. And my math teacher heard about it somewhere, it happened on the weekend, and he came in Monday morning and told us all about it. He was very upset."

"Were you very upset?"

"Not exactly," Jack said. "I just couldn't understand how it had happened. He was famous, and famous people weren't supposed to die. I'm not making any sense."

"You're making some," Linda said. "They do die, though. She died. I know you were fond of her."

It was, Jack thought, a very Linda-like phrase. "Fond of her." What would that mean, if it meant anything? Had he been "fond of" Kendra Rhode? He really didn't know. He thought that most people who had come into Kendra's orbit might have the same kind of confusion. Kendra wasn't a person that you liked or disliked. It was far more fundamental than that.

"They don't say what it was," he said. "On the television, that is. They don't say if somebody killed her, or if it was just an accident."

"She fell down the stairs," Linda said.

"I know."

"She fell down these stairs, right here," Linda said.

Jack turned to look at her. He had the bed propped up. It was one of those mechanical ones you could operate with a little handheld thingee. Linda was sitting in the chair without her back touching it. She was sitting straight up, the way grown-ups always wanted children to in church.

"She was in the room," he said finally. "She was standing right over there, by the window."

"You mean she came to visit you?"

"I guess. I got the impression that it wasn't on purpose. She hadn't come out to the hospital to visit me."

"Just the impression? She didn't tell you why she was here?"

"We didn't talk about why she was here. We didn't talk much at all. She stood over by the window. Then she got up and left and went down the hall. I could hear the footsteps. Or not. I don't know. There was something about her leaving. And I got angry."

"Did you? At something she said to you?"

"Not exactly." Depression was different from being tired. When you were tired, you just wanted to sleep. When you were depressed, it was as if you had been weighted down with lead. You tried to get up, and there was too much weight you had to pull with you, weight that didn't belong to you.

"I was angry a lot the last few weeks," he said. "Since we got back from Vegas. We got back. Listen to me."

"It was 'we,'" Linda said. "You all went out together. You all came back together."

"It still wasn't 'we,'" Jack said. "And it doesn't matter, I guess. But she was here, and she was being a pain, and then she left. And I got so angry I got up. I know I wasn't supposed to get up, because of the hand—"

"It wasn't because of the hand," Linda said. "It was because of the drugs. You'd been given some kind of drug. Too much of it, Mike Ingleford said."

"I know." Really, Jack thought. Lead weights. It was exactly as if somebody had sewn lead weights into the skin of his back and the back of his legs. "It was because it was the wrong drug. People who don't know anything about drugs don't know how they work. They pick the wrong ones for the job they want to do. Do you see what I mean?"

"Yes," Linda said.

"It doesn't matter," Jack said. "I knew all about the drug. I just got angry and I thought I'd catch her, I'd catch up with her, I'd talk to her. So I got out of bed. It was really hard. I got myself out of bed and then it was hard to walk. I was stumbling all over myself. I don't know why I kept on with it. I just kept going. It was like that."

"Did you catch up to her?"

"I called out to her and she heard me and she stopped. That was right at the fire doors. I've been wondering all morning where Leslie was. I mean, it's not like this ward is a busy place. It's empty. She must have heard me. Leslie must have heard me. Kendra heard me. Why didn't Leslie come?"

"She was in the bathroom or something," Linda said. "And then things got crazy. Marcey Mandret found her. Found Kendra Rhode. And the silly twit, instead of getting somebody at the hospital to do something, she ran all the way across town to the inn and blurted the whole thing out to a press conference full of idiots. And then you had, you know, what's been on television all day."

"There's supposed to be something else on the Internet," Jack said. "They've been talking about it all morning, but they won't show it. I passed out on the floor. In the corridor. I just lay down and went out like a light."

"I know," Linda said.

"I wish they'd say whether it was an accident or murder," Jack said. "I just wish they'd say. I was so angry. It's almost as if my anger reached out and broke her neck."

"They're never going to know what broke her neck," Linda said. "The paparazzi stormed the scene, and it was contaminated, and now they can't get any evidence at all. It wouldn't matter if you'd stuck a knife in her heart. They couldn't catch you on it."

"I didn't stick a knife in her heart."

"I know," Linda said.

"I know who did this to my hand," Jack said. "I knew at the time. I know who gave me the drugs. They don't make you forget things, the drugs. They don't put you all the way out until the end."

"Carl Frank came to see me," Linda said. Then she got up out of the chair and walked to the window where Jack had last seen Kendra standing. She was not like Kendra. Not even a little bit.

Up on the television set, the issue was now whether or not Kendra Rhode had had a will, which it was possible she had had, since she came from a wealthy family, and had money of her own, and lawyers, who would insist. The talk went on and on, filling up time, filling up space. There was a war in Iraq and trouble in the economy and wildfires in California and it was as if none of it was happening. The only thing anybody wanted to talk about was Kendra Rhode, and what had happened to her.

"I should have gone to law school," Jack said.

"What?"

"I should have gone to law school. That's what most people do when they go to a good college and get a degree in history. Law school. A partnership somewhere. I thought about it. I really did. It just seemed too, I don't know. Too everyday. I wanted something more . . . significant, I guess. Something that would mean something."

"Taking pictures of Kendra Rhode and Marcey Mandret is more significant than what you could do with law school?"

"There was this cartoon I saw once, in the *New Yorker*. One of those Hamilton cartoons with all these Waspy people at a cocktail party. This woman and this man are talking and the woman says, 'You're a lawyer? Everybody's a lawyer.' And that was the problem. It was too everyday."

"Carl Frank came to see me," Linda said. "He's looking for some pictures he thinks you have. Pictures of the Vegas trip that haven't been published anywhere yet."

"There are pictures of the Vegas trip that haven't been published anywhere yet," Jack said. "I don't see what Carl Frank wants them for."

"He wants them," Linda said, "and that ought to be enough. I don't like that man. I think he's dangerous. I don't like the things he does to people."

Jack put his head back as far as it would go. They were past the will now. They were talking about the funeral, even though it was obvious in no time that they had no actual news.

"It's like a drug addiction," Jack said. "They can't stop. They don't want to stop. They talk and talk about it."

"Jack."

"Never mind Carl Frank," Jack said. "I can take care of Carl Frank."

FIVE

1

Carl Frank was an official interview, and because of that it was to take place in an official venue, by which everybody meant the Oscartown Police Station. Putting it like that would have made anybody on Margaret's Harbor laugh even twenty-four hours ago, but a lot had changed overnight. The death of Kendra Rhode had galvanized the Massachusetts State Police in a way the death of Mark Anderman had not. There were dozens of them on the island now, in patrol cars in the streets, at points of interest on foot, in the police station, as if Oscartown had suddenly become West Thirty-third Street. They were even staking out the stairwell where Kendra Rhode had died, although Gregor couldn't for the life of him see what good that was going to do now. Maybe murderers returned to the scene of the crime in Massachusetts, the way they did in romantic suspense novels, and the staties were just waiting for their suspect to turn up and turn himself in.

Silly or not, there was something reassuring about all these professional law enforcement people. Gregor didn't do a lot of thinking on

Big Subjects. That was Father Tibor's department, and Father Tibor never seemed to come to any specific answers to any specific questions where both the answers and the questions wouldn't change next week. What Gregor did know, however, was that civilization was fragile. It took nothing at all to turn a place of comfort and safety into a hellhole, and rampaging hordes from the eastern steppes were not required. The paparazzi almost were rampaging hordes, but it wasn't their rampaging that worried Gregor. It was their state of mind. They seemed to live in a world where common human decency had been abolished, as a matter of policy.

There was a young policeman on duty at the front desk when Gregor walked in. This was better than the first time he had visited the Oscartown Police Station, when there had been nobody on duty at the front desk, and only one comfortably padded, sleepy local policewoman watching the jail cells in the back. It said something about the survival of civilization, in a good way, that Arrow Normand hadn't just got up and walked out one afternoon because she was tired of being in jail.

The policewoman recognized him on sight, and stood up. "Mr. Demarkian. Mr. Frank is already here. He's in the conference room."

"Is that the same room I was in this morning?" Gregor asked. "Biggish table, peeling veneer?"

"I couldn't say for sure," the policewoman said. "But I'd be surprised if this place had two conference rooms. It's like a fairy tale around here, don't you think so? I'm used to Boston. We have real law enforcement there."

Gregor was sure that Jerry Young was "real law enforcement," just at a level Margaret's Harbor usually required, which was different from the level Boston usually required. He said nothing about it, though, and let the policewoman lead him down the narrow back corridor to the door he was sure he recognized. She swung it open and he looked inside. It was the room he had been in with Arrow Normand. This time, there was only one person waiting for him. Carl Frank had declined to bring an attorney.

The policewoman shooed Gregor inside, and Gregor let himself be shooed. He heard the door close behind him just as Carl Frank stood up, being polite in a way that very few people bothered with anymore. He was an interesting man, especially considering the people he worked with. His clothes were expensive without being fashionable. In fact, if Gregor had had to guess, he would have said that Carl Frank's clothes were expensive because they were not fashionable, that he had gone to a lot of trouble to blend into the background in one sense while being impossible to ignore in another. He was, in other words, a very serious person. He was not the public relations flunky for a minor motion picture.

"Mr. Frank," Gregor Demarkian said.

"They aren't going to bring in that local kid in the cop uniform?" Carl Frank said. "I suppose that's all to the good. He's a nice kid, but he doesn't have a clue."

Gregor Demarkian pulled out a chair and sat down. Carl Frank sat down again at his own. Most people couldn't stand the sound of silence. If the investigator just shut up, they would start talking and find themselves unable to stop. They would confess to the present crime and to a few more they'd committed, right down to the Raisinets they'd stolen from their lab partner in high school biology. Carl Frank was not one of these people. Gregor was ready to believe he would be able to stay quiet indefinitely.

"You know," Gregor said, "if somebody had introduced me to you before any of this happened, and told me that you were the public relations man for this movie, I wouldn't have believed him. You're not the public relations man for this movie."

"Oh, but I am," Carl Frank said. "I'm good at it too. It's where I started in this business. Although we ought to be clear. I'm the public relations man for this filming. It's not the movie I'm concerning myself with, it's people's behavior while they're making it. After the film is made, it's no business of mine what kind of publicity it gets."

"All right," Gregor said. "Let me try again. You're not just the public relations man for this . . . filming. And that's not your principle job here."

"No."

"Are you what you're rumored to be?" Gregor asked. "Are you Michael Bardman's hit man?"

"Sometimes. When it's necessary. It isn't usually necessary. Michael Bardman is the most important producer in Hollywood, maybe the most important Hollywood has seen in fifty years. It's not just that everybody wants to work for him, it's that most people can't afford to piss him off too much. Too many of the movies that do get made are his productions."

"All right," Gregor said. "Then let me ask you something off topic a bit. What does Michael Bardman want with this movie? I'm not entirely clear on it, but from what people tell me it sounds like something fairly minor. Much lighter than Bardman usually produces. No science fiction. Few special effects. So what are you doing here?"

Carl Frank didn't blink. "The script was written by Christa Hall Grande."

"And?"

"Christa Hall Grande spends her real life as Mrs. Michael Bardman."

"Ah," Gregor said. "All right."

"Not that Michael is an idiot," Carl Frank said. "This movie is expensive, but not particularly expensive. It will come in under sixty million even with all the screwups, unless you're intending to arrest Marcey Mandret for murdering Kendra Rhode. Which, by the way, is the kind of rumor I hear."

"She's a person of interest," Gregor said. "She would have to be. She was on the scene in both deaths. In the second one, she was right there."

"She was drunk the first time and coming out of a bad chain reaction the second," Carl Frank said. "And I don't have to hear rumors about that one. That's the kind of thing I check out myself."

344

"Assuming she wasn't," Gregor said, "would you think she'd be capable of it?"

"It depends what you mean by 'it,'" Carl Frank said. "Pushing Kendra Rhode down some stairs? Hell, yes. I was capable of it. The woman was a pest. Shooting Mark Anderman in the head? I doubt it. Drugged up and scared and crazy, a spur-of-the-moment thing, anybody could do that. But anything that took even a second more thought, and from what I hear this took at least that much, no. Not at all. She may be a charter member of the Twits Club, but her real problems are ignorance, disorganization, and a complete lack of self-esteem. Or self-respect, for that matter. She was the one I wasn't opposed to hiring when this project started, if you want to know the truth. She gets seven point five a picture and she can almost always be cajoled into behaving like a professional. I'll admit I underestimated the amplification effects of having the other twits around."

"Let's go down the list," Gregor said. "Stewart Gordon."

"He gets five," Carl Frank said, "and he's worth it. He has a cult following that's hard to beat. He's thoroughly professional. Gets to work every day on time, knows his lines, knows his moves, gets the job done, stops at a bar for a couple of beers on the way home, keeps it to a couple of beers. I wish every actor in the world was like Stewart Gordon. If they were, there'd be no need for me."

"Could he have committed these murders?"

"Could he? Sure. But why would he? I know he's been playing father-mentor to Marcey and sometimes to Arrow, but he's not so old-world that he'd kill off their boyfriends. Never mind kill off the men pretending to be their boyfriends. I think he thinks he's going to convince the both of them to go back and finish high school. Or something. It's that kind of a relationship."

"What about Arrow Normand?"

"Ah, the principle twit," Carl Frank said. "Well, she's getting fifteen for this movie—"

"Really?" Gregor was surprised. "I don't keep up with these

things, but I'd gotten the impression that her career was somewhat on the wane."

"If you mean that she's in a downward spiral without much choice but to self-destruct, your impression is entirely valid. My guess is that that girl has about another year, or maybe two, before she becomes radioactive. And with all this, it may happen sooner. Five years ago, she'd have gotten thirty million to make a movie."

"Fifteen is still not minor money."

"No, it isn't," Carl Frank said. "And I wasn't the only one who told Michael he could get her for less if he held out for it. I think he felt sorry for her. That Michael felt sorry for her. Hell, pretty much everybody does. She's young, and 'stupid' is giving her more credit than she deserves, but she's a nice enough girl, she's not a raving bitch to people or anything. It's just that she was always just one of those things. She's not particularly talented. She can't act worth a damn, and her singing voice is weak. It has to be teched up when she records and when she performs. She's not even particularly pretty. She was just young, that was all, and she was in the right place at the right time, and she was willing to wear not much in the way of clothes when she made music videos, and for a few years there wasn't much in the way of competition. Now she's not as young as she was and there are people coming up who are younger and better looking and actually talented. She hasn't released an album in two years. She hasn't made a movie or a video, either. And she's got a family that spends money like water."

"But you don't think she killed Mark Anderman."

"No," Carl Frank said. "And neither do you. She wasn't even available to kill Kendra Rhode, although I think she could have done it and made a case for justifiable homicide. The woman was absolutely poison to someone like Arrow Normand. Arrow could never understand that people like Kendra could get away with things that she herself couldn't."

"Like getting caught without wearing underwear?"

"Exactly like getting caught without wearing underwear." Carl

Frank stared at the ceiling. "Of all the things that have come down the pike these last five years, that's the one I'm never going to understand. Do these girls get it at all? Do they understand that showing that part of themselves and getting it caught on camera is toxic to any hope they ever have of being taken seriously? Do they have mothers?"

"Let's try one more person," Gregor said. "You."

Carl Frank stopped looking at the ceiling. "Me? What makes you think I'd murder Mark Anderman? Or even Kendra Rhode."

"You had opportunity, in both cases," Gregor said. "In fact, you're the only one who did have clear opportunity in both cases. I don't see that the means would have been difficult for you to obtain. You'd know where to get a gun. And as for motive—well, there's the movie. You've said yourself that your job here is to make sure the filming goes smoothly and with no bad publicity. It was to hold off bad publicity that you got rid of Steve Becker."

"I got rid of Steve Becker by getting him a far better job on another movie," Carl Frank said, "and I didn't do it because he was making the filming go screwy. I did it because Arrow went off and married him in Vegas, and Arrow has too many liabilities already to pull that kind of stunt and get away with it. Remember when Britney Spears married that childhood sweetheart or whatever he was and then got it annulled four days later? It didn't do her any good, and a similar stunt wasn't going to do Arrow any good, so I made it go away. If I'd wanted Mark Anderman to go away, I'd have done the same kind of thing."

"Maybe he refused to go away."

"There was nothing for him to refuse to go away from," Carl said. "He wasn't dating Arrow Normand. Oh, I mean, he was in public, they hung out, but that was one of those little things Arrow was doing for Kendra Rhode. It was Kendra Rhode that Mark Anderman was married to in Vegas."

"I know," Gregor said.

"And you think I'd lift a finger to keep Kendra Rhode out of trouble? Why? She wanted a part in this movie, you know, and she asked for it several times, but she never got it, and she wasn't going to get it. That one, Michael promised me. Not that he was keen to have her. I mean, for God's sake. And as for Arrow hanging out with Mark Anderman—why not? It made people forget about Becker. There was nothing to discover about Arrow and Mark. It was the perfect arrangement, before somebody put a bullet through his head. The last person in the world I had a motive to shoot was Mark Anderman, and it would have been beyond counterproductive to do it in a way that got Arrow Normand thrown in jail and the filming stopped for a week and a half."

"Did you have a motive to shoot someone else?" Gregor asked.

"I keep a list," Carl Frank said. "I'm going to wait until I have my fuck-you money, and then I'm going to get a machine gun and have at it."

2

For the next interview, Gregor had gone back and forth in his head between protocol and practicality. It often made good sense to interview someone outside the official institutions of the law, to do it in a way that stressed humanity and not the function of a witness or a suspect. For Linda Beecham, Gregor thought it would be better to be as official as possible, and as serious. He didn't think she was worried about being a witness, and he was sure she had no idea that she might be a suspect. He did think that she resented the fuss and bother made over people like Arrow Normand and Kendra Rhode, and that she was sure that Jack Bullard's problems would go unresolved because they were the problems of someone nobody important would have any interest in attending to.

Gregor had asked for the file on Jack's attack to be sent up to him, and it arrived in the hands of another young state policewoman almost as soon as Carl Frank left the conference room. Gregor spread the contents of the file on the conference table in front of him. There wasn't much to see. Linda Beecham had, indeed, reported the attack on Jack to Jerry Young, and Mike Ingleford had sent over a medical report, but so much else had been going on over the last few days that nothing had been done to identify the person or persons who had made such a mess out of Jack's hand. And it was a mess. The tips of the fingers of the right hand were almost entirely ruined, and the palm had been cut in a dozen places, seemingly haphazardly. The left hand was clean. It was the drugs that were the most confusing thing about the incident. Date rape drugs were not the sort of thing most people had lying around the house, and they weren't the sort of thing that would first come to the mind of someone who needed to knock somebody else out to—what? Mutilate him? What had been done to Jack, exactly? He didn't know, and so far, nobody had tried to find out.

Linda was five minutes late for the appointment. Gregor considered that mildly interesting, since she didn't seem to him to be the kind of woman who was often late to anything. She came in just as he was gathering up the papers to put them back in Jack's file. She caught a glimpse of one of the pictures the hospital had taken of the hand before it had been worked on, and made a face. Then she sat down. Her eerie calm was still in evidence, except that it wasn't really calm, which is what made it eerie. It didn't matter that Gregor had met other people with this same dead flatness of affect, and that none of them had been mass murderers or even petty thieves. There was something about being in the presence of a person like this that made the nerves beneath his skin begin to jump.

Linda folded her hands on the table in front of her and waited. She could wait forever. Gregor knew that. You might goad somebody else into talking just by staying silent, but you wouldn't goad her.

"It's funny," he said.

"What's funny, Mr. Demarkian? I don't see anything funny in any of this."

"I was just thinking how alike you are to Carl Frank," Gregor said. "Not really, of course, but you have one thing in common and it's an unusual thing. And with unusual things, the fact that they're unusual makes people think that they must also be important."

Linda sat there, with her hands folded. Nothing about her moved except her eyes, and they weren't particularly active. She was small and gray and compact and incredibly neat. She was not particularly interested.

"Aren't you interested in knowing what you've got in common with Carl Frank?" Gregor asked.

"Not really. I thought that if you thought it was important, you'd tell me. But I don't know him, do I? I'll probably never see him again after all this is over. I don't see why I should care that we share some characteristic in common."

"Do you care about Jack Bullard?" Gregor asked.

This time, her eyes got a little more active. If Gregor believed eyes could narrow, he would have imagined hers had.

"I've known him half my life," Linda said. "I've known him all his life. I remember him as a baby in a carriage in town. His father used to walk him in on the weekends and buy bait and go out fishing with Jack in the carriage beside him. He was the cutest thing on wheels."

"Which doesn't answer my question."

"Your question is impossible to answer. I suppose I care about him. I'm fond of him. He's—there's something very innocent about Jack. Not just naive, but innocent."

"Was it innocent, going out to Las Vegas with Kendra Rhode and Arrow Normand?"

Linda flicked this away. "Jack wanted to be a photographer, a celebrity photographer. It was his chance. The whole filming thing was. His chance to take a shot at getting out of here and doing something with his life."

"Do most people want to get out of Margaret's Harbor? I thought this was where rich people went to retire."

"Which is fine if you're a rich person," Linda said. "Jack wasn't, any more than I am. If you're a year-rounder, the Harbor is deadly dull and deadly ended, if that makes any sense. Jack went away to college, and we thought that would be the last we'd see of him, but he came back. His father was ailing. Not that that lasted long. The man keeled over and died within a month, but Jack never seemed to be able to get the momentum going to get all the way out, if you see what I mean. Then they came and there it was, his shot. So he took it."

"You didn't mind?"

"Why would I mind?"

"He is your employee," Gregor said. "Going off to Vegas for a weekend had to cut into the time he had to work for you."

"Oh, for goodness' sake," Linda said. "Really, Jack's taken weekends before. And it's not as if it was in the season, when we've got a lot to do. Margaret's Harbor in the late fall is not a hotbed of news that has to be rushed to the printers."

"Not even with the film people here?"

"I didn't run stories about the film people," Linda said. "And I'm not going to run them now, except to report on the criminal investigations, and the trials, if we ever get to those. I am running a story about what happened to Jack. I wrote it myself. It will be out at the end of the week."

"What will it say?"

"It will say Jack was attacked," Linda said, "which is more than any other paper will say, anywhere. Nobody is much interested in Jack Bullard's hand when they've got Kendra Rhode to talk about, or that other one. I didn't mind Kendra Rhode so much. She was at least local."

"I thought she came from New York."

"Local as in from a Margaret's Harbor family. A summer family, but a family." Linda shrugged. "I'm sorry. I'm a snob. It matters to me."

"Do you want to tell me what happened to Jack Bullard?"

"I don't know what happened to Jack," Linda said. "How could I know? I only know about finding him."

"Where did you find him?"

"In back of the Home News Building. There's a place back there, a little open space between our building and the Coach store on the other side, the Coach store on Melville Street. We put the garbage out back there and then on garbage day we wheel it out to the front. Well, we do at the *Home News,* and the people at the Coach store do, but Bill Grady that has the pharmacy takes his stuff to the dump in his truck. It makes me crazy. It's a pharmacy, for God's sake. It's not like he's some widower fisherman living on his own in a cabin. But you can't talk to Bill Grady. You never could."

"Do you know what Jack was doing out in back of the building? Was he taking out garbage? Had he gone to meet someone?"

"He'd gone out for air," Linda said. "He was up in my office, and he started to feel sick to his stomach. Or he said he did. And he got up and went out back to get some air. He was away for nearly half an hour and I got worried. So I went back there to see if I could find him."

"And?"

"And," Linda said, "I did find him. He stumbled into the building, and there was blood everywhere. It looked to me like somebody had tried to take his hand off. Then I went to look at the other one, to see if somebody had tried to take that one off, too, but of course it had the glove on it."

"Why of course?" Gregor asked.

"Because it was cold," Linda said. "It's freezing up here this time of year, Mr. Demarkian, in case you hadn't noticed. But you can't operate those cameras he has with a hand in a thick leather glove, and you can't go without the gloves completely or your fingers fall off. So he wore the glove on his left hand and kept his right hand free to work the cameras."

"And it was his camera hand that was attacked," Gregor said. It was not a question.

"I think it was one of those other photographers," Linda said. "One of those people from New York or Los Angeles. Jack is a very good photographer. I think those people didn't like the competition from somebody local, and then of course there was all that stuff about the Vegas trip, where Jack was the only photographer to be asked along. I think they're jealous."

"I think they very probably are," Gregor said. "Somebody I talked to in town said that Jack had a crush on Kendra Rhode, or possibly on Marcey Mandret. That he was emotionally involved."

Linda Beecham shrugged. "He was, of course he was. He was way out of his league in terms of the personalities. They all seemed special to him. You couldn't tell him otherwise. And I suppose, to someone with limited experience, they did seem special. They are special. They're, I don't know, shinier than the rest of us."

"But not better?"

"Better at what?" Linda asked. "They're not very bright, at least not the ones I've talked to, and I've talked to most of them these past few months. They tend to be rude, and to think they can do whatever they want without consequences. They're rich and they're spoiled, but so are a lot of other people on Margaret's Harbor. They get their pictures in the news a lot, although I've never been able to figure out what for. I think that for Jack, there was just too much dazzle and he was just too unused to it. He'll figure it out in the long run."

"You don't think he had a particular crush on any one of the group of them?"

"I don't think Jack's ever had a particular crush on anybody."

"All right," Gregor said. "What happened after you found him behind the building?"

"I went back into the building and called the hospital," Linda said, "and then I called Jerry Young, because it was obvious that what we had was a crime scene. It was a criminal attack. It had to be. I mean, there he was, drugged up like that, and his hand bleeding all over everything. But Jerry didn't come out, not right away. He had to wait until somebody came in to babysit Arrow Normand."

"Was that illegitimate?" Gregor asked. "He couldn't leave Arrow Normand in a cell without supervision, could he?"

"Why not?" Linda asked. "This isn't Rikers Island. We have people in those jail cells all the time without supervision. Not in the summer, of course, but during the off-seasons. Drunks, mostly. Nobody bothers to get somebody to sit around and babysit them. And what did Jerry think Arrow Normand was going to do in his absence? Stage a jailbreak? Commit suicide?"

"Maybe," Gregor said.

"Don't be ridiculous. Arrow Normand wouldn't commit suicide unless she could be guaranteed ringside seats at her own funeral, and if she staged a jailbreak she'd be caught in a minute and a half when she stopped to pose for the first set of photographers. It wasn't that. It was just that Jack is Jack and not some Hollywood celebrity. It's like a virus everybody's been catching around here. Jerry Young had too much to do to actually investigate a crime."

"Are you saying he didn't come to the scene at all?"

"He came, at the last minute. By then the ambulance was already there, and they were loading Jack into it. They had to do that. Jack was alive. It was an emergency. They couldn't just leave him lying in the snow while Jerry took his own sweet time showing up."

"Did anybody else show up?"

"Some of those photographers poked their noses in when the ambulance first got there, just to see what the siren was about, but they didn't stay long. There isn't much money in photographs of Jack Bullard with an injured hand. There isn't much money in photographs of Jack Bullard. They went away."

"And then what?"

"Then the ambulance took Jack to the hospital, and I stayed around for a while, and then I went looking for Clara Walsh," Linda said. "And then I met you, come to think of it. But none of you were much interested in Jack either."

"We did come and interview Dr. Ingleford, on the spot."

"And then Marcey Mandret turned up drunk and you all went running," Linda said. "It's embarrassing, really, the way you all behave.

He was lying there in bed, unconscious, or something like it, and you were all more interested in Marcey Mandret being drunk. What does that woman do, anyway? She's supposed to be a movie star, but I never see her in a movie."

"I haven't either," Gregor said. "But what did you do when we all went to see about Marcey Mandret? Did you stay with Jack?"

"Yes, I did. For another half an hour, at least. And then I went home."

"Did anyone else come to see Jack when you were there?"

"No."

"Did he get any phone calls? Did anyone inquire about him?"

"No."

"Did you see anyone coming into or out of the hospital when you left?"

"Well, there were a million people around the emergency room entrance," Linda said. "They looked like one of those invading armies from the *Lord of the Rings* movies. But there was no one on Jack's ward, no. Even Dr. Ingleford left."

Gregor was about to say that she couldn't fault Dr. Ingleford about that, since he seemed to be the only full-fledged doctor on duty at the time, but he let it go. Linda Beecham only seemed to be dead flat and without emotion. In truth, she was angry to the point of explosion, and keeping control of it by a continual act of will.

He wondered what happened when the will broke down.

Then he didn't wonder anymore, because he realized he knew.

SIX

1

Stewart Gordon was glad to hear that Carl Frank had moved Arrow Normand and her mother out of Annabeth Falmer's living room. He'd thought the entire idea was cracked from the start, because there was no way Annabeth's house could be "secured" against paparazzi in any meaningful sense, and because the paparazzi wouldn't be back in force for at least another day or two. There was also the problem of Annabeth herself, who wasn't used to people like Arrow Normand, and who really wasn't used to people like Arrow Normand's mother. Besides, the paparazzi hadn't really disappeared. They'd only gone into hiding. They were waiting for the moment when it would be safe for them to return in force, or impossible to resist, whichever came first. At best, Stewart gave them another twenty-four hours. It would be less if somebody was arrested for causing the death of Kendra Rhode.

Stewart was less glad to hear that Marcey Mandret had not left Annabeth's living room, and didn't seem to be intending to.

"She's lying on the couch with a blanket, drinking tea and reading

W. B. Yeats," Annabeth said when Stewart called to say he was coming over.

"She can't be reading Yeats," Stewart said. "She won't get any of the references."

"I'm explaining things," Annabeth said. "And really, Stewart, you can't complain that much. It's better than having her drunk in the middle of the day and falling out of her clothes where photographers can catch her at it. I mean, I admit I would have started her on Byron maybe, or even Dickens, but she liked the cover on the Yeats."

"Isn't there something somewhere about not judging books by their covers?"

"I don't know if she knows that one," Annabeth said.

"I just got a call from Carl Frank," Stewart said. "He said Gregor Demarkian was asking him about my suitability as a suspect for these murders."

"You are a suitable suspect for the murders," Annabeth said. "You're a more suitable suspect than Arrow Normand. I don't think that young woman could plan her way into a peanut butter and jelly sandwich."

"Possibly true," Stewart said. "But there's no malice in her."

And that, he thought, as he made his way from his house to the boardwalk so that he could walk along the beach to Annabeth's, summed up his entire position in this endless mess. The twits were twits, but with the exception of Kendra Rhode they had no malice in them. They were ignorant, and vulgar, and shallow, but they wished no one harm, and they tried to be nice to the people who had to work with them. Maybe it was too much to ask them to behave like thoroughgoing professionals at their ages and their levels of experience. Had he been a thoroughgoing professional at the age of twenty-one? Well, actually, he probably had. He'd just left the Royal Academy then, where they'd trained his voice, already too deep by half, until it sounded like a foghorn. But he hadn't had the disadvantages these girls had had. He hadn't been famous at fifteen, or surrounded by adults whose only purpose was to suck money out of him. He'd had a decent home life with two people who had worked with their hands and been paid for it, and who didn't take any nonsense from "teenagers." Stewart tried to imagine his father referring to anybody at all as a "teenager," and failed. His father was not fond of fads. Not even a little bit.

Annabeth's house was easy to reach, and there was nobody on the boardwalk this afternoon. Stewart wouldn't have cared if there had been. His policy had always been to treat fame as if it didn't exist. He employed no bodyguards. He didn't travel with an entourage. The only assistant he'd ever had had been the one the studio hired to help with his fan mail while he was playing Commander Rees. She'd been a very nice, sensible, middle-aged Scotswoman whose idea of a night on the town was shrimp and pasta at an Olive Garden followed by three stiff shots of unadulterated whiskey when she got home. Mrs. Mackindle, her name had been, and Stewart still sent Christmas cards to her place in Aberdeen.

He got to Annabeth's house and knocked on the door. Annabeth had *The Well-Tempered Clavier* on the stereo. It was a good stereo, a Bose, that her sons had bought her because she liked music. The disc of *The Well-Tempered Clavier* she was playing featured a harpsichord, which was what it was supposed to feature, instead of a piano, which most of them did. He knocked a second time, just in case she hadn't heard him, and the door opened.

"Hello," Annabeth said. It was a door to the kitchen, not the one to the living room, because that one faced the sea. "I've got more tea on. You look good. This is very odd."

"I want to talk to you about something," Stewart said.

Annabeth was already headed back toward the stove. The kettle was blowing, but not sounding, because she had put the whistle up.

"I think Marcey may have fallen asleep," she said. "I really don't know what to do about the mood she's in. I mean, you can't just make up ten years of schooling in an afternoon. Not that I'm necessarily wedded to the idea of education taking place in schools. But you can't go from not reading anything at all except menus to reading Yeats just like that. I finally got her to give it up and gave her Elizabeth Barrett Browning. She likes Elizabeth Barrett Browning."

"She probably thinks it's song lyrics," Stewart said. "Is she going to stay here all day? Is she moving in? She does have a house to go to."

"Oh, I know," Annabeth said. "I think she's just worried about the publicity, you know, and the photographers. I mean, she does realize they're not much in evidence today, but she seems to be sure they'll be back any minute. Is that right? Will they be back any minute?"

"Sooner rather than later," Stewart said, "which means it makes even more sense for her to be in her own house instead of here. She's got at least some security in that place."

"She's also alone. She said she always used to have people with her, but Carl Frank made them leave."

"They all travel with huge groups of people," Stewart said. "Paid friendship, if you ask me. Anyway, the huge groups of people don't usually come to work with them, and Carl Frank had had enough of the schedule going to hell, so he packed them all home. I live alone. You don't worry about something happening to me."

"Of course I worry about that. But you can take care of yourself. You'd probably do pretty well in hand-to-hand combat. She seems a lot more vulnerable."

"I can take care of myself," Stewart said. "But right now, there's something I want to talk to you about, so if she's asleep, that's all well and good."

There was a sound from the living room, and Stewart realized that what he was hearing was Marcey Mandret, moving around. The disc had finished playing. He heard clicks and whirrs and then the sound of another disc, still *The Well-Tempered Clavier,* starting up.

"Well," Annabeth said. "She must be awake. I've got those Moravian spice cookies you like over there in that tin. Let's bring them into the living room and relax."

"Let's not go into the living room just yet," Stewart said. "There really is something I want to talk to you about."

Annabeth turned to look at him, quizzical. "You aren't going to confess to a murder, are you? Because I did think about you and Kendra Rhode, and you didn't seem to have time. Or maybe I'm wrong. About the time."

"I don't know," Stewart said. He reminded himself that, for all her perfections, she was still an American. Then he admitted to himself that he often rather liked Americans. Next to the Brits he was used to dealing with at home, they had a terrific work ethic.

"Listen," he said. "I was thinking. In spite of all this mess, the filming can't go on here longer than another two to three weeks. After that, I've got three months before I start another project. I think we should go to Australia together."

"What?"

"Australia," Stewart said. "You know. We've talked about Australia. You said you'd like to see it."

"I would like to see it."

"So," Stewart said, "we should go together, and on the way, we should stop in London and get married."

"Married," Annabeth said.

"I know it's a little quick," Stewart said, "but we're neither one of us teenagers, and we both have children who probably don't want to see their parents jetting off all over the world with a paramour. Or, you know what I mean. My children are all in and around London—well, except for Andrew, who's in the Amazon, but that's a long story. We'll get him out of there long enough to attend the wedding—and we can fly your boys in, and then we can take off and call Australia our honeymoon. Go see the fairy penguins. That kind of thing."

"Married," Annabeth said again.

Stewart had a sudden feeling that this was not going well. He didn't think he could have been that far off in judging the emotional climate between them. Why wasn't it going well? He was beginning to feel a little panicked.

"When I'm not filming," he plowed on, "we could travel wherever you liked. We could go to Rome. We could travel across the United States and see the places you want to write about. We could go to China."

Annabeth had stopped making tea. She had the hot water half poured into a yellow and white polka-dot teapot, and she was still standing next to it, holding the kettle in the air, staring at him. Stewart had begun to feel like Jack the Ripper.

"Or not," he said, in a last desperate bid to get a response out of her. "If you don't like traveling, we could stay home. In Scotland, if you wanted. Or in Los Angeles. Or London. Or even, ah, here."

"Oh, for God's sake," Marcey Mandret said. "You've got to go down on your knees or have a ring or some flowers or do something romantic. Don't you know anything about anything?"

Stewart turned, feeling his face go brick red in a way he hadn't since he was a third-former caught with a copy of a girlie mag in his Latin workbook. He was only somewhat mollified by finding that Marcey was not in her usual strappy little dress, but wearing sweats that covered everything as thoroughly as a burka. She was not, however, making fun of him. She was deadly serious.

"If you're going to get her to marry you," she said, "you've got to do something romantic. You've got to treat her like she's worth doing something romantic for."

This seemed to do something to Annabeth, who until then had been frozen in place. She looked at the kettle she was holding and then at the teapot. She poured more water into the teapot until it was full. She put the kettle back on the stove. She bit her lip. Stewart had the terrible premonition that she was about to give him one of those lectures about how they would always be friends.

Instead, she said, "It's all right, I think. I don't need anything romantic, at least not right now. I'll marry you."

"Don't do it," Marcey Mandret said. "Not till he at least comes across with flowers. If you don't insist, he'll just go on forgetting to do anything romantic for the next fifty years."

"We don't have the next fifty years," Stewart Gordon said.

"Make him get you flowers," Marcey said again. "Do it."

Annabeth put the top back onto the teapot and brought the teapot over to the kitchen table. She put it down and then sat down in front of it. The cat was there, waiting, the way it always was. Stewart didn't understand what it was about cats.

"We can take the cat," he said. "We can even take him to Australia if you want to. I don't mean to separate you from the cat."

"Okay," Marcey Mandret said. "You can go back to saying yes. He's lost it."

2

There were times when Carl Frank honestly thought that the majority of human beings should be prevented by law from viewing any kind of popular entertainment. Viewing it, or reading it—in Carl Frank's world, books were not thoughtful histories of America's role in the post–World War II reconstruction of Europe or insightful analyses of the iconographic elements in Caravaggio's *Death of the Virgin*. Books were like movies, and like television, and all three were engaged in an orgy of conspiracy theories and simple hyperbole that left nothing of reality untouched. Look at it, Carl thought, climbing carefully along the boardwalk as it started to get rocky and badly cared for. Look at the people, the otherwise sensible people, who believed that Kennedy was assassinated by a cabal led by Lyndon Johnson or that the Twin Towers came down on September 11 because George W. Bush had the CIA blow them up. Reality wasn't good enough for them anymore. The messy, stupid pointlessness of it didn't ring true. Maybe that part predated popular entertainment. It seemed to him that people had always preferred conspiracy theories to reality. That was why religions were so popular. No, it isn't a matter of chance and circumstance that you're here on this earth, or that your five-year-old child died of leukemia, or that you lost your job when the plant moved manufacturing operations to Taiwan. No, it isn't chance and circumstance at all, it's a plan, a vast cosmic plan, and you're a very important part of it.

The boardwalk here was really awful. It was true in Oscartown as it was true everywhere else that the rich got better treatment than the poor, even when it came to public services. Someone ought to come out here and do a good job of snow removal and then sand and paint the thing, and replace the rotten boards. He thought about Gregor Demarkian, and his head hurt. Did a man like that, a man who had worked with presidents, who had headed up one of the most important sections of one of the most important law enforcement bodies in the world, did that man really think that movie producers sent henchmen around to murder prop boys and second assistant grips when they got in the way of finishing a motion picture? What about a bad motion picture? There was a story about G. Gordon Liddy that Carl had heard just after he left college. He had no idea if it was true, but it was a perfect illustration of what was wrong with everything and everybody these days. The story went like this: In the last days before the Watergate mess had unraveled, when the break-in was still secret but didn't look as if it would be for long, Liddy had shown up at the White House and asked to talk to Halderman and Erlichman. "All right," he was supposed to have said, "I know how this works, and I'll make it easy for you. I'll be on the corner of K Street and Connecticut at twenty minutes after midnight tonight, and I won't do a thing to stop you from taking me out."

Carl remembered hearing that story the first time and thinking how funny it was, thinking that it summed up Liddy's goofiness even if it wasn't true. Life was just not like that, and sane people knew it, but nobody seemed to be sane anymore. Why ever would someone like Michael Bardman, who could eat the cost of a failed minor movie out of his own checking account, bother to pay somebody to murder somebody like Mark Anderman? You could say anything you wanted about Michael Bardman—and Carl had said a lot of it; in some ways, the man was a loon—but he was the most important producer in the history of movies, and not just movies in Hollywood. He was practically a force of nature. It wouldn't hurt Michael Bardman's career if Arrow Normand went down in flames, or even if the movie did. There was a difference between not wanting a failure and needing not to have one.

The boardwalk had come to an end. Carl looked up and around himself. He was in an area of small, low houses, the kind that looked, from the road, as if they were too low to stand up in. Here and there he saw a pickup truck parked in a drive next to one. He couldn't see any proper garages. There was a lot of snow, and a lot of what seemed to be random items piled up on porches that didn't look long for this world. People fished here, not for relaxation, but for money. People chopped cordwood and cleared other people's driveways and mowed lawns when the fishing wasn't good. People used whitewash instead of paint. Carl could remember houses like this. They existed on the edges of every small town in rural America, existed and not much more. He found the sign that said Bellwether Road and counted down from it until he reached number 6. The ocean was here, right here. It came right up to the back doors of half these places, and yet none of them would ever be described as "waterfront property" in any real estate brochure. It was funny how that worked.

He stepped off the boardwalk onto Bellwether Road and was very careful of his shoes, which were not made for wading through the snow. People like Michael Bardman had a certain amount of responsibility for the way everybody was acting these days. They made the movies that used conspiracy theories as their foundations: the ones where the crop circles really were made by mysterious aliens; the ones where Kennedy really was killed by Lyndon Johnson's undercover dirty-tricks operators; the ones where everything you see and everything you know and everything you do is just code for something else, something darker, something more sinister, something secret. Maybe it had always been like this in one way or another, although he doubted it. He was fairly sure that, at least for his parents' generation, there had been times when most people would have rejected this kind of thinking in favor of living in the mundane day to day. Entertainment had simply become so big a part of everything, so integral a part of everybody's day-to-day lives, that nothing else felt real anymore. Carl's professors in college would have called it the "narrative instinct," although Carl didn't think it was an instinct. Lately, though, he'd understood what they'd meant better than he had when he'd first heard them. Human beings were narrative animals. They liked stories. Their brains were hardwired to think in stories. Nothing sounded true to them if it didn't fit into a story. The Michael Bardmans of the world made it possible for people to live in stories, all day, all night, all of their lives. It took training and practice to learn to think logically. Nobody who spent his life at the movies was ever going to get that far.

"Then we turned the entire country into a high school," Carl said out loud, "and nominated our own popular crowd."

He felt better after he'd heard the sound of his own voice. He wished there was somebody around here, even though it meant he would have to be more careful doing what he had to do. It was true, what he'd said, about high school. First they made the stories the most important things, and then they made the people who acted out the stories the most important things, because those people would have to be. The paparazzi didn't chase Arrow Normand and Marcey Mandret because they were idiots or because the editors of the tabloids were terrible human beings or even because the public was stupid. The paparazzi chased and the editors published and the public paid attention because these were the people who defined the stories that defined their lives. And defined was the right word, Carl thought, picking his way carefully over a little mound of snow and ice that cut across the road with no way to go around it. Stories were how people defined themselves as well as each other and the world they lived in. Identity was a story. In very traditional societies, the stories were myths and legends. In very religious societies, the stories were religious ones. In this society, the stories were at the movies, and on television, and in music videos, and without those stories the whole damned thing would fall apart. He'd spent a lot of his time in college rolling his eyes, wondering how anybody could spend his time worrying about this kind of bullshit, but now he saw that it wasn't bullshit at all. It was the most important thing. "Identity narratives," his professors had called them, and that was what he had spent his life doing. He had spent his life in the care and maintenance of the only identity narratives most Americans would ever know.

"Probably most people in the world," he said, aloud again. His voice echoed slightly, and the street felt uncomfortably still. Here was a narrative for you: a man alone on a strangely deserted street, where things seem to be moving just out of sight, in the shadows, a man destined to meet evil face-to-face before he even knows what hits him. It was not a terribly inventive narrative. Some version of it had probably existed forever, since long before human beings knew how to write things down. Maybe all narratives had existed forever. That was why people couldn't walk through cemeteries without getting the creeps, and couldn't stay long in an empty house without putting on some music or the television. Maybe all narratives started in raw emotion, the kind of raw emotion people were helpless to control. Maybe they started in the conviction that being alone was so awful a thing, it was better to deny that it could ever be true.

He found the mailbox that said "Bullard" and looked up and down the street again. He might as well not have bothered. There was nobody here. He wondered where all the people were. They couldn't be off on vacation, or at jobs in Boston. In either case, their houses would be better than these were. Besides, it was obvious that the houses on this street were not shut up for the winter. He looked around yet again. Maybe there were people here, but out of sight, behind curtains, lurking at windows. If anyone was here, he would know that Carl Frank did not belong, that he had no right to be trying the door at one of these houses. Would it matter? There was only the one town policeman. The state police had other things on their minds.

Carl walked up onto the front porch. It was a wide front porch, but the wood was old. Something would have to be done about the porch floor soon or Jack Bullard would find himself falling through it. There were planters hanging from hooks in the porch ceiling. The plants inside them were dead. There was an old glider up against the porch wall just outside a row of small windows. The glider was broken, and the fabric that had been used to cushion it was torn.

"He doesn't take care of his place," Carl said, out loud again, because he really couldn't help it. He tried the door and found it locked, but not locked in any serious way. He jiggled the handle a couple of times and felt the door rattle in its frame. He gave it one good push with the side of his hip and it popped. He wondered if there was a problem with theft in this neighborhood. Idiotic as it had always seemed to him, theft was a big problem in poor neighborhoods. There were thieves—apparently, thieves who couldn't count—who preferred to steal from poor people rather than rich ones. Maybe it was laziness. Maybe poor people's houses were just easier to break into than rich people's houses. Maybe fewer people cared.

He stepped into the living room and looked around. The house was full of stuff. There were things piled everywhere, not important, not expensive, but plentiful, as if Jack Bullard spent money for the sake of spending money. Maybe he did. Carl knew very little about him, except that he wanted to be a celebrity photographer and he'd spent a lot of time following Kendra Rhode and Arrow Normand around. Well, a lot of people did that. That wasn't unusual.

He picked his way through the old furniture and the boxes full of things that had never been used and made his way into the kitchen.

The kitchen looked much more lived-in than the living room did. It was obvious that somebody had been using the stove. There was a coffee cup on the round kitchen table, still half filled with coffee. If this had been summer instead of winter, the coffee would have gone to mold.

Carl turned around, and looked, really looked. There were cabinets, but the ones that were open seemed to be half empty. There was a sink full of dishes. They may have lain there, dirty, for weeks. There was the stove and the refrigerator and the sink. He opened the refrigerator and then the freezer. That was an old writer's trick, from the days before digital, when a single manuscript copy might be all you had. You put it in the refrigerator when you weren't working on it, because that would save it if the house burned down. There was nothing in the refrigerator but old food, almost all of it rotting and gone to mold.

Carl went to the line of cabinets and opened one. There were a couple of plates, a couple of coffee mugs of the same kind as the one on the table, a couple of small bowls. He opened the next one and found what had to be two dozen boxes of family-size beef Rice-A-Roni. He went to the next one and hit pay dirt: regular folders, accordion folders, loose photographs, documents held together by paper clips. There would be order to this mess that Jack Bullard would understand without thinking about it, but for Carl it was just a mess, and it would stay that way. He took out the three largest accordion folders and dumped them onto the kitchen table.

He would not kill anyone for Michael Bardman, or for a movie, and nobody would. By and large, people were just people. They did the small and usual things, and the really big ones, like homicide, were outside what they could work up the imagination to conceptualize. Violence didn't even occur to most people most of the time, and the people to whom it did occur on a regular basis generally had too little control of themselves to hold a job for a week, never mind to launch and carry out a conspiracy that required the suborning of presidents. Carl Frank didn't want Mark Anderman dead. He didn't even want Steve Becker dead. He just wanted Jack Bullard's pictures of the wedding, so that no matter what came out in the press, he'd have the upper hand for damage control.

"It's as simple as that," he said, out loud again, just to hear the sound of his own voice. He wasn't talking to himself this time, though. He was talking to Gregor Demarkian, even though Gregor Demarkian would never hear it.

All he wanted was the pictures of the wedding, and it was good luck for him that Jack Bullard was temporarily incapacitated and unable to prevent a little foray into his own house.

SEVEN

1

At the Oscartown Police Department, Gregor Demarkian was still sitting at the table in the conference room, but the other side of the table was occupied by Clara Walsh, Bram Winder, and Jerry Young, and Gregor had a big piece of paper to write on.

"Your problem," he said, not looking up to see if they were paying attention, "is that you had a series of events that had to be explained to make sense of what happened, and they couldn't be explained in the usual way. Real life is not like a detective story, no matter how much we want it to be. Real murderers are messy. They're haphazard. They panic. Most of them can't plan their way out of paper bags. And murder for hire is a lot more rare in the real world than it is on *CSI*. Here are your problems."

He passed the big piece of paper across the table. On it, he had written in capital letters:

MURDER OF MARK ANDERMAN
ATTACK ON JACK BULLARD

GUN IN ANNABETH FALMER'S HOUSE
DEATH OF KENDRA RHODE

"My problem," Gregor said, "was to assume that life was never like a detective story, because the four things on that list could not have been committed by the same person."

"Do you mean there was an accomplice?" Bram Winder asked. "There's nothing odd about that. Perpetrators have accomplices all the time."

"There was no accomplice in the ordinary sense," Gregor said. "This wasn't a plot hatched by two people, or even a case where person A commits a crime and gets person B to help him cover it up. If it had been, the attack on Jack Bullard would never have happened. Or if it did, it wouldn't have happened the way it did. As for the gun in Annabeth Falmer's house"—Gregor shrugged—"I suppose that could have happened the way it did, but it was a stupid move, and unnecessary, and did more harm than good."

"The forensics came back on that, right?" Bram said. "It wasn't even the right gun. I don't understand why anybody would want to plant it in Annabeth Falmer's house, if somebody did plant it there. What was the point?"

"The point was that it was Jack Bullard's gun," Gregor said.

"Do you mean somebody was trying to implicate Jack?" Clara Walsh said. "That doesn't make sense. It would make more sense to mail the gun to the police station, or to me."

"Nobody was trying to implicate Jack," Gregor said. "Turn it around, and see what you have. First, the person who planted the gun in Annabeth's house thought that it was the gun that had been used to kill Mark Anderman. Second, the person who planted the gun in Annabeth's house knew that both Arrow Normand and Marcey Mandret had been in that living room all the afternoon of the storm. The idea wasn't to implicate Jack. It was to implicate Arrow Normand."

"But she was already in jail," Clara Walsh said.

"She was in jail, but not for long," Gregor said. "In fact, even you admitted to me, yesterday, that you couldn't understand why she was still in jail. She has good legal representation. She could have been out any time she wanted to be. The only reason she wasn't out was that she didn't want to be. She used a few days in jail to hide from the crazy people around her, and having met her, and several of the crazy people, I'm not entirely unsympathetic. I don't think anybody, anywhere, thought that you were going to end up prosecuting Arrow Normand for the murder of Mark Anderman, not as things stood, at any rate. And nobody thought you'd ever get a conviction. But the person who planted the gun didn't care whether you got a conviction or not. The only point was to get you to concentrate on Arrow Normand and not on anybody else."

"We didn't have anybody else to concentrate on," Clara Walsh said. "I wish we had."

"So let me get this straight," Jerry Young said. "First the perpetrator murdered Mark Anderman. Then the perpetrator attacked Jack Bullard. Then the perpetrator hid Jack's gun in Annabeth Falmer's house—"

"No," Gregor said. "The perpetrator murdered Mark Anderman, but since then, everything we've been looking at has been the work of somebody else. It's been smoke, pure and simple. And that was what I had to get past before I could understand what was happening. It wasn't the work of only one person, but it also wasn't the work of one person and an accomplice, because the person who killed Kendra Rhode wouldn't have agreed to the attack on Jack Bullard, and if that person had known about the planting of the gun, the gun wouldn't have been the wrong one, or it wouldn't have been planted at all. And as for Kendra Rhode, the last thing the murderer of Mark Anderman wanted was the death of Kendra Rhode."

"You keep saying 'death,'" Bram Winder said, "not 'murder.' Wasn't Kendra Rhode murdered?"

"I don't know," Gregor said. "I don't think the person who killed her knows. My guess is that there was a single murderous moment, but I know there was no planning, and no conscious intent. Which is very different from the murder of Mark Anderman, which was not only planned but plotted out, and then followed up. It had to be, because if it hadn't been it would have been too obvious. So I'll hand over to you the murderer of Mark Anderman, and tell you how it happened, and lay out what you need to get your conviction, but the death of Kendra Rhode is going to be solved only if the person who killed her tells you about it, and I have no idea if that's going to happen or not."

"So where do we go from here?" Jerry Young said. "We've got enough staties in town to open a barracks, and the paparazzi are going to be back, and you know it. What can we do about any of this?"

"We can go and ask one more set of questions," Gregor said. "Why don't you all come with me. I need to have you along. With any luck you'll be able to make your arrest before the paparazzi get back, and then you can try to equip the Harbor with advanced security equipment to keep them under control."

"They haven't actually left the island," Jerry Young said gloomily. "They're just hiding. And not doing that good a job at it."

"If we're going to go somewhere, we ought to go," Clara Walsh said. "Where are we going?"

"To see Jack Bullard," Gregor said. "I talked to Mike Ingleford half an hour ago. Mr. Bullard is up and around and due to go home as soon as Dr. Ingleford stops stalling so that we can get there first."

2

The Oscartown Hospital was actually named the Betty Larkin Halle Memorial Hospital. Gregor had no idea how he had missed that the first time through, especially since it was spelled out in shiny letters over the hospital's front door, and then again in the glass next to the emergency room entrance. Then again, he only noticed it now because he was looking at the places in which the glass was broken and boarded over, a relic of the half riot of just yesterday. Gregor looked up and down the street as Clara Walsh's car pulled to a stop right in the middle of the curving front drive. He had no idea why they had driven from the Oscartown Inn, which was close enough to see from where they were now, but Clara had insisted, and here they were. Nobody else was here, though, at least as far as he could see. Linda Beecham was not entirely wrong when she said that nobody was interested in somebody like Jack.

Gregor got out of the car and waited for the rest of them. Bram Winder looked disgruntled. Jerry Young just looked depressed. It was colder than Gregor thought it ever got in Philadelphia.

"So," Clara said. "What are we going to do, charge Jack with ruining his own hand?"

"Maybe," Gregor said.

She walked past him and in through the big plate glass doors. It occurred to Gregor that the United States was the least security-conscious of nations, in spite of the way they hyperventilated about it in public. There were so many glass doors, everywhere, that couldn't be defended with less than an army at hand. There were so many windows, too.

They went through the lobby, waving at the woman at the desk, and to the elevators. The entire place felt as deserted as it had the first time Gregor had been there. The elevator was sitting on their floor. Clara shooed them all into it and then punched the button for the third floor.

"Honest to God," she said. "I thought you were going to have me arrest Marcey Mandret. Wouldn't that have been a show?"

Gregor didn't say anything. The door was opening at the third floor. Stepping into the corridor, he could see Leslie at her desk—he guessed she would never leave her desk during a shift again, even if it meant she would have to urinate in a Dixie cup—and then, looking left, Mike Ingleford standing near a door at the end of the hall. Gregor looked from Ingleford to the fire doors at the end, and back to

Ingleford. That was going to work out, but it was something he should have checked out before.

They were halfway to Jack Bullard's room when Linda Beecham came out, holding one of those big paper shopping bags with handles.

"Now what?" she said. "Don't tell me you want to question him now. He's going home. He'd have been home in an hour. Go away now."

Clara Walsh had puffed on ahead of the rest of them. She reached Linda Beecham first.

"It's all right," she said. "It's something of an emergency, that's all. For goodness' sake, Linda, you saw what happened yesterday. You can't believe they've gone away for good. I've got half the state police force on the Harbor this morning and I still don't feel safe enough. Let's get this over with before there's more trouble."

"He's been unconscious for most of a day," Linda said. "He's been drugged. How is he supposed to remember anything?"

"He wasn't drugged on the night of the storm," Clara Walsh said. "Come on, Linda, stop playing the mother hen. This will only take a minute. Won't it, Mr. Demarkian? You're not intending to give Jack the third degree, or whatever it is? I don't know why people say 'the third degree.' I haven't got the faintest idea what it means, and I don't think anybody else does, either."

The rest of them had reached the door where Linda Beecham and Mike Ingleford were standing. Gregor said hello to the doctor and went inside. Jack was standing near the windows, looking out at Oscartown, his back to the door. The room was bare except for a small bouquet of flowers in a thin glass vase. Gregor wondered if Linda had brought it, or if one of the nurses had, uncomfortable at how barren and sterile Jack's room was.

Jack turned around and looked at them. He was young and good-looking in the way that only young men of a certain age can be. He was very tired.

"Well," he said.

"Do you know why I'm here?" Gregor said.

"I think so," Jack said.

"Does she know?"

Gregor meant Linda Beecham, and Jack understood him.

"She knew before you did," he said. "She's a very strange woman."

"She could have gotten herself into a great deal of trouble. She might have been wrong. You might have pressed charges."

"But she wasn't wrong, was she?" Jack said. "She's never wrong, if you want to know the truth. Wrongheaded, sometimes. Lots of times. This time. But never wrong."

"You're still drugged to the gills," Linda Beecham said. "You shouldn't let them do this to you. They're only trying to railroad you because it's better for them to get hold of you than to get hold of one of those people. They're afraid of those people. They've got money."

"I wanted to have money once," Jack said. "That's how this started. Did you know that?"

"Yes," Gregor said. "But it wasn't where it ended."

"No," Jack agreed. "If what I'd wanted in the end was money, I could have had it. I've got a stack of photographs from the Vegas trip back at the house. They're worth a fortune. Literally. Arrow Normand. Marcey Mandret. Kendra Rhode. In clothes and out of them, at the weddings, in bars, everything. Absolute exclusives. Nobody else has them, or anything like them. I could have done a seven-figure deal with any one of the tabloids. But even before we went to Vegas, it wasn't about the money anymore. And she knew it."

"Kendra Rhode knew it," Gregor said. It was not a question.

"Of course," Jack said. "I knew her a long time before anybody else did. Did you know that? She used to come here summers as a child, when we were both children. She used to play out on the beach by the Point. Her mother used to bring her into Oscartown for ice cream, along with her sisters. She always looked like that, you know. Blond and slim and tall. They don't all look like that. Even her sisters don't all look like that. But she did. As if she'd been created just to represent—well, whatever it was."

"It was rich twits," Linda Beecham said. "You were born on the Harbor. You should know that."

Gregor was fairly sure he was now the only person who was listening to Linda Beecham. Clara Walsh, Bram Winder, and Jerry Young were all staring at Jack Bullard as if they'd never seen him before. Jack was not staring back. He was still looking tired, more and more tired as the seconds ticked by. He moved away from the window and sat down in the single vistor's chair.

"It was the storm," Gregor said. "In case you're wondering how I knew. The storm created the opportunity, because it meant you were free of your fellow photographers. Nobody was going out in that mess if they could help it, and at the time it didn't look like there was anything new to see. The papers had enough pictures of Marcey Mandret getting plowed and falling out of her clothes so that a few more weren't going to be worth risking your life for. But you weren't risking your life. You'd been in nor'easters before. You'd grown up on the island. You could follow them without that much trouble, even in the mess the weather was making."

"She wanted him dead, you know," Jack said. "Kendra did. She wanted him dead, or disappeared, or something. She didn't marry him because she loved him. She was stoked on Ecstasy and in one of those moods. Well, stoked for Kendra. She'd had like half a dose. She never took whole ones."

"She told you she wanted him dead?" Gregor asked.

"No," Jack said. "She just talked about him. To me, at first, but then there was the picture. I had to sell the picture. I had to make enough money to cover my expenses out there. She could never understand that. She could never understand why people needed money. So she stopped speaking to me. They all did, except for Marcey, on and off."

"So you followed them out—wait," Gregor said. "They were who? Arrow Normand and Mark Anderman and Kendra Rhode? All together, at first."

"Yeah. It was the middle of the morning, but Arrow and Mark had been drinking. They'd all been on the set, even Kendra, and it was going to hell because of the weather, and Arrow had something in her trailer, and they all went in there. Carl Frank went crazy trying to keep Kendra off the set, but he never could do it. Anyway, they left there and went off in the car, and Marcey had had some kind of huge fight with Kendra over something, I don't know what, they all fight with each other all the time and it's impossible to figure out why. And I followed them. But I didn't follow them because I meant to, I mean, you know. I just followed them."

"You had the gun," Gregor said.

"I'd had the gun for weeks. I carried it everywhere after she stopped talking to me."

"To kill her with?" Gregor asked.

"To kill him with," Jack said. "There was this big charade going on, that he was Arrow's boyfriend, that he had nothing to do with her, but he did. They were married. He had legal rights and things, and she liked being with him, even though she wasn't supposed to. She liked—I don't know what. I don't know what any of them see in anybody. I don't know what they see in each other. But it shouldn't have been Mark she married out in Vegas. It should have been me. I was the one she went out with."

"Went out to Vegas with?" Gregor said.

"Yes," Jack said. "Three couples. That's how we put it when we went. Arrow and Steve. Marcey and Mark. Kendra and me. Only when we got there, things went wrong. Marcey couldn't really stand Mark, and she got too high not to show it. Then I was the one with the camera. They weren't going to get pictures unless I took them. Then—I don't know. I don't know. I only know it was supposed to be me, but then it wasn't."

378

"So you followed the car and there was an accident," Gregor said.

"She spends all her time in California," Jack said. "She didn't know how to drive in the snow. She skidded and went sideways down to the beach. It wasn't a bad accident. Not bad in the way they can get, you know. She wasn't stupid enough to try to go really fast in that weather. She wasn't stupid at all, really. People only thought she was."

"Kendra Rhode was driving," Gregor said. "Mark Anderman was in the front passenger seat. Arrow Normand was in the backseat."

"Yes."

"They went over onto the beach and you stopped to check them out," Gregor said. "But you had the gun. You'd brought the gun."

"I told you. I always had the gun. I'd had it for weeks," Jack said. "I hadn't thought about what I was going to do with it. The truck was on its side. A purple truck. Who buys a purple truck? I went down there and I helped Kendra get out. The driver's side was up. I got her out and then I stuck my head in to see the two of them, and there he was, on the other side. He'd been banged up a little, and he was pissing and moaning, and suddenly I thought, here I was, here we all were, it was the perfect opportunity. Because they would never give me up. They couldn't. And they knew I knew it."

"So you got out the gun and shot Mark Anderman in the head," Gregor said, "and the blood went back, into the backseat, all over Arrow Normand."

"I'd forgotten she was there," Jack said. "I got out of the cab and opened the back door and pulled her out and she was screaming her head off. And Kendra—Kendra was just standing there. I've never seen anybody so still in all my life. And Arrow was screaming and screaming. And Kendra turned around and slapped her, hard, so that the sound was louder than the sound of the bullets had been. Arrow stopped screaming. And Kendra looked at me and said, 'If you think this is going to get you anything you want, you're out of your mind.' And then she just walked away. Down the beach. That was the second to the last time I saw her in person."

3

In the rest of the room, there was a sort of buzz, not really conversation, just an under-the-breath, not-exactly-articulate hum of dissatisfaction. Linda Beecham had stopped talking. She was not a stupid woman. Clara Walsh, Bram Winder, and Jerry Young had started talking, but Gregor knew they would stop at any moment. They were all probably ready to brain him.

"All right," Clara started. "You said, not half an hour ago, that there were four problems that had to be solved, and the next one after the murder of Mark Anderman was the mess somebody made of Jack's hand. You're not trying to tell me that Jack made a mess of his own hand? And he couldn't have put that gun in Annabeth Falmer's house. And—"

"I want to know about the truck," Bram Winder said. "When Stewart Gordon took his pictures of the truck, it had been cleared off, or a lot of it had. The windshield had, and the door, and most of the hood."

"I cleared the truck off," Jack said. "Right after I fired the shots, I went off down the beach. I was just sort of running in the bad weather, and I tossed the gun, and then I thought about it, about the pictures. And I came back and took them. A couple of dozen pictures. And then Mr. Gordon came down with some woman and I had to run."

"He took the bullet, too," Gregor said. "It wasn't hard to find. It was stuck in the glass. Look at the official pictures one more time. You'll see the hole. It isn't big enough for the back of the bullet to go through."

"But that wasn't the gun Annabeth Falmer found," Clara said. "What was that gun doing in her house? It was Jack's gun."

"Linda Beecham thought it was the gun," Gregor said. "She knew Jack must have killed Mark Anderman. She was trying to make sure he wasn't suspected."

"By putting his gun where Annabeth Falmer could find it?" Jerry Young said.

"She didn't put the gun where Annabeth Falmer could find it; she put the gun where Arrow Normand had been. Which she knew, just the way everybody else on the planet knew it, because that was one of the details that's been all over the Internet and the tabloids. But she did a much more important thing to make sure Jack couldn't be arrested, never mind convicted, of that murder. She got rid of the fingerprints on his right hand."

"What?" Bram Winder said.

"She didn't have to worry about his left hand," Gregor said, "because when he's out in the cold, Jack wears gloves. But when he's photographing, he wears only the glove on his left hand, because he needs his right hand to operate the cameras. So she was fairly sure that on the afternoon of the murder, Jack would have had the glove on his left hand and no glove on his right. But since he's right-handed, that meant that the hand without the glove, the hand free to leave fingerprints on the gun, would be the hand he would use to fire the gun. So she dumped a bunch of Rohypnol into Jack's coffee one day in the office, asked him out back on some pretext or the other—"

"To help her move the new garbage bins," Jack said.

"To help her move the new garbage bins," Gregor repeated. "Then, when Jack started to pass out, she went after him with what was probably a small knife. Go look at his injuries. They're concentrated almost exclusively on the fingertips. The fingertips are slashed up to the point where wounds and scar tissue will make it impossible to match Jack's fingers to anything he imprinted before the attack, unless he's given prints for some other purpose—"

"No," Jack said. "I've barely had parking tickets."

"But where would she get Rohypnol?" Jerry Young said. "I know it's supposed to be floating around all over everywhere, but most people wouldn't know where to get it to save their lives."

"She got it from me," Jack said. "I gave it to her for safekeeping after I took it off Mark and Steve one night at Cuddy's. They were going after one of the waitresses, a girl who was the younger sister of one of the girls I knew in high school. They had a lot of it."

"I don't think you can charge her with anything, unless Jack here wants to press charges for the attack," Gregor said, "and I don't think he will. She was just thinking the best of him. She was just thinking that he'd gotten stupid one night and done something that was going to ruin his life, and she didn't want him to ruin his life. She's very maternal when it comes to Jack. And she's a very angry woman, which somebody ought to pay attention to sometime soon."

"I've never heard such nonsense in my life," Linda Beecham said. "Do you think I killed Kendra Rhode too? Jack couldn't have killed her. He was a mess. He was drugged up and weak. He couldn't have gotten to that stairwell to save his life."

"He was found in the hall, not half a foot from the stairwell door," Gregor said. "We do know that he got that far."

"And collapsed," Linda said. "He was right there, on the floor. I heard all about it. I came to the hospital and complained. It was typical. All that fuss over Kendra Rhode, and Jack lying in the corridor passed out and nobody paying any attention to him. Leslie didn't pay any attention to him until she'd finished with Kendra Rhode. It was more important to take care of a dead celebrity than a live local boy."

"Leslie didn't know that Kendra Rhode was dead," Gregor said gently. "And she knew Jack wasn't about to be. There isn't much staff at this hospital this time of year."

"You didn't answer my question," Linda said. "Are you going to charge me for the death of Kendra Rhode? Because Jack couldn't have killed her. He wasn't physically capable."

There was a strangled sound from the other side of the room. Gregor turned to see Jack smiling at them, a calm smile, a beatific smile, the kind of smile people got in the movies when they were bathed in a divine light.

"But I did kill her," he said. "I caught up to her in the stairwell, and I grabbed her, and I threw her down, and when she started falling I went back through the doors and passed out. But I did kill her. And I meant to. It was the only thing I could have done, after everything that happened."

EPILOGUE

1

Stewart Gordon and Annabeth Falmer were married in St. Andrews, Scotland, on the twenty-eighth of February, in a snowstorm bad enough to make the nor'easter on Margaret's Harbor look like spring. Marcey Mandret arrived by private jet to Heathrow and private car to St. Andrews, or rather cars, since it took a second one to carry her luggage. Coming up the walk of the university chapel ten minutes before the wedding was due to start, she was still trailing four wheeled suitcases, three carry-on bags, and a trunk. Fortunately, she had hired several luggage people to deal with them.

"What is that woman doing?" Bennis Hannaford asked, looking out the window of the "apartments" they had been assigned for the duration.

Gregor Demarkian and Stewart Gordon came to the window to look out. Stewart Gordon laughed.

"Ah," he said. "That's just Marcey. She thinks she's traveling light."

Bennis let that one pass, and went back to trying to do something about Gregor's bow tie. Gregor could feel the exasperation coming off her in waves. First the bow tie would be all right, then she would turn her back, then the bow tie would not be all right again. There was that, and there was the little pile of information from Box Hill Confections lying on the dresser on the other side of the room. She'd been going on about the chocolates for more than three-quarters of an hour.

"All I asked you to do was call her when you got to Massachusetts," Bennis said. "Was that really so hard? I know you were working, and I do understand that there was something of a crisis, but would a telephone call have been so much? You could have done it from anywhere. I gave you the cell phone."

"I don't see what difference it would have made where I called her from," Gregor said. "It's a phone call. It's not as if I was actually in Maine and could go to see her."

Stewart coughed the way cannons bark when they're fired, and said, "I still don't understand the timing of it all. It still seems a lot for him to have done in such a short time."

"It wasn't such a short time," Gregor said. "That's what was hard to get straight, even for me. There was probably between forty-five minutes and an hour between the time Jack shot Mark Anderman and the time you and Annabeth got to the truck to discover the body. There was more than enough time for Kendra Rhode to get back to the Point and for Arrow Normand to get to Annabeth's house, and, most important, there was more than enough time for Jack to get back to his own house, realize he'd missed an opportunity, and go back to the truck himself. He was probably no more than five feet away from you and Annabeth when you got there. It was an incredible risk."

"He took a lot of risks, if you ask me," Bennis said. "Why would he do something like that? And why didn't one of them say something about it?"

"Arrow Normand may not have known," Gregor said. "The best I can understand, from her statement to me at the time, and her statements since, she may have been asleep before the gun went off. Or passed out, which would make things more confusing. And of course

Kendra Rhode wouldn't turn him in. The chances were too good that she'd get arrested herself, as an accessory, as something. And annoying as that woman was, she had good reason to suspect that under this particular set of circumstances, her celebrity would work against her instead of for her. She was in no danger from Jack, because he couldn't say anything about her being in the truck without implicating himself. She was in no danger from Arrow, because Arrow couldn't remember what had gone on and was half convinced it was her fault."

"Not because it was," Stewart said, "just because Arrow is always half convinced it's her own fault."

"But he had to have the pictures," Gregor said, "because he was still operating on the assumption that he was going to be able to go on as he had before. He still had a life he wanted to live. And that life included being a famous photographer."

"You mean a famous paparazzo," Bennis said. "I thought you told me that all this was about him being obsessed with Kendra Rhode, and wanting Kendra Rhode for himself. Do celebrities marry paparazzi?"

"Why not?" Gregor said. "They marry everybody else. Women celebrities especially. Anyway, he was always careful to have a backup plan, so he went back to the truck to take pictures, and he cleaned off the hood and the windows to make that possible, and then he left again. We found the pictures in his apartment. Some of them, at any rate."

"Why only some of them?" Bennis asked.

"Because somebody had gotten there before us," Gregor said. "The files had been rifled through, and a number of things were obviously missing. For instance, they contained no pictures at all of Arrow Normand, and very few of Marcey Mandret."

"Carl Frank," Stewart said solemnly.

"Or somebody connected to Carl Frank, yes," Gregor said. "Not that that's going to help us any. And now Jack has what he wanted, of course. He's famous. That's what this was about all along. It was even the reason he wanted to be with Kendra Rhode."

"He's not famous for killing Mark Anderman, though," Bennis said. "He's famous for killing Kendra Rhode. And he isn't even going to be charged with killing Kendra Rhode."

"Nobody can be charged with killing Kendra Rhode," Gregor said. "There wasn't enough left of the scene to provide any uncontaminated evidence."

"So that leaves the question," Bennis said. "Did he actually kill her?"

Gregor shrugged. Something happened to his bow tie. He wasn't sure what, but it seemed to have exploded. "I don't suppose it matters if he did or didn't," Gregor said. "Contrary to what Linda Beecham wants us to believe, he was probably capable of it, if he had a strong enough motivation, and he probably did. Kendra was doing this dipsy doodle around town, trying to get in for a meeting and out again with a minimum of fuss, so she was going through back doors and in and out of alleys. One of the other things I kept forgetting was that Kendra Rhode wasn't one of the film people. She hadn't shown up on Margaret's Harbor just to make a movie. She'd been coming there here entire life. So she knew where to go if she wanted to keep out of sight. My best guess is that she thought she would cut through the hospital and then go up Birkwell Road, which is right behind it. But I'm not the best person to ask. I don't know the roads that well. But she was trying to cut through the hospital, and Marcey was admitted to the emergency room—"

"Again," Stewart said. "That girl spent the entire picture getting admitted to the emergency room."

"And a lot of paparazzi came with her," Gregor said. "So, to get away from the paparazzi, she went upstairs. She was looking for a stairwell and a way out without paparazzi all over it. I don't know if she went up to see Jack in his room on purpose or if she saw him incidentally as she was passing through, but she went in to talk to him."

"And got him so angry that he leaped out of his bed of pain and threw her down a flight of stairs?" Bennis said.

"I think he'd probably been angry for quite a long time," Gregor said. "Angry at her. Angry at Arrow and Marcey. Angry at the entire setup, the entire thing he was involved with. Angry at not having been born at the right place in the right time to the right people. And he didn't have to throw her down a flight of stairs. He only had to fall into her at the right angle, or push her. For whatever it's worth, I don't think he meant her to end up dead. That wasn't the idea at all."

"Was there an idea?" Stewart said.

"Sure," Gregor said. "It was rather like Pinocchio. He just wanted to be a real boy."

"You're making absolutely no sense at all," Stewart said.

But Gregor was making sense, and he knew it.

"If you hear a tree fall in the forest, but nobody notices you did," he said, "did you hear it at all?"

Stewart Gordon looked like he wanted to brain him, but it was time to go, and they went.

2

Sitting in the chapel, Gregor Demarkian considered the various ways in which this wedding would be very much unlike his own. For one thing, it was taking place in a religious setting, even though it wasn't religious. That was something Father Tibor could not find a way to allow, although everybody—including Father Tibor himself—wanted Gregor and Bennis to be married at Holy Trinity. Things were apparently much more relaxed among the university Presbyterians, or whatever they were, in Scotland. The wedding would take place at the altar, but be performed by some kind of government functionary, and nobody would say anything about God. Gregor thought this was good, since Stewart was likely to start lecturing if somebody mentioned God, and Stewart could lecture in a voice it was impossible to overcome.

The other way it was different was in the people who were attending, which in Stewart's case included dozens he didn't like very much but couldn't avoid inviting: agents, managers, producers, God only knew what. Marcey Mandret had found a seat with Stewart's children and Annabeth's sons. Stewart's daughter, Caroline, was an enormously sensible woman in tweeds, and she seemed to have taken on the role of mother hen to a mentally deranged chick. At least, Marcey Mandret looked mentally deranged. It would take mental derangement to show up in the middle of a snowstorm in Scotland in a dress that barely went to the bottom of her bum and had neither sleeves nor much of anything around the neckline. The plunge of the neckline had excited the interest of all four of the young men, both of Stewart's sons and both of Annabeth's, and Stewart's youngest, the tanned one that looked like he had just come in from hunting lions, had managed to get himself right up behind her so that he could whisper in her ear. Marcey Mandret seemed to like what she was hearing, but Gregor thought that was no indication of anything. She was primed to look like she liked what she was hearing.

"Look," Bennis said. "Your friend Stewart was right. She's got a book with her. Do you know what he said it was?"

"What?" Gregor said.

"Milton's *Paradise Lost.* Did you ever have to read that thing? It makes graduate students cry."

"Maybe whatever his name is will explain it to her," Gregor said.

"Colin," Bennis said. Then she shook her head. "No, maybe that's the other one. I didn't know he had children. Did you?"

"Yes, I did. He's made a point of making sure most people don't know about it. Trying to save their privacy, I'd guess, or their sanity."

"Is that Jack Bullard person insane?" Bennis asked. "He sounds insane. How can anybody really not know if he's really real?"

Gregor thought he had met a lot of people who didn't know if they were really real, and that those people had included all the serial killers whose cases he had ever been involved with. He wished Father Tibor were here, instead of back on Cavanaugh Street being driven to distraction by Donna Moradanyan Donahue. It was not a matter of belief in God or lack of belief in God, or of belief in an afterlife and the supernatural or the lack of it. Gregor had known murderers who were believers and murderers who were not believers. He had known saints who were believers and saints who were not believers. It was not so simple as what sort of philosophy people had come to accept as some sort of conscious act of the will. Most people felt real, and some people just did not. The people who analyzed serial killers got it wrong most of the time. Serial killers did not think they were the only real people in the world. They didn't think they were real at all. They killed because—

"But he wasn't a serial killer," Gregor said.

"What?" Bennis said.

"Jack Bullard," Gregor said. "He wasn't a serial killer. Even if he did really kill Kendra Rhode, with intent, I mean. He wasn't a serial killer."

"I'd noticed that," Bennis said. "Or I would have, if I'd bothered to think about it. The ceremony is going to start any moment. They're fussing around at the back there for the bride to come in."

"I was thinking of the way murderers think," Gregor said. "There's a piece of conventional wisdom about serial killers, that each of them thinks he's the only real human being on earth. I've been thinking these last few weeks that that's exactly backward."

"You mean that they don't think they're real themselves? Gregor, for goodness' sake, if that was what made somebody a serial killer, we'd have thousands of them roaming around the landscape. A lot of people don't think they're really real these days. That's why they'll take their shirts off for *Girls Gone Wild* or go on *Jerry Springer* and admit to sleeping with their daughter's husband. There's got to be something more to it than that."

Gregor was sure that there did have to be something more to it than that, but he didn't know what, and Annabeth Falmer was proceeding up the aisle carrying a big bouquet of hothouse flowers. The organ was playing, too, and he didn't know when it had started. He tried to imagine his own wedding to Bennis in a few months' time, but realized that there was too much he just didn't know. Was there going to be an organ? Were the bridesmaids going to be in special, hideous dresses? Annabeth had no bridesmaids at all, and she looked just fine.

"You'll notice," Gregor said, whispering into Bennis's ear much as Stewart's son was whispering in Marcey Mandret's. "It took them a few weeks, and it's a lovely wedding."

"Tell that to Donna Moradanyan," Bennis said. "And then duck."